Praise for *Sw[...]*

W9-BMZ-668

Finalist for the 2010 Strega Prize

"A beach read for strong-willed, independent souls."

—*Kirkus Reviews*

"Readers will devour this richly detailed, sensual bildungsroman."

—*Booklist*

"Avallone's engaging debut novel explores the troubled friendship of two sexually precocious young girls. . . . Avallone does a good job of capturing the intensity of lifelong female friendship and concomitant jealousies."

—*Publishers Weekly*

International praise

"Powerful. As trenchant as it is true."

—*Le Parisien*

"A galvanizing social novel, spacious and strenuous, like a film that would have been cosigned by Ken Loach and Gus Van Sant."

—*Libération*

"With Silvia Avallone, we are in the presence of a natural, original, and untutored talent, capable of capturing the contradictions of her own time in a rebellious, heartbreaking way. But the greatness of [*Swimming to Elba*], at once carnal and chaste . . . lies in the powerful way that it identifies beauty and friendship as the two decisive, all-encompassing emotions of adolescence. It is a book that demands love, in its truthfulness, in its refusal to turn away from the life-giving breath of poetry."

—Giuseppe Conte, *Il Giornale*

"A masterpiece of fine writing, literature in its purest state, as if the words had flowed like molten steel out of the blast furnace to recount perfect characters and a magnificent story."

— Caterina Soffici, *Il Riformista*

PENGUIN BOOKS

SWIMMING TO ELBA

Silvia Avallone is a published poet who was born in Biella, Italy, in 1984 and now lives in Bologna. This first novel—published in Italy as *Acciaio*—won second place in the 2010 Strega Prize competition, was a #1 bestseller in Italy, and rights have been sold in twenty languages.

Swimming to Elba

silvia avallone

TRANSLATED BY ANTONY SHUGAAR

PENGUIN BOOKS

PENGUIN BOOKS
Published by the Penguin Group
Penguin Group (USA) Inc., 375 Hudson Street,
New York, New York 10014, U.S.A.

USA | Canada | UK | Ireland | Australia | New Zealand | India | South Africa | China
Penguin Books Ltd, Registered Offices: 80 Strand, London WC2R 0RL, England
For more information about the Penguin Group visit penguin.com

First published in Italy as *Acciaio* by RCS Libri S.p.A., Milan 2010
First published in the United States of America by Viking Penguin,
a member of Penguin Group (USA) Inc. 2012
Published in Penguin Books 2013

THE LIBRARY OF CONGRESS HAS CATALOGED THE HARDCOVER EDITION AS FOLLOWS:
Avallone, Silvia, 1984–
[Nuoto all'Elba. English]
Swimming to Elba / Silvia Avallone.
p. cm.
ISBN 978-0-670-02358-5 (hc.)
ISBN 978-0-14-312365-1 (pbk.)
1. Girls—Italy—Fiction.   2. Female friendship—Fiction.   I. Title.
PQ4901.V34N8613 2012
853'.92—dc23
2011043895

Printed in the United States of America
10 9 8 7 6 5 4 3 2 1

Hand lettering by Kristen Haff

To Eleonora, Erica, and Alba

My best friends

And to everyone who makes steel

The best things shimmer with fear.

Don DeLillo, *Libra*

Adolescence is an age of potential.

PART ONE

Best Friends

CHAPTER 1

Within the round blur of the lens, the body, headless, shifted slightly.

A backlit wedge of flesh pulled into focus.

From last year to this, that body had changed, slowly, under its clothing. And now, this summer, in the binoculars, it was bursting into view.

The distant eye nibbled at the details: the strap of the swimsuit, the swimsuit bottom, a strand of seaweed on the hip. Muscles flexing just above the knee, the arc of the calf, an ankle dusted with sand. The eye swelled and reddened with the effort of burrowing into the lens.

The teenage body leaped out of the field of view and plunged into the water.

A moment later—the viewfinder now repositioned and the focus recalibrated—the body reappeared, topped by a gleaming blond head of hair. And a burst of laughter so violent—even from this distance, just the sight of it—that it shook you down to the ground. It felt like you had tumbled into that laugh, past the white teeth. And the dimples on the cheeks, and the hollow between the shoulder blades, and the indentation of the belly button, and all the rest.

She was playing like any girl her age, without a hint of suspicion that someone might be watching her. Her mouth opened wide. What could she be saying? And to whom? She sliced into a wave, emerging from the water with the triangle of her swimsuit top askew. A mosquito bite on one shoulder. The man's pupil constricted and dilated as if he were under the influence of narcotics.

Enrico continued watching his daughter; the impulse was too strong to resist. He spied on Francesca from the balcony, after lunch. He was off his shift at the Lucchini steelworks. He tracked her, studying her through the lenses of his fishing binoculars. Francesca scampered over the wet sand and through the splashing waves with her friend Anna. They chased one another, tagging, touching, pulling each other's hair, while he, from his vantage point high above, motionless with a cigar in one hand, stood sweating. His giant bulk, his sweat-drenched T-shirt, eyes staring, intent in the crushing blast of heat.

He was just keeping an eye on her, or that's what he said. He'd been doing it since she started going to the beach with those older boys, those characters that he found deeply suspicious. Boys who smoked cigarettes; boys who most likely smoked joints, for that matter. And when he talked to his wife about them, about those troublemakers who were clustering around his daughter, he shouted like a psychotic. They smoke joints, they snort coke, they deal pills, they want to fuck my daughter! He actually never uttered the last phrase. Instead, he pounded his fist on the table, or punched the wall.

Maybe he'd started spying on Francesca before that, though: when the body of his little girl suddenly seemed to slough off its old skin, gradually taking on a specific flesh and odor, new and, perhaps, savage. His little Francesca had suddenly sprouted a mocking ass and a pair of irreverent tits. The bones of her pelvis had developed an arch, forming an angled spillway between her ribs and her abdomen. And he was her father.

Just then, he was watching his daughter thrash to and fro in his binoculars, hurl herself forward with all her force to catch a ball. Her wet hair clung to her back and sides, to the expanse of flesh pebbled with salt.

The teenage boys were playing volleyball, in a circle, surrounding her. Francesca was lunging, lean and in constant movement amid a frenzy of shouts and splashes where the water was shallow. But Enrico ignored the game entirely. Enrico was thinking about just one thing: his daughter's bathing suit. Christ, it doesn't hide a thing. There should be a law against bathing suits like that. If just one of those fucking bastards dared to lay so much as a finger on her, he'd be down on the beach with a baseball bat.

"What do you think you're doing?"

Enrico turned to face his wife, who stood in the middle of her kitchen, watching him with an appalled look on her face. Rosa felt appalled, withered inside, at the sight of her husband holding a pair of binoculars at three in the afternoon.

"I'm checking up on my daughter, if you don't mind."

Meeting the gaze of that woman was sometimes difficult, even for him. A relentless accusation was leveled in his wife's stabbing gaze.

Enrico furrowed his brow, gulped uncomfortably: "It seems like the very least. . . ."

"You're ridiculous," she hissed at him.

He looked at Rosa as if all he saw was an annoyance, something calculated to make him lose his temper, fly into a rage.

"Oh, you think it's ridiculous to keep an eye on my daughter, in this day and age? Have you noticed who she's going around with at the beach? Who are those boys, you want to tell me that?"

Whenever Enrico lost his temper—and he lost it frequently—his face turned a mottled purple, the blood vessels in his neck swelled and throbbed. It was frightening to see.

When he was twenty years old, before he let his beard grow and put on all that weight, there was no anger. He was a handsome young man, newly hired at the Lucchini steel mill; from childhood he'd sculpted his muscles by hoeing and digging the earth. He had become a giant in the tomato fields, and, later, shoveling coking coal. Just an ordinary man who had left the country with a rucksack on his shoulders to come to the city.

"Can't you see what she's up to? And at her age . . . Look at the fucking way she's dressed!"

Then, over the years, he had changed. Day by day, too gradually for anyone to notice. That giant who had never ventured outside the boundaries of the Val di Cornia, who had never seen another scrap of Italy, had gradually frozen inside.

"Answer me! Can you see the way your fucking daughter is dressed?"

Rosa said nothing, and just gripped the towel she had just used to dry the dishes a little harder. Rosa was thirty-three years old, had callused hands, and had stopped taking care of herself the day of her wedding. Her beauty, the beauty of a southern Italian girl, had washed away, drained into the suds of the detergent, the dish soap, the perimeter of that floor she'd scrubbed every day for the past ten years.

Her silence was stony. It was a closed silence, a form of attack.

"Who are those boys, huh? Do you know them?"

"They're perfectly nice boys. . . ."

"Oh, so you do know them! But you don't say a word to me, do you? Why doesn't anybody tell me anything in this house? Francesca talks to you, doesn't she? Sure, she talks to you for hours and hours. . . ."

Rosa threw the dish towel onto the table.

"See if you can figure it out," she huffed, "why she never talks to you."

But he'd already stopped listening.

"Nobody tells me anything! Nobody ever tells me a thing, god damn it to hell!"

Rosa bent over the basin full of dirty dishwater. When summer came other women her age still went out dancing. She'd never been in a discotheque in her life.

"So what am I, huh? An idiot? You think I'm an idiot? She's walking around dressed like a slut! Is that how you raised her? Well, congratulations! But one of these days, let me tell you . . ."

She lifted the basin and emptied the dishwater into the balcony sink, staring at the specks of grime as the water swirled down the drain. She wished he would drop dead in front of her, just fall to the floor and slowly die.

"Fuck you and fuck her, fuck the both of you! This is what I'm working for? For you? For that little whore?"

Then she'd run over him with the car, grind him into the asphalt, smash him into a pudding, into the worm that he really was. And Francesca would understand. Murder him. If only I'd never fallen in love with him, if only I'd tried to get a job, if only I'd walked out of here ten years ago.

Enrico turned his back on her and leaned his gigantic body over the railing, in the sunlight that at three in the afternoon poured down like molten steel, crushing everything beneath it. The sand, on the far side of the road, teemed with beach umbrellas and loud voices. A flesh pit, he thought to himself. He relit the dead cigar stub he clutched in his fingers. Stubby, short, red, callused fingers. The fingers of a manual laborer who works without gloves, even when he's testing the temperature of pig iron.

On one side was the sea, teeming with young people in that brutally hot hour of the afternoon. On the other, the flat façade of the public housing projects. All the slatted shutters rolled down over the windows along the empty street. The motor scooters parked in ranks along the sidewalks, handlebar to handlebar, each with its own decal, each with its own phrase scribbled in colored marker: "I love Francesca."

The beach and the walls of those giant barracks, in the blistering June sunlight, looked like life and death howling angrily at one another. There was no way around it: Via Stalingrado, if you didn't live there, seen with the eyes of an outsider, was depressing. Worse: It was poverty.

. . .

One balcony up, on the fifth floor, another man was leaning over the rusted railing and looking out at the beach.

He and Enrico were the only human shapes looking out.

The sun was stunningly hot. The plaster was flaking off, tumbling earthward.

The short, bare-chested man had just snapped shut his cell phone. He was a midget in comparison with the giant holding a pair of binoculars on the fourth floor. For the entire duration of the phone call he had shouted— not because he was angry but because that was how he talked. He had talked about money, astronomical figures, and he had never taken his bright beady eyes off the beach, as he searched for something that, at that distance, without eyeglasses, he couldn't make out.

"One of these days, I'm going down to the beach myself. And who's to say I can't? After all, they fired me from my job," he cackled to himself, speaking aloud.

From inside the apartment someone shouted.

"Wha-a-a-at?"

"Nothing!" he replied, remembering that he had a wife.

Sandra appeared on the little balcony, her mop dripping ammonia.

"Artù!" she cried, brandishing the mop. "What's going on, have you lost your mind?"

"I was only kidding!" he gestured with one hand

"Kidding? You think this is something to kid about? Right now, we've got the dishwasher to pay off, the installments for your son's car radio . . . a million lire and change for a car radio! I ask you, and now you start with your jokes. . . ."

It was no joke. He'd been caught stealing drums of diesel fuel from the Lucchini steel mill.

"Go on, move aside. I need to mop."

Since the day he'd been hired, Arturo had been stealing diesel fuel from Signore Lucchini, for no particular reason—just to fill up his tank and sell a little extra to the farmers. No one had noticed a thing, for three good years. But now, fucking hell . . .

"I said, get out of my way, this floor is a mess."

He stepped aside, whistling a tune. He stepped into the kitchen. He was a cheerful, expansive little man: He had plenty of friends. They could fire him, he might be saddled with debts, but he still whistled.

He grabbed a plum from the fruit basket on the table and bit into it as he mused contentedly. He was successfully pulling off incredible deals in his imagination: barely lifting a finger, and raking in profits.

"Aren't you done cleaning? You never do anything but clean house!"

"Oh, yeah? And if I stop, who cleans the house . . . you?"

Arturo had had some intermittent experience of hard work, the kind of work his wife had been doing since she was sixteen, that allowed them to pay the rent every month and raise two children. He had been, in chronological order: a purse snatcher; a factory worker at the Lucchini steel mill, at the Dalmine mill, at the Magona d'Italia mill; and then a foreman back at Lucchini. He was born on the island of Procida near Naples, and at nineteen he had emigrated to Piombino for a factory job, a new way of life: finally legal, finally honest. He looked down on the members of the metalworkers' union—the FIOM—as so many losers. There was only one certainty in life: Work is hard.

"Where's Anna? At the beach?"

"Yes, with Francesca."

"What about Alessio?"

Definitely: Tomorrow he'd win big at poker, and with his winnings, he could start to make some real money. He could feel it. How to put it? It was fate. And with the money he was going to make he'd buy a diamond for Sandra, a . . . what do you call it? A De Beers . . . a "forever."

"I think he's at the beach too."

"I need to give your son a talking to. He thinks he absolutely has to have a VW Golf GT. . . . Why does he need a Golf GT?"

Sandra looked up from the already dry floor and stood there, in the sunlight—"Let him talk; anyway, he doesn't have the money"—sweating for a few moments.

She walked back into the apartment and sat down at the kitchen table. She started observing her husband carefully: In all these years, he'd never changed. "Starting tomorrow . . . ," he always said, and she fell for it every time.

"Your son votes for Berlusconi," Sandra said, with a forced smile. "He wants a car, not social justice. He wants to dress up, show off, brag about how well he's doing. . . . But how can you lecture him when your own car cost fifty million lire? By the way, did you pay this year's road tax?"

"Road tax?"

The forced smile vanished instantly from her face: "Before you start worrying about your son and his money, why don't you make sure you don't gamble away your own money."

"Oh, now you're starting up with that again?" Arturo puffed out his cheeks and snorted like a bull.

"That's right, now I'm starting up with that again." Sandra leaped to her feet and started windmilling her arms in the muggy stagnant air that filled the kitchen. "It doesn't do you any good to act all put upon, you know. You're not fooling me. What happened to your last paycheck?"

"Sandra!"

"It never even made it into the bank account! You lost it at cards—go on, admit it! Even before you could deposit it in the bank, you gambled it away. . . . Do I have STUPID written on my forehead? I don't think so." She tapped her index finger twice on her sweaty forehead, her hair rolled up in curlers, her ineptly plucked eyebrows.

Arturo threw open his arms. "Come on, give me a kiss. . . ."

That was what he always did, that man. When he had no arguments and no excuses left to offer, he turned affectionate.

The two of them vanished into the interior of the apartment.

Now Signore and Signora Sorrentino's slatted shutter was rolled down like all the other shutters in the building (all but one). It was rolled down, but it jammed halfway.

"When are you going to fix that broken shutter, *Artù?*"

Silence. Then, from the bathroom came the sound of water running from the tap, the clack of a razor on the edge of the sink. And Arturo started singing. His favorite song, *Maracaibo*: *Maracaibo, mare forza nove, fuggire sì ma dove? Za-zà.*

At three on a June afternoon the old people and the children lay down for a nap. Outside, the light blistered everything it hit. The housewives, the retired husbands in acetate tracksuits who had survived a lifetime working the blast furnace, nodded off, half asphyxiated, in front of the television set.

After lunch, the façades of those giant dormitories, one next to the other, all identical, resembled a wall of cemetery vaults, stacked from floor to ceiling. Women with swollen calves and ass cheeks bouncing like beach balls beneath their smocks trudged down into the courtyard and sat around plastic tables. They played cards. They fanned themselves furiously and talked, mostly about nothing.

The husbands, when they weren't at work, didn't poke their noses outside the apartment. They sat vacantly, dripping with sweat, remote control in hand, clicking from one channel to the next. They didn't listen to a word those assholes said on television. They only had eyes for the *veline*, the scantily clad tarts who assisted the television show hosts, and who were the exact opposite of their wives. Next year I'm installing an air conditioner, at least in the living room. If they don't pay me my overtime tomorrow, I swear I'm going to give them a piece of my mind.

Arturo carefully shaved his chin, singing a song popular in his childhood, when the public housing authority had built the giant barracks lining the beaches for the workers at the steel mills. Even metalworkers, according to the views of the local Communist administration, had the right to an apartment with a view. A view of the sea, not a view of the factory.

Forty years later everything had changed: the lira had given way to the euro; you had to pay for cable TV; there were GPS navigation devices; and the political parties of his childhood—Christian Democrats and Italian Communists—had both vanished. Life was completely different now, in 2001. But the barracks were still there, as was the factory, as were the beach and the sea.

The beach of Via Stalingrado, at that time of day, was jam-packed with screaming kids, cooler bags, and umbrellas piled one atop the other. Anna and Francesca took a running start down the sand and tumbled into the sea with victory cries, splashing water in all directions. Swarms of adolescents leaped all around them, every muscle straining, after Frisbees or tennis balls.

People said it wasn't much of a beach: There were no luxurious clubs; the sand was mixed with rust and garbage; sewer pipes ran down the middle; and no one went there but criminals and the poor folk from the public housing.

Mound after mound of seaweed, and no one in city hall ever bothered to have it cleaned up.

In the distance, two and a half miles across the water, the white beaches of the Isle of Elba gleamed like an unattainable paradise. The inviolate domain of the Milanese, the Germans, the silky-skinned tourists in black SUVs and sunglasses. But for the teenagers who lived in the huge barracks of public housing, for the children of all the nobodies dripping with sweat and blood at the steel mills, the beach across the way from their front doors was already paradise. The only truly real paradise.

When the asphalt was oozing in the heat of the sun, the muggy heat was corrupting the air, and the smokestacks of the Lucchini steelworks were coughing out filth that lingered overhead, the residents of Via Stalingrado went barefoot to the beach. They had only to cross the road, and then run down to belly flop into the water.

No one had ever seen Anna and Francesca leave the water. It was a little eerie to watch them swim—two parallel wakes in the water—out to the farthest buoy. One day they'd make it all the way to Elba—"We'll swim the whole way," they said—and they'd never come back.

The twentysomethings would gather in the bar before going into the water, the young men clustering in broad circles. They moved in packs, herds, flocks, usually congregating around some simple common thread: the street address of the apartment building; the degree of violence involved in their work lives; the quality of the narcotics; and—last of all—the soccer team for which they rooted.

They felt none of the frenzied eagerness that drove thirteen-year-olds to plunge into the water. First a drink, a smoke, a poker game. Some of them had abs and pecs, others had enormous guts spilling over their belts. They were like Olympic deities. And while their little brothers dreamed about modified mufflers and discotheques they were still too young to get into, they lorded it over everyone else, with their voices and their fists, driving tricked-out rides with spoilers, and on Saturday nights—windows rolled down, elbows resting on the sill—rocketing past at close to 120 mph.

Girls didn't pull their punches either. They were ruthless, especially when the prize at stake was a smooth young guy like Alessio. Summer was when it happened, along the boardwalks running between the changing huts, their hair hanging loose. For the girls who could risk it, the girls who were old enough and had the body to pull it off. Making love inside the darkened changing booths. No rational forethought, no condom, and if you got pregnant and he agreed to stick with you, then you'd won.

"It won't be long now," Francesca and Anna whispered to one another. When an older girl zipped up to the beach astride a gleaming new scooter, they flicked her off the saddle with their imaginations and took her place. "It won't be long." On Saturday night other girls went out with shimmering glitter on their cheeks, lip gloss, and high heels, while they stayed home, trying on clothes with the stereo blasting at full volume.

They were waiting for the world to come. The world arrives when you turn fourteen.

They hurtled into the foaming waves, side by side, and when a ferryboat

went past, vast ripples began to carve into the water's skin. They had been
the subject of idle conversation in the cafés for a couple of years now, around
the tables where the older boys sat: The word was that they weren't bad,
not bad at all. Wait'll they get a little older and you'll see.

Anna and Francesca, *thirteen going on fourteen.* The brunette and the
blonde. Down there, in the distance, surrounded by all those males, those
eyes, those bodies, zooming out, receding into the water in a uniform,
undifferentiated mass of silent, eager bodies. One of their favorite games
was to steal the soccer ball just as one of the boys was about to kick it
through the goalposts, two wooden stakes jammed into the wet sand. And
with a furious kick, laying triumphant claim to the goal.

They ran freely through the crowd, turning to look at one another, joining hands as they ran. They knew that nature was on their side; they knew
they were powerful. Because in certain settings, certain places, all that
matters is whether a girl is pretty. And if you're not, if you're a loser, you
go nowhere, you have no fun. If the boys don't write your name on the pillars in the courtyard, if they don't slip notes under your apartment door,
then you're nobody. You're thirteen years old, but you already wish you
were dead.

Anna and Francesca splashed smiles in all directions. Nino, who carried
them up and down the beach, letting them ride on his shoulders, could feel
their crotches warming the nape of his neck. Massimo, before he hurled
them into the saltwater, assaulted them relentlessly, tickling and biting. In
front of everyone. And they happily let anybody who happened by do what
he wanted, without shyness, without hesitation, without the slightest
awareness. Effortlessly, since the world was there, within reach, and to hell
with anyone who hung back and watched.

They weren't the only girls experiencing new sensations in their bodies.
Losers, dogs like Lisa cowering under her beach towel—wished they could
roll around on the wet sand in front of everybody, breathlessly run headlong into the waves.

The way that Anna and Francesca ran, slamming into arms, smiles, and
tennis balls, their swimsuits half undone, amounted to a challenge, a dare.
If you watched them, you couldn't help but envy their breasts, their asses,
their shameless smiles that said: I exist.

In the shallow water the sand mixed with the seaweed, creating a pulp
underfoot. They ran, the blonde and the brunette, into the sea. They could
feel male eyes prying and probing. And that's what they wanted: to be seen,

stared at. There was no exact reason. They were playing, you could tell, but they were also deadly serious.

The brunette and the blonde. The two of them, always and only the two of them. When they emerged from the water, they held hands like a pair of fiancées. At the café they went into the bathroom together. They cut along briskly up and down the beach, turning—first one then the other—to acknowledge frank compliments. They tossed their beauty in your face. They wielded their beauty violently. While Anna might, occasionally, give you the time of day even if you were a loser, Francesca never said hello, never smiled. Except to Anna. Except at Anna.

No one could ever forget the summer of 2001. Even the collapse of the Twin Towers was, in the final analysis, for Anna and Francesca just a part of the orgasmic thrill they were experiencing as they discovered that their bodies were changing.

By now only one slatted shutter remained open. Only one sweaty man leaning on the balcony railing, a pair of binoculars in his hand.

Enrico stubbornly continued searching for his daughter's blond head in the waves, among the welter of teenage bodies playing volleyball, soccer, beach tennis. He isolated Francesca's torso in his lens in that tangled mass of arms, breasts, and legs, focusing on it, staring in a state of animal wariness as she moved in contact with the sea.

Francesca's shoulders, covered with dripping wet blond hair. Her round bottom: something you should never look at, something no one should ever look at. But Enrico was looking, drenched with sweat. That lithe, perfect body that his daughter had magically produced, without warning, in front of everyone.

CHAPTER 2

Instead of a hard hat he was wearing a threadbare Chicago Bulls baseball hat, one with a couple of chrome-plated studs punched in at either side of the visor.

He had just taken a jab at the little asshole's face. He'd even unhooked the shoulder straps of his overalls so he could swing his right fist with greater ease. The hanging load, hooked on to the giant winch of the overhead gantry crane, was swinging in the oppressive heat like a pendulum. His muscular upper arm was still poised, tensed like his whole face, filthy with pig iron.

"Repeat what you just said," Alessio shouted over the roar. "Say it again, you fucker!"

The punk reached up to touch the bruise Alessio had just stamped on his face.

"You see this?" he slapped his hand on the gritty side of an eighteen-ton mill crucible.

The punk wasn't even sixteen years old yet.

"What did you say my sister does?" He hocked a chunk of phlegm onto the ground. "You see this thing, you see it? The next time I hear you . . ." And he reached out to pat the crucible again. "I'll drown you in this."

Twenty-eight hundred degrees Fahrenheit is the melting point of steel alloy. Steel doesn't exist in nature, it's not an elementary substance. It's a secretion of thousands of human hands, electric meters, mechanical arms, and every so often the skin of a cat that's tumbled into the molten alloy.

The boy looked down at the floor. He'd just been hired; there were maybe a dozen whiskers on his smooth chin.

Everyone looked hard at him, his fellow millworkers approving the punch-out.

"I'll drown you in it," Alessio snarled, a second time. Then he paused to light a cigarette.

An older man, from the maintenance crew, scrambled up onto the crane to check the cables and shouted down a string of insults at Alessio for leaving the mill crucible swinging unsecured. Another man turned the page of the *Maxim* calendar, which was still at May. He replaced a brunette in a thong looking back over her shoulder with the massive tits of a blonde straddling a motorcycle.

Alessio stripped off his sweat-soaked undershirt. No one, not even his best friend, could dare to say that his sister . . . The word that the punk had spoken flashed into his mind again. He had to swallow a huge gob of spit and iron filings to keep calm.

They were standing in the middle of a clearing covered with dry grass, a steppe running between the piles of bundled steel rebar and the black tower of the fourth blast furnace. Alessio flicked the cigarette butt onto the ground, and moved quickly to crush it under his boot. Anything could catch fire at two in the afternoon. He turned off the keyboard controlling the system of weights and counterweights on the crane, forty feet high and eighty feet across. It's an entire zoo in here: pig iron everywhere, cranes of every species and variety. Rusted animals with horned heads.

"Asshole!" the maintenance guy yelled down at him.

When Alessio jammed the brake on the crane cables he had come close to shearing the maintenance guy's foot off.

The dense black sludge of molten metal was bubbling in the crucibles, potbellied swiveling barrels running along on the mill trains. Giant tanks on wheels that looked like primordial creatures. Alessio's shift was over. He let a bottle of water gurgle over his head and neck.

Metal was everywhere, in the process of birth. Unceasing cascades of steel and glistening cast iron and viscous light. Torrents, rapids, estuaries of molten metal coursing through the flow lines, into the ampules of the ladles and pouring out into the tundishes to drain into the molds for furnaces and trains.

If you looked straight up you'd see greasy fumes and robotic sounds merging murkily. Raw materials were being transformed at every hour of the day and night. Ores and coal arrived by sea, were unloaded at the industrial port from huge freighters docked there: Fuel hurried along on overhead conveyor belts, midair highways, and overpasses, running and traveling the endless miles from the docks to the coal towers and the coke ovens, and then headlong into the blast furnace. You could feel the blood rushing through your arteries at a fantastic velocity in there, and from the arteries to the capillaries, while your muscles built up in tiny fractures: You were regressing to the animal state.

Alessio was small and alive in this vast burgeoning organism.

He shot a quick glance at the blonde on the *Maxim* calendar.

Constant yearning for sex, in the mill. The reaction of the human body inside the titanic body of industry: It's not a factory but material changing form.

It has a name and it has a formula: $Fe_{26}C_6$. The artificial insemination took place in a test tube as tall as a skyscraper, the rust-flaked urn of A-Fo 4—AltoForno4, or BlastFurnace4—that has hundreds of arms and bellies and three horns in place of a head. But that wasn't enough. It demanded other bellies still: converters, rolling mills, dozens of dizzying hot sacs, the tubes, the gaseous follicles of duty.

Half naked, he headed out through the south plant exit, the young blond man who still had two hours of boxing ahead of him after finishing eight hours on the crane, and Tuesdays, Fridays, and Saturdays at the club. He thought of his sister, Anna. About the way she and her friend Francesca were overdoing it, with the lipstick, the skimpy swimsuits, the afternoons holed up somewhere with boys. . . . He'd have to keep an eye on her or, maybe he should say, put some reins on her.

He walked across the steel rebar yard, embankments piled high with rebar and steel rod; in comparison he was a midget. Outside the plant no one knew it. But inside there were guard booths and service stations, intersections, plazas, and ramps. Alessio stepped over a pair of tracks without worrying about the torpedo ladle cars that emerged every fifteen minutes. He waved to the truck drivers waiting in a long line in the hot sunshine, windows rolled down, legs stretched out on the dashboard. They were waiting for loads of rebar, slabs, billets. They'd leave the steel mill and head out for all the cities of Europe, driving semitrailers the size of elephants with a luminous plastic Jesus, in green or hot pink, in clear view on the dashboard of the tractor-trailer's cab.

He swung one foot to kick aside the rotting corpse of a rat.

He reached the secondary service road, the one where Cristiano liked to stage Caterpillar tractor races.

He could feel the pressure of it at the nape of his neck, the black tower of the A-Fo 4, a giant spider that digests, ruminates, and belches out. He could feel them looming over his head, the partly ruined smokestacks and the ones that were still alive, spitting flames like so many dragons.

Bluish fluorescences, toxic clouds in volumes sufficient to poison not only the Val di Cornia but all of Tuscany.

Behind him was the heart of the plant: the gas tank. If it blew up it'd take all of Piombino with it, the posthumous carcasses of the three blast furnaces that hadn't yet been dismantled, and, down there at the far end, the coke oven where men shoveled coal by hand, by arm, as if it were still the nineteenth century.

There was no sky. There was an aviary: the purple flames of the furnaces; the swinging arms of the cranes; the tons of metal slung from the hooks beneath the hoisting tackle. The endless rows of sheds, workshops, bunkers. A self-sufficient obsession. The smokestacks, both active and extinct. Overhead, the constant crackling of flames: purple, red, black. The arms of hammerhead cranes swinging around, yellow, green, tons of metal whirling like birds, yellow clouds of carbon smoke, black at the mouths of the smokestacks. It's called continuous integrated steel production.

As Alessio walked he crushed nettles and chunks of refractory brick underfoot. Metal saturated the ground and his skin.

More truck drivers, more tractor trailers arrived. An enormous sinuous worm of waiting semitrailers stretched out, and as usual something had gone wrong. Time stretched out, dribbled away. They turned off their motors.

If you tried to count the leaks in the system, you'd run out of fingers and toes.

Alessio walked briskly, consuming fluids and miles in the scorching heat of this parallel city. Millions of pistons pumping in continuous excitation were shuttling furiously, synchronized at a dizzying rate, the elementary motion of machinery that is no different from life. At times, to withstand the boredom or the fear, you have to sit in a corner and unzip your fly.

Alessio was irritated; he was thinking about his sister, about his dream car, the VW Golf GT. If there was anyone he really couldn't stand it was those drooling loser leftists. The Democratic Left, Refoundation, all those Communist show-offs: the poses they struck, they way they reeled off complicated words. At the elections on May 13 he had voted Forza Italia. Berlusconi. He was sure of it: Words were useless, no good to anyone.

There were oddly twisted signposts at the turnoffs. The plant workers twisted them around intentionally, a form of sabotage to mislead truck drivers and outside inspectors. He'd done it once himself, with Cristiano:

They'd sent all the outsiders to the rail yard instead of the billet yard. Just one of the numerous entertainments in this rust-flaked amusement park—half dismantled by now, but thirty years ago twenty thousand people worked here, the market was undergoing a spectacular expansion, the West was reproducing the world and exporting it.

Now there were just two thousand of them left, including the subcontractors. The owners were moving production to the East. Some sectors of the plant were dying; smokestacks and industrial sheds were being demolished with dynamite. They were selling off everything for what the market would bear, grasping whores that they were.

Still they, the seventh-generation millworkers, had their fun, riding the power shovels like bucking bulls, their transistor radios blaring out at full volume, an amphetamine tablet dissolving under their tongues.

You adapt. And no one adapts better than cats. There were hundreds of cats in the cellars under the cafeteria, all of them mangy and sick, all of them calico, with black and white patches, from the relentless inbreeding.

Alessio was walking through the wastelands of the last big industrial sheds now, toward the last stages of the manufacturing cycle. When you get to the point of shaping a railroad track, space expands and grows sparse: That's where the canebrakes, the marshes, begin, and you could breathe a sigh of relief.

I'm not voting for those losers, I refuse to vote for them. We need to send them packing, off to play bocce ball with the other retirees. All Communists and their so-called honorable workers are jagoffs.

Alessio punched out on his time card, said good-bye to the faded woman behind the reception window, stepped outside.

Where the sea awaited him.

When shifts changed, a swarm of blue-collar workers emptied out into the parking lot. Before getting into his car, a Peugeot with two side spoilers and a spoiler in the rear, Alessio stopped to look at it for a moment. To look at the blast furnace. Call it by its name: A-Fo 4. Distort it to UFO: Everybody else does. A giant unidentified object. Even with a world war raging around it (it actually happened in 1944, when the steelworks was occupied by the Nazis), there it stands, imperturbable, industrious. And it always gets a smile out of you, a smile of fear and astonishment. Just like the smile on Alessio's face as he looked at it.

Its long, coal-sucking proboscis, the testicles where it cooks up the steel, the three-horned snout, the massively powerful skeleton of a brutal cathedral at its commencement. The beginning. Just as his sister's pink and downy body was commencing, developing breasts, hips, starting to attract. The blond peach fuzz of her crotch, and under her armpits. The animal scent when she came home from the beach and unfastened her swimsuit to take a shower.

He couldn't believe it, couldn't wrap his mind around the fact that Anna was already sneaking into cabanas with boys. And getting into Christ knows what kind of trouble.

CHAPTER 3

I t was a game, and it wasn't a game.

Over the sink, the mirror spotted with toothpaste, the blonde and the brunette look at the reflections of their most brazen selves. They're motionless, waiting anxiously. Pretending to pout, hair hanging loose. A little portable stereo is perched on the washing machine, volume turned all the way up.

It's blasting one of Alessio's old CDs from the nineties.

Anna and Francesca, when no one's home at Anna's house.

The two bodies pulsate like the sound, together with the sound.

They wait for the end of the intro before they start unbuttoning.

The window is open. They've locked themselves into the bathroom. They do it every Monday morning in the summer, when school is out and everyone's at work. They roll up the slatted blind; they pull open the curtains. They stand there half naked in the middle of the bathroom. And in the apartment building across the way nobody's home but retirees and fuckoffs.

They've made up their faces, gleefully overdoing it. Mouths smeared with lipstick, mascara dripping in the heat and clumping their eyelashes together, but they don't care. It's a little private carnival for them, a provocation they launch out the bathroom window. Deep down they know perfectly well that someone might be spying on them, someone might be unzipping his trousers as he watches.

As soon as they hear the female vocalist, Anna and Francesca fling themselves furiously into the dance, barefoot. They improvise dance steps worthy of Britney Spears. They're spectacularly successful, to judge from the number of eyes watching them from the windows across the way.

The summer is magic, is magic. Oh, Oh, Oh . . . The summer is magic . . .
Anna, in the rectangular window, is the one you see first. She's put on her
mother's lace bra. A woman's brassiere, which clashes violently with the
pink panties decorated with daisies.

Francesca hides in the shadows behind her. She's wearing a white camisole that offers just a translucent glimpse of her small breasts. She's taking
a risk, but she's still dressed. She doesn't smile. The top of her thong peeps
out over her lowrider denim shorts: You can tell that she's wearing a thong,
which is exactly what her father doesn't want.

The yearning to do something she shouldn't, something the world has
to look at.

The summer is magic. Oh, Oh, Oh . . . The summer is magic . . . They're not
really singing. They're just moving their lips. And after the refrain has been
repeated for the hundredth time, Anna unhooks her bra. She's dancing. Or
maybe we should say she's rocking her pelvis. She's playing with the hem
of her panties. She's tossing her hair vaporously, blowing stray strands that
fall over her eyes. She sees her breasts and her belly in the bathroom mirror,
nakedness framed in the window, in the morning sunlight that angles
down on that side of the building.

The stifling air seethes in the cement.

They pretend not to know that men they meet in the stairwells are now
watching them.

Francesca follows her. She slips the camisole off over her head. She's bare
chested, an almost masculine nude. She's pale and angular. Everything in
her is bright and clear, even in summer. She doesn't tan, she doesn't even
look Italian. She dances in her own way: slow, tough.

Francesca doesn't melt. Her face is serious; she wants to provoke, but she
doesn't open up. She looks at her best friend, she follows her moves. She
reaches for her hands, she grabs one, she kisses it.

*This is the rhythm of the night, the night . . . Oh, yes. The rhythm of the
night . . .*

The music is echoing off the ceramic tiles, adding to the clutter of noise
rising from the courtyard and emanating from the balconies. The bathroom tiles are green, the ceramic is flaking off on many of them. Lisa's
uncle is leaning on the windowsill; he lights a cigarette. And watches them.

They have an absurd conception of a striptease. They blend the videos
they see on MTV with the dances the showgirls do before commercial
breaks on *Striscia la Notizia*. But they're thirteen years old; they have no

idea. In an apartment complex with four buildings facing one another across a courtyard, there are at least a hundred windows with a fine vantage point from which noses can be stuck into that bathroom.

Which is what they want. They play the game Monday morning at ten-thirty. And people talk about what they're doing—in the hallways, in the stairwells, in the elevators.

There are people having breakfast at that hour of the morning. There are people who get up by now just to see it.

Francesca turns her back to the mirror, she gathers the shock of blond hair at the back of her neck. The mirror—filthy, rusted at the edges—reflects an adolescent back and an adolescent bosom, one beside the other, in perfect equilibrium.

Her spinal cord arches slightly. Francesca bends over to unbutton her shorts. She slips them off. Anna does the same with her panties.

If my father ever knew about this.

They move like a pair of tentacles; they've stopped looking at one another. Across the way are married women beating carpets over the side of their balconies. The same undulations of the pelvis, the same caresses from belly button to breast, and lower down they slip in a finger, then another finger. They embrace. They fit together perfectly, like serpents. Skin to skin. Eyes shut.

Francesca rests her face on Anna's shoulder, between her arms. She grazes her neck with her lips, slowly, behind her ear. And Anna tips her head back. She has a disquieting smile on her face.

The first thing you felt like saying was: Who the fuck do these two think they are? The second thing: They're perverts.

They embrace in front of the mirror. They aren't dancing anymore now. They embrace, and nothing more, moving slowly. You can't tell where one ends and the other begins. They stroke each other's face, run their hands down their sides, their hips, down their spines. Maybe they're afraid. They dig into one another with nose and lips; they become tender and distracted. *This is the rhythm of the night, the night . . . Oh, yes. The rhythm of the night . . .* Someone's spying on them from behind a curtain in the building across the courtyard. It doesn't bother them in the slightest.

They're undifferentiated; they're nude. There's the sort of fury that surges through your body at the beginning of everything, when you're thirteen years old and you don't know what to do with yourself. There's your dearest friend, right in front of you, rubbing her belly against yours.

They put their clothes back on and sit there, cuddling. They slip into a slow, animal trance, a state of forgetfulness.

Anna's eyes are closed; she's smiling. They nuzzle, rubbing noses, cheeks, faces against each other. Anna grazes Francesca. Francesca opens her eyes. Anna caresses her, and Francesca holds her. Her face quivers ever so slightly. She digs her fingernails lightly into her best friend's flesh. Anna places her lips on Francesca's.

Oh, yes. The rhythm of the night . . . But the enchantment is suddenly shattered. At a certain point, they pull apart. They turn off the stereo and pull the curtains closed, across the window.

It was always Anna who broke away. They couldn't, they didn't know how to go beyond this point. But the men who'd been watching them didn't stop. Lisa's uncle got up early just to masturbate to the sight of the thirteen-year-old girls in the building across the way. Even Lisa, turmoil roiling in her chest, would pull the curtains closed and close the shutters, and sometimes she felt like crying.

Anna looked out, nude as she was, framed in the rectangle of the window, her elbows on the sill. She watched a wooden spoon stirring a pot, in a kitchen at random in building 8, and a robust woman cleaning and chopping long stalks of celery.

In the building across the way, on the far shore of the courtyard, the one infested with shouting brats, there were plenty of women already at work on lunch. Around here spaghetti sauce was simmering by midmorning. Anna looked down and watched the little boys playing soccer, a young couple arguing on their balcony: He kicked a flowerpot with a basil plant in it.

Then there was the blue sky.

She loved that place. She could see the big bunkerlike buildings, the mess, the noise, Emma coming home with her bags of groceries, pregnant at age sixteen, and felt that she was a part of all this.

"It's insane, if you think about it. We'll be riding motor scooters to school! We'll take the hill road to Montemezzano. . . . You know how fast that is? My brother says he'll give me his SR; he's not using it anymore." Francesca was huddled in the shadows, perched on the bidet.

"They won't give us a hard time anymore; they won't be able to tell us we can't go out!"

Francesca's legs were askew, her eyes were looking at the floor.

"I'd love to see them try to catch you, if you had a scooter. The old baboon tells you: You aren't going out tonight. And you hop on your scooter, you zip away from Piombino, and you never come back!" Anna was radiant.

Francesca wasn't. She was afraid.

"You don't give a damn that we're going to be separated," she snapped. She suddenly got to her feet and looked at Anna with a sullen glare: "You don't care."

The oppressive heat stagnated in the barrackslike apartment buildings, settling in every room, transforming it into a swamp.

"What the fuck are you saying?"

Francesca turned toward the mirror.

It annoyed her that Anna was so galvanized at the idea of the future. Worse, it hurt her feelings that Anna was leaping with joy at the thought of going to a school that wouldn't be her school, to a class that wouldn't be her class. That they couldn't see each other during recess anymore, that they wouldn't be able to share their snacks.

Then there was the fact that Anna would be going to the *liceo classico* with the other smart kids, that Anna had finished middle school with excellent grades, and that she liked to study.

Anna didn't have any reluctance letting boys kiss her; she didn't have bruises on her back and belly. Francesca didn't like studying at all.

"Don't forget that the IPS Institute is across the street from the *liceo classico*," Anna said to her. "That in the morning we'll go to school together, and that we'll come home together, too."

"How nice!" laughed Francesca, rubbing makeup remover over her eyes.

"God, I hate you when you're like this. . . . When you pretend to be a bitch. You're not thinking about all the changes; you're just thinking about bullshit."

"Get out of my way. I have to pee."

It was past twelve noon. Mothers were starting to lean out the windows and call their children to come upstairs.

"So what, you can't pee now?" Anna laughed.

"Not if you stare at me." What does it mean to grow up in a complex of four big tenements shedding sections of balconies and chunks of asbestos into a courtyard where little kids play alongside older kids dealing drugs and old people who reek of decay? What kind of vision do you get of the world in a place where it's normal *not* to go anywhere on vacation, *not* to go to the movies, *not* to know anything about the world, to never read the newspaper, to never read a book, and that's just how life is? The two of them, in this place, sought each other out, chose each other.

Now Francesca looked down, listened to the rush of water from the toilet, and felt like laughing. Anna was looking at her again. Francesca tore a length of toilet paper off the roll, crumpled it into a ball, and threw it at her. And she threw it back at her with a laugh.

"Shower?" asked Anna, turning the faucet.

They'd already made peace.

Francesca smiled and stepped into the shower stall with the glass door that stuck. The sense of sight and smell were clouded under the spray. All that remained was the sense of touch, one girl's bottom against the other's.

They weren't talking anymore. Words are no good; they mostly start fights. They washed themselves carefully with the shower sponge and were astonished at the differences between them: a mole; the oblong or blunt shapes of their fingernails. They were astonished, as if witnessing something that made no sense.

Why did Anna have broader hips and bigger breasts? And why was Francesca's bottom higher and rounder? Why was her belly button deeper? "Why aren't we the same?" asked Francesca, as she massaged Anna's curls.

"Because we're different, but we're still the same."

"But why?"

"Because we were born together, we live together, we'll die together, and we'll do everything together."

"How are we going to die together?"

"I don't know."

They dried off in a hurry. They didn't want to get caught by Sandra, who might be home at any minute.

When they stepped out onto the landing, their hair still damp, Francesca stopped at the edge of the stairs. Her face looked different now. She looked at her friend with eyes that had grown larger.

"I don't want to go home. The old baboon's home for lunch today. . . ." Francesca, in the half light of the dusty, foul-smelling staircase, was teetering on the edge of the top step, and she wasn't crying, because she'd never liked crying.

Anna stepped closer to her and caressed her, trying to instill courage in her friend.

"Look, I'll see you later, at two o'clock on the dot. . . ." Her voice had become gentler, softer.

"Okay," Francesca said. But she wasn't moving. She stood there and seemed to grow thinner, frailer.

From the stairs, from the darkness of the long hallways, shouts and the sounds of fists came echoing every five minutes. A child would burst into tears. A mother chased her son on the landing, tearing from his hands the Super Liquidator he had just used to spray her. She spanked him hard and then retreated with him into their apartment, slamming the door behind her. It wasn't clear why these parents were constantly angry, always losing their tempers: After all, these little boys were just playing cops and robbers on the stairs.

"I'll come get you as soon as I'm done eating, and we'll go straight to the beach."

"Okay, but make sure you come in. Don't stand outside the door."

"Can't you stay here and have lunch with us?"

"As if!" Francesca tried to smile as she said it, but it didn't quite work. "That'll really set him off. . . ."

Kids shouting. BB gun pellets chipping the walls. And the thuds of things, the dull thuds of hands. There was a man shouting angrily at his wife in a high-pitched keening voice: "You're nothing but a whore!"

CHAPTER 4

S
he went back into the apartment.

Anna knew.

She mopped the bathroom, dried the floor, and cleaned the hair out of the shower drain. She didn't want to hear her mother screaming at her.

Anna knew, the only one who did.

But she didn't know what to do.

She started setting the table; she put a pot of pasta water on the stove. She wanted to make her mama happy, let her find everything ready for lunch. She laid out the napkins carefully, to the right of each plate. But her thoughts never veered away from Francesca.

She picked up the remote control and hit 1. Punctually, the theme music of the TG1, the midday news program on Rai-1, blared out.

The roar of the midday news theme music blasted out from all the television sets, all the open windows in the thousand or so apartments on the Via Stalingrado. She loved that theme music; it made her feel like a grown-up, part of something bigger. Rome, Milan—the Italy that she had never seen, even though she lived in Italy.

"You're a darling," said Sandra, as she opened the door and saw her daughter stirring the pasta. "If it weren't for you . . . With that idiot father and miserable brother of yours!"

She was tired. She put down her grocery bags and stretched for a moment. Her back was sore.

Then she hurried over to open the door of the washing machine she'd run that morning before leaving for work.

Anna loved her mother. She was a woman who worked hard at her job but who still found the energy to leaflet and help organize the annual Communist festival, the Festa dell'Unità. And she read left-wing newpapers, *La Repubblica* and *Liberazione*, and always told Anna to study hard, that one day she'd be a member of parliament, the Honorable Anna, a lawmaker. Part of Anna even believed it.

"Go ahead and drain the pasta," her mother shouted. "Those two won't even be home for lunch today." Sandra hefted the basket of wet sheets, socks, and underwear onto one shoulder and stepped out onto the landing to call the elevator.

While she was waiting, she looked around. All up and down the stairs was a clatter of clogs and the shouting of various oaths, all ending in *madonna*.

Relations with their neighbors weren't especially good. They were willing to declare open warfare if a sock flew onto their balcony. But Sandra had studied a little, and she was no pushover: She insisted on handing out leaflets that few if any bothered to read for every election campaign.

When she got up to the roof, on the twelfth floor, the sky was so powerful it hurt. At first, she closed her eyes.

There was the summer, chirping with millions of hidden insects.

She slowly opened her eyes again: a vast field of blue, the blue of the sky and the sea together. So much color it made her stagger. The clean, clear silence of the sun, the blue silhouettes of the distant islands, truly dragged out a smile of bafflement, of liberation. Even if you didn't feel like smiling at all, even if you were never going to set foot on Elba, Capraia, and Giglio.

Here, among the tightly stretched clotheslines and the hanging laundry, Sandra recognized Francesca's mama. She saw her busily hanging out laundry, between the white of one sheet and the next, in the wind that was tossing her hair and blowing handkerchiefs away.

"Rosa!" she called to her.

Rosa turned slowly, fearfully. She was wearing down-at-the-heels clogs and a stained smock over a black housedress. She dresses like my grandmother, thought Sandra. But Rosa was ten years younger than Sandra, and she did wear a pair of flashy earrings.

"You hang up laundry at this time of day, too?" she asked, just to strike up a conversation.

Rosa's eyes, darker than her hair, lit up.

She didn't move any closer; she stayed where she was. But it was clear that she wanted to stop and talk.

"I'm sorry we never see each other . . . ," said Sandra. "Why don't you come to my house sometime for a cup of coffee? I don't have to work on Saturdays." Rosa stiffened slightly.

"I'd like that. . . ." The left-wing activist and the housewife studied one another, warily approaching one another as if they were two animals from different species.

One was trying to draw the other forward as she retreated, while the smell of boiled caggage wafted up from below.

"Okay, I'll expect you!" Sandra called out, encouragingly.

She knew how to talk to people: She was a woman who dreamed of addressing political rallies, even if she had never done anything but distribute leaflets.

"It's a pity. We're neighbors, our daughters are such close friends, and we hardly know each other."

"You're right," smiled Rosa. "I'll come by to see you one of these days. . . ." Then she went back to folding her sheets, avoiding Sandra's gaze. Sandra considered the other woman's petite person. She knew almost nothing about her, and yet, without knowing, there was something she knew.

"If you like, I'll bring a cake," Francesca's mama ventured, brightening a little at the thought. She was so different from her daughter; she didn't look a bit like her.

"Good idea, bring a cake, I don't know how to bake at all. Anna yells at me. She says that a mama who doesn't bake cakes isn't a proper mama at all." She laughed.

Rosa felt a mixture of fear and attraction for that woman: She was so energetic; she put on makeup every day; and she wore sandals with heels even when she went to work. An intuitive sympathy, like when she was back at school. She hadn't had girlfriends since she'd moved from Calabria to Tuscany, when she was eighteen. And then she got married.

She overcame her shyness: "Anna's gotten to be so pretty."

"Let's hope she doesn't notice it, or she'll turn obnoxious on me. . . ."

Sandra snorted. "Francesca's gotten pretty, too. I was watching her come back from the beach in her swimsuit yesterday and I thought to myself: Goodness, she's grown!"

Rosa's eyes gleamed.

Elba gleamed too, and Corsica and Capraia in the distance.

The two women went on hanging sheets on the few unoccupied lines on the roof.

"Your husband? Everything okay?"

Rosa dropped the basket of clothespins she was holding. Clothespins scattered across the roof.

"Yes," she said. Her expression had changed.

Sandra noticed, and she glimpsed a mark on the woman's neck.

Silence. A wind sprang up from the sea. It played havoc with the laundry.

Rosa was kneeling down, picking up clothespins. She was in a hurry to go now.

"Then I'll expect you, okay?" Sandra said again.

Rosa nodded as she stood up, but she hurried immediately to the stairs and almost didn't say good-bye.

Her slender figure moved hesitantly. She seemed to be afraid she'd be attacked at every step. She looked at the ground; she clenched her fists. She was pale. But up on the roof, with summer in the fullness of its power, that woman seemed for a moment to have realized that she was still young and, perhaps, even pretty.

Then she stopped and stood there, poised at the door. She turned with determination toward Sandra.

"Ciao!" she cried. "So, I'll come see you!"

Sandra smiled as she hung up the last of the socks.

"I'm counting on it!" she answered in a strong voice.

Rosa felt happy. After all, what's so wrong about wanting a friend?

CHAPTER 5

At two on the dot Anna rang the doorbell of the Morganti apartment. The mother opened the door. She cracked it open just far enough to see who was outside, and stood there, at the threshold.

"Hello. Is Francesca ready or is she still eating?"

Rosa didn't know what to say for a minute.

She stood there toying with the security chain on the door, and couldn't seem to bring herself to undo it. Slender, uncertain fingers. She avoided locking eyes with the impatient young girl standing in front of her.

"If not, I can come by later. . . ." Anna looked hard into the darkness to get a better glimpse of that segment of a woman, rigid as a sentinel, between the edge of the wall and the edge of the door. She had the impression that Rosa was trying to block her way and block her view.

She'd never entered that apartment. The two girls had been friends since they were born, and they'd never let her in.

She noticed that the woman had something strange on her face.

A purplish shadow on one cheek, under the eye that was staring at her now. A liquid eye, petroleum dark.

"Francesca can't come to the beach today."

"Why not?"

Rosa jumped at the sound of that "why not?" spoken like that: uttered mouth and face wide open, by a young girl in a swimsuit with sandals on her feet, plastic clips in her hair, strawberry lip gloss that she could smell from where she was. She saw—incarnated in Anna's body, the backpack on her shoulder full of lotions, beach towels, and nets to catch sunfish—the world that her daughter would have had every right to inhabit. And so she smiled, for a fleeting instant, disarmed.

"She doesn't feel well; she'd better stay in."

"But it's June! What's wrong with her?"

Anna wasn't going to swallow it.

"Tomorrow . . . I'm sure that Francesca will feel better tomorrow."

From the interior of the house, in the meanwhile, not a sound, not even the buzz of the television set.

From the way she compressed her lips and narrow-focused her pupils, Rosa understood that Anna had understood.

She cut the conversation short: "I promise she'll come tomorrow."

Then she shut the door and thought to herself that that wasn't a promise; it was an act of justice to be undertaken.

She thought that as soon as the monster was gone, she and her daughter would talk. She'd tell Francesca that she deserved to go out like all the other kids her age. Enough, they'd put up with enough now. She was strong enough: She'd find a job and report the monster to the police. No question. And divorce him.

The problem was the job; Francesca had to understand that. The problem was money, and nothing else. That she hated her husband, and she'd never let him do her harm again.

Anna stood waiting for a few seconds, motionless in front of the closed door like a cat caught in terror in the headlights of a car.

Now what do I do? I don't want to go to the beach anymore. That piece of shit baboon . . . She wanted to punch him in the face. Why do there have to be fathers? Meanwhile, from behind the door, not a sound. In fact, the silence of a tomb. So she went downstairs to the courtyard, kicking a pebble across the pavement. Then she tossed her backpack to the ground and sat down on a skeletal bench.

Until *France* comes outside, I'm not moving.

Farther along a few old women were enthusiastically playing cards, fanning themselves energetically. They were talking about the latest episode of *Inspector Derrick*. Anna gave them a surly glare.

She couldn't knock on their door again. She'd seen that woman's face, and she'd understood: the beatings and everything that went with them. She clenched her fists hard. She was alone in the fierce heat, in the middle of a cement courtyard. She wanted to get over this feeling of helplessness. Do something, anything, clamber up the drainpipe all the way to Francesca's window.

But she was afraid of that man.

She started looking at the walls: ten stories high, blocking the view on all sides. She liked to look at things. She liked to examine details. The windowsills were cluttered with stuff: withered plants, shoes, newly washed pots and pans set out to dry. You couldn't see the water from here. You could see pieces of flaking plaster, rusted sections of rebar that stuck out jaggedly like broken fingernails from the reinforced concrete pillars.

Mama had explained it all to her: There are two classes in society. And the social classes are at war with one another because there is a bastard do-nothing class and it oppresses the good class that works hard for a living. That's the way the world spins. Mama belonged to Rifondazione Comunista, she was a member of that 5 percent of the Italian population. That's why Alessio called her a pathetic loser. Her father worshipped the myth of Al Capone and the godfather, Francis Ford Coppola's *Godfather*. Her brother was a member of the FIOM, the metalworkers' union, but he voted Berlusconi. Because one thing is for sure: Berlusconi *is no loser*.

Anna examined the courtyard with interest. This was her world. She saw Emma go by with her big pregnant belly: She'd gotten married in a rush to Mario; he was eighteen. All the people from the apartment buildings got together and threw a big party the day they got married, with potato chips, Coca-Cola, and confetti, sort of like at school when it's someone's birthday.

She thought to herself that she wasn't convinced of what her mother said, or of the things that her brother yammered on about, and least of all the crap that old baboon spouted. She was convinced of her courtyard, that and nothing else. She was convinced of the beams, the pillars, the reinforced concrete. She liked the architecture of those huge, cratelike buildings, with all their tiny cubbyholes. She didn't envy people who lived downtown or in the row houses outside of town; she just ignored them.

Why don't you come downstairs, *France?*

This wasn't the first time: "She doesn't feel well. . . ."

A flat, open courtyard without so much as a spot of greenery. They played soccer there; they cooled off. It was always a noisy, rackety place, at any hour, except on summer afternoons.

Then it looked like a desert, the most arid desert you could imagine.

Anna'd been born here, but she realized that the wastepaper, the cigarette butts, the occasional used syringes on the cement were a bad sign. That everyone pissed at the base of the pillars: dogs, children, junkies. That there was a stench there that you'd have to hold your nose. That a man shooting a dose of heroin into his arm or his neck in front of little children isn't a nice thing to see. But if you spat on those things it would be like spitting on yourself. Sometimes, with certain junkies she'd meet in the apartment buildings, she'd stop and chat.

Anna knew that no man is a monster. Except for Francesca's father.

Why doesn't she come out? What had he done to her? She started reading the graffiti on the bench. A geological stratification of loves and quarrels, including her own. "Francesca U R the best by Nino" was the first X-ACTO knife carving that she deciphered. Then she recognized her own handwriting, with a uni-POSCA paint marker: "Anna & France together forever."

The buzzing of grandmothers in clogs corroded the asphyxiating silence of the cube at the edges. Anna was now completely absorbed in reading the bench.

"Marta + Aldo = love." "Sonia you're a gigantic whore" ("whore" erased). "Jennifer and Cristiano 4-Ever." She smiled proudly when she found a new graffito: "Anna U R HOT 2 bad U R my best friend . . . By Massi '84." She laughed out loud when she saw: "Alessio = 9 1/2 in." And, immediately beneath it: "I love you—your Sonia."

My brother's great, she thought.

Certainly Sonia, who watched porno movies with Alessio in his bedroom, wasn't exactly to her taste. If they'd at least put on a little background music . . . but nothing, so you could hear everything. And she'd have to go into the kitchen and wait until they were done. But that was the price you paid for having a brother who was so cool. Just think, What if he'd been a loser? Omigod! She was proud of Alessio. She could hold her head up high with a blond, muscular brother like him.

Sonia, Jessica, and all the other big girls always said hi to her; they would invite her to go for a ride on their scooters with them; they'd apply nail polish for her and teach her how to put eyeliner around the contours of her eyelids. All of this, of course, was just so they could extort information from her about Alessio.

"Cia-o A-nna." Anna turned suddenly in the direction of the voice.

Donata, struggling with immense effort to lift one hand to wave ciao, was coming over to her in her wheelchair, pushed by Lisa. Her hand, which refused to respond to her commands, dangled in the air like an inconclusive claw.

"Ciao, Donata," Anna responded, totally unnatural. "What are you doing?" No one fell for it: Her smile was obviously uncomfortable.

She didn't even exchange a hello with Lisa.

"I-I-I'm ge-etting some coo-ool air."

In order to utter a word, just one two-syllable word, she gathered all her strength, as if she were about to toss a javelin. The left side of her mouth and jaw were numb and lame forever; she couldn't smile. Her legs wouldn't move at all. And for the past year, neither would her left arm. That arm had curled in upon itself. The hand clenched into a fist, couldn't seize objects, couldn't wave, couldn't pet cats or caress people. It just trembled, with harsh jerks, like the rest of her body.

Anna tried not to look at it, that fifteen-year-old body that wasn't a fifteen-year-old body.

"What a-are you-ou do-ing? Wh-why a-aren't you a-at the bea-each?"

All the same, despite her injured body, you could see it with the naked eye: Donata had a thirst for life. A desire to move, to go, to talk to other people, to learn something about the world in the years she still had before all her muscles went numb for good: all of them, from her finger muscles to the muscles of her eyebrows, to her abdominal muscles, and gradually, to the muscles of her heart.

Anna was sure of it: In her place she'd never have left the house. The minute she had the chance, she'd throw herself and her wheelchair down the stairs.

"I didn't feel like going to the beach today. . . ." She glanced up at Francesca's window, then added, darkly: "I need to think."

"You-ou're a philo-sopher the-en!"

Donata was joking with her; she'd even tried to laugh. And pretty Anna, with her name written by Massi on the bench, felt as if she'd been turned over a knee and spanked.

"Let's not exaggerate. . . . But I'll be studying philosophy, too; starting in September I'll be in the same school as you." If you looked carefully into Donata's eyes, you couldn't say that you couldn't see the pain.

"The-en you-ou'll be in Li-isa's cla-ass!"

Anna smirked. "Is that right?"

She barely dignified her with a glance, that loser Lisa. She decided that the one thing she didn't need in her class was that one.

The sun was beating down. People started coming out of the buildings, carrying chairs and folding tables down into the courtyard. It was a hostile time of day. People took shelter in the shade and chatted.

Dozens of portable radios in the background. It wasn't easy to get comfortable on the seething cement, but it was still easier than sitting cooped up in those apartments that turned into kilns in the summer.

Donata was forcing her lips, her tongue, her throat to manage to expel the words that she had inside her. Inside there was an endless font of words: complete, ringing, directed at all the lovely, healthy people like Anna. It was just that the muscles of her mouth distorted them, twisted them, made them ugly and dolorous. Donata knew that: She was fighting a war.

Now she was explaining in broad outlines what philosophy was, first Greek philosophy, then Latin, the subjects that Anna would be studying before long. Plato's myth of the cave, with the chained servants. And after that, *The Iliad* and *The Odyssey*, the great creations of humanity: all this in the midst of the din and chaos of Via Stalingrado.

Anna understood some of it, but some of it she didn't. To see the sweat pouring down her temples from the sheer effort of talking was like a fist to the solar plexus. She was interested in what Donata was telling her, she liked Donata, but . . . someone like her just can't live in this world.

This world was hard enough for her, even with the tits and the shamelessness that God gave her. It was hard, even with all the boys her age prostrate at her feet and a fantastic best friend like Francesca. She always had to hurt someone else to keep from taking the hurt herself. Donata shouldn't have existed at all.

And so the minute she saw Nino drag his gleaming new motor scooter into the shade of the concrete pillars, drop the kickstand, open his tool kit, and pull out a monkey wrench, it took Anna only a split second to say 'bye to Donata, to say nothing to Lisa, and to rush away from them and straight to the side of the blond sixteen-year-old who was handsome to die for.

If you had a sister like Donata, you wouldn't be so high and mighty, thought Lisa as she watched Anna jump onto Nino's back out of the corner of her eye. And went on pushing the wheelchair.

Lisa would study herself in the mirror, at length, in the bathroom with the door shut. If she detected a zit on her forehead, she felt a sharp stab of fear in her chest. If she realized that her belly and hips and chubby thighs weren't likely to turn slender, she was swept by a wave of fury. . . . She felt ugly. And she was ugly, with her pointy, mousy little face, her oversized, downturned nose, and her thin, drab, sparse hair. . . .

Then Lisa would think about her sister. She'd wrench her eyes away from the mirror and feel a sense of guilt.

Now she was wheeling Donata around the courtyard and—a little bit—hating her. No, not hating her, hating her disease. And when she remembered that Donata wouldn't live more than a few more years, she felt a burning sense of injustice inside her. What did Anna know about it? That girl didn't know a damn thing about pain and grief, not the real kind.

She wanted to punch the whole world in the face, beat the whole world senseless.

It was hard to push that wheelchair around, hard to be part of the sickness, in front of everyone: in front of a couple of mean little shits like Anna and Francesca, who were laughing and talking with the boys, rubbing up against the boys, and even letting themselves be kissed by the boys.

Shits, the both of them. Lisa was biting her lip, tamping down her anger. Those two damned turds—when they got their periods, you'd think no one else in the world had ever menstruated.

And Maria, and Jessica, and that other idiot, Sonia: cocks this and dicks that, and blow jobs here and cocksucking there. Cocksucking? She didn't even know what all this famous cocksucking was about.

She just knew that it wasn't fair. That in this world there are people who have everything and people who have nothing. Nothing at all.

She saw them in the distance: Nino and Anna stretched out on the pavement underneath the motor scooter, focused on disassembling the muffler. She heard them laugh in a way that she'd never laughed. And she rushed through the front door of her apartment building, number 8, across from Anna's bathroom window, through which you could see everything.

In the waiting room of the doctor's clinic father and daughter sat wordless, ignoring each other. Their bodies were rigid and icy in the flat fluorescent light.

Enrico had argued with Rosa to let him take Francesca to the doctor. He wouldn't take no for an answer.

He knew that if Rosa went, she'd say too much. She'd burst into tears, who knows what she'd dream up. Words were the one thing there couldn't be too few of. Few words and, most important, only convincing words.

Francesca's eyes were empty. She was staring into an abstract point in the middle distance, and she wasn't going to shift her gaze. She was pressing down hard with her right hand on the inexpertly applied bandage wrapped around her left wrist. The cotton was slowly saturating with blood.

To the doctor's clinic, not the emergency room. At the hospital they would have started asking questions.

They'd been waiting for an hour; there were still seven or eight people ahead of them. Neither Enrico nor Francesca was in a hurry. If anything, they seemed strangely absent.

I know Doctor Satta. He won't get nosy; he'll mind his own fucking business. He'll do what he needs to do and nothing more. That, more or less, was running through Enrico's head. His thoughts were focusing on practical matters, strictly practical, basic: the stitches, the disinfectant, the gauze, and Francesca shouldn't take off her T-shirt. The doctor shouldn't examine her.

Suddenly, the door to the doctor's office swung open, and a little old man wearing sunglasses, his arm wrapped around a diaphanous blonde, emerged; she had a distinct Eastern European accent. The old man was smiling and showing her off to the other old men sitting in a half circle in the waiting room.

"Oh," said one, "but wasn't he married?"

The old man had barely gone out the door before the other old men who were still waiting started in.

"His wife must have died, I think, two years ago. . . ."

"Ah, I see!"

One or two of them actually stood up. One old man closed his copy of *Il Tirreno* and set it aside.

"Blondes, yep, they're not like the women from here in Piombino. . . ."

"If my wife died, knock on wood, never want it to happen," he reached down and grabbed his balls to ward off evil, "but if she did, I think I'd get me a blonde!"

Father and daughter, immobile, just kept on staring at the toes of their shoes.

"Well, sure. Italian women want you to take 'em out to dinner, to the movies, and they won't come home with you, they won't wash your socks for you, no."

"Well, though, they tell me that Russian girls drink, they drink too much. . . ."

"Nice firm asses, though!"

"And they don't bust your chops."

"And they'll give you seconds, and thirds, too . . . Ukrainian women."

Enrico wasn't listening. He was maniacally rehearsing the three phrases he had to say to the doctor; he was designing them, scheming, polishing them, practicing them to the point of obsession. Francesca, in contrast, was listening. She was looking into the middle distance, eyes wide open, staring, but she could hear perfectly. And she felt an impulse to vomit—a physical, piercing desire to vomit at the idea that one of those old men over there, with their filthy shirts and circular sweat stains under their armpits, could mount a young girl who had immigrated from who knows what poverty.

"Russian women aren't bad. There's plenty of them in Piombino."

When she walked in, they'd all looked her up and down. Then her father had walked in, and they'd all looked studiously away.

"Boys, you've got to save your pennies! Your pension isn't enough. You've got to pay her, buy her jewelry, dresses, shoes. . . ."

"For now I just hope my wife holds on a little longer."

Francesca wasn't there or anywhere else. She was flipping distractedly through old issues of *Novella* 2000. She lingered over the photographs that showed *veline* on Formentera, half-naked girls with professionally curled hair posing in all the chic spots in Milan, the glittering shop windows of New York behind them . . .

But she would never be able to escape. *He* would thwart her; he'd hunt her down wherever she went. When she was eighteen, maybe. Yes, at eighteen she could compete for Miss Italy, be noticed by someone, and leave. With Anna. But now? She couldn't dream; she lacked the strength. In fact, now she only desired one thing: her father's death. The death of the disgusting old men in front of her, who smelled bad and expected to have a woman who would clean them on the bidet, a Ukrainian stolen away from her home.

She was sure of it: She'd never get married. Men disgusted her. That was one thing that was clear in her mind: that men disgusted her, that she'd never let one touch her, ever, as long as she lived. She'd just leave, someday, with Anna. Just the two of them, no one else, forever.

Now Enrico had stopped thinking. He'd learned the three phrases by heart, and he felt okay. The bovine gaze. He wedged things into his brain the way the various phases of the production cycle fit together, the temperature of the steel, the cooling times, the roller that shapes the hot bar, the rail that comes out. Like the different steps involved in fishing: Assemble the rod; spool line onto the reel; tie on the hook; impale the worm.

His binoculars.

His daughter.

His daughter, who can't turn into a whore. His daughter, who this afternoon had seized a kitchen knife, a big meat knife, and carved her wrist open in front of his eyes.

I'll have to say that she fell on barbed wire.

The metal was clean; it won't cause an infection. The cut was deep, she had lost a lot of blood, but her veins are intact.

That's the important thing.

The old men had quieted down now. One by one they'd been admitted to receive prescriptions for the medicines they needed to take on a daily basis: the heart pill, the blood pressure pill, the pill to keep their glucose levels stable. On their way out each of them said good-bye in a faint voice, gripping the prescription in a trembling hand. Their bodies, they knew perfectly well, weren't really functioning properly anymore; there were leaks and weak spots everywhere. The illusion of a Ukrainian woman wasn't enough to put things right: It was as much as they could do to hobble down to the pharmacy without pain.

Francesca: the one good thing he'd created in his life. He remembered every minute of her existence, since she was born. The first time she stammered "Papa." The time she won the school swim meet. Her tiny face, impossible to describe, no bigger than a fistful of rice, newly glimpsed as it peered out from the incubator. But his hands were too big, his fingers too hard; he couldn't handle her with sufficient delicacy.

When they were called they stood up in perfect lockstep and walked into the doctor's office together, without hesitation. The doctor smiled at them. Enrico smiled in turn. Francesca's lips remained set. She looked hard at the man with a pair of eyes that said nothing more than: Stitch me up. Then Enrico started in on his explanation, as best he could. He was untutored, intimidated by doctors. But he knew how to be persuasive, when necessary, by gesturing with his hands.

The doctor understood; he asked no questions. He took Francesca's wrist, removed the cotton gauze, sodden with blood, and cleaned it with alcohol. He began to suture a flap of skin with a large steel needle.

Francesca watched, expressionless, as he reknit flesh to flesh. Without particular interest: Her flesh lay open, the blood continually soaked up by patches of gauze. Motionless in the surreal silence, she allowed herself to be stitched up, good as new, in Dr. Satta's walk-in clinic.

"We don't need a full physical examination, Doctor. There's no need for that."

The doctor understood; he asked no questions. This wasn't the first girl covered with bruises he'd treated in his clinic. He didn't really want to uncover an array of bruises. The last thing he wanted was to mingle with those people. Animals is what they are, it's well-known. He was just a general practitioner assigned by the public health service to this part of town. Not a social worker, not a policeman. It wouldn't have made any difference, anyway.

"In a week we'll remove the stitches, all right, signorina?"

Francesca nodded, impassive.

As they walked out the tallest smokestack of the steelworks expelled a puff of carbon monoxide into the air. It hung there, still against the clear sky. Then a strong gust of wind sprang up from the far side of the promontory and swept the sky clean.

Nothing had happened.

Looking out the passenger-side window of the car as they drove down from the scenic road and out onto the Lungomare Marconi, along the waterfront, Francesca watched the island glitter. So near, yet unattainable. There's a scheduled ferry service, but I've never been there, never laid eyes on it. Just three miles. Me and Anna could swim it.

Enrico drove calmly, respecting the speed limits and the traffic laws. If the sign said "30 mph," he kept the car at 30; if the sign said "20 mph," he kept it at 20. He had a certain gift: He could forget what his hands were capable of. Never think about the complicated things, only think about one thing, separately, without linking it in time and space to other things.

The light began to sink back, relaxing against the horizon. And the villages on Elba turned into so many tiny manger scenes that, glimpsed from afar, no longer seemed to belong to this world.

Today I stood up for myself. Today, for the first time. Like Anna says: You have to stand up for yourself, you have to make it clear to him that you're not his chattel, not a piece of property he owns; you are a person.

Anna knows how to use words properly. Standing up for yourself. Chattel; piece of property. Person. I don't know how to use words, though. I wanted to kill myself. Like hell: I wanted to kill him. And what happened? Nothing. We're both still here. Now we're pulling into the garage, he's parking the car, we slam the doors. Anna, why aren't you here with me? Why don't we run away together? Now he's locking the garage, putting the key in his pocket; we avoid looking at each other, we walk upstairs in silence, we say hello to mama, and we sit down to dinner.

CHAPTER 6

Arturo was there, peering out at six in the morning. He was alone. He was leaning on the low wall by the little marina. He was feeling his wrist, looking for the Rolex that wasn't there anymore. His eyes were puffy and his mouth was gummy with nicotine.

He gawked at his wallet in astonishment: Yesterday there was two million lire in there; now there's ten thousand five hundred lire in coins and one-thousand-lire notes. How could that be? In one night. I piled it up in a heap and burned it, in one night. Shit, that was my last paycheck.

Across the water the island's streetlights flickered one last time, and then went out, at 6:30.

Arturo couldn't believe his eyes. He counted and recounted the money, arranging it in orderly piles on the low wall; he emptied his empty wallet. He took off his summer raincoat; it was already hotter than hell. He unbuttoned his shirt and stood bare chested, his fine gold chain and crucifix glittering amid his chest hair.

Suddenly he heard someone whistling. He whirled around like a wild animal that's been bitten.

"Why the fuck are you whistling at this time of night? Everyone's asleep, idiot!"

The retiree, who had just stepped out of his house, froze to the spot and took a good look at the thug who must have been up all night and was now shouting at him.

The old man extended both arms: "Ya drunk! Look at the sun; it's broad daylight!"

Arturo looked up at the sky. Christ, it's daytime! What day is this? Do I have to go to work? No, that's right: I don't have to go back to work anymore. I have to call Pasquale, that's what I have to do. The paintings were supposed to get here today, right? That's right, it was today: Saturday.

He pulled his two cell phones out of his rumpled trouser pocket and noticed that they were both turned off.

"Excuse me, could you tell me the time?"

This guy's crazy, thought the old man. He had left his house to go buy a loaf of bread and a copy of that morning's *Il Tirreno*, and he found himself confronted by this individual who starts by shouting at him, then turns all courteous, and has the eyes of a drug addict.

"A quarter to seven."

Arturo gulped: Now Sandra's opening her eyes, turning over toward my pillow, and seeing that no one's there.

For a few instants he stood there, silent and off-kilter. His face expressed the concept: My wife is going to strangle me.

"Sorry to have to say this, mister, but you strike me as retarded," laughed the old man in his undershirt.

Arturo was standing with his wallet turned inside out in one hand, his two dead cell phones in the other, and ten thousand five hundred lire neatly arranged on the wall. He couldn't manage to move a muscle; he was stuck. That was because he was thinking of his wife. And the dishwasher, and his son's car radio, and his debts with that bastard of the Monte dei Paschi bank.

"You tie one on?"

"Not even. I'm done for. . . ."

"Did your wife catch you with your girlfriend? Or else maybe you lost big at poker?"

Arturo was astonished: Grandpa's pretty perceptive.

"Not the girlfriend, it was the poker. . . . But all the same . . ." and color began to return to his cheeks, "I've got enough money left for breakfast."

In the meantime, on the wharves of the little harbor, crates filled with squid, sea bass, and gilthead bream were beginning to stack up. The fishermen were reckoning up their catch aloud, and the fish, still half alive, were becoming salable merchandise. Wholesalers were crowding onto the docks, the shopkeepers were standing in small knots and shouting at one another, and the restaurateurs were carefully examining the gills of the tuna fish.

In less than fifteen minutes it was a mob scene. The refrigerator trucks were parked pretty much everywhere, at crazy angles. The scooters of the street sweepers zipping through the center of town, Maghrebis with blank expressions and sorghum brooms in hand. Brushing against certain walls, down the narrow lanes of the old part of town, past certain small open windows with potted geraniums on the sills, you could hear the Moka coffeepots puffing away on the gas burner and demitasse spoons tinkling in the espresso cups.

Now that Sandra was raging through the apartment, kicking doors, kicking the walls with the wallpaper that had been peeling off and tattered for years now, Arturo took the time to think of her with a swelling sense of tenderness. "Where the fuck has that bastard gone?" she was screaming like a lunatic at her son, who had just returned from a night out in the discotheque. "He never came home last night, you realize that? Do you understand that he never came home? Where is he? Where the fuck is he?"

Arturo knew that she was telling Omnitel to go fuck itself because it was informing her that her husband's cell phones were turned off; he knew she was cursing the Madonna because her husband had flushed a huge pile of their money down the toilet at a poker table for the umpteenth time.

He walked into the Caffè Nazionale with his new eighty-year-old friend.

"Two espressos and two pastries. Ah, with a splash in the espresso, if you please."

"The usual?" the barista asked his longtime acquaintance.

"Yeah, Sambuca." He turned to the old guy: "You like Sambuca, don't you?"

For Arturo, making friends was a fine art. He could pick up anyone on the street. The crease in his trousers off center, his hair encrusted with brilliantine, he immediately won people over.

"I like everything," the old man replied, "when someone else is treating me."

Arturo was convinced that he was the cleverest of them all. All he had to do was show off his Ray-Bans, reel off a joke or two, leaning against the bar on one elbow: He was the king of Piombino.

Sandra, in fact, *was* cursing the Madonna. And Alessio, who had just gotten home in the sagging final stage of the drugs, had no idea where his father might be and no interest in listening to his mother.

"Will you shut up, for the love of Christ? Just go to work and stop moaning!"

"I will kill him. I swear I'm going to kill hi-i-m!"

She was wandering around the apartment in a rage. Half the time she was assembling the things she needed to go to work: her overalls, her hair-net . . . and where did she put her mascara? Half the time she was just tossing everything across the room: her stockings, her lipsticks, everything she laid hands on went slamming straight against the walls.

A half-naked figure appeared in the hallway, at the edge of the door. She was rubbing her sleepy eyes.

"Mama, what happened?" she mewed.

"Go back to bed."

"Mama . . . ," mumbled Anna, her face puffy with sleep, her feet bare on the chilly tiles. She had all those curls tumbling chaotically down over her bare shoulders, her big eyes glistening, empty of any accusations. She'd been startled into wakefulness, but she was still calm, in her undergar-ments, ready to help if she could.

"What's happened is your father is an idiot," Sandra snapped out unceremoniously. "Now that you know it, you can go right back to bed." Anna turned and went into her bedroom without a word.

She watched her brother take off his T-shirt and the chains he wore around his neck. You could see a mile away that he was exhausted, so from just across the room it was glaringly obvious. He'd gotten wrecked, as usual, on a Friday night. His hair, smeared with gel, was no longer cohering; it was flopping over and sticking up in all directions.

Anna looked at him the way you might stare at a chimp behind bars in the zoo, half curious and half heartbroken. What on earth had he been doing all night? She may have been born just the day before yesterday, true enough, but she was nobody's fool. When you live in certain places—where the only law is the law of the strongest, with no plea bargains on the side, and with the kind of father that destiny had assigned her—well, she knew something about the world.

She drew closer to him, stood up on tiptoes, and gave him a lip-smacking kiss on the cheek. Alessio responded with a smile of martyrdom. Dead tired.

His shift started at two o'clock, and he felt like breaking into tears at the thought of it. He felt too weak after ten hours of pounding music, pills, and fistfights to break into a stream of profanity, as he usually would. He undid his jeans, looked over at Anna, half naked, in front of him.

He hadn't realized that his sister was all grown up, she wasn't a little girl anymore, and she'd turned into a tremendous babe, too. He only saw it now, in the midst of his amphetamine hangover. And in the train wreck that was his family, with his piece-of-shit father, his sister would become his problem from here on in.

These thoughts shot through his mind in a split second. The time it took to kick his combat boots off his feet and across the room. He collapsed onto the bed in his boxers. You've got five hours to get some sleep, shave, smoke a quick joint, and then: fun, fun, fun on the crane! He collapsed face-first, his big tanned body, case-hardened by steel, thudding into the mattress like a corpse.

Anna lowered the slatted roller blind and turned on the fan—it was already stifling hot. She stood there bare chested like him, hovering, taking in her little pink bed and her brother's broad shoulders in the other bed.

Her mama went on shouting, outside the bedroom, slamming every door in the apartment.

Maybe I shouldn't, she mused, maybe it's not okay anymore. But then she swatted that mosquito of a thought aside with one hand. Sure, she laughed. And she catapulted herself onto Alessio's bed. She scooted over beside him, her head lodged under his armpit, her nose pressed against his skin. That was her brother's body: her reef. And sometimes she fastened herself to him, like a scallop on the rocks.

The two of them lay there, motionless, wedged together, on the perennially unmade bed, the swaybacked single mattress.

They wrapped their arms around each other, despite the heat and daylight sifting in through the blinds, and plunged into sleep. Sandra slammed the front door violently as she left for work. The glass panes of the windows shivered; they never even noticed.

They were used to it by now. Just one more reason that even at their ages, they still shared a bed every so often.

"So just what did you say you do for a living, Arturo?"

"Me?"

"Yeah, you!"

"I . . . well . . ." Arturo neutralized in a fraction of a second the surge of confusion that filled his head, then he cleared his throat and spoke: "I'm a businessman . . . an art dealer."

Men dressed in white walked past the Caffè Nazionale, lugging baskets of bread.

Sure, you're an art dealer, thought the old man, *and I'm a Rockefeller.*

Shopkeepers rolled up the metal shutters all along the Corso Italia, one after the other, with a loud clatter and screech. The news vendor, the corner mechanic. The guy who fixes bicycles, the Neapolitan who crowds the whole sidewalk with carts overflowing with bric-a-brac. He would talk to every one of them: the businessman, the art dealer. He'd stop to chat about this or that, he'd cadge himself lunch one way or another, and he'd carefully avoid the bank and his wife.

He would roam the city, from one end to the other, without a cent, without a watch. He'd hole up in the old phone booth on Piazza Bovio, with the letters of the old phone company still stenciled on the side.

And he'd take his last thousand lire and challenge fate with a Scratch & Win.

CHAPTER 7

Early on the morning of the following day, while Sandra was at work and the kids were sure to be asleep, Arturo crept cautiously across the courtyard. He slipped, furtive as a cat, into the ground-floor door of building number 7.

It was where he lived, sure, but technically he wasn't allowed in.

Most important: He mustn't be seen, while he rummaged through his own apartment, to make off with a few indispensable items, like his cell phone charger and, if he found it, one hundred thousand lire.

He went upstairs, looking around as he climbed each step. He didn't like what he was doing, let that be clear, but he really had no alternative. With his heart in his throat, feeling guilty as hell. Just a couple more days, just let him get a few things squared away, and he'd be back home, head held high; he'd have a talk with his wife; he'd embrace both his children. Now, though, he had to slink along, shoulder brushing the wall, and sneak through the shadows up the stairs, holding his breath.

Preoccupied as he was, his nerves on edge, he reached the turning for the fourth-floor landing.

When Enrico loomed up in front of him, Arturo practically screamed.

They ran into each other. They weren't expecting it, in the gravelike silence of the apartment buildings at that time of day. They stood there, uncertain in the half light, eyes wide open.

Enrico had never liked him. He'd heard about him; he knew he was Anna's father. A questionable individual. A guy with shady dealings. And his daughter was no better than he was, a little slut trying to steer his Francesca off the straight and narrow.

He noticed that Arturo was uneasy, looking around him, nervous as a burglar, smiling foolishly up at him as if to say: I'm innocent, I swear it. But Enrico didn't give a damn about him. He was leaving for work, the way he did every day; he just wanted to get to the steel mill on time and do his job right.

He said, "Hello." And went past him.

Arturo replied, "Hello."

They'd been exchanging hellos and nothing more for a lifetime.

Arturo resumed climbing the stairs, a bad father, a bad head of household, and when he reached the fifth floor, a few yards short of his front door, he stopped to rummage through his fanny pack for his keys. Actually, he was stalling for time and working up his nerve, because he was anything but excited about what he was getting ready to do. Before slipping the key into the lock, he thought to himself that he'd never liked that Enrico one bit.

He was a stupid man, you could see it from his eyes: round and flat, like hen's eyes. There wasn't an ounce of brains in his head, a giant though he might be.

He thought back to that one time when he'd overheard him talking to a plumber: He said the same thing a hundred times just to explain that the meter wasn't working right. The plumber nodded blankly, astonished that anyone could be so damned dumb.

It was such a basic thing, a tiny lag in the meter. But he just kept saying the same thing over and over, unable to link it to the thing, the broken thing he couldn't pin down and the words that couldn't describe it.

Enrico, on the other hand, who was turning the key in the door of his white Fiat Uno, wasn't thinking about a thing. Except for his drive to the steel mill: He'd go through three traffic lights and three roundabouts. Then he'd park in the big lot across from the entrance on the Via della Resistenza, punch in his time card, change into his overalls in the locker room, and then arrive at his destination: the coke oven.

There was something immobile in his gaze, like an animal staring intently at its prey's throat. Nature performing its daily task: the hard work of steel, hands firmly gripping the steering wheel. If there was shoveling to be done, he'd shovel. If there was quality control to be done, he'd control. He'd jot down the temperature in a notebook, swing the shovel into the coal and lift it: It didn't make a bit of difference to him.

They thought they were so smart. That Arturo, nobody knew how he'd become section foreman, Arturo, who never lifted a finger except to steal diesel fuel. Those other idiots, the young guys, swinging from cables like they were vines in the jungle. Instead of worrying about steel production they were trying to be Tarzans. But that's not the way, that's not right.

Enrico knew the right way to do things. In fact, he kept his eye on the temperature of the steel. He'd check the thermometer three and even four times. To make sure. To do his job right. He'd fill his lungs with coke, breathing in carefully, without allowing himself to be distracted from the job, and perform the same gesture for eight solid hours.

As he was driving, the only image in his head was of Francesca. Not her anger-reddened face when she'd jammed the knife into her wrist. No, the half-naked body on the beach, the one that was escaping his control, the one that had to be set straight.

He had to get her back into focus, back inside the outlines, his little girl. This was not good.

They'd knock her up, if this kept up. One of those bastards. Pregnant. His little girl. This never should have happened.

CHAPTER 8

Francesca turned around, shouted something to Anna that was swallowed up by the thunder of the exhaust pipes. Something like: I'm happy. Without a helmet she was getting a mouthful of hair. She was laughing because the wind under her camisole, and between her legs straddling the scooter, was tickling her. She turned again, clinging to Nino's body, and laid her face on his shoulder, rubbing her cheek against him.

Massi was twisting the throttle knob furiously to try to catch up to them, but Nino's Aprilia SR was ripping along, pulling away at fifty-five miles per hour, and Massi's Piaggio Typhoon couldn't reach that speed. Anna, unaccustomed to coming in second, was urging him on, smacking him on the back of his neck, punching him in the back. Instead of hugging him, she was hitting him.

The four kids were zipping along the scenic road. Heading out of Piombino. It was the time of day when all the mothers are at home, the fathers are at work, and the kids their age were at the beach. Anna and Francesca watched the road vanish among the tough hillsides covered with holm oaks and the smokestacks of the Lucchini steel mill. The factory was laying siege to the sky.

They smiled in silence. They felt powerful, their arms wrapped around two beautiful men.

When they reached the intersection with the state highway the sea had already vanished, along with the houses, the beaches, the shops shut up for the afternoon. Now the factory was looming up, enormous in front of their eyes, exhaling a remote vibration in the gas pipes and larger pipelines; it was throwing its arms to the sky, its furnaces coated with soot. Nino turned left, Massi followed close behind him. Their destination wasn't far now.

Without helmets, keys, money, wallets. If you stayed home, you were a loser. If you went out, the greatest thing was to be going at top speed on the saddle of a souped-up scooter, heading for a secret destination.

Nino turned left again, Massi stuck close to his rear wheel.

And now they were inside.

Cotone, the steel quarter. Bare as a grave site. Not a bakery, not a grocery store, not a newsstand. Maybe the metal shutters, rolled shut and locked, of a machine shop.

You could feel the light coating of coal dust filtering into your lungs, sticking to your body, blackening your skin. The two scooters zipped along without slackening pace past houses that had long ago been torn apart. They were houses from the turn of the twentieth century, those shattered ruins now inhabited only by third-world immigrants.

Just a few feet from the border.

Two dark-skinned children, leaning over the railing of a balcony, each with a ball in hand, were the sole human presences. But stray cats were everywhere; they piled out of the rotten walls and emerged from the fields that had deteriorated into dumps, and you had to be careful not to run them over. There must have been a time when this place was full of life, but now it was reduced to rubble. The few pieces of laundry hanging out to dry at the windows were gray. Weighing down the streets and court-yards was the heavy silence of phantoms. A mute memory. Rats and thorn-bushes everywhere; a prehistoric setting.

Nino and Massi scootered along the factory fence for three miles. It wasn't the monster it had been thirty years before: twenty thousand em-ployees, a veritable city. They'd cut staff and dismantled a number of smokestacks, and the monster had shriveled a little. Via della Resistenza, 2, the main entrance. Something like twenty-five hundred acres. In block print: LUCCHINI S.P.A.

Francesca and Anna opened their eyes even wider, because two eyes weren't enough to take in the sea of coal bunkers, power shovels, smoke-stacks, dead tracks, the rollers of conveyor belts. The body was pounding hard along with the metals in the furnaces. Rebar, slabs, billets: along with the heart, the arteries, the aorta. It was impossible to find order, to make sense of it. And they were only thirteen.

Nino braked to a halt near a hole in the chain-link fence.

They turned off the motors. They jumped off the scooters and stood there, all four of them, in silence. The incessant, raucous lament of the steel mills—you could feel it vibrating deep in your bones. They felt a blend of fear and wonder at that place on the margins of the world.

A place of arid red dirt, transformed, at two in the afternoon, into a furnace. Where not even a blade of grass could come up. Not even a rat here, just reptiles. That dirt, dried up over time, resembled asphalt pavement. Lead and the heavy scent of iron burned the lungs and the nostrils.

Not a fly was buzzing.

Nino was the first to climb through. The others followed him through the tear in the rusty chain-link fence. It must have been the hundredth time. They went there when they wanted to be alone or when they were skipping school. They were the only ones, in all Piombino, to venture beyond the threshold. The only ones with the balls to do it.

Now that they'd crossed over, they were inside, for real.

That dead branch of the factory had been reduced to a carcass of rusted metal. They stood there, all four of them, paralyzed for a moment. Dazzled by the light glinting off the metal. Their throats dry. Their bodies bathed in sweat; their small bodies alive. Panting against the cement giants.

It was a little bit like being inside an aquarium. In the distance the steady flow of steel from the blast furnace inflamed the sky, infecting it with toxic fumes and mists, and you could feel yourself liquefying. You were sweating; your heart beat crazily.

In front of you, the ruins of a smokestack. Farther on, an abandoned industrial shed. In the middle, an excavator with a twisted arm and an upside-down bucket. Dead and seething with heat.

Nino shouted, for no good reason, just for fun. All four of them started forward into the industrial cemetery, running headlong in every direction, like newly freed animals.

Everything was allowed in there.

They darted from one side to the other, climbed up onto the bucket of the crippled steam shovel, onto the fallen blocks of the smokestack, and then jumped down. They weren't afraid of cutting themselves on the rusty metal or tripping in the ruins of the railroad tracks or old tires. They shouted over the colossal buzz of the factory, and, for a moment, they were stronger than the monster.

Nino grabbed Francesca by her arm and dragged her into the darkness, into the abandoned shed.

"Now tell me what you did to your wrist."

"I told you, nothing."

You could hardly hear the breathing or see the outlines of things in that giant womb. You couldn't see where you were putting your feet, what you were treading underfoot.

"You're an idiot," said Nino.

He moved his body closer to the body that was breathing next to him.

"Maybe I am," she whispered, taking a step back.

Nino imagined the sarcastic expression, the smirk of intolerance that so often twisted Francesca's lips, and he felt a rush of blood through his body.

"You're an idiot, . . . but I have to kiss you."

He took her hand. When they touched he felt a slow forest fire burn its way through the blood in his arteries. He drew her to him with the sweetness of someone who knows he can't wait.

There was no light, not even a thin filament of moon.

Francesca pulled away. Untangling herself from that male body, too big and intrusive, she stood there, stiff and enclosed, like an egg. In silence.

"Why are you like this?"

"Just because."

"Then why did you come, if you didn't want to?"

He almost couldn't hear her breathing. The imperceptible pounding deep in the chest, as if she were hibernating. Nino grabbed her wrist again, the bandaged one. He was panting, and his body was in tumult. He held her tight, hurting her. He did it on purpose. And this time she emitted a brief sound, as if she were underwater, without putting up any resistance.

She vanished into Nino's big arms.

They were both trembling, though trembling differently.

"What's wrong?"

"Nothing."

"You can't just always say nothing; you're going to piss me off. I want to know what you did to your wrist."

He was stronger than she was. That grip, his hands, the body of the most beautiful boy she'd ever seen in her life—a boy who grew up with her, who had played and splashed and swum with her—frightened her now.

It repelled her to touch him. The contact disgusted her. She could feel Nino's heart pounding away, powerful enough to enter, to shatter her empty thorax, and she felt inadequate.

His beauty was pointless; it couldn't move her.

Now he placed his wet lips on her lips. And she couldn't keep from feeling revulsion. She liked Nino: when he came home from his job at the garage, dressed in his dark blue overalls, his hands smeared with engine grease; when he popped wheelies on his scooter to attract her attention. But when he kissed her the way he was doing now, in the big shed, her muscles immobilized her. It unleashed a war inside, in her belly. And she had to hold out, make an effort: relax her lips and let him enter, at least a little.

Because that was what was right.

Anna did it, with Massi: They kissed each other, openmouthed.

This time, though, Nino didn't try to force open her lips. He stopped short. He took her face in his hands and turned it ever so slightly upward.

He was hopelessly in love. In a way he'd never be again for the rest of his life. Before turning into the asshole that everyone now knows, that day, in the Lucchini industrial shed, as he took Francesca's face between his hands, he'd been on the verge of weeping.

He practically couldn't see her face at all. An impenetrable, pale face that he yearned to devour, gobble up.

All he could see were the two seething blades of her eyes.

"*France . . .*"

She had her arms lying lank, dead, at her sides.

Nino was trying not to say it, but he was going out of his mind. He felt rejected, and he couldn't accept that. He was completely lost in love with her. He had to do something, something big. He was upset, restless, on the verge of exploding. He couldn't hold it in. Okay, now. No, I can't. Oh, yes I can. In fact, now I'll tell her, now I'm telling her . . .

"I love you."

Francesca shuddered.

She hadn't been expecting that; no one had ever spoken those words to her. For a fleeting instant she came back to life: life, full of blood and flesh. Warmth flooded her face. But she had no answer to those words.

But now Nino had said it. It had cost him an inhuman effort and there was no longer any way out, no way to unsay it, nothing to hide behind. He pressed his warm body hard against her closed, narrow body. He let his hands slip from her face to her shoulders, from her shoulders to her breasts, the cotton of her outfit, the scent that physically hurt him. What did it smell of? Of skin, her skin.

He was going out of his mind.

"I'll wait forever for you. . . . I'm willing to wait," he laughed, "until marriage!"

Francesca laughed, too. She wanted to laugh, wanted to feel normal somehow.

She allowed herself to be embraced by the good-hearted boy who had watched her grow up from the window across the way, through the cement pillars in the courtyard and the bars of the gates at school. He had told her, I love you. And what he wanted was to thrust right into that body.

Nino could have done a thousand different things right now, but what he did was kiss her on the forehead.

Francesca jammed her mouth and nose into his chest, and finally managed to stop pretending. She let herself dissolve into tears, practically without a sound. He was no longer asking for explanations. But, as he embraced her, he'd had an erection.

He couldn't know. She couldn't let him see: the marks under her clothing; the purple shadows of the bruises, of the beatings. Francesca knew it perfectly clearly: She could never fall in love with a man.

Outside, in the meantime, in broad daylight Anna and Massi had chased one another and played hide-and-seek, around and behind the dunes of pig iron and coal. They were high on light, their bodies perspiring, and they showed off by leaping off the ruins of the smokestack.

Suddenly, now, they stopped.

Anna let herself fall off the upside-down bucket scoop of the steam shovel. She was covered with dirt and panting hard. Massi stripped off his T-shirt, tossed it onto the arm of the Cat, long since eroded into a skeleton by the elements, and crouched down. He felt like rolling on the ground, covering himself head to foot with dust, and practically dying—his lungs were exploding in his chest.

They stayed there for a while, catching their breath and looking at each other.

Massi was handsome. He was dark and swarthy; he looked like a Taliban. He was slightly knock-kneed, his leg muscles prominent like a professional soccer player's. He was seventeen, about to turn eighteen. His eyes were cutting and dark, dreaming of the major leagues. His face was hard, southern Italian.

The white light turned the dirt, the iron, and the unbreathable air into a placenta. You had to squint your eyes almost completely shut or it hurt.

Anna lifted her head, leveled her irises straight into his irises, and burst into laughter right then and there. It was her way of starting something.

Massi laughed back. He could sense something was about to happen and he moved, without taking his eyes off her. He pretended to study for a living. He attended, occasionally, the Pacinotti vo-tech school. And that year he'd flunked out. Anna's freckles were the detail that drove him crazy. Her curly mass of hair, always unruly. She'd put on some light makeup today. She'd outlined her eyes with a little dark eyeliner. But she was still a little girl, and he liked that, too.

The light was dazzling them. There was the low and constant hum of the factory, radiating up from under the ground. And the flat, organic smell of coal. The smell of rust, iron, damp—just like when it starts raining. Anna stretched out on the back of the excavator bucket and felt as if she were on the verge of something nameless.

Massi wasn't her boyfriend; he was more like an older brother. She needled him and badgered him, and he played along. She didn't even mean to flirt with him; it just came naturally. It was just that now her thoughts were confusing and hard to pin down. She could feel her muscles relaxing and her whole body accelerating. She pulled her camisole off over her head; she unhooked her bra. It had always been like this, ever since they'd been kids together, playing at undressing in the basement.

They'd be naked in the dark. The door of the storage closet locked behind them, the strong smell of dust and neglected forgotten things. They'd look at each other, pointing out parts of the body, saying their names out loud. Every body part made them laugh: her nu-nu, his pee-pee, her titties. Then they'd get dressed again and go back upstairs to play with the other kids.

Massi was there. Anna could feel him drawing nearer, breathing. And an unruffled terror spread through her arteries, penetrating every capillary in her body, clouding her eyes. The light was melting her, the piles of discarded tires, the mountains of iron filings.

She liked lying there, bare breasted, waiting, her arms crossed behind her head, her eyes closed. She knew that he was looking at her now.

So much had changed in recent years, and especially in the last two weeks, things they had been unable to understand or react to. He no longer felt like laughing when they undressed. They'd started feeling embarrassed when they changed into or out of their swimsuits in the dressing booths at the beach. Something new had happened, something stronger than them.

Massi couldn't take Anna's naked breasts. He looked at them, motionless, in the daylight, and nothing could be more tyrannical. He had to grab them, plunge his face into them, he had no alternative. The sweat streamed down the back of his neck, drenching his hair, a rivulet running down his spinal cord. Nothing he could do about it. It was happening and he couldn't conceal it. He took off his belt; it was bothering him. He walked over to her, covering her with his shadow. He wondered if Anna was feeling the same thing. . . .

She wasn't moving. Stretched out, her legs akimbo, her skirt hitched up a little. She just smiled at him as if to say: Yes, you can.

He slowly lowered himself, covering her with his entire body. Now he closed his eyes. Now it was dark for both of them. Everything slipped into a blurry uncertainty, into an acrid taste, the smell of a bird's nest. He relaxed his body between Anna's knees, onto her warm breasts. And she clamped her arms and legs around him, like a Snugli.

It just so happened that in the whole world there was only one place where Massi really felt happy, really felt safe, and that place was Anna. His next-door neighbor, the obnoxious little girl who used to drop water balloons off the balcony.

He didn't always want to be at war—with the teachers at school, with the guys his age, with his parents. And acting tough with her, with his gestures, the way he looked at her, the way he showed off. Knocking himself out to score a goal every Sunday at the soccer match, working relentlessly to soup up his scooter to the max. There were times when he just felt like curling up and falling, naked, into that girl.

He'd only recently discovered Anna's body. Too well-known, so deeply changed, it could have been his sister's body; anyway, she didn't have thorns.

Anna was kissing him, and she couldn't think straight. I'm not in love; it isn't true. It's a game, but it's more than a game. She clung to his shoulders. She wanted to do something, but she wasn't sure what. She let him slip one of his hands in. She shouldn't let him, but she was letting him. Because he was touching her exactly the same way she touched herself before falling asleep at night.

The first time they'd French kissed had been two weeks ago.

He'd swung by on his scooter to pick her up on the last day of school. They'd stopped on the scenic road and sat on the bench overlooking the sea. It was noon.

Massi had opened her lips and slipped his tongue in, and Anna was scared. Then he'd embraced her tighter, and as he wrapped his arms around her, he'd grazed her between the legs. She'd felt a sudden strong desire to pee, and she'd slapped his face.

Now, though, and she wasn't sure why, she felt like letting herself be grazed between the legs. A little, just a tiny little bit. She wasn't so afraid now. She wanted to find out more about this strange thing, this thing she liked but that hurt her, too. And Massi pushed aside the hem of her panties, just with his fingers, with just one finger, barely. Because she was trembling she'd opened her eyes, and those eyes were asking: What was happening now?

When they heard their names being called, they stopped short. They hurriedly put their clothes back on without looking at each other and emerged wrinkled and rumpled from behind the power shovel.

Francesca and Nino were gesturing to them.

Before climbing back onto the scooters, Francesca looked at Anna in a way that frightened her. Her glare was a sort of sullen forest fire. Anna couldn't take it; she turned and looked away.

CHAPTER 9

"**W**hat did you do with Massi?"

"*France*, don't be a pain! I'm not in love with him, don't worry."

"Okay, but what did you do?"

Before going upstairs they'd sat down side by side on the staircase.

Francesca grimly piled on one question after another while Anna laughed so loudly that she could be heard throughout the building.

"I hate it when you act like an idiot."

Anna sobered up immediately. She didn't like being called an idiot.

"We did what you did."

"So you kissed."

"Right."

"And that's all?"

"That's all."

"Did he touch you?"

"No!"

"Are you in love with him?"

"Fuck, no! I don't give a damn about Massi. I've known him all my life." A surge of annoyance swept over her. "We're friends, we play together, . . ." her voice rising, "and you're jealous!"

She got up to let a swarm of shouting children go by; the kids had them covered with submachine guns. The kids didn't want to go by. They aimed the guns at them. They were waiting for the two girls to surrender.

"I'm not jealous." Francesca leaped to her feet as well, her eyes uncertain whether to flash lightning or cry.

"You are too! You're trying to pick a fight. Why? What do you care if I kiss Massimo?"

Four little boys with skinned knees stood there waiting, grave and silent, for the girls to raise their hands or say something along the lines of: We surrender. But Anna and Francesca weren't paying the slightest attention to them, didn't even glance at them; if anything, they seemed completely focused on glaring at one another with incandescent gazes. Disappointed, the children lowered their submachine guns and went on up the stairs.

It was obvious that she was furious at Anna. She felt like punching her. Because she'd understood when she saw the two of them half undressed that Anna had done something serious with Massi.

"Look," Anna began confidently, "even if you kiss some boy, and I kiss some other boy, nothing changes between us."

She stopped for a second. A tactical pause.

A rivulet dripped from the landing above them, where a little girl squatted, panties stretched around her knees, skirt hitched up. Peeing on the stairs was normal here.

"Eventually, we're going to be in relationships, both of us. I'm not saying with Nino or with Massi, but in general, we're going to be in a relationship. We're going to make love with our boyfriends, we'll spend lots of time with them, and we'll go dancing, hand in hand, and we'll get engaged, and get married, have lots of kids, I'll go to some school far away from here, you'll win Miss Italy, and just by the nature of things, for a certain period of time, we'll be separated."

Francesca listened, deeply offended.

"It can happen, *Fra*, it's going to *have* to happen. But we'll never really be separated. We can't lose each other, you understand?"

Francesca was still wary, defensive, but something was beginning to dissolve in the grim expression on her face. Anna saw it. "We're different, but we're parts of one single thing." She smiled. "We're sisters!"

Francesca gave in suddenly.

She hadn't liked being lectured about boyfriends, about being far apart, by Anna. In fact, it had made her tremble inside. But in the end, when she'd heard that word—filled with esses in English, *sisters*, but els in Italian, *sorelle*—she'd felt an explosion deep inside her chest. She leaped at Anna and wrapped her arms around her.

She couldn't wait, truth be told; she needed to hug her. She wanted her back, wanted to be able to call Anna hers. And, after all, Anna wasn't in love with Massi, she didn't give a damn about him.

"*France*, seriously . . . now listen to me."

She took both hands in hers and gripped them tightly.

"First thing: I'll go with you when you get your stitches removed. Second: I promise and I swear to you, that monster won't hurt you again. And if he does, you'll come live with me. And if my father pulls one more fucked-up caper, and my mother doesn't throw him out of the house, we'll both leave and find a place to live together."

Francesca was doing her best not to burst into tears.

"Because it's not right," Anna shouted. "It's not fair that our lives should be ruined by a couple of assholes!"

Let them hear her, everyone in that fucked-up apartment building.

"A couple of assholes who can't do a fucking thing right and are worth less than nothing!"

Let Francesca's father hear her.

When she walked into the kitchen, a totally unprecedented thing: Sitting at the table was . . . her father.

"Daddy!" Anna cried out instinctively.

Actually, there were storm clouds on the horizon. Sandra was slamming spoons and ladles around, and she hadn't even turned around to glance at her. When Arturo saw his daughter's ringleted figure, he recovered from his awkwardness and threw out his arms.

The theme music of the TG1 news began. For a moment Anna had the impression that she lived in a normal home. There was her mother, finally waving hello with a pair of pot holders in her hand, ready to pour the pot of boiling water into the sink. There was her father, who'd been on the lam for three days, smiling at her. And there wasn't her brother, okay, but that was normal too: He was busy shaping white-hot slabs of steel into long sections of track. The table was neatly set; the day's news was being clearly announced by the voice of an attractive lady.

She didn't want to see that her mother's nerves were on edge. She didn't want to notice the nervousness with which her father was tearing at his fingernails under the table. She leaned over to give him a kiss and then sat down to a steaming bowl of fusilli.

Arturo swallowed his first forkful and then burst into compliments for the excellent sauce. Apparently cheerful and at his ease, he commented on some of the news items with a laugh, without emphasis, at random, indifferent that someone had been arrested or someone else had been killed in a construction accident. Anna seized on that appearance with all her might. She agreed that the sauce was tasty. And Sandra sat in silence, looking down into her bowl.

"So? What's new, where have you been?" asked Arturo, once he was done chewing.

"Around," Anna replied.

"Sandra, could you pass me the salt?" His wife, her face twisted with pain, picked up the salt that stood near her bowl and set it down, rudely, in front of his bowl.

"Thanks." Arturo swallowed, then turned to address his daughter: "Didn't you go to the beach today?"

Anna looked at her father's smiling face and felt as if she really did love him. In spite of everything. She was happy that the three of them were sitting down to dinner together. The fitting conclusion, she thought, to my day.

"No, we didn't feel like going to the beach. So we just hung out, you know, me and Francesca."

Arturo looked a little harder at his daughter's face, then his expression changed. His face darkened suddenly, and he interrupted her before she could finish.

"What's that black stuff on your eyes?"

Anna said nothing.

"What is this? Have you already started? Now you're going around with makeup on?" He threw his napkin violently down on the dining room table and turned in a blazing rage toward his wife. "Sandra!" he thundered. "Tell me you don't let her go around like this!"

The peace had lasted all of four minutes. Great, thought Anna. She'd lost her appetite. The baboon has already lost his temper. That's how it always was with her father, a crapshoot. There she sat, her stomach twisting with rage, disappointment, and a strong desire to tell him to go fuck himself—she couldn't stand it anymore.

"Look at her, Sandra, have you seen her? Her face is two inches deep in makeup! She looks like a whore, goddamn it!" He stood up in a blind rage.

Sandra suddenly sat erect in her chair.

"Don't you ever dare to say anything like that about *my* daughter again!"

Anna sat there, eyes wide open, heart beating crazily. Her parents seemed like a couple of dynamite bombs with timers, ready to devastate the apartment at any second. By now the pasta was cold in the bowls.

She was tempted to shout right into his face: You could have just saved yourself the trouble of coming home at all, you asshole. Why didn't you just stay wherever it was you were? Every time you come home you just unleash hell on us. Why the fuck? You're pissed at me because I'm almost fourteen? You jerk, you've fucked up everything you've put your hand to—what right do you have to bust my chops?

Of course, she sat there without saying a word.

Her father, who was there but wasn't there, who smiled and then flew into a rage: She'd had enough of his tantrums. Why did he have all the power?

She didn't move from her chair.

"Anna!" he exploded. "March straight to the bathroom and wash that stuff off your face. And you'll be sorry, young lady, I swear, you'll rue the day! If I ever catch you looking like that again. . . ." He reached out blindly and grabbed the salt bowl and threw it ferociously against the wall. "You'll never walk out that door again!"

Anna stood up, relieved that she'd been given permission to leave the table. She slammed the bathroom door loudly, and when she was face-to-face with the mirror, her hands on the sink, she ground her teeth. She hadn't even eaten.

Well, look at this asshole who just appears out of nowhere one night and decides he's going to be my father. And he thinks that being my father means chewing me out because I have a tiny bit of makeup on my face. Well, fuck him!

She turned on the water and plunged her head under the stream; water poured into her ears. She never wanted to hear his voice again, the fucking baboon, who was still shouting: "Until you're eighteen years old, you aren't putting that shit on your face, do you hear me? You aren't putting it on, you understand?"

"Don't shout so loud," hissed Sandra, as she started to clear away the dinner plates, "and stop waving your horns around the room. You'll break something. Your daughter can put on a little eyeliner if she wants to. That's the least of the problems."

There was no way Anna was going back into that kitchen. She was too pissed off. She went into her bedroom and shut the door behind her. She turned the stereo on full blast. She thought about Francesca. Maybe it really was time to leave, for good. The two of them, in secret, with a detective's trench coat and a head scarf, a bundle at the end of a stick like in the cartoons, and a pair of sunglasses, on a pier down at the port, waiting for the first ferryboat for Elba.

But she wasn't the one who needed to leave: It was him.

Why didn't her mother kick him out of the house, throw him out on his ass?

If she went back in there right now, she would see her father, calm and amiable, sitting in his comfy chair, laughing as he stared at the TV screen. That's how Arturo was: After one of his tantrums, after he'd broken a few things, he'd immediately turn sunny and docile.

Not Sandra.

She stepped out onto the balcony to shake out the tablecloth. She filled the sinks with hot water and dish soap. She thoroughly scrubbed the dishes and the pots and pans, rinsed them, and set them out to dry. All this in a silence that verged on the religious, without so much as a glance at her husband, who was enthralled by the buffoons and their big-breasted show-girls on *Striscia la Notizia.* She swept the floor, gathered up the crumbs. She tied off the garbage bag, and even went downstairs into the street to deposit it in the Dumpster.

I've got to get outside, or I'll strangle him.

She went back in.

Arturo was still there, in his easy chair. He never lifted a finger; he never moved an inch.

"Listen." She uttered the word with great calm, as she slowly sat down face-to-face with her husband: a word so charged with catastrophe.

Arturo looked at her; she had an unmistakable expression on her face: I'm ready, let's do this.

"Now you're going to explain to me," Sandra began, "why you haven't come home to sleep at night for three days, why for the past three days the phone has been ringing off the hook with calls from the bank, threatening things that you know about but I didn't, and why there's three million lire missing from our account." She took a deep breath. "But most of all, you have to explain to me how we're going to pay for the dishwasher, your son's car radio, and fourteen million lire worth of debts without getting evicted from this apartment."

For a fleeting instant Arturo felt a stabbing pain in his chest that might resemble a heart attack. For an infinitesimal split second, as he gazed at his wife's weary, impassive face, he felt like a complete piece of shit. But it was, in fact, only for an infinitesimal split second.

"All right, Sandra. I'll tell you. Now, if you let me speak and you don't interrupt after three seconds, I'll explain everything, and you'll see that there really are no problems at all."

No changes appeared in his wife's expression. With superhuman patience, and superhuman weariness, in the cramped living room of their apartment she prepared herself to listen to him yet again, after twenty years of marriage, and yet again to pretend to believe him.

"It's true, I quit my job."

She felt as if she'd just been slugged in the belly.

"But Sandra, objectively . . . Look at me!" Arturo got to his feet, extended a hand. "Objectively, I couldn't exactly go on working my fingers to the bone in that steel plant, putting up with all kinds of abuse, for the starvation wages they were giving me. . . . That is . . . ," he gulped, stalled for time, desperately searching for better words, "I've had some opportunities . . . some high-class opportunities! A new job, Sandra, a good job, I swear it, and I guarantee you, this is a high-class job!"

"Exactly what is this *high-class* line of work?"

"Sales, Sandra! Antiques, artworks. A solid field of activity, earnings that constitute an investment," he went on as he worked up his enthusiasm. "You know that I've always been interested in these things, that buying and selling are what I've always been good at . . . and now I've finally got the opportunity."

He believes it, thought Sandra. He actually believes the things he's saying.

"A dear friend has extended this offer to me, Sandra, an offer to become his partner. Antiques. It's a market sector that's experiencing growth, sharp growth."

"Antiques," Sandra echoed him in a faint thread of a voice. "And exactly who is this dear friend of yours?"

Arturo cleared his throat, coughing slightly.

"Pasquale."

His wife turned white as a sheet.

"Pasquale*eee*?" she shouted. "Pasquale who? Pasquale who spends half the year in jail, regular as clockwork? The one who spends more time in prison than at home?"

Arturo ran his hands through his hair. For an instant, for a brief instant, he felt like a piece of shit again. Then he recovered.

"Nooo! You've got it all wrong. Pasquale is a good guy, he's got a heart of gold, it's just that . . ."

And he was starting to explain again, justifying and launching into his spiel, when Sandra told him not to say another word, putting up a hand in exhaustion. She wearily got up from the chair she was sitting in.

"Reality, *Artù*," she said, placing a hand on the table. "There's a big difference between reality and bullshit."

That night Sandra slept with her arms around her husband. They slept hand in hand in the big bed, the way they slept when they first met and they were dreaming of their lives together: a home, children, vacations in Sardinia or even just on the Isle of Elba.

Before falling asleep she lay there for a long time, caressing the hair of the man she had married and that no one else—neither now nor ever, unfortunately—would ever be able to replace. In reality she was thinking seriously about divorce.

She was responsible for her children, for her home, for the concrete things in her life. She could feel all of it on her shoulders, that responsibility. She would request a trial separation without waiting much longer. But also without denying, at least for this night, the feelings that she still had, in spite of everything, for this man.

She let herself sink into her pillow. She'd request a trial separation. It couldn't go on like this. She closed her eyes. Outside, voices and noises stabbed through the silence of the night. A car horn, a car tearing past at reckless speed.

It would be great to be able to cancel everything, hit clear, and see nothing but zeroes. Have another nine or ten lifetimes ahead of her.

She thought back to her father, a man who had received a medal from the hands of the president of the Italian republic, a hero of the resistance movement, someone who had worked hard all his life, who had lost a leg in the factory where her husband had been fired.

She thought back to that momentous summer night in the middle of August, more then twenty years ago, in the pine forest of Follonica—that was where she had met Arturo for the first time. And right then and there she had understood, from the way he lit his cigarette, the way he talked about phantasmagorical opportunities and projects, that he was a man who would never amount to anything.

Sandra realized that there are things that you don't decide. Things that world capitalism, the history of nations, or the Italian republic decide for you.

There are other things, things that you do decide, she thought. Things that depend on you and you alone. Like what you do, what you decide to become. A person who's born where I was born can either be a thief or a factory worker, work at the deli counter at the Coop or be a hooker on the streets. A person can choose to think with their own mind; they can vote for X or Y. They can read *La Repubblica* or watch a reality show.

Last of all, there are things that nobody can decide. Like the fact that I'm lying here under the sheets with this man who has always disappointed me, always failed me, with my arms wrapped around him, and I feel at home, I feel like I'm on earth, and tomorrow, I swear it, I'm calling the lawyer, I swear I'm going to do it. The things that I am and the things that I wish I could be.

CHAPTER 10

Alessio was driving at an insane speed down the deserted road through the center of the industrial port, past streetlights at distant intervals. It was 11:00 P.M. The stereo was pumping in the desert.

You could recognize Alessio's Peugeot from a long way off, because he had installed three Batman-style spoilers on the back. He'd even chopped and channeled it four inches lower to make it look more aggressive. But his dream was still the Golf GT.

Sitting next to him in the passenger seat was Cristiano, his lifelong best friend, seat belt unbuckled, elbow stuck out the window. They couldn't speak to each other: The music was too loud. For that matter, Alessio wasn't much of a talker when he was alone with another person.

At 10:00 P.M., when the shift was over, he'd taken a quick shower, sandpapering the black coke dust off his skin, he'd punched out at the time clock, and he'd hopped into his car. He was exhausted after eight hours in a row on the crane unloading bottle cars piled high with steel into the ladles. But there's no way I'm going to bed; it's Saturday night, it's summer. And the discotheques are brimming over with pussy.

He'd swung by to pick up his friend, then they stopped by a pizzeria to eat a couple of slices and drink a beer standing at the counter. And now they were slingshotting at top speed into the darkness, heading for the wilderness of the outlying province. He was zipping along the perimeter of the Magona, roaring past the worker housing quarters and the first few yards of the industrial port. He was driving with his usual spectral concentration.

"Why don't we go to the Gilda?" shouted Cristiano, to be heard over the erupting lava of the speakers.

Alessio felt a terrible surge of power when he jammed his foot down on the accelerator. He was twenty-three years old; he'd been working in various positions in the steel mill for seven years now. His first job was to transport pig iron from the blast furnace to the converters; then for a time they'd assigned him to shovel coal; and in the end they'd put him on the crane. He could feel the blood pumping through his arteries when he drove with that insane music, straining the speakers to the point of destruction. He liked to listen to hard-core in the steel mill, with his MP3 player. He'd watch the steel pouring out from under the tundish in the continuous casting strip, hot steel, the color of blood, and the obsessive thump-thump in his ears made him feel as if he was at war, in a combat zone.

"*Ale!* I said, Let's go to the Gilda!"

He turned the car into a narrow side road, went roaring up the crumbling switchbacks. There were no more streetlights here, and he had to click on his brights to cut through the dark.

"No, let's go to the Tartana," he finally replied, after a long silence.

Mill trains are the most dangerous things there are, because there's never any coordination between the people who dispatch them from the central office and the guy driving the train. It's all disorganized. It only takes the blink of an eye, and you're crushed under the wheels. On his identity card they'd written: "Licensed to drive industrial vehicles."

The car reached the summit; he jammed on the brakes beneath the dish antennas and the signal repeaters. This was where they'd been heading. Anyone in Piombino who is or has been a bad boy knows about the Tolla. From up there, like nowhere else, you can hold the entire plant and the port in the palm of your hand, in your fist.

That night, luckily, there were no couples necking in cars parked off in the shadows, no fogged windshields. None of the usual punks hunched down smoking marijuana.

Luckily, they were alone.

To Cristiano's disappointment, Alessio turned off the stereo. And an unreal silence, with the distant buzz of the Lucchini mill carving a trench through the bottom of that silence, filled the interior of the car.

"Why don't you want to go to the Gilda?"

"I don't want to give money to a whore."

"Sheesh, you're so dramatic!" Cristiano took it hard. "And what's at the Tartana tonight? For sure, there's not a fucking thing. . . ."

"I don't give a damn what there is or isn't. If you want, we'll go to the Tartana; if not, I'll drop you off and you can walk."

His friend quieted down. He knew Alessio; he knew it was a bad idea to insist when he heard that tone of voice. He pulled a dose out of his pocket, removed the rearview mirror from the glass of the windshield, and began the ritual operations of Saturday night in a religious silence.

Alessio didn't bother to look over at him. He was sunk in the upholstery of the driver's seat, staring fixedly out at the man-made sea of lights and purple flames through the windshield. By night, seen from above, the plant was quite another thing. Right now he was tumbling headfirst into it with his eyes, indifferent and mute. He was tired, and he was pissed off, too.

Cristiano leaned forward over the mirror with a ten-thousand-lire banknote rolled up in his nostril. Before he snorted he realized that he had invested his entire May paycheck in cocaine, but this time it would turn out right: It had to turn out right; there was no other way. He'd taken a risk, no question, a big risk. But the coke was so good that he'd pocket at least six hundred thousand lire of pure profit.

Cristiano had a terrible yearning right now for music blasting into his ears, into his head. But he didn't dare ask Alessio. When he lifted his head and snorted again he saw his friend out of the corner of his eye, in a trance, his eyes wide open and fixed on an abstract point somewhere out in the night. That point, in reality, was the tower of the blast furnace.

Alessio hadn't turned, hadn't lunged, hungry as a wolf, over his line of coke. He just sat there, remote, without moving a muscle. Something had definitely happened to him. He was definitely pissed off. But it would have been ridiculous to ask him what it was.

He wasn't the kind of guy who confided in you.

Cristiano handed him the mirror. Alessio took it, but then he didn't move.

It's full of cats. That's what Alessio was thinking.

Nobody outside of the plant knew it, but down there, in certain sheds, especially around the cafeterias, there were huge colonies of cats, hundreds and hundreds of cats. Cats that have never seen the light of day, cats that don't know what a blade of grass looks like. They're like mutants—tailless, one-eyed, all the same. Absurd.

He'd always been amazed by this presence of cats. It struck him as unbelievable that cats could live in steel, in pig iron. Not that they were thriving, poor things. They were unhealthy, some of them were mangy, hairless, scary to behold. Look them in the eye and they struck you as practically human. There were people, and Alessio was one of them, who fed those cats.

But Cristiano didn't give a damn: about the cats or about the Lucchini steel mill, which he saw every blessed day. Very simply, he was sick of them. The drug was starting to take effect and he had only one thought in his mind: the blonde in the skimpy bathing suit on the billboard at the Piombino city limits.

He wanted to go to the Gilda tonight. He wanted to get right down to business, without wasting time, with the stunning blonde who'd do it for money; he didn't want to chase after some spoiled young girl on the dance floor at the Tartana. Those bitches aren't giving it up, anyway. They think they're all this and all that; they won't even let you kiss them. He wanted a handful of enormous tits. Paying a little extra, in a private room, you could go all the way. And this guy, this nut sitting next to him: Who could say what he was thinking about?

Actually, Alessio was struggling to keep from thinking at all. But that damned scene kept coming back to him, flashing before his mind's eye like a recorded message replaying endlessly.

That afternoon, around four o'clock, one of those fucking cats, a kitten practically, wound up under the mill train, and there was nothing he could do about it. It had crushed the cat into a smeared clump of blood and fur. He'd climbed down and started kicking everything in sight. I'm an idiot, he thought now, I'm a moron. Because after that the floor boss, rightly, chewed him out. He'd run straight at him, yelling: "What the fuck are you doing? Asshole!" Instinctively, he turned around and swung his fist right into the floor boss's face.

I'm an idiot, he kept telling himself. I lost my head over a cat. But that cat was an uncomfortable reminder of a friend of his, one crushed under a roller two years ago. He didn't want to remember his friend, crushed to death right under his eyes. He didn't want to remember the face of the man who had been on the train and couldn't stop it.

Now the kitten, his friend, and the horrified face of the man on the mill train were all just one thing inside his head.

Cristiano had gotten out of the car to go take a piss in the thornbushes. And Alessio still hadn't made his mind up to snort the line of coke. He was staring into the heart of it: the brightly lit tower where they melt pig iron and steel, hoping they'd never fire him—that he'd never be the one driving the train when it razed someone to the floor.

What you could never imagine from outside, really, is the inside. Everyone knows, everyone takes it for granted, that inside the Lucchini plant, deep down in the bowels of the place, the flesh of human legs, arms, and heads is stirring. They know it, but they could never manage to encompass this gargantuan effort. Someone from outside couldn't understand what it means to transform metric ton after metric ton of raw material. The hardest matter that exists. And you can't even begin to imagine the disproportionate number of sexy calendars and posters of naked women hanging everywhere in the steel mill.

They even stuck a woman with big tits up on a bulldozer.

Suddenly he bent down over the line of coke and sucked it up into his nostrils with all his strength. Cristiano got back into the car and looked at him, as if to ask: Well, what do you think?

"*Cri*," Alessio said, "have you ever seen the fox in the cokery?"

Cristiano raised his eyebrows. He worked for an outside company, on the exterior, running an excavator. Loading slag for recycling.

"No. Why? Is there a fox in there, too?" He laughed.

"Think of that. . . ." Alessio laughed with him. "A fox in the pit! I've seen it plenty of times, but it only comes out at six in the morning."

That's what they've always called the cokery: the *pit*. To the point. This name for the place is one of the few things that's been handed down from generation to generation.

"You better now?" Cristiano ventured.

"I got in a fistfight with my boss today."

"Oh, damn!"

There was a chart on the wall with a blackboard and a graph of plant accidents, but it was never kept up-to-date. People wrote all over it, whatever they thought would get a laugh: like that someone was dead, only they weren't. They'd write: I'm dead; the rollers have crushed my balls. And everyone would laugh and laugh.

"From up here, it's almost pretty."

"What is?"

Alessio pointed down at the sea of lights.

"A pearl of loveliness!" Cristiano exclaimed.

At 5:00 A.M. they'd leave the disco, and at 6:00 A.M. they'd head straight back into the Lucchini plant.

"So it's the Tartana? Not the Gilda, you're sure?"

"Jesus Christ, *Cri*, I told you already!"

A reddish light invaded the black sky for a few minutes, like a hint of apocalypse. Molten steel, continuous casting.

"Do you think it makes sense?"

"What?" Cristiano stopped playing with the display on his cell phone and looked over at his friend.

"Working in there your whole life."

"Sure, if they paid you five or six million lire a month. It'd make a lot of sense!"

By now Cristiano was pretty hopped up. He was impatient: He wanted to get moving; he wanted to get out into his own Saturday night, his moment of glory.

Alessio noticed it and started the car. He was starting to feel the effects of the coke himself. He turned on the stereo. He pushed away the image of the clump of blood and fur, the image of his crushed friend, the incredulous face of the man who had killed him, the man who was his uncle.

He went screeching down off the top of the Tolla. No, they'd never fire him. Down toward the Aurelia highway, along with thousands of other cars racing through the Saturday night, toward a Tartana under siege by German girls on holiday, toward the warm white breast of a girl, of any girl, just a breast to rest on, put an end to the race.

Alessio was driving like a reckless lunatic, and Cristiano was bobbing his head to the rhythm of the thumps.

Alessio was passing other cars, thinking about girls. The girls that came to see their husbands at work, with little kids in their arms. They stayed on the far side of the chain-link fence, pointing out the fathers, filthy black with pig iron, to their sons. The little boys were thrilled with the excavators and the bulldozers. They'd clap their hands in delight, as if they were at the circus.

He'd have applauded, too, if he'd had a father on those bulldozers—he'd have been proud of him. And the girls with the children in their arms, they might not be as pretty as the girls at the discotheque, but they had a smile, faces free of makeup, a pallor, something about them that was like an enchantment. Elena, if she hadn't left him, if she hadn't gone to the university, would have come to see him, would have stood on the far side of the hurricane fence, and she would have shown their little boy just how ferocious a power shovel could be.

He was gripping the steering wheel hard in his fist. The fist that came easier to him than any words ever did.

A pale white breast where he could rest his head. That, at least, made sense to him.

CHAPTER 11

The minute she saw the water, Anna would go crazy.

She'd drop her backpack and towel wherever she happened to be, gather her strength, and run. She'd run until the water was too deep, until her lungs were bursting in her chest, and then she'd dive. She'd scrape her belly against the undulating surface of the seabed, and then she'd resurface many yards farther out, where she couldn't touch bottom even with the tips of her toes. She loved the feel of that sea bottom, rough and soft at the same time. Touching it with her hands, digging her fingers into it—underwater, where the noises of the world become a placenta, where the salt burns your corneas, where the only sound you can hear is your own breathing, no longer yours.

In contrast, Francesca took her time.

Her sharply defined silhouette against the light was the most luminous point on the beach. She let the eyes of the whole beach graze upon her, nibbling at her as she turned golden in the light.

She lingered for a while where the waves washed up on the shore, digging her big toe into the wet sand. She entered the water by degrees, dripping water on herself with her hands, first on her belly, then on her arms. Finally, when Anna had almost reached the buoys, she dove into the water, with the perfection of a mermaid.

Now Anna was tumbling and rolling on the beach, smearing her hair with muck and filling her swimsuit with sand. Francesca watched her with amusement, but she didn't dare imitate her.

"Come on, *Fra*, jump in!"

Anna didn't seem to notice. She was walking on all fours, covered with seaweed, her bathing suit vanished between her butt cheeks. As if it were the most natural thing on earth. And she was laughing for no good reason.

But the boys noticed. They tore at top speed across the sand at her, Massi picked her up by the arms, Nino by the legs.

"One, two, three . . ."

And they hurled her into the water. She shouted happily. She drank a little saltwater, coughed up the rest. She was back on her feet in an instant, panting, uncertain whether to go back to rolling on the sand or to swim underwater to the buoys in twenty seconds.

When the boys stuck poles into the wet sand and one of them tossed the soccer ball into the air, announcing that the match was on, Anna and Francesca went wild.

When Nino, Massi, and the other eighteen-year-old boys from Via Stalingrado were playing soccer, they didn't give a crap about anyone else. You could see them frantically engaged in their game, shouting: "Pass it, pass it! To me, to me!" and they only had eyes for the ball. But Anna and Francesca couldn't take being sidelined. Inflamed, they leaped onto backs and shoulders, grabbed all the players.

Someone like Lisa, by contrast, who was farther up the beach, sweating on her beach towel and hoping she'd turn up a decent card in her game of gin rummy, could only feel her nerves surging up inside her. She watched the two of them running in among the guys out of the corner of her eye, letting the top of their suits dangle open in front of prying eyes while pretending to cover themselves up with the other hand, as if they were playing capture the flag. Playing cards wasn't that much fun.

Then a person wonders why nobody can stand a couple of girls like that.

The other girls their age, the losers who were slipping into a total crisis of confidence every time they stood in front of the mirror, just wanted to spit when they saw them. Anna and Francesca slapped you in the face with the fact that they were pretty. They had to prove it, every blessed minute of the day, that they were better than you, that they had won, hands down, once and for all.

Lisa realized that she would never be there, in the middle of the crowd of males, the center of their attention. She wrapped herself up inside her beach towel, the deck of cards in her hand. She hissed: "They're just a couple of sluts."

Donata, on the other hand, was enjoying the spectacular view: the sparkling water and the two girls leaping and dodging in the midst of the boys. She couldn't do anything more than watch from her wheelchair. It was rare and unlikely for anyone to take the trouble to get her into the water. They left her in the shade of the beach umbrella, but she never felt as if she'd been abandoned. She watched and reflected. She had no hard feelings toward either Anna or Francesca. If she'd never contracted this disease she would have wanted to be exactly like them.

Anna came out of the water. She walked right in front of Lisa and the other homely dogs without bothering to glance in their direction. She did twist her face into a nasty little smile when she stepped on one of their beach towels, as if to say: poor things. Then she waved to Donata.

It's not automatic, Lisa thought to herself, that if you're pretty you have to be cruel, too. If a wave swept Anna off the rocks right now and she was disfigured for life, it would only be fair and right. It would be simple justice if Francesca's metabolism suddenly spun out of control and she found herself with a pair of grossly fat and cellulite-ridden thighs.

If you're relentless enough, with enough brushing of the ass as if by accident, enough climbing on backs and flaunting of tits, eventually you'll find a male who falls for it hook, line, and sinker.

Nino gave up chasing after the soccer ball and turned to run after Francesca, in the direction of the dressing rooms.

"Nice work, *France*, nice work," Lisa puffed in exasperation. "A round of applause for *France*! What are you going to say when you're in the Miss Italy pageant? 'I'm just a soap-and-water girl, the girl next door. . . .'"

"Yeah, stop showing off, why don't you!" muttered another exasperated young girl; she, too, had a beach towel wrapped around her waist to cover her fat thighs.

Francesca, unaware of all the venom, slipped under the shower and gave a show.

"You just can't do that," Nino laughed, but he was only laughing to a certain point. "You can't inflict certain things on a man. . . ."

"Look at the imbecile," Lisa and others commented indignantly, vinegar mouthed, "like a ripe pear falling off the branch!"

Francesca was rinsing her hair, massaging her thighs to scrape away the salt, and looking directly at Nino through the stream of water. Nino was doing his best to control himself, but it was more than he could take. He suddenly leaped under the spray, wrapped his arms around her, and gently sank his teeth into her neck.

"You nut! Everyone's watching us. . . ." Francesca shoved him away, out of the spray, laughing as she did.

That was what she had wanted; she'd achieved it: Nino, begging, at her feet. She planted a kiss on his lips as a reward. It was as if she were standing on a stage in the middle of the beach; she could feel a million pairs of eyes focusing on her. In front of everyone, she had conquered all her shyness.

Then she ran away, again into the water, and caught up with Anna. And with that poor sap Nino hard on her heels, like a dog.

Every day, every blessed day, it was the same thing. The endless back and forth, Francesca and Anna, from the water to the changing rooms, from the changing rooms back to the water. Under the showers, behind the bar. And then back into the water. An endless back and forth, up and down, Anna and Francesca in front, and the males trailing along behind them. The homely dogs watching from a distance. Lisa and those pathetic losers; to make things even worse, they had bodies that were starting to change, too.

But they weren't the only ones watching. There was someone watching from the fourth floor of building number 7, watching with an unblinking gaze.

The bar was beginning to fill up at that time of day. Around the plastic tables branded Algida, in the shade of the big tattered umbrellas, the bigger kids sprawled out, sipping alcoholic beverages.

Maria, who had both her legs on the tabletop in a posture that was hardly the height of couth, observed Anna and Francesca coolly for a few minutes, then lit a cigarette. "Those two," she pointed them out to the others, "if they keep it up, will be pregnant by the end of the year."

"If!" laughed Jessica. "Her brother will kill her."

"Someone ought to tell him. Look at how *stoopid* she's being with Massimo. . . ."

Cristiano pulled his lips away from his glass of Southern Comfort.

"Oh, witches!" he called out with a smile. "Are you done? Let her be, why don't you? What were you guys doing a few years ago? I seem to remember . . ."

Everyone burst into laughter.

Sonia was there, too, the diva, the one who'd carved Alessio's name into the bench, the one who sometimes went into Anna's bedroom with Alessio to watch porn movies with him. She sat down and crossed her legs, and the skimpy pareo she was wearing left little to the imagination. She was sort of the ex-Francesca of the Via Stalingrado. Now she worked as a salesclerk at Calzedonia, selling stockings and beachwear, and no one remembered when she was pretty.

All the people were waiting for him. And finally he appeared.

At 4:30 in the afternoon, with his blond hair spiky and on end, his blue eyes concealed behind his aviators. Jessica and Maria swooned when he showed up. Sonia looked down, smiling. And Cristiano stood up to slap him on the shoulder, with his usual swagger and bluff.

He walked in bare chested: Alessio, two steel chains around his neck, his jeans half unbuttoned, the hemmed waistline of his boxers in clear view. He dropped into a chair.

He lifted his sunglasses, looked every member of his crew in the face. Said: "Life just exhausts me."

This was his attitude, as king of the forest. He had the physique and he knew it. He had the money, money he got from selling coke and stolen copper. And he had free run of many of the women in the quarter.

Anna recognized him all the way from the buoy. She swam across the water in thirty seconds flat. She ran as fast as she could, weaving past beach umbrellas and cooler bags. Drenched with saltwater, she threw her arms around his neck. Right behind her, as always, was Francesca.

"Anna, god damn it! I really wasn't planning to take a swim today. . . ."

"*Ale!*" Anna crushed him in a bear hug. "Tell me I can come out with you tonight!"

"You get why she's so thrilled to see me?" he said in a stage aside, exasperated, to the rest of his crew.

"There's a party at the roller rink, you promised me . . ."

"No, I have to work tonight. Absolutely no way."

"But you said!" she protested and, begging: "C'mon, *Ale* . . ."

"No," he repeated, flatly.

"Why don't you let her go . . . ? What's the worst that could happen?" Sonia broke in. "We'll keep an eye on her."

Anna gave her a glare that meant: Don't stick your nose in where you're not wanted, stupid.

"I said no. You can go to the party on Ferragosto, August fifteenth: they're having another. At least I'd be there for sure."

"August fifteenth? That's in the next century!" she protested, bitterly.

"Listen, I'm a wreck, I've only had an hour's sleep, I just got here. Don't bust my balls, and get the fuck off me."

Anna stomped off with a scowl. Francesca, still right behind her, was relieved; it meant her friend would be home that night, just like her, and not out somewhere doing who-knows-what with who-knows-who.

You want me to stop busting your balls? Anna brooded as she stepped on beach towel after beach towel, kicking over pails and destroying children's sand castles as she walked. What about you, then? You're the one who's busting my balls.

She was walking without looking where she went. A child looked up to see his marbles ring destroyed and burst into tears. But Anna was furious. You want to keep me in a cage? Me? I'm almost fourteen years old! Well, in a month I'll have my own motor scooter, and then I'd like to see you try! I'd like to see just what you do if I run away on my new scooter if I have a new boyfriend twice your size. I'd like to see what the fuck you do then, you and that baboon of a father, of *your* father. They don't get it, they don't see I'm growing up now, that I have a brain to think with and I'll fuck all of you *up!*

"You're so tough, *Ale*," Sonia smiled.

"I'm not tough. I just know how things work. If I didn't have to work tonight, I'd go to the roller rink, too. But since I can't keep an eye on her, she stays home."

"What harm could she do?" asked Jessica.

"No, she wouldn't do anything, no way. But you know me. . . . If I hear about anyone laying a finger on her, I'd just beat the shit out of them. And since *her* father doesn't pay any attention to these things . . . I'm the one that has to tell her no."

They were standing in a circle, getting high on joints and alcohol, under a big skewed beach umbrella. On either side of them other circles of kids were draining beers, passing a one-hitter around, groping the thighs of the girls who were intentionally sashaying between the tables, sucking ice pops.

"Jesus, Francesca is hot!" Cristiano suddenly said, out of the blue.

They all turned to look at her. Her pale body, the way she moved through the crowd, had little kids with water wings and boogie boards, and wrinkled old guys with sun hats turning to stare in astonishment as she went past. The way she intertwined her slender, graceful body with Anna's, wrapping one arm around her waist, resting her face on Anna's shoulder. She was the magic spell of Via Stalingrado, the kind of beauty you see once every three or four generations.

"You know what we should do, *Ale*?" said Cristiano. "Let's go to Baratti and pick up some wallets from German tourists! P-tooie," he spat, "those fucking Germans . . ."

In Via Stalingrado, of course, not even the shadow of a tourist, not even a lost tourist.

But Alessio, who'd been massaging Sonia's inner thigh under the table, was making other plans in his mind. He didn't even bother to reply. He took Sonia's hand, pulled her to her feet with the slightest effort. And Cristiano understood instantly.

He didn't give a shit about Sonia. The thing is this: You have to have a lot of women in the quarter if you want to be number one. You have to mark your territory; you have to command respect. She let him pull her by the arm, she let him take her behind the beach cabanas while the others shouted out the usual acid wisecracks.

"Full throttle, *Ale!* We want to hear you guys!"

Alessio pushed her back against the creaking wall of a beach cabana, in broad daylight, in full view of passersby. They huddled back in a cone of shadow. Her sarong pushed aside, his zipper unzipped in a split second, and she let him slip into her. A little knot of young boys with water pistols got the drop on them. No one panicked. The kids turned the corner, let them finish in peace.

That afternoon Sandra came down to the beach, too, together with other women from the neighborhood. It was a Thursday, but she had the day off. Lots of mamas had brought down folding chairs and gossip magazines, and they'd started chatting.

Not Rosa. Rosa had stayed home, as usual, sitting in her easy chair looking at the television, thinking and tearing at her fingernails: her face as white as a sheet, her feet swollen in her slippers, sealed into the airless vault on the fourth floor. As she sat there her husband was leaning over the railing of the balcony, and she knew what he was doing.

Sandra scanned the beach umbrellas for Rosa and was sad to register her absence. Rosa hadn't knocked at her door. Even though it had been days and days, she hadn't come by with a cake. Sandra was no fool; she could guess the reason.

Now she proudly unfolded the day's copy of *La Repubblica*. She was probably the only woman in the apartment buildings to read a newspaper every day, and it made people look at her with mistrust.

She hungrily skimmed the headlines and the columns of type. "Berlusconi wins confidence vote in the Senate. Berlusconi references *Alice in Wonderland* by Lewis Carroll." She furrowed her brow. "The prime minister of Italy pointed out that this is not Wonderland, and more importantly, that he is not Alice . . ."

Sandra was eagerly reading the section on domestic politics when Anna came over, stopped in front of her with a pout, and tore the newspaper out of her hands. They would oppose the government's line with all their force. They'd bring down this administration in less than a year. Anna, in the meanwhile, was telling her that she was going to the roller rink tonight no matter what he said, whether her brother liked it or not.

"Well, let's just see if I slap your face, young lady!" She grabbed back her newspaper with great irritation.

She let her daughter spout five or six curse words, then she plunged her head back into the pages of the newspaper. She resumed leafing through it, moistening the tip of her index finger with the tip of her tongue to make it easier to turn the pages. Both fists raised, when she was a little girl, she'd sung songs from battles that had vanished into the mists of the past century. Anna looked at her mother and felt as if she was at war with the world. They'll see. Oh, they'll see! They'll see what I'm capable of. . . . I'll run away from home, she decided, as she walked away. I'll kick up a cloud of crazy. You won't be able to hold me back anymore: You'll have to let me go.

Then Francesca tripped her on the wet sand, grabbed her by an ankle, and laughed as she dragged her into the waves. Francesca . . . Sinking underwater, her arms wrapped around her best friend in the world and in the universe, Anna suddenly forgot about the roller rink and her fucked-up family.

Now she was running through the crowd of boys playing soccer. In cahoots with Francesca she implemented a vast series of well-tested disruption techniques. Like leaping onto Massi's back, making him stumble and fall just as they were passing him the ball.

For an instant she stopped to catch her breath. Eyes wide open, looking out upon her world.

She saw Donata sprawled motionless under her beach umbrella, twisted in her sickness. She would have liked to take Donata into the water with her, but she couldn't: She lacked the courage. She saw that loser Lisa eating ice cream. Her mother laying down her newspaper, gesticulating with animation to the other women. Who knows where her father was? It'd be better if he just never came back. Alessio's seat was empty at the bar, and Cristiano was trying to hook up with some girl. She saw the beach teeming with people. And then she saw Francesca. The finest thing. Her soul mate, her best friend. She'd just turned a cartwheel in ankle-deep water, and now she was smiling radiantly at her.

Her sister, that's right. More than a sister.

If Anna had looked up and turned her gaze far away, up at the gray walls of the bunker she lived in, she might have noticed a man looking out from a fourth-floor balcony.

Enrico, with his binoculars in hand, was observing the scene. He was sharpening his focus on his daughter's swimsuit. He was sweating. This time, he'd seen it all. His daughter was climbing up some boy's back, her arms wrapped around his neck, that filthy bastard who lived in the building across the way. And he was embracing her underwater, out of the water, any old place. He'd seen them racing across the sand toward the dressing rooms, hiding between the cabanas.

His hands were shaking; veins were pulsing on his neck. He was ready to stomp down there, rush out onto the beach. Then he saw them come back, just a few minutes later, back with all the others. That's why he hadn't taken matters into his own hands. No point in creating unnecessary scenes. He'd wait for her to come home. Before he had to leave for his ten o'clock shift he'd pound it into her head, whether she liked it or not, that she couldn't act like a little whore.

Oh, he'd make her understand this time, her and that little bitch friend of hers, the one who was steering her into trouble.

Look at them hugging each other. What are they doing? What the fuck are they doing?

The binoculars dropped to the ground. And there was darkness inside the lenses.

PART TWO

Seaweed

At midnight on August 13, 2001, Alessio hoisted himself to the top of a rusted pole along the old high-tension line, securing himself with a lineman's belt. He'd scampered up the trelliswork like a cat. He was wearing his overalls from work and the usual Chicago Bulls cap. From high atop that pole he could see the whole promontory and the sea, not far away, warm and dark.

Two pylons farther along, wearing shorts and a short-sleeved shirt, Cristiano was holding up his cable shears and gesturing for him to get started. He'd wrapped both legs around the pole. He hadn't even brought a cable to secure himself. Cristiano wasn't afraid of a thing. In his chest his heartbeat was altered, and he felt the usual thrill, his inner thirteen-year-old, of doing something reckless.

The night was clean. And deserted.

They stared each other straight in the eye, determined not to leave a single power pole unshorn. Alessio's heart was pumping blood and cocaine, as always when he and Cristiano were sneaking onto private property to steal something.

They were inside the barbed-wire perimeter of the Dalmine-Tenaris plant, which was at the center of an expanse scattered with stands of reeds across from the WWF Oasis. Nearby, the gigantic ENEL power plant projected its towers straight up, emitting bright white shafts of light identical to the stars. They were the highest things along the coastline. The moon was filtering the mists from the marshes, turning them into a slime. Then there was nothing but brushwood, short stands of holm oaks, and thornbushes. After that, the sea; then nothing.

There were just the two of them, hard at work, in the industrial infrastructure. Maybe a couple of foxes, the occasional warthog, and lots and lots of mosquitoes. They hadn't brought flashlights. The silvery moonlight was more than sufficient: It didn't attract the attention of the Dalmine security guards.

From here, too, from anywhere, A-Fo 4 was clearly visible. The tower of the blast furnace glimmered motionless over the promontory. Standing sentinel. And a cruise ship, lit up like a party boat, would sail by every so often like a dream.

Groups of kids were clustered on the beaches not much farther away, like every year, in loose circles around bonfires. It was the week of Ferragosto, nearly everyone was on vacation, and all the different groups had organized their beach parties along the Via della Principessa, drinking beers and smoking joints. There was a contingent from Via Stalingrado, too, the roughest, bumpkinest-looking of them all. Sonia and Jessica were there, wondering where the two of them had wound up tonight; they couldn't even imagine.

Alessio rolled up the first bundle of copper and signaled okay with thumb and fingers. We're good.

Cristiano replied by tossing an enormous cable into the air like a cowboy tossing a lasso, pretending he was riding the power pole like a bucking bronco or something. What an idiot, thought Alessio, shaking his head.

Just a few days earlier, in the Lucchini cafeteria, one particularly sly employee let slip the fact that there was still plenty of copper inside the grounds of the Dalmine plant. He said it with a wink, aloud, without realizing that there were silent listeners, listeners who had more than a nodding relationship with copper. "They haven't dismantled them all yet, the old electric lines." They'd grasped the concept easily. What's more: They'd beat him to the punch.

That night, headlights off, they'd skirted the perimeter of the pipe factory along the dirt lane of the field where the quail-hunting dogs were trained. They'd hunted for the exact right spot, where the canebrake thins out and the swamp is shallow. They'd cut through the chain-link fence, and they'd ventured in like a couple of nocturnal animals.

The black market for copper: that's one sector that was booming. As they worked they looked up every so often to make sure no one was coming out of the Dalmine building. It was all deserted, all silent. It had been that way for a good solid hour.

Then Cristiano noticed something moving through the vegetation. He froze. It was coming toward them. Alessio stiffened, watchfully.

A car was moving slowly through the canebrake, its headlights on bright. *The police!* was the first thing they both thought. They followed the noise of tires on gravel and peered down at the silhouette of the car parking not far away. They held their breath.

The engine stopped, but no one got out. They went on holding their breath for two minutes. Tense, ready to move fast. Two more minutes. The headlights went out. Okay: The car was starting to rock. Gently, like a cradle. Back and forth, like a porch glider.

Alessio smiled, sensing the tension uncoil inside him all at once. Cristiano waved a hand, visually telling them to go fuck themselves. Why tonight of all nights? And with all the empty coastline available, why here of all places?

Well, that's better. They were definitely not cops, and they definitely would not call the cops. They had better things to do than that, the lucky dogs. The car pulsed away happily; the windshield was starting to fog up.

They had some strange company.

Meanwhile, Alessio and Cristiano went back to clipping cable and sweating. Their T-shirts were sticky, clinging to them. Humidity was creeping up from the sea, clogging up their mouths and nostrils, turning air into water.

Down below, on the state highway, long lines of cars were moving at walking speed toward the port. Cristiano could see them from high up on the pylon: a serpent of yellow headlights and rumbling engines. Tourists anxious to board the first ferryboat for the Isle of Elba in the morning. He didn't envy them in the slightest, all those big-city snobs who'd sail to the island tomorrow morning to celebrate Ferragosto in a hotel, under a beach umbrella on a blinding white beach.

The lives that tourists lived were another world, another way of life, crowded and ordinary. Here he had adrenaline; there was even a couple fucking down below. There were security guards lying in ambush, mosquitoes, pounds and pounds of copper—that is, money—just lying around to be picked up.

Cristiano looked over at his longtime friend, his best friend, who was leaping down onto the ground and rolling up a thick length of cable, up to his knees in muck. He looked down at him with a special smile.

Because. Just because, when they were twelve years old, they'd sneak into the construction sites along the new Aurelia highway and wait for one of the workers to walk away. They'd mutter under their breath: "Go on, asshole, go take a piss." And if he really did step away, they'd say: "Ready, set, go." Then they'd make a dash for it, scramble up into the operator's seat of a bulldozer or a power shovel, those mastodonic pieces of equipment that they would drive for the rest of their lives.

Alessio looked up and glanced over at the car.

"They still at it?" He pointed. "My compliments!"

He wiped the sweat off his brow with one arm and took a deep breath, filling his lungs with brackish salt air. He felt like laughing.

Stealing copper in the middle of the night: something he'd tell girls about. Alessio knew the way girls were; he knew that at a certain point in the story that funny little smile would appear on their faces. Lips compressed, stern, obstinate, but detectable, as if in filigree, already willing to be kissed. For that kind of kiss he was willing to do anything; for that exact kind of girl, who would fall in love with crooks and thieves and then wind up marrying a guy who works in a bank.

Anyway, here he was—he tried to smile—on top of a high-tension power line and, to tell the truth, he was having as much fun as a little kid. How much fun does a bank teller have, all day, at his little window? And if one day, by chance (though that day would have to come, sooner or later), he happened to run into Elena in the street, that's what he really would say to her: "Good for you, I hope you're happy, go on and get married to that slobbery toad from the UniCredit branch office. You know what? I'm proud of what I am. I may bust my ass, but I'm alive."

At last the car engine started up again, then the headlights switched on, and the car slowly disappeared, crunching away down the gravel lane.

"It's been a pleasure!" laughed Cristiano.

Alessio pretended to applaud.

They looked each other in the face: They were a disgusting mess. They looked at their watches. Nothing to laugh about. So, back to shearing cable, their hands torn and bloody, their legs numb and tingling, with the absolute satisfaction of having already piled up an industrial quantity of copper.

They went on working like that, perched high in the sky, shears in hand, for five hours. As dawn approached they both had such a strong urge to shout out loud that their lungs felt as if they were exploding. They hadn't made a sound all night, out of fear of the security guards, out of fear that one of the truckers sleeping on their steering wheels in the entrance parking lot of the Dalmine plant might wake up and start honking his air horn.

When they got down off the pylons they were drenched in sweat, and their arms felt as if they had multiple fractures. By now there weren't even the headlights of stragglers or lost partygoers. Nothing, nothing at all. Soon the workers in the plant would finish their shift and go home, and others, from all over the Val di Cornia, would start arriving by bus and car to start the next shift.

They waded through the muck in their rubber boots, carrying the last rolls of cable over their shoulders. When they got to the car they crammed the trunk full of cable, piled the backseats high, wedged cable in everywhere there was room, right up to the windowsills. Then, with the headlights off and the suspension compressed under the weight, they drove along parallel to the state highway.

A black sign with orange lettering announced that they were driving through an ARTISANAL ZONE. Or used to announce. Because someone, an unsung genius, had recently blacked out the ARTIS part of the lettering. The sign was much more accurate now.

Alessio was driving unhurriedly, carefully avoiding potholes and rocks on the road. Frogs were croaking, insects sounded like helicopters, and those damned mosquitoes blew in the open car windows along with billows of dust.

Scratching and scratching their calves.

Alessio shifted into fourth when they finally got past the grounds of the Dalmine plant, and then fifth, kicking up a huge cloud of dust. He turned and looked at Cristiano with a galactic smile.

Cristiano responded by punching the windshield. A triumphant, happy punch. He turned on the stereo: *I'm blue, da ba dee da ba die*, turned it up louder, *I'm blue, if I was green I would die.* The speakers were thundering; they both stuck their heads out into the rushing wind. They both shouted at the top of their lungs, on the empty Via Aurelia, against the hillsides.

"Three thousand lire a kilo, multiplied by?"

"Something like . . ." Alessio glanced in the rearview mirror.

"Something like half a ton!" Cristiano exulted, turning to look at their plunder.

When you added it all up, in a single night they'd pocketed a month's salary from the Lucchini plant.

"We dismantled their asses, and not a single alarm bell!"

"They were asleep, or watching a porno. . . ."

"*Ale*, look at me." At the stoplight they stared into each other's weary, glistening eyes. "Tomorrow night, we're going to the Gilda, and I don't want to hear any crap."

Alessio's car was the only vehicle out and about in the sleeping city.

They felt like thieves when they got out of the car in Via Stalingrado, and the garage doors made a tremendous clanging crash as they swung shut. They weren't laughing when they stowed the copper in the garage, warily eyeing the apartment windows, afraid of seeing lights turned on.

They tiptoed across the courtyard, then each of them scampered into his own building. On the stairs, the only sound was men snoring and a newborn baby wailing. It was like invading a foreign kingdom. And the baby who was crying was Cristiano's son, in his ex-girlfriend's apartment.

Cristiano stopped and pressed his ear against the door: Until she got up to cradle the baby in her arms, he'd stand there, listening to it cry. He felt something powerful and unbridled in his chest. Maybe he should have knocked at the door. He couldn't bring himself to. He slipped away into the darkness, galloping up the three remaining flights of stairs.

Alessio did his very best to keep from making noise. He'd taken the precaution of removing his shoes. He decided not to turn on the light. He tried to grope his way through the darkness to his bedroom.

It didn't go well.

He bumped into a chair in the kitchen. The noise echoed, surrealistically, throughout the apartment. In no time at all he heard the click of a light switch. He cursed inwardly. And his mother appeared right before him, her face puffy with sleep.

There stood Sandra, rigid as a broom handle, staring at the motionless figure of her son at six in the morning—in his work overalls, his face smeared with mud, looking like nothing so much as a Vietnam grunt in *Apocalypse Now*.

"Now you're going to explain to me," she started to say. She opened her lips, glued shut by sleep, and beneath the translucent flesh of her forehead a muscle tensed. A stranger's voice came out of her mouth, and she was unable to finish the sentence.

Alessio looked at his mother: a woman in a dressing gown, her shoulders curved with weariness. She was old now, in fact; she was ashen and beaten down, this woman with eyes filled with sadness, who was closing those eyes now to keep from seeing what was in front of her.

He hadn't realized that his mother was a woman with way too much to worry about to put up with his bullshit. She had her hands full with that bastard father of his; the bastard world they lived in had already hurt her enough. If anything, he should have tried to give her a little happiness.

"Mama," he found the courage to speak, "go back to bed now, try not to ask me any questions. I swear to you, you have nothing to worry about."

Sandra kept her eyes shut, and stood in silence.

"Mama," he said, "forgive me if I'm filthy. . . ."

He took that body in his arms, hugged her to him as if she were a baby or a girlfriend. In spite of his aching back, he conveyed all his physical strength to her.

"I'm not asking," said Sandra, shaking her head, "you just promise me . . ."

"Sssh!" Alessio didn't want to hear the words.

"Promise me," Sandra said again, her face turning pretty again, "that this is the last time you go out doing who-knows-what in the middle of the night."

Alessio laughed. They laughed together, in a weary embrace, by the light of the hanging lamp and the dawning day. Just then, from behind the edge of the door, Anna appeared. She didn't say a word. She just stood there, barefoot and clean. She looked at them, unseen, like a small angel in summer pajamas. In her alphabet, that was a beautiful thing. Her mama's face pressed into the hollow between her brother's neck and shoulder, was perhaps the finest thing. Something that was perhaps worth it, a reason in life not to cheat or lie.

CHAPTER 13

Tiny mosquito larvae bobbed on the water's surface. A dense, luke-warm broth teeming with barely living creatures.

Francesca and Anna were making their way barefoot through the canebrake, emitting little, scarcely human bursts of giggles. Every step was a spasm of tickling around their ankles, and they loved it.

The cuffs of their tracksuits were rolled up to their knees; their running shoes were tied around their waists. Anna's small face searched through the reeds for Francesca's. They were playing hide-and-seek amid the mists and swooping insects.

"Are you sure that you're still going to love me next year?"

"Christ, *France*, what a pain in the ass!"

They were just a pair of excrescences on that murky landscape. With every breeze the swamp released a blizzard of pollen. The light too seemed to stagnate. The sun hung in the middle of the sky, swollen and enflamed. It refused to set.

Why did they even bother to shower, knowing they'd just get dirty again?

Their damp hair, scented with shampoo, was gradually being impregnated with another odor: a mixture of sweat and sap. The downy growth on the surface of the plants caused their skin to itch. It felt as if they were walking through wool.

They'd gone there every evening, after dinner, for years. They had to be home no later than ten.

There was no other way to get there: You had to clamber over the wall, hold your nose as you went past the sewer outlet, and then wade through the marshes, dense with filaments and slime.

But when you emerged, and you saw the sea spreading out before you, a feverish urge to run swept over you, like nothing else in the world. There was no one down there; it was deserted. You could strip naked and shout out the worst obscenities, strings of filthy words, without shame.

The beach was piled high with seaweed. Logs and stranded boats, their hulls covered with downy growth, tumbled up by the waves. Fishermen came here to leave the broken hulks of boats to save money on dumping fees.

They loved stepping into the gooey mass of the seaweed, pushing their feet in up to their calves, feeling the empty seashells that stuck out like fangs and bit their feet. Balls of neptune grass by the million, all tossed up by the sea right there. On the shore they broke down into a black mucilage, a muck that reeked of pee and fresh bread. This was their secret beach.

Anna clutched her bundle of leftovers from dinner in her hands and strode briskly along the water's edge. She was radiant: She was thinking of Ferragosto, tomorrow, the fifteenth of August. She looked straight ahead of her, staring at the fat red disk of the setting sun. The sensation that everything was within her grasp.

Francesca hung back, dawdling along on her long slender legs. Deep in her chest she was nurturing a promise, a promise she might keep. A promise to herself that she'd made in silence at the dinner table, as she sat eating between her parents. But now she wasn't so sure she'd be able to live up to it. When the time was right, she felt certain, her courage would fail her.

When they reached the exact spot Anna stuck two fingers in her mouth and emitted a shrill, masculine whistle. They waited.

"I'll bet you one's missing. . . ."

They'd sworn to each other never to bring anyone else down there.

They didn't even know why, but there was something naked about the place that made them feel at home. Francesca, maybe back in fifth grade, had suggested the pledge: "This is only for us." And Anna had immediately agreed. She'd sworn an oath: "Only you and me."

It didn't take long for cats to materialize from every direction, from the pores of the boats and from the nearby underbrush, loyal to the girls' signal.

"One, two, three, four . . . ," Francesca counted. "They're all here!"

Bringing them food, dislodging the creatures from the bowels of hedges and broken hulls before nightfall, before climbing into bed and thinking back on the day's events, allowed them to regress to a childish state. They chewed on the seaweed. They rubbed their faces in the cats' damp, rough fur, ugly beasts that they were. One was missing an eye. Another was missing a tail. Countless fleas.

Long ago, maybe more than a century, this was a harbor. Now, for the two of them, it was a nest.

Anna set her bundle of food on the ground and unwrapped it; she was immediately enveloped in mewing. That dead zone of the coastline was reduced to a primordial broth of things. Francesca liked searching the ruins for evidence that someone had been there before them: a ladle, a ceramic tile. She'd hunker over her digging and shout if she unearthed anything human.

That day, too, she squatted down by a pile of ivy and rocks. Only this time she wasn't concentrating. She was digging with one hand at random, and as she delved she hefted and weighed her promise, examining it from all angles. There was one thing she was sure of: This was the right place. As for the time, tomorrow would be too late.

She lifted her head and stopped to watch Anna, her *best friend*, at the center of a swirling welter of tails and paws. She had to tell her now; she just had to make up her mind to do it. A baker's dozen of cats were wreathing their bodies between her legs, and she let them, bending down to pet them, turning them on their backs and stroking them where their fur grew pinkish and sparse.

Francesca stood there, in turmoil. She felt something flowing beneath her flesh like a warm, vibrant plasma, at once irradiating and frightening her. Anna lowered her nose to the damp noses of those wild creatures, and Francesca noticed how greatly she'd changed, she couldn't say whether over time or just now. Something had liquefied in her actions and her eyes. She'd become feminine. Her voice had turned husky, a step lower in tone; now that she was talking, Francesca couldn't grasp the meaning of her words. Something was coming unlaced deep inside her mute, angular organism.

That mysterious effect. That ineffable feathering that Nino was unable to trigger in her.

She had to work up the courage, had to tell her; the time for concealing it was long over. She hated time: It had created a distance between them. When they were little girls they'd been a single thing, a whole. Now the distinctions were proliferating. As this fission was progressing, as Anna pursued her galactic ambitions—"I'm going to be a magistrate, a lawyer, a senator"—Francesca hung back, unsettled. When Francesca hugged Anna, if Francesca grazed the tip of Anna's finger, Francesca's body responded in a way that was new. Francesca wasn't stupid. She might be covered with bruises, but she wasn't stupid.

When Anna took a seat on the rusting skeleton of a boat and stared out at the sea, backlit, dark, and tinged with red, Francesca went over to sit next to her, wrapping her arms around her knees.

"*France*," Anna said without turning her head to look, "my mother is a frustrated woman. She thinks I can't see it, but I do. You must think I'm a jerk but . . . I want to get out of this place. I want to be famous!"

Francesca gulped: "There's something I have to tell you."

Her friend was enraptured. She was staring at the line of the horizon, at the spiky silhouette of the island, with the eyes of someone driven to conquer, someone with a frenzied sense that time was running out.

"I don't want to be a failure," she went on. "Sonia, Jessica. Even my brother . . . They work from dawn to dark, they get wasted on the weekends, and then they die. And what's happened? Nothing. No one even notices they were there."

"Then the thing to do is get on TV. . . ."

"That's not it! I have nothing but respect for *veline*, dancers, and show hosts . . . but Fabrizio Frizzi is not going to go down in history!" She punched the air with a fist. "He's not somebody who matters!"

She collected herself. "You said there was something you wanted to tell me?"

As Francesca listened to her, her pupils dilated, eager to capture every tiny variation of her profile: every last beautiful expression on her face. A very specific word was flooding into her brain, burning her temples, but she couldn't bring herself to utter it.

"No, nothing, nothing important." Francesca's face was pale. "But . . . you know, someone who's born here, there's not even a decent movie theater, you grow up in this shitty neighborhood, you think they can go on to make history?"

"You don't understand. You're a pessimist at heart. Let's say I become a labor organizer, and I get pissed off at the Lucchini management, and I call a strike so total and absolute that they have to shut down the blast furnace, that'd be awesome, wouldn't it?"

No, Francesca didn't think anything of the sort was possible. The only thing she really thought about the Lucchini steel mill was that, if her father died in there, she'd heave a sigh of relief.

Anna was talking about Rome, Milan, law school, all the distant things that she was yearning to do and learn, probably without her. And Francesca could feel her chilly body growing warm and formless. She felt a stirring desire to suffocate Anna, keep her from talking, keep her at her side, crush her close.

Francesca also turned to look out at Elba, the gigantic silhouettes of the mountains, the iron quarries. In a quarry carved out of the side of a mountain: That's where she wanted to hide her.

"I feel like I want to become somebody, *Fra*, and there's no two ways about it," she smiled, "I practically can't believe that they're letting us go to the party tomorrow, at last. . . . Everything's changing."

She was going to go away. She was going to leave her all alone. What could she do without her?

Anna: the first word she'd learned to write, after *mama*.

She wasn't actually listening to her at all: She was just looking at her. And she couldn't seem to restrain this thing that could only have one name. It was pointless to try to find another name for it, to pretend anything different. It's useless, Francesca, to keep holding it in, over the days, months, years. How much longer can you keep it up? You can't do it: Your body's already decided for you.

"I want to be somebody, but I want you to be somebody, too."

In that *you*, *too*, pronounced with the tongue pushed sharply against the tip of her teeth, Francesca felt herself explode and subside, once and for all.

"You," a magnificent, freckly smile, with the lips gently tooth marked and shiny with saliva, "are the most special person on earth."

Boom.

The world. Francesca was closing her eyes.

You have to say it. You have to do it.

She opened her mouth and perceived the aftertaste of cat fur mixed with seaweed that densely pervaded that place. She perceived it, and soon she felt it, it changed into an emotion.

You have to utter those words.

She was yielding.

You have to pronounce the whole phrase, pronoun, verb, and pronoun. Or you'll die.

Once she got home Anna changed into her pajamas immediately. She hurried into the bathroom to brush her teeth, and she brushed so hard that she made her gums bleed. She raised her eyes from the sink to the mirror and looked hard at herself, the way she was: her face smeared with toothpaste; her eyes wide open, staring.

She begged herself: Tell me that I'm normal, tell me that nothing bad has happened, please, I beg you, let me be normal!

Francesca's sick. No, it's not true. I didn't just lose my . . . Oh, come on, you know perfectly well that's not how you lose it. Then why are you upset? It's nothing, it's ridiculous. Now calm down, go to sleep. Tomorrow's Ferragosto, tomorrow's the party. It's all her father's fault, that monster.

She gargled and gargled with mouthwash, then spit it violently into the sink. She dried her face, her mouth minty fresh, and tried to smile at herself in the mirror. It's all over, it's okay now.

But when she got into bed her supplications and false reassurances came back to haunt her. Her heart was pounding in her chest; she could feel the heat rushing to her head. Enough, that's enough, you've got to cut it out. From outside her window came the shouting and laughter of grown-ups, along with the moon and the car horns. The night was full of life, and she didn't know anything about it.

Not for long, though: In a few hours, tomorrow, everything would change. . . . But then why (the fuck!) couldn't she feel happy just anticipating the party, the way she'd felt before dinner? Why wasn't she filled with eager excitement at the thought of the roller rink and the boys and the dance music, and why were other things keeping her awake? She knew perfectly well why.

Nice. You claim to be a world beater, you want to become the president of the Italian republic, but now you're wetting your pants.

In the meantime, in the darkness of her room, Francesca was closing her eyes, holding her breath, and thinking intensely about Anna. She was clutching her warm, living body tight to her pillow. Warm and alive in a way she'd never been before.

It's true, she'd made a tacit promise: *Nothing* happened, and we won't ever talk about it again. Still . . . still, now, in the secrecy of her room, she could do it: explore, relive, and put a name to that nothing. At least here, inside of herself. Because that nothing had happened. And Anna had gotten mad afterward; she'd even given her a rude shove. But *before that* . . . Francesca opened her eyes and projected on the ceiling, over and over endlessly, that *before*.

She heard a plate or a glass shatter. Her father started shouting.

She wasn't a fighter, Francesca. She wasn't determined to be a world beater, like Anna. She wasn't Anna. She wasn't like the other girls in their neighborhood, or like other girls in general. And she'd always surrendered, since first grade. She didn't love this world.

But she loved Anna.

She did her best to ignore the shouts, the filth. The sounds that her father's hands made against her mother's body, and her mother's soft, continuous sobbing. It couldn't be all that terrible, what she'd done. It couldn't be truly wrong if at least, at night, in the safety of herself, before falling asleep . . . She would deny them and repress them, these feelings she had, she'd conceal them the way she did the bruises, the beatings, the horror. Dark, savage Francesca. But even she was capable of a tiny modicum of warmth. Her pores, her follicles were quivering.

When silence fell a luminous sequence of images began crowding into her mind: cold milk with mint, first of all, in the tall glass, stirred with a spoon, that made a tinkling sound. Snack time with Anna, one afternoon many years ago. The first time they'd discovered the seaweed beach, and Anna had said: "Oooh!" The land tortoise. The white stain in her panties that she tried to conceal. Okay, she was almost asleep. The seashell that Anna used to put to her ear when she was eight, pretending she was making a phone call: "Hush! The sea has something important it wants to tell me."

Her true dream wasn't runway fashion shows. It was taking the Toremar Ferry to Elba, the first one in the morning. Leaning over the bow and hugging Anna close to her, watching as the island drew closer. She'd wear her prettiest outfit that day. She'd pack her diving mask, her flippers, and her Rollerblades. She'd take care of everything: cooking, washing, dancing. In the little house inside the iron quarry.

Anna, on the other hand, couldn't sleep. She tossed and turned in her sweaty bed, begging: stop, please stop. Her head was buzzing like a fan turned on maximum. So she took it out on her sheet: She attacked her pillow ferociously. At a certain point, in desperation, she turned on the overhead lamp and grabbed a school textbook at random: Read the text. History of Italian literature, 3. She opened at random and started reading: Giovanni Pascoli.

She loved Francesca, that much was certain, even now. She might not have loved anyone as much as she loved her in her whole life, because . . . well, they'd grown up together, they'd done everything together, and they knew everything there was to know about each other. *But.* And there was a *but.*

"Digitale Purpurea." From *Primi poemetti*, free verse.

Anna forced herself to read, kept herself from reiterating in her thoughts what had happened just an hour earlier on the secret beach. And yet gleams, threads of that minute, or five, or ten minutes, wormed their way into what she was reading, and hurt her. Remembering. The sun, halfway hidden behind the island, and the island black and alive. She'd been breathless. She'd found her nostrils filled with the scent of her, the scent of hazelnut, almond, and cat fur. The mist coming off the sea. She felt the sea water smoothing out the surface of things, breathing.

Analysis of the style. Analysis of the text.

Two young women seated. One gazing at the other. One / slender and blonde, simply dressed / simple in her gaze; but the other one, slender and dark, / the other one . . .

It can't really be happening, she thought while it was happening. Francesca had spoken *that* word, had done *that* thing, and she had surrendered. She couldn't understand. Or really: She understood perfectly. But she was curious.

She remembered Francesca's green eyes. She wasn't innocent, not at all.

The cats, the ones that were still there, had stretched out on their bellies between the boats and closed their diseased, cataract-ridden eyes.

Then she'd realized. And when she did, she started running for her life. And she, too—Francesca—started running barefoot in the opposite direction. They'd both forgotten their gym shoes, lying abandoned in the seaweed, between the planks of the fishing boat.

Running with her eyes closed, the wind, the darkness thickening, condensing between them, and all those shards of glass nicking cuts into her feet, Anna had thought everything and more than everything: that she hated her, that she loved her, that she'd never speak to her again as long as she lived.

In the end, though, as she emerged onto the paved road, she'd seen Francesca by the wall, leaning against a lamppost, bent over, trying to catch her breath. She'd waited for her.

"November" was written by Giovanni Pascoli in 19 . . .

When they got back they'd walked in silence along the flaking walls of the garage. Above their heads the massive silhouette of the bunker apartments told them: You're safe. The windows, brightly lit in their hundreds, called out one to another. Swollen with shouts and cooking smells, the windows of their overcrowded, familiar world. They'd avoided looking at one another.

They were a little dazed when they walked into the courtyard. There was Nino, sitting on the saddle of his scooter, waving hello. Cristiano, revved up as usual, shouting, "To the Gilda! To the Gilda!" and making obscene gestures with one hand. At the far end, sitting on a bench, Sonia and the other girls were grouped in a circle, talking intently and launching subtle glances. The stars were invading the sky like freckles, and the two of them—filthy, wet, and chilled—were walking side by side without looking at each other.

"Okay, then, tomorrow, at two o'clock . . ."

A calm, neutral voice, smooth as the surface of a lake, scarcely audible in the crashing wall of noise that came from a car door swung open, a car radio turned up to the highest possible volume.

"At two o'clock, but we can't go to the beach. We're going to try on our outfits."

A difficult smile, eyes wide open, pupils dilated and tremulous.

They wouldn't go back to feed the cats, of that much Anna was certain.

She closed the book and her eyes. She decided that, after all, those cats could take care of themselves. The sliced-up soles of her feet stung painfully.

Too bad about the running shoes; they were practically new.

CHAPTER 14

I   t was around midnight when Francesca and Anna fell asleep. But outside their bedrooms the world was still busily humming along.

Rosa was staring at herself in her bathroom mirror, applying pressure to a cut on her cheekbone with an alcohol-soaked cotton ball. She had two black eyes so dark that you could barely see the crusted blood on her skin. In the next room Enrico the giant was sprawled out comfortably in front of the television set, watching a rerun of *Super Quark* on Rai 1. There was no expression whatsoever on his broad, unkempt face. His feet were propped up on a cushion, the remote control was perched on his belly. His big hands rested idly at his sides.

Sandra was watching television too: a news special on sudden infant death syndrome. The fan was running, blowing air straight at her. She was drumming her fingers on the armrest of the armchair. She felt like calling someone, but she didn't know whom. She was marveling at the fact that already, at age forty-three, she was forced to stay home alone on a Saturday night.

She was furious at him, and was bearing a grudge, but still she missed him. She almost hoped that tomorrow, at least for Ferragosto, Arturo would come home.

Meanwhile, leaning against the counter of a bar up the coast, in San Vincenzo, in the midst of a crowd of small businessmen, motorboat dealers, and owners of automobile dealerships, her husband was talking on his cell phone. There was a new watch on his wrist and, to judge from the way he was dressed, things were going well for him. He was a good-looking man, charming and attractive despite his diminutive stature. He could have had plenty of women, if he wanted.

But he didn't want women. In fact, what he wished he could do right now was go home, with a present under his arm for Sandra. Say to her: "Come on, get dressed." And take her out dancing. But he wasn't ready yet. He had no desire to get into a fight with her. A gentleman refilled his glass with *spumante*, and he smiled as he drank. He had a few big deals on the front burner: This time he really had turned his life around. Instead of serving him with a writ of divorce, Sandra was going to ask him to marry her again. On Capri, or in Positano.

What he wanted to do most right now, though, what he couldn't put off any longer, was to call his son. He had a burning need to hear his voice, a sort of frenzy to make sure he was all right. It wasn't obvious, he realized, but he cared so deeply about that stubborn young man who obstinately kept working like a donkey at the Lucchini steel mill, busting his hump in that shit hole. And then there was his baby, his little girl, Anna . . . but she was certainly asleep at this hour.

He flipped open the banged-up clamshell of one of the two cell phones he carried in his breast pocket and he punched in Alessio's number. A happy smile, a special daddy smile, appeared on his face as he listened to it ring.

But nobody was listening to the ringing of Alessio's cell phone. It lay forgotten in the backseat, drowned out by the thumping hi-fi and the road noise in the Peugeot hurtling along at speed. It illuminated the upholstery for just a moment. Then it went dark.

They parked outside the pine grove of Follonica. Their jeans were tight fitting, their back pockets stretched by the wallets stuffed with cash from selling all that copper cable. They got out of the car and slammed the doors behind them. Look out, here we come.

Cristiano had overdone it, with his drinking and his clothing. He was wearing an orange shirt, emanating such an intense stream of photons that nobody could miss it. *Like a superhero!* he was telling himself, in his mind. He wished he'd been able to give his son a kiss before heading out for the night, because his ex wasn't at home. But he'd lacked the nerve, and now he'd canceled all thoughts of that minuscule human being. He was whistling and kicking a pinecone along as he walked.

Alessio was handsome, with a smoulder. He was walking along behind Cristiano, slightly unsettled. His white shirt was neatly pressed, the collar was turned up, his eyes were almost gray. Earlier that evening, at the bar in Piombino, a couple of cops had told him: "Why don't you do a screen test for Canale 5, instead of selling stolen copper on the black market? What kind of fools do you take us for?"

Crowds of kids went zigzagging through the pine forest. So many crackling flames, redolent of aftershave and whiskey, emitting ululating shouts launched straight up like rockets between the trees. Where the forest grew denser and pine needles filtered down like rain, there was a chill in the darkness. They picked up the pace, moving along briskly through the resinous scent and the turgid mists of night.

Through the branches they could just make out a dot of light, which gradually took on the outlines of a luminous sign. Some of the letters were burned out, but the word was still legible. As they got closer they could distinguish the stylized figure of a pinup girl inviting them to continue in that direction. They could see a pair of neon nipples blinking in the dark.

They'd have to wait in line.

Cristiano snorted in annoyance. Alessio patted his jeans pocket and realized he'd left his cell phone somewhere.

Waiting in line makes it sound civilized. It was a random milling crowd, a traffic jam, a crush. A swamp of overheated drunken males who were shoving each other one minute and hugging each other the next, and it was unclear where they were all headed. In the general confusion one little punk was doubled over, vomiting on the asphalt path. Another one, who looked like he was fourteen at most, had his underwear pulled down and was shouting: "I'm John Holmes!"

Nobody was paying attention to him. There were lots of kids more or less the same age and as noisy as he was mingling with the older guys, maybe out to get their cherries popped. The only old guy—in a vignette that was almost entirely lost in the chaos—turned to look with a hint of envy gleaming in his eye.

This was the only SEXY DISCO SEXY—as the sign advertised—between Grosseto and Livorno. A sign at the entrance warned prospective customers of the elevated erotic content of the club: It discouraged anyone from entering whose sensibilities might be easily offended. Alessio and Cristiano stopped, read the sign, and—like all the others—laughed at it. After waiting in line for thirty minutes and paying a cover charge of thirty euros, they finally threw open the door and walked in.

They were greeted with a damp, solid gob of smoke, noise, and stench.

Even before their eyes adjusted enough to see, the Gilda emitted a blast of its hot, nauseating breath in their faces. The air was so dense that it felt as if they'd been jammed into a laundry hamper full of dirty clothes. Their heads were spinning with the aftertaste of disinfectant, vomit, and sweat that was oozing out of every pore in the place. There was an impenetrable wall of overheated men. Low ceilings, bluish lights: It was like a cellar, almost like a coffin.

The summer is magic. Oh, Oh, Oh . . . The summer is magic . . . went the song, pumping out of the speakers at top volume.

Far off, at the end of the room—Cristiano was savoring it in advance, rolling it around on his tongue—was a pair of dizzying thighs. There was a woolly glow of exposed pubis.

They elbowed their way to the bar. They glimpsed through the silhouettes of a couple of bald heads the silhouette of a nude self-propelled figure. As they moved a little farther forward they glimpsed the brown flesh of a pair of nipples and the glitter of a metal G-string. At last, as they emerged at the edge of the stage, there she was in her entirety: a magnificent brunette gyrating languidly, gripping a steel pole with both hands. Next to her was a minute, translucent blonde, working her own pole, twisting and contorting, dressed in scales.

It was with immense satisfaction that they took their seats at a table that might have been wobbly but still commanded a view. They stretched their legs and ordered a couple of Negronis.

Cristiano stabbed a couple of violent glances in the direction of the two females with absent, distracted faces. He reckoned the circumference of their hips and breasts. A couple of sides of meat hanging on a hook at the slaughterhouse. But what the hell, yeah, they were hot! And he joined the chorus of hoots and cheers.

They ordered two more Negronis, and after that, two more.

No one seemed to notice that the ceiling plaster was flaking, that there was a black mold spreading out from the corners. No one except for Alessio took into consideration the state of neglect of the swaybacked sofas, the upholstery worn thin by hundreds of knees, thighs, and elbows, intertwined and pressed. The big spherical chandelier reduced to a barren skeletal structure, with only a dozen or so crystals still dangling from it. Who knows how many times a week, or a month, the cleaning crew vacuumed that stifling dump, Alessio wondered, as he nursed his drink. Without making any comment, he eyed the face of the noticeably tired brunette. He deduced that, No, after all, she wasn't magnificent at all.

Her lap dance was apathetic and unsurprising. That woman must be over thirty; her cheeks were pockmarked by acne under the heavy layer of foundation. Alessio didn't have a hard time imagining, behind her movements, her dissolving a tablet under her tongue in the dressing room before starting the night's work. It was harder to imagine the rest of her life: the furnishings of her bedroom, her hobbies, how she spent her time in the daylight.

He couldn't bring himself to go for it; he'd never liked that place.

The smiles of the hooker bunnies wandering among the tables in search of fifty-thousand-lire banknotes were sad. Those smiles dragged out of his gut all the sadness and gloom that he'd built up in twenty-three years.

He even tried to fake it; he launched the occasional empty comment, a laugh, and he did it only for his friend.

Some friend . . .

Because Cristiano, at a certain point in the throes of overexcitement, had recognized his employer in the throng. He'd jumped to his feet and started waving his arms. His boss, a guy in his early sixties wearing a Hawaiian shirt barely covering an enormous belly, was busy stuffing a solitary banknote into the G-string of the blond pole dancer. Cristiano called him by name and the man turned around. He yelled: "Hey, jerk-off!" And Cristiano had gone running like an idiot.

Alone now, Alessio was watching in silence.

The revolting sight of Cristiano gnawing at crumbs his employer had dropped on the floor. A leftover thigh, a bit of breast. "The bastard who underpays me, the bastard who exploits me," he used to say. Alessio watched the movements of that big hairy man's hands on the fragile, possibly anorexic body of the blond girl. He had the impression that from one moment to the next that body might just crumble like a cookie.

She was young, very young. There was something foreign in her features. Alessio realized with astonishment how closely that adolescent resembled Francesca. Identical: perfect and obscure, just like her. The same water-green eyes, the same tense lips. He could feel his flesh crawl at the mere thought.

He put down his glass and finally felt free to be sad. Deeply and truly sad.

While Cristiano was leading Francesca's doppelgänger toward the filthy curtain of a private room, Alessio lurched to his feet, bumping the table and overturning his chair. He saw Cristiano jam a bill into her hand, into the hand of that synthetic creature, a child—not even eighteen, now that he looked even more closely. He watched as the disgusting old man followed them behind the curtain, into the lurid den where she'd put on her show. A predictable routine, for cash. The two of them would flop down onto the Naugahyde ottomans, and she'd let them talk her into coming a little closer.

A towering sense of revulsion and rebellion drove him briskly toward the exit. He'd gladly report them to the police, sons of bitches trafficking in underage girls from Eastern Europe. But since he was no hero, in fact nothing more than a poor asshole who'd had too much to drink and needed to vomit, once he was outside he collapsed onto the walkway.

When he finally lifted his head from the slimy puddle, he felt like a fourteen-year-old at his first party. He got back to his feet and smiled at himself. The clearing was empty now, the night was creaking with crickets and stars. He rested his face on the cool breeze springing up from the sea. And he feebly shuffled forward toward the pine grove.

There he gingerly lowered himself onto a bench. The night was clean and spacious between the branches spread open like long slender fingers and the sudden, harmless collapse of a pinecone. He wanted to gather his strength, take a moment to recover, clean himself up a little, get back to his car, and leave. Alone. Tonight that guy could get home on foot, or else wait for the first bus in the morning, whatever—that was his problem. It would be sickening to see him again, smeared with the lurid pigments of that girl.

His stomach was a bubbling cauldron of vicious gastric fluids; his head was spinning just slightly. In the humid heart of the pine grove, he gradually felt better. The scent of resin was bracing. He closed his eyes and summoned, inwardly, as if to cleanse himself, some nice image, anything, as long as it was nice.

And in fact an image surfaced from an obscure recess of his memory and swept, hot and bright, into his temples.

He saw himself: disheveled hair, face filthy with iron dust, standing beneath a clear sky, perhaps bluer in his memory than it really had been that day. He was wearing dirt-smeared work boots and orange three-quarter-length work pants, the kind with phosphorescent stripes.

He'd slipped out of the cafeteria during the lunch break. He remembered distinctly the way his heart was racing, pounding in his chest, and the way every part of his body was smiling.

Behind him, Corso Italia was teeming with pedestrians. He was standing, rooted to the spot, in front of the plate-glass window of the Scognamiglio jewelry store.

It was noon. A young mother had grazed him with the wheels of her baby stroller, and he'd turned sharply, saying, "Excuse me," even if he wasn't the one who needed to say excuse me.

It was July 12, 1998. The sun wasn't burning in the sky, but it was illuminating everything with generous clarity. The jewels were glowing as if alive behind the shop's plate-glass window. He stood there, helpless and hypnotized, with his lifelong Chicago Bulls cap, twisted and tortured in his hands. He was as emotional as a little boy; he seemed retarded.

Until a woman, the proprietor of the jewelry store, came to the front door and asked him, with a broad, friendly smile: "Can I help you?"

He would have needed a crutch just then to keep from keeling over. And a glass of whiskey to steady his nerves.

He walked into the jewelry store as he was, dressed for the Lucchini steel mill, red-faced, completely intimidated. He put himself in that woman's hands; he said in a subdued voice: "I'd like a ring."

The wind was tossing the branches of the pine grove a little more softly now, like a sleeping animal or perhaps someone who wanted to sit with him, keep him company without disturbing him. He looked straight ahead at a specific point in the middle distance. He knew he had to face it head-on, that memory that scraped away at his esophagus, his throat, his hard palate.

Elena. Sitting across from him in the restaurant—the Vecchia Marina. Her chestnut hair was pulled back at the nape of her neck; she had a faint dusting of light-blue eye shadow on her eyelids. She'd just finished the *liceo* and she'd taken top marks—a sixty—on the final exam. She was wearing a white cotton dress the way she wore them, no plunging neckline.

She was telling him the story of the final oral exam in great detail: how she'd read perfectly in Greek until she reached that verse, and then she'd stumbled over that aorist (*aorist*! He even remembered that). And while she went on about the exam and while he cared less than nothing at all about those details, he'd wondered for the umpteenth time how on earth he, a shithead like him, had wound up with someone like her, who spoke in complicated sentences and enunciated clearly and distinctly all her consonants.

Because she wasn't from the quarter. Elena was the daughter of the head physician of the hospital of Piombino. They made love constantly, anywhere, even in the bathrooms of their junior high school in ninth grade, and between the lockers in the changing room at the gym. And he was her first and only boyfriend.

She went on talking, she didn't expect . . . she couldn't expect it. She was uttering those rounded, full words of hers, those nicely balanced sentences, flowing, uninterrupted. . . . And at a certain point, he'd interrupted her.

"Listen," he'd said.

He didn't know yet that she was about to enroll in the university—an MBA program—and that she was going to rent an apartment in Pisa with her girlfriends from the *liceo*, and that her educational commitments would only allow her to return to Piombino now and then. He hadn't given her time to tell him any of that.

"That is," he'd gulped, "I mean to say . . ."

She'd looked at him in surprise, arching her eyebrows. Perhaps she already sensed it, that she was going to become someone and that he would remain nothing but a steelworker, a good-looking one maybe, but two million lire a month isn't much.

"It's been a while now and I . . . This might be a little intense for you, but . . . That is, I . . . uh, you and me, we've been together for a long time, now, since junior high school, is how long, but so I was thinking that maybe . . . if you wanted, that is, I thought I'd tell you . . . Oh hell . . ." He'd smiled. "In the sense that you're done with school now," a slight discomfort, a shyness, "while I'm not done with shit, okay, well . . ."

Elena sat silently and let him speak.

"I just had to tell you." He slipped a hand into his pocket and pulled out a velvet ring box.

He'd snapped it open: the ring box. And she'd shuddered.

He never thought he could do it, he never dreamed he'd utter that idiotic phrase. But he did, he'd been such a pathetic jerk: "Elena, will you marry me?"

He felt someone tap him on the shoulder, and he snapped out of it suddenly. His thoughts recoiled in a flash. Alessio said, motionless, with sullen menace: "I don't even want to look at you."

"Oh, then it really is you!" said a voice that wasn't Cristiano's. "What are you now? The brooding poet of the Gilda?"

Alessio turned around sharply. He gasped, stunned. Incredulous, for a moment he didn't seem able to move his jaw muscles. Then the first real smile of the evening appeared on his face.

"I don't believe it! It can't be!" he lunged at him, grabbing him in a hug, crushing him to his chest, practically in tears. "You don't know how much time I spent trying to find you, piece of shit bastard!"

"Hey," the other guy laughed, "you've turned sentimental. . . . What are you doing in the pine forest? Did they wear you out in there?"

"Where the hell have you been all this time, eh? You forgot about me . . . son of a bitch!"

"You know I recognized you from all the way down there, from behind! Think about that."

They pulled away and looked one another square in the face.

"You haven't changed at all," they each said, practically at the same time.

"Where'd you go?"

"You won't believe me if I tell you."

"Come on, let's hear it, spit it out!" Alessio was practically jumping up and down.

"To Russia. To the Black Sea, on the freighters."

"Shit! That's fucked up . . ."

"Yeah, I guess," he laughed, "but now I'm back. Do you still work at the Lucchini?"

"Where else?"

"What section?"

"Crane."

"Congratulations," he extended his hand, "let me introduce you to the new rebar technician . . . starting next week!"

"Nooo!" Alessio hurled himself into a chest bump and hugged him, overjoyed. "Until two seconds ago this was a totally shitty night, let me tell you, so shitty that I vomited, and now you show up! And you're going to be working with me! But why did you just take off like that? I told you to fuck off billions of times, in my mind."

The other guy gestured with one hand. "Forget about it, bad times. How about you . . . Elena? Does she know that you're here being a bad boy?"

Alessio suddenly changed expression: "Don't say the name. . . ."

"Of God in vain. Okay, don't tell me about it. I'm an atheist, anyway."

"Don't you start trying to ruin my night, please," Alessio snorted in frustration. "Cristiano's already taken care of it."

"Ah, Cristiano! Is that jerk still alive?" Mattia made light of the situation.

But Alessio was too excited to be sad. He hadn't seen him since 1998. Both of them had vanished from his life—Mattia and Elena—without warning and simultaneously: Then and there he'd been ready to shoot himself. Now, though, he had at least one of them back.

"Listen to me, and listen good, you bastard," he said. "Now you're leaving with me, I don't want to hear any bullshit. You're going to sleep at my house, too. That's the way it's going to be: the very least you can do, after everything you put me through."

"That's cool, boss, I'm walking, so that's good." He looked around. "Did you come alone tonight, or are you here with that asshole?"

Alessio shot a furtive glance at the entrance: "Come on, run!"

The friend that Alessio had just grabbed by the arm and with whom he was now running at breakneck speed through the pine grove to his car, the friend by the name of Mattia, at the time was practically a criminal.

But they'd grown up together. Mattia was from Via Stalingrado. Mattia was the classic cool guy with a penchant for trouble. When he was sixteen he'd been in trouble with the law on charges of breaking and entering. Then, in 1998, he'd gotten into bigger trouble, and he'd been forced to flee the country. At this point he was no longer a minor, and he wasn't looking at being sentenced to public service, cleaning toilets at the assisted living center. He'd be going straight to hard time in the adult penitentiary in Livorno. Through a fairly shady network of acquaintances he'd managed to get on a freighter, and from there he'd found a job with a Russian shipping company on one of those enormous LNG carriers that transports natural gas from Ossetia to the rest of Europe; he'd had to go all the way to the Black Sea to learn how to work.

Not that he was a bad kid, not at all.

"Are you sure you want to leave him without a ride?" asked Mattia, as he got into the car. "That'll piss him off something ugly . . ."

"Well, let him get pissed off!" Alessio shifted into reverse. "He should have thought of that first, the shithead. But if a guy goes off with his boss to fuck an underage girl, leaving you there alone like a stray dog? He should just count himself lucky that I didn't break his nose for him."

As he looked in the rearview mirror, Alessio saw a blinking light on the rear seat and finally noticed his cell phone.

He reached out his hand to pick it up and saw it: eight missed calls.

Papa.

He shoved the car into gear and took off, revving at top speed.

CHAPTER 15

At first she moved only her head, abandoned sideways on the pillow. The ringlets quivered in disarray. Then she stretched her legs under the sheets, rotating the outstretched tips of her feet. Slender, shapely small feet, toenails covered with hot pink polish, poking nakedly out at the end of the bed. She stretched her arms, and the blond peach fuzz covering those arms glimmered dimly. Without opening her eyes she seized the hem of the top sheet and thrust it down, uncovering her torso.

She was wearing white cotton summer pajamas, dotted with a minute pattern of red strawberries. A crescent of breast protruded from her camisole top.

She'd outgrown those pajamas; they were tight on her. The practically adult curves of her hips clashed with the tiny red strawberries, or perhaps they went together all too well.

The minutes tiptoed past and she didn't notice a thing. Someone was observing her very closely. There was an intruder in her bedroom, a man, and she didn't know it yet. She'd turned over onto her side, facing the window. The sun filtered softly through the blinds, in a mixture of light and airborne dust: It looked like sugar.

It was nine in the morning. Mattia had been watching her for more than half an hour. He was careful not to make noise; he was focusing his total attention on capturing every last tiny movement she made. And he couldn't take his eyes off her.

She would have looked wonderful in baby doll pajamas, he decided. See-through black lace. But then he changed his mind: she wouldn't be this pretty even in baby doll pajamas. Fragrant and clean in the peaceful early light.

A nice scent was wafting off of her. Not some artificial perfume, not a deodorant. She smelled of milk. Gently, slowly, he breathed it in.

Evidently, she had an itch somewhere, because she slipped her fingers under her pajamas and scratched in a certain place, then elsewhere, behind her shoulder. She smiled, who knows why. Finally, she opened her sleepy eyes just a little.

Anna opened her mouth, separating her lips, damp with saliva. She smiled again, a smile filled with all those straight white teeth of hers. She sat suddenly bolt upright, swept back her vaporous hair with one hand, looking first straight up at the ceiling, and then down at her alarm clock. And when she opened them wide and looked straight ahead of her, she screamed.

Hazel eyes, flecked with yellow.

Her eyes are freckled, just like her cheekbones, thought Mattia. And he smiled at her, not even slightly embarrassed; if anything, he was just dazed by such beauty.

A stranger was sitting comfortably on the chair pulled out from her desk, staring at her with mocking eyes. Anyone would be alarmed.

"Who are you?" Anna shrieked, and hastily covered herself with the sheet.

But she did a bad job of covering herself, and the crescent of breast remained bare. He noticed it, and his smile grew. He waited, a tactical pause, before answering. He wanted to enjoy her alarm in full.

Anna turned toward her brother's bed and saw that it was empty. She stared with worried eyes, alternately at the stranger and then the empty bed, and struggled, unsuccessfully, to grasp the situation.

"My name's Mattia," he said, amused. "It's a pleasure to meet you."

He held out his hand and she glowered at him, without venturing to touch his hand.

"Actually, we've met, but you were just a scrawny little bird, eight or nine years old. . . . Maybe you don't remember." He continued to hold out his hand, and he couldn't help laughing. Anna blushed visibly, but she didn't realize half her tit was out of her pajama top.

"Mamaaa!" she screamed.

"She's not here," he shook his head. "You're trapped."

Seeing that he was making fun of her, and above all that he was staying put, like a good boy, Anna calmed down a little. "Where'd she go? Where's *Ale*? And why are you here?"

Mattia withdrew his hand, ran it through his dark brown, curly hair, and then cleared his throat as he crossed his legs. He had no reason to put on airs: He had airs by birth. But it amused him to make an impression on that child-woman, and he was taking his time, standing up, examining the Britney Spears poster hanging on the wall with feigned interest. He was a born actor.

"Your mother's gone out, and it just so happens that she's invited me to stay for lunch. She was very nice to me. . . ." He took his eyes off Britney and turned them to Anna: She was standing openmouthed, twisting the hem of the sheet. "Your brother is downstairs fighting with Cristiano. And I'm an old friend of his, just recently back in town."

"What do you mean 'fighting with Cristiano'?"

"Well, it's a manner of speech. . . . But they're having a discussion," he laughed, "a lively discussion, I believe."

Mattia was moving from one point to another in the half light of the bedroom, and Anna followed him with her gaze, moving her head like a character in a cartoon.

"When did you get here?"

"Around five this morning."

"Where did you sleep?"

"Right here. Right on this chair." Mattia pointed at the chair with the utmost gravity.

"Then you saw me sleeping!" A hot blush appeared on Anna's face.

Mattia noticed it, drew a little closer, and with a mischievous smile he whispered, "Oh, I assure you, you were marvelous. . . ."

Big emerald-green eyes, hard fleshy lips.

Both of them had curly hair.

Anna leaped out of the bed and ran barefoot to the window. She pulled on the strap that raised the wooden roller blinds, hauling them all the way up, and the bedroom was flooded with daylight. Then she turned, dazed, to look at the illuminated face of the new boy who was just stretching out on her bed.

Leaning back, Mattia had hungrily breathed in the smell of her between the sheets.

"Maybe it's true, maybe I do know you. . . . I don't remember exactly, but I've seen you somewhere before," said Anna, standing in front of him, gesticulating more than normal.

Mattia was thinking that she truly had nice legs, and that for age thirteen she was quite tall. Very well developed. He said: "You must have seen me a million times. But you were always too busy with your Barbie dolls and your little girlfriends to pay any attention to yours truly."

Anna blushed. Along with the sunlight, heat had invaded the bedroom, and she would have liked to get undressed. There was a boiling hot August out there, and an incandescent ember inside her. No man who wasn't her brother or her father had ever seen her in pajamas before. She felt naked and embarrassed, like in one of those dreams where you go walking dressed only in your underwear down a boulevard crowded with people.

It was slowly dawning on her just how handsome that young man was. And strong, and grown up, and sure of himself. The dark face, with the square jaw and the high cheekbones, seemed to have been carved out of marble. There was something tyrannical about the eyes. And something inviting about the slightly feminine lips. The large gnarled hands didn't gesticulate like the hands of anxious boys. He must be six foot three. His shoulders looked as if he'd carried the whole planet for days.

"Where do you live?" Anna was becoming curious in spite of herself.

"I live alone, not far from here."

"Why alone?"

"Because I like being alone." It wasn't true; he coughed for effect.

He added: "I'm a sea wolf."

Anna fell for him, dazzled. As if a young version of Santiago from *The Old Man and the Sea*, her personal myth, had appeared before her.

"I just came home to Piombino. I was in Russia for three years, on the Black Sea."

Finally Anna realized that her camisole was on askew, that she was practically half naked, and that she was wearing a ridiculous pair of pajamas. Doing her best to conceal her embarrassment, she advanced vaguely toward the armoire and pulled out a sweater at random. It was a winter sweatshirt, and considering the heat, it wasn't the right choice. But by now she was completely frazzled, and she put it on.

Of course he noticed it, and he stifled a boisterous laugh that was tickling his throat. He didn't want to intimidate her, at least any more than she already was. And he liked her: so inexperienced, so cute.

"And you? What do you do for fun in life?"

"I go to school." She no longer felt either hot or cold. But her knees were knocking slightly.

She decided to sit on the bed, too.

At a certain distance from him. . . . He was ten years older than her, so he deciphered all her movements with great ease. Still, he had to admit it: He was finding her performance more amusing than he'd expected.

When Anna dropped onto the bed near the pillow, Mattia moved an inch or two in the same direction. It was a secret war of position, and they were distinctly unequal adversaries.

"In fact, this September I'm going to the upper grades. I'm starting *liceo . . . liceo classico.*"

"Damn . . . Then you're quite the student!"

"I like to study. . . ."

"Good for you. Don't follow Alessio's example." He looked at his watch. "Well, looks like Cristiano chewed him up and spit him out."

When she saw him look at his watch, Anna felt a strange shiver run up her spine.

"And did you study?" she hastened to ask, as if to detain him.

"I have my diploma." There was no need to engage Mattia in conversation to detain him, "but I don't think I ever studied. I was warming a chair, more than anything else. . . . But I've always read a lot of poetry. . . ." He said it, obviously, to make an impression. Mattia, reading poetry? As if. But she was completely dazzled.

"Like Pascoli?" she smiled.

"Exactly! Pascoli. And also Carducci, Baudelaire, and Dante. . . ." He tossed out a few names at random. "On the freighters, before falling asleep, I liked reading them. . . ."

Anna imagined Mattia in the half light of a hold, stretched out on a pile of sacks with a candle flickering at his side, a stormy sea, a book read avidly aloud in a faint voice. Her heart began pounding in her chest.

They were both on the bed. Anna was sitting cross-legged, Mattia stretched out full length, with his arms behind his neck. They were looking at one another, studying each other. And she was astonished at the way her whole body was palpitating, while he was amazed by the effect his friend's baby sister was having on him. She was thinking that she'd like to reach out a finger to touch him and see if he was real. And he was thinking that he'd like to kiss the nape of her neck.

This is a bolt from the blue, Anna realized. Yikes! But she didn't have time to realize it a second time before her brother burst into the bedroom shouting: "That guy is nuts!"

Alessio didn't pay the slightest attention to how his friend and his sister were positioned: On the bed, staring into one another's eyes, talking quietly and closely, smiling continually. He went straight over to Mattia, got him to his feet, and made him examine his black eye.

"Look at this!" he shouted. "Look what that fucker did to me! If I go back downstairs I'll break him in half, I swear I'll kill him!"

Mattia inspected Alessio's furious face: "Put some ice on it. . . . Come on—tonight you'll clear it all up. . . ."

"What am I supposed to clear up? You must be kidding! I drive him back and forth every blessed day, and the one time I leave him without a ride, what does he do? He punches me in the face!"

Anna watched the scene, bewildered. She didn't understand a thing that was happening. At the same time, she discovered that she was annoyed: Alessio had come back too soon. And now? Would he take Mattia away with him?

"You know what he said to me? That I've never taken a bus at six in the morning. . . . Nooo, of course not! I've taken a bus that early a billion times!"

Anna remembered that her mother had invited Mattia to stay for lunch and she suddenly livened up again. Alessio left the bedroom in search of ice, and Mattia followed him out. Before he closed the door behind him, though, lady-killer that he was, he stuck his head back in and gave her a wink.

As soon as the door clicked shut, Anna, electrified, put her hands in her hair and started whispering, "Fuck fuck fuck fuck." She started jumping up and down. She couldn't believe it. She took off that horrible winter sweatshirt. The first rational thought that she managed to have was: I have to tell Francesca about this immediately.

A second later, though, while she was putting on her shoes to go tell her friend everything, a surge of distaste stopped her fingers just as she was tying her laces. She decided against it. No, I don't really have to tell Francesca anything.

She let herself fall back on the bed. He was the most beautiful man she'd ever seen. She smiled at the ceiling. He was the man of her life. From now until lunchtime, she was going to lock herself in the bathroom, try on all the makeup and clothes she could think of, and come to the kitchen table looking beautiful. She wondered if he'd come to the party tonight. For sure, he'd have to come, for sure!

Life was wonderful. She was overjoyed, crazed with happiness.

Francesca. Of course. But right now she didn't want to think about her. She looked at her watch: It was 10:30. She rushed to her armoire, rummaged through all the drawers, and pulled out everything. Impossible to think that a guy like him, an older guy, could have looked at her like that. That he'd watched her sleep. Oh God, what if she snored?

While Alessio and Mattia talked intently in the kitchen, smoking cigarette after cigarette, Anna bustled to and fro between her bedroom and her bathroom, making at least ten round-trips. Every time she went down the hallway she looked into the kitchen. Pretending she wasn't doing anything in particular, she would look at him. And if he noticed her, she would scamper away barefoot, stifling a giggle.

"What the fuck is my sister doing?" Alessio furrowed his brow. "Is she spying on us?"

"Mat-ti-a," Anna enunciated the name in front of the mirror. She'd locked herself into the bathroom; she'd turned the key in the lock. I'm an idiot, she told herself. Then she started: She turned the music on full blast. *Me and you . . . La la la la, la la la.* She tried out at least fifteen facial expressions: from sullen to amused to sensual. She decided that the time had come to pluck her eyebrows a little, narrow them down, and she caused herself a great deal of pain with a pair of tweezers.

She never stopped dancing the whole time, nor did she stop reminding herself over and over of the exact spelling of that name. She painted her lips variously red, pink, brick red, and fuchsia. She painted her eyelids green, gold, sky blue, and purple. She pilfered some mascara from her mother's handbag. She looked at the resulting concoction and decided that her face looked obscene at best.

She hurried to take a shower. In all her life she'd never experienced such a sense of jubilation, such a razor-sharp sense of joy.

Before lunch she opened her diary and circled that day's date over and over again: August 15, 2001. She wrote, filling the whole page, big as a house: "MATTIA." With a pink uni-POSCA, the kind you can't erase. Underneath that she inserted about six feet of ellipses: dot-dot-dot.

Incredible: She felt as if as of 10:30 this morning she'd begun living a different life.

At exactly two o'clock Francesca rang the doorbell. She came in. She said hello to Sandra, Alessio, and a guy she'd never seen before. But even before she came in and greeted everyone she'd noticed Anna's outfit from the threshold, the plunging neckline, a party dress, certainly not something to wear around the house, and her made-up eyes.

No one on earth could come close to imagining with what trepidation, or how eagerly, Francesca had been waiting for this moment.

She'd tossed and turned all night, waking up repeatedly. Around four in the morning she'd gotten out of bed to open the window and cleanse the sweat from her brow with some cool night air. After breakfast she'd lounged in her bedroom for hours doing nothing. Applying polish to her fingernails, she'd tried to imagine—with twinges of fear—just what Anna must think of her now, and how she would respond to her that afternoon, with what expression on her face, what tone of voice. Her fingers trembled; the nail polish wouldn't apply neatly.

She didn't care about Ferragosto, about their first night out dancing. She imagined Anna chilly and distant. Maybe it would become necessary to have a discussion, clear up the issues between them, but as with her father, she wouldn't be able to come up with the words; she'd fall silent. Maybe Anna would tell her: "*France*, you're sick in the head." Or else she'd embrace her, like yesterday, and they'd kiss again. . . .

It was nothing like that at all. Anna was completely normal. She took her arm as usual, pulled her laughing into her bedroom, whispering the usual things in her ear: this skirt, that top, which hair clip? As if nothing had happened.

But she was wearing that pink outfit, too short and too cute to just wear around the house. Why had she put on eye shadow, and why had she chosen that color? Just for lunch? Francesca was no fool. She could put two and two together. She could ask her something, offhand, like: "That's quite a look you've got today."

But she didn't comment on it at all. She didn't ask a thing. In fact, she took great care not to notice a thing.

As for the rest of it, she'd barely given the new guest a glance. For that matter, she secretly hoped that Anna's changes, her excitement, were actually for her.

They spent the whole afternoon together, in the bathroom with the door closed and the key turned in the lock, trying on clothes and putting on simpering expressions, the better to meet boys with. The window wide open as usual. Peeing together as always. Not even a hint of conflict. Not the slightest sign of any new wrinkles.

But there *was* something new—with a vengeance. It oozed out of every pore on Anna's body: She was affectionate and remote. Gradually it dawned on Francesca that Anna's mind was wandering. And while the day was giving way to the long-awaited hour, Francesca wondered if she could really tolerate an entire lifetime like this: never being A nor B.

It was much harder than she'd expected. And it took all the effort she could muster, at a certain point, to keep from breaking down in tears.

CHAPTER 16

The minute Anna left the apartment Sandra stripped the rubber gloves off her hands, emptied the bucket of dirty mop water into the toilet, and went out onto the balcony. She calmly lit a cigarette and took her time looking at the Isle of Elba.

A ferryboat was going by. A flock of seabirds followed the boat, swooping around it in broad circles. The light was dissolving along with the clumps of clouds and the contrails of planes overhead, coagulating in the pinpoint lanterns of fishing boats that dimly punctuated the surface of the water.

Suddenly, on the island, a handful of streetlamps blinked to life. They flickered like live flames. As if responding to an invitation, Sandra began to imagine the evening strolls for which those streetlamps were lighting the way. The shopwindows, open after nightfall, the clumps of tourists coming and going along the waterfront. Portoferraio in August must be wonderful, with its little street fairs, orchestras playing in the evening air, restaurants glittering with silverware, toasts being offered and drunk.

She thought of those Milanese or Roman society ladies she'd seen through the windows of cars lining up for the port. She decided it must be nice to have that kind of life. Going on holidays, renting a room with a veranda, with a view, with breakfast brought up by room service.

She'd been to Elba once in her life, when she was twenty.

As soon as they landed, Arturo was fixated on tracking down that friend of his, Pasquale, whom they absolutely had to see. There'd been no two ways about it: They spent the afternoon in the back room of a warehouse, and then sitting in a café lined wall-to-wall with video poker slot machines. They kept it up until it was time to catch the ferryboat back to the mainland; she sat wordless in a corner the whole time. She hadn't seen a thing, not even Napoleon's house.

She flicked the cigarette butt into the street below. The sky was darkening, and she had a pile of clothes to hang out to dry. She was forty-three years old.

She turned and went back inside. The sound of her clogs dragging on the floor made her smile.

As she leaned over the door of the front-loader washing machine, she swatted away those pointless thoughts. She piled the sheets in her laundry basket. The age of believing that the world is a gold mine, that it's enough to grow up and leave home . . . That time had ended long ago for her, and where had it left her? Enough: She had plenty of other things to think about. There was the Rifondazione festival to organize; next week she had to invite her honorable comrade Mussi to come deliver a talk about the welfare state.

It was a quarter to nine.

Francesca and Anna were walking in silence, side by side, through the deserted city.

Most families were still sitting down to dinner. Through the many windows thrown wide open you could glimpse the light-blue smears of television sets, and a great clatter of pots and pans and silverware startled the girls every time they walked under another window.

They walked across the deserted parking lot of the Coop supermarket and left the Salivoli quarter behind them. Another neighborhood similar to theirs began here: Here, too, enormous gray bunker structures and cement courtyards alternated without any apparent logic with wooden shacks and poorly kept vegetable gardens. Over the partition nets red clusters of tomatoes pressed; bunches of apricots dangled from overarching branches, fragrant and orange. Anna reached up and grabbed an apricot, and then another; she offered it to Francesca.

They practically hadn't exchanged a word since leaving the house. When they walked by the city nursery school, though, Anna smiled at Francesca and took her hand. They each cherished their own thoughts without wanting to know the other's, as the sun spent its last rays on the boulevards, stretching out the shadows of the trees like taffy.

No cars, no pedestrians. That silence was sweet; the sensation that the streets and the neighborhood were a private spectacle staged for the two of them alone. When they came to the corner of a rusted old playground,

Francesca stopped suddenly and pointed, turning to look at her friend. A faint smile, the product of an unexpected memory, played on her lips.

"You remember?"

There was plenty of time before the party. The two girls walked onto the tiny field, which was almost completely enclosed by a hedge. The grass was a tender green in spots and sun-yellowed in others. The twin trees seemed to be struggling to remain erect: Ivy had almost engulfed them, and was strangling them. The swings and the slide were so ramshackle and neglected that they looked as if they'd been there for centuries.

How many years had it been? Anna wondered, as she cautiously walked forward. She ran a hand over the flaking rust of the merry-go-round, then gave it a light shove. It turned, creaking, a slight shaft of sound in the lowering silence. Then Francesca called her name.

Down at the far end was the little log cabin. The two girls walked toward it, practically on tiptoe.

There was dirt everywhere inside the cabin, and there seemed to be an anthill under the space between two of the floorboards. But you could still smell that dank scent of wet wood that they loved so much. They wanted to go inside, crouch down beneath the angled roof the way they had when they were little, but they were big now, they didn't fit anymore. They started laughing—till their bellies hurt from the contortions each saw the other undertaking. By now the space was far too constricted; they couldn't stay there with their knees pressed up against their chests.

They reemerged into the light, with a few ants climbing up their legs.

"And to think that was going to be our home someday!" laughed Anna.

"I certainly remembered it as bigger," Francesca admitted. "Or else we're twice the size we were then. . . ."

They exchanged an enduring glance of complicity, a look that summed up all the things that had been lost—or maybe they weren't lost after all.

Then they ran to the swings. Each of them took a seat on a creaking one. Francesca simply let herself dangle, barely moving, her forehead pressed against first one chain, then the other. Anna, knees wide apart, pumped herself sharply up into the still bright sky.

Everything was poised motionless in that place, as if it had been buried in an aquarium. The two young women, as they ran from one piece of equipment to the next, became animated, like the two little girls they had once been. When Francesca was too frightened of her father, when Anna's father shouted at her without stopping, they decided to run away from home. They had ventured as far as the Diaccioni quarter. It was the first time they had gone that far from home, and they had discovered this secret garden.

It had always been like this: empty. It had always been a little paradise in honor of Anna and Francesca.

They came back here every afternoon after school for months. They came here to play house: They pretended to cook, do the wash, and then hang the clothes out to dry, as if they were a couple of imaginary newly-weds in their wooden playhouse. But one day the old baboons noticed they'd gone missing, that they weren't playing in the courtyard anymore, and who knew where the fuck they'd been hiding, they never got home until eight in the evening: That wasn't right, not with all the child molesters out on the streets these days.

They'd both caught a beating from their fathers.

"It's weird to look at it now," Anna said. "Look at the hedges, look at all the thorns . . . Places get old, too."

Francesca dropped onto a patch of grass that was dotted here and there with the white puffballs of dandelions. She picked one and blew away the white fuzz into the warm evening air: "It's not older . . . ," she smiled, "it's just more secret . . . and I like it better this way. I like to think that in all these years nobody's been here, that it belongs to us alone."

Anna went over and lay down next to her. She looked up to where Francesca's eyes were focusing: on the white contrail of an airplane dissolving in the blue sky, just like the clouds in the slanting sunlight and the dandelion fuzz between Francesca's fingers.

"It's been years."

Francesca turned toward her on one hip and started tickling her cheek and nose with the tip of a dandelion stem. "Time is just so strange."

"You think?" Anna looked at her with amusement. "Stop it, you're tickling me!"

As she reached out to grab the dandelion stem, she found herself with the tip of her nose half an inch from Francesca's.

"I don't want to grow up, A," Francesca said.

For a few seconds they remained motionless like that: big eyes wide open, staring into one another, hair tangled together, filled with blades of grass and pollen from the flowers. Nostrils full of each other's scent. The scent of apricot and the scent of chestnut, unmistakable. Equally unmistakable were the shapes of the ears, the arcs of the eyebrows, and even the curls and colors of their eyelashes. Then there were the dimples in the cheeks of one, the cleft in the chin of the other. And the complexion of the skin, the small tip-tilted noses, the heart-shaped bow lips, and the freckles!

So many times Francesca had played the game of counting those little dots of color on Anna's cheekbones and nose. She alone could testify to every variation of that face. She alone could distinguish the pigments that time had not touched. She had seen that face open and unfold; she had caressed it and helped it to bloom. She had seen it palpitate, watched it put together one by one words, phrases, dreams. She was the only one in that whole world on the other side of the hedge who knew what had remained unchanged in Anna.

"A," she whispered, "I wish we could rub noses the way we did when we were little girls . . ."

Anna, who was completely caught up in that present moment, had forgotten the party and the night that were both impending. She rubbed her nose against Francesca's, smiling Francesca's identical smile. She could feel that every fiber in Francesca's body was hers, as she grazed and drew closer to her over and over again, until she had nearly all of her within her grasp.

Even the purple shadow of a hematoma beneath her breast—she felt that that, too, was hers. She felt an excessive, boundless love: Yes, it was definitely love that she felt for that creature gazing at her with such complicity, with whom she could feel infinitely close and cozy and yielding and warm and dark . . .

Their clothes were stained with dirt and grass; they didn't care how dirty they got . . . the smell of laundry soap gave way to the smell of rusted metal.

"A," Francesca whispered, in the moistness of mouths close together, "I don't understand it, but I feel like kissing you."

Anna leaned over her friend's face, placed her mouth lightly on hers. She liked feeling her friend's hot breath mingle with her own; she liked feeling the veil of wet saliva coating her lips. She liked it. And nothing, no one, could change that.

Francesca closed her eyes.

"We can't do this," said Anna, without pulling away. "Something about it's not right."

Francesca's dark green eyes flew open. "Why not?"

"Because we're not little girls anymore. If we kiss, it's not like it was in elementary school, it doesn't have the same meaning." She hesitated for a second. "Things happen to me . . . that shouldn't happen to me with you."

"But they only happen to me with you!" Francesca smiled, in a way she'd never smiled before. "I don't like Nino, I like you!"

That name, Nino, dropping suddenly like a stone into their little paradise, startled Anna into remembering Mattia, the party, and the others, and she sat up.

Francesca sat up, too. Then, taking Anna's hand, her eyes filled with fear, she asked the question she'd been too afraid to ask that afternoon.

"You like that new guy, don't you? The guy who was at your house for lunch."

Anna made a quizzical face. "But I don't even know him!"

Francesca grabbed hold of that lie and held on for dear life. She shyly drew closer to her best friend.

"But you don't like me, do you? I mean, you don't *like* me, in that way . . ."

Maybe it was the effect of that place, the overwhelming impression of all that golden dying light on Francesca's beautiful face, but Anna felt completely disarmed, and she allowed herself to be swept into the moment. A delicate joy filtered through the air, the clouds, the playground equipment in that park where the little girls they'd once been were now buried, and that joy injected itself into her blood like a drug.

"*France*, maybe I do love you. But it can't be part of real life. It's something that goes against my whole future. And even if it's true, now, when I'm saying it to you, the minute we leave this place, I'll know that it can't be, and I'll just take it back immediately, and I'm so ashamed . . ."

The light was gone now. They could hear the first few roars of speeding motor scooters passing in the street and the usual assortment of loud noises and shouts, the usual curse words of kids on their way to a party. Anna, who had bitten her lip over what she'd just said, was seized by a frenzy to go and at the same time not to go. Francesca would have preferred to head straight for the port, to take the next ferry to Elba and never return.

They embraced. Hiding their faces in each other's hair, hugging each other tight. Because they were telling each other good-bye.

When they finally unclasped, darkness had fallen in the little hollow of the secret garden and was nibbling at the margins of the swings, the slides, the two trees. There were no lamps down there; you could hardly see a thing by now. They got to their feet and left that place with regret for something that was impossible to put into words, with flower stems and blades of grass tangled in their hair.

They didn't say another word.

At the entrance to the roller rink there was a crowd clamoring to be let in, on the brink of a riot.

Chaotic rows of motor scooters heaped against each other and cars kept pouring in, wedging into the tiniest chink of a parking place. There was something hostile about so many people all in one place. There was even an ambulance with a couple of guys from the volunteer emergency response office sitting on the hood and snorting in annoyance. There was a guy pissing against a tree.

Here it was, the turning point. The moment they'd fantasized about for years, described for hours in thousands of invented details. While they were stretched out on the empty hull of a boat, having fun imagining the future—together. "When we're grown up," they'd whisper, "we'll come live here." And they hugged each other tightly, curled up in the dark, in the tiny wooden cabin.

It was all there.

They moved forward, in small shuffling steps, jarred and shoved by the arms and legs of strangers, pushing against strangers' necks and backs. At a certain point they were forced to stop, to wait for the tide of people to subside. They were surrounded by unbuttoned shirts, T-shirts drenched in sweat. There were words they'd never heard before. The harsh white light of the spotlights showered down on all those heads, like a weed killer. And the music pumped throbbing up out of the ground, mixing with the loud conversations nearby, leaving Anna and Francesca slightly stunned.

These were the last few dwindling minutes. Then each of them would go forward toward their future, each of them on their own. They were already beginning to feel that strange sensation, that feeling of suddenly finding yourself completely alone.

When they walked in, a few people held their breath. Mattia, for instance, unseen, fell under their spell for a moment and lost track of what he'd been saying.

An expert eye would have immediately sensed that this kind of beauty lasts for only a moment in the course of a lifetime. But in that crowd there were no expert eyes.

There was everyone.

Massi with Nino. Separately, on a bench, Sonia, Maria, and Jessica. There were all those losers, Lisa and her girlfriends, sitting up on the bleachers. Donata wasn't there. There was Emma with her husband, her sixteen-year-old body deformed by her pregnant belly. At the bar, in the distance, there was Alessio, Cristiano, and Mattia. There was a tidal wave of unfamiliar people, condensing and blurring until it became an indistinct material.

Anna and Francesca plunged forward, into that magma. They hurried straight to the roller skate rental booth, huffing in annoyance because there was a long line snaking up to the cash register. They wanted to believe it, that this was it, the culmination, the apex. Each of them, in her own young girl's mind, convinced herself that this was the perfect life.

In reality it was just an old roller rink that had needed new varnish for decades, fixed up with money from local civic volunteers. The amplifiers pumping out music were the same ones that had been used over and over again for the Festa dell'Unità. The rickety little bar that was selling beer and orange drinks for two thousand lire, hard liquor for three, was just a prefabricated stand. And the streamers and festoons decking the railings made it look like an old school party.

Alessio was at the counter, leaning on one elbow. Every so often he took a sip of his beer, which had gradually gone from cold to lukewarm. That was the only motion he made for a good solid half hour.

People kept pouring in, either strapping on skates and crowding the rink or else clustering around it to watch. The bleachers were packed as well; so was the gazebo where a rudimentary discotheque had been set up. The bar, on the other hand, was practically empty. The couple of dozen tables were mostly abandoned. Only a few bored-looking grown-ups were sitting there, playing cards; a few other unfortunates were watching instead of participating in the festivities. There was even a toothless little old man, and the sight of him finally tipped Cristiano over the edge.

"It's ten o'clock," he complained in exasperation. "Can we leave now?"

He was sick and fucking tired of sitting there waiting. Plus, he'd already gulped down two amphetamine tablets.

Alessio ignored him: He had a specific reason for being there, and he was keeping that to himself. He stood at the bar, straight as a ramrod, rooted to the spot, waiting. Cristiano glowered at him; he felt as if he were being defrauded of his Ferragosto. You tell me: The one week of vacation I'm going to have all year, and I'm standing here watching twelve-year-olds roller skate. Tomorrow I'll be breaking my back again on that fucking power shovel.

"Look, in case you didn't hear me: Can we move our asses out of here?"

Once again, Alessio pretended he hadn't heard. More than a plan, he had a premonition. He never lost sight of Maria, Jessica, and Sonia sitting on the bench under the tree. There weren't any other trees. Cristiano was draining one whiskey after another. It was beginning to dawn on Mattia that the situation could turn ugly.

Just then, on the top tier of the bleachers, there was someone else who was watching in silence and wallowing in bitter rancor. Actually, there were plenty of people who had left their houses thinking they'd find America in a roller rink but were now lonelier than they had been at home.

The only boys and girls who count here are the ones who spin, leap, and take to the air, pirouetting and whirling, competing to be the most spectacular, racing along at terrifying speeds. Slender, athletic girls who may not do anything else for the rest of their lives. But what does it matter, because at the perfect moment of their adolescence, here they are: at the center of the rink, in the middle of the party, in the spotlight. It's an unequaled moment of glory.

There were boys with spiky, gel-smeared hair, six-pack abs under their shirts fluttering in the breeze, seashell chokers around their necks. Boys and girls who anyone would want to kiss, who'd never be lonely wallflowers like Lisa, despondent on the highest tier of the bleachers, sitting far from the crowd, watching other people have fun.

She was sitting in total shadow, legs crossed, in the company of two girls who were, if anything, worse off than she was. And with the sensation of losing something colossal, of the earth swallowing her up right then and there.

This was Lisa's first night out at a party, too. She'd spent the whole afternoon in front of a mirror like the others, but the only appreciable result was a worsening of her inferiority complex. After all that, she just put on her usual pair of too long, too loose jeans, the usual shapeless T-shirt. And now the timid veil of pencil with which she'd lined her eyes was melting, only making things worse.

She cast a sidelong glance at her companions: She suddenly had the impression that she was not only on the outer margins of the roller rink but of the entire animal kingdom. I'm not a loser, she said. Even if everyone was constantly telling her she was one, even if the bastard at the front gate had called her a homely dog to her face and she'd felt as if she wanted to die. Even if, sure, she wasn't exactly beautiful, she was still alive, and she felt like skating, and dancing, and kissing someone. Even if she was pretty much dressed like a mushroom she was no different inside after all than Anna. Anna, who at that very moment, about thirty feet away, was about to enter the roller rink tightly wrapped in her square inch of camisole and her half a square inch of pink miniskirt.

Suddenly she thought of her sister. Donata would never have indulged in all this drama, all these scenes. If Lisa had had the courage to bring Donata, she would have had the best time. She would have sung along to the music, moved her arms and head as much as she was able, even danced in her way in her wheelchair. But Lisa hadn't brought her; once again she'd been ashamed that her sister was an invalid. As if Lisa somehow had Donata's disease. As if, after all, the world was easier to take without Donata.

Lisa stared at Anna's short skirt, Anna's long legs.

Donata was at home, parked in front of the television set. And here she was, right in the middle of a huge party, but instead of skating or doing anything healthy, she was just sitting there rotting away, fixating on Francesca's lithe, slender body, which was joining Anna's radiant body at the edge of the roller rink. Neither of those two bodies was hers. But even if the whole world was a sink of injustice, for the first time it became clear to Lisa that this couldn't be a justification.

In the throes of a sudden rebellious impulse, she leaped to her feet. She'd been sitting on that bleacher gathering mold since nine o'clock; now it was 10:30: Enough is enough. She wouldn't take it any longer.

To hell with the bastard world, to hell with the son-of-a-bitch bouncer who'd given her shit at the front door, to hell with her own miserable, slight, hump-shouldered self . . . and that wasn't all!

Scraping together every ounce of courage she possessed, beaming with a triumphant smile, she looked down on her companions, stunted and hunched in semifetal positions: "You know what? I'm going to go do some skating."

For the first time in her life she started running as hard as she could, running flat out. Toward the center of the light and the noise, toward—she fooled herself into believing—the center of life. She undid the scrunchie that was holding her hair back and laced up her roller skates quickly to keep from losing even a gram of that sudden, unexpected courage that had swept over her.

She headed down toward the entrance to the skating rink where, unattainable but now a little closer, Anna and Francesca were zipping around the floor.

Even Mattia couldn't wait to get onto the roller rink, but he was forced to cool his heels in that miserable little bar, inventing the worst imaginable wisecracks, saying the worst imaginable bullshit in an attempt to distract Alessio from that fucking obsession of his, and especially to try to calm down Cristiano.

Trying to defuse the situation—easy to say! Alessio's face was dark, blank: like a brick wall. And Cristiano's face was scarlet. His annoyance and irritation just added fuel to his resentment about what had happened last night. Mattia wasn't responsible for any of it. They were standing there like three cowboys in a saloon.

Perhaps attracted by their demeanor of sullen, mute rage, girls—of varying degrees of ripeness—began to drift over, strolling past repeatedly, meaningfully. Emitting the usual series of whimpers and giggles, they loitered hopefully in the general vicinity, practically wagging their tails. The three males, of course, didn't even see them. And each of them, from a state of irritation, drifted increasingly close to the rapids of fury.

"The place is full of pussy, sure . . . from a distance!" Cristiano started in again. "When you get close enough to see them, you'd put a bag over all their heads."

Mattia set his second glass down on the bar and shot a desperate glance at Alessio: He was just standing there, rooted to the spot, staring at Sonia, Maria, and Jessica, and no one could say what thoughts were whirring around in that mind of his.

"*Ale* . . ." he started to say, trying to intervene in diplomatic terms, "listen, maybe we should . . ."

But Cristiano, brash and less diplomatic, broke in.

"Do we have to stay here much longer? Say the word, because we're at your orders here. . . . Since we're relying on your car for transportation!"

Alessio stared over for the last time at the bench where absolutely nothing was happening. Maria and Jessica were still deep in conversation, and by now Sonia had stopped glancing over at Alessio with a worried expression. Her glances had impressed him as a signal, a form of proof. Very simply, he'd tricked himself into believing.

He tore his gaze away and turned it toward Cristiano's face, mottled red with anger. The face of a gigantic dickhead. Along with his hopes, he lost his temper once and for all.

"Why don't you go fuck yourself?"

Cristiano, cracking his knuckles, shot him a wry little challenging smile. But it wasn't a challenge, it was just the amphetamine in his bloodstream.

There's always a certain set of expectations in everyone's mind at a certain kind of party. It was logical that the situation was precarious and could deteriorate. Cristiano hadn't even wanted to come to the roller rink; as usual, he wanted to go to the Gilda. And Alessio had been focused, staring, fixated on that fucking bench for the past hour. It was logical. Still, Mattia didn't know what to come up with anymore; he was watching them lock horns, raising their voices, starting to pepper each other with insults, and he was thinking: *Let them punch each other out. What do I care?*

The unfortunates sitting at tables had all looked up and turned to stare in their direction. Eagerly, they smoked their cigarettes and settled back for a show. Mattia shook his head, demoralized: Not a fucking thing ever changes around here. Not the people, not the steel mill crushing the balls of one and all, not these two assholes about to lose it.

Everything was the way it had been before he fled the country. *Everything was disgustingly the same*, he thought suddenly, *all except Anna*.

"I'm warning you, you're going to piss me off."

Cristiano burst into laughter, right in Alessio's face.

"Go ahead and be pissed off, it won't change a thing. Face it: *She's* not coming."

Who's *she*? Mattia was baffled.

Alessio was seeing red.

"Get out of here," he hissed through clenched teeth. His face transfigured.

"Where am I supposed to go? It's your car!"

"Get out of here!" he roared.

Cristiano stood his ground, making no signs of yielding, with the grinning face of a doped-up pill popper.

The toothless little old man was especially enjoying the scene, and from his table he shouted: "Go on, hit him!"

But there was nothing funny about the situation. There was nothing to be happy about in this scene, thought Mattia. *It was straight out of the worst outlying slums of the soul.* The tattered Italian flag, which still fluttered limply, in spite of everything, at the entrance to the roller rink, struck him as emblematic, uncannily so.

"She's not coming!" Cristiano was taunting him now. "I'm not going to ruin my Ferragosto because that slut isn't coming! Oh, she's probably *coming,* but in bed, with someone else, so deal with it."

Even before he'd finished the sentence, Alessio had seized Cristiano by the neck. He answered him with a succession of vicious head butts—one, two, three. He'd probably have killed him if Mattia hadn't gotten between them with his full two hundred pounds of weight on a six-foot-two-inch frame. Someone would probably have called the Carabinieri if the two of them, seething with fury, hadn't broken their clinch at a certain point. And if Cristiano, with a lump the size of a grapefruit on his forehead, hadn't turned to leave.

"Go! No one's keeping you here," Alessio shouted at him, as if he'd lost his mind. "Maybe, instead of going after a bunch of whores . . . Just maybe, instead of knocking up another fifteen-year-old girl, you might act like a man tonight, do one decent thing in your whole shitty life," he raved like a lunatic now. "*Cri,* instead of going to the Gilda, why don't you go see what your son's fucking face even looks like for once?"

Your son.

Mattia felt the blood freeze in his veins.

Cristiano, who had taken a few steps, turned in disbelief.

A moment of general amazement went by; no one knew what to say. The rubberneckers, themselves astonished at such a massively uncomfortable outcome, lowered their heads and hastily returned to their decks of cards. Alessio, face-to-face with his friend's cadaverous expression, an ashen visage with two smoldering embers instead of eyes, already regretted saying something that he'd never have dreamed of in a clearheaded moment.

Cristiano, on the other hand, said nothing. He twisted his lips in a grimace of disgust and then, driving his pupils hard into Alessio's eyes, he summoned all the saliva available to him and spat furiously on the ground. Then he turned and was gone.

It should immediately be said that if Alessio hadn't been picking a fight with Cristiano he would have noticed sometime earlier that a slender figure with long chestnut hair had joined the three girls sitting on the bench under the tree.

It should also be said, to be faithful to the historical truth, that the fifteen-year-old girl that Cristiano had knocked up was named Jennifer, and that evening she wasn't at the party like all the other girls her age but at home trying to wean little James, who was deeply uninterested in taking a baby bottle in place of his mother's tit.

In fact, Sonia, Maria, and Jessica were waiting for precisely the person that Alessio suspected. Under the tree. They'd agreed on that rendezvous by text message. They, too, were about to give up when Maria felt someone tap her on the shoulder.

She really had come. Despite the location and the provincial crowd sweating en masse there, in the end she really had come, after all. Now she was looking at them, smiling, courteous, and slightly off-putting.

She, in fact, had nothing in common with *them*. She'd never worn one of those denim miniskirts that barely covered the crotch, or those belts covered with studs, and especially not the lavish volume of cheap costume jewelry around the neck. When she sat down she didn't sprawl, legs wide apart. She didn't shout filthy words. Just the material of her lilac sheath dress dug an unbridgeable trench between her world and theirs.

Sonia, Maria, and Jessica sat there a moment, rapt, watching her with a blend of attraction and mistrust.

She had learned the alphabet even before she was enrolled in elementary school, and she knew how to count to a hundred. Her parents had taught her to read, and they'd explained to her the importance of books and how many different professions there are in the world—things that not everyone in Via Stalingrado had a chance to understand. She'd never run unsupervised through the streets in the working-class projects; she'd never hidden in the cellars to try her first cigarette; she'd never let boys touch her behind the reinforced-concrete pillars. No one had ever hoisted her skirt at age eleven.

Still, there she was, and her oval face wore a disarming smile. And, all things considered, they were glad she'd come.

She said she was sorry; she couldn't stay long. They were waiting for her out front. She couldn't leave without saying good-bye, though. She really did love those three young women, though they probably liked her only up to a certain point.

The first time that he'd brought her home—everyone still remembered it clearly. It was part of the legend: the way she walked, careful not to get her heels stuck in the sewer grates, a little squeamish at the sight of the giant cement apartment buildings. They'd mocked her brutally. When she was introduced she'd reached out courteously to shake hands, saying: "Good evening, pleasure to meet you." Good evening? Pleasure to meet you? Not even the postman, not even the doctor indulged in all those niceties.

Now, though, they'd known each other for years, and the four young women concealed behind the tree talked about holidays, work, her job search (which she'd begin once she graduated), maybe in Pisa, or perhaps in Piombino, starting in September; the underpaid part-time employment the other girls were struggling along with; graduating from middle school was the height of their achievements, and they worked stints as cashiers at the Coop supermarket and at Intimissimi, the lingerie chain, the kind of jobs that don't have paid vacations.

After a while, though, Maria felt obliged to whisper in her ear that *he* was there tonight. She pointed him out to her, standing atop the man-made hillock. Elena looked up in that direction with a blend of astonishment and fear. She immediately identified the blond figure in the distance and stood, as if in a trance, saying nothing for a few moments.

"How is he doing?" she asked at last, wrenching her eyes away.

"How do you think he's doing?" replied Maria sarcastically.

"And Anna?"

"Now she's doing well! She already has a few boyfriends on the side. . . ."

"Oh, yes?" Elena tried to put on a knowing smile, but what came out was an off-kilter grimace.

"She's enrolling in the *liceo classico*, just like you."

Elena had always nurtured a special fondness for that young girl; she hoped Anna wouldn't wind up like the others, behind the bar in a pub having her ass grabbed by drunks.

"She must be around here somewhere." Jessica looked around. "Now that you mention it, we should go take a look around for her. Otherwise, her brother'll kill us."

"Come with us, you can say hello to her. . . ."

She avoided the offer: "No, really, I can't. Say hello to her for me."

"You don't even want to say hi to *him*?" Sonia ventured.

She sketched out a bitter smile. She said nothing. She hugged them one after the other. "We'll see you again in September, when I get back from Paris."

"Okay, and make sure you send us a postcard!"

At last, in the very instant that she was leaving, at the exact moment when she turned to walk toward the gate, by pure chance, and without a shred of hope, Alessio turned and looked in that direction.

He turned pale.

His pupils narrowed.

He swayed.

Mattia, thinking that he must be feeling sick, started shaking him. Alessio ignored him: He looked as if he'd been shot. But he recovered immediately.

Except of course for the one person who most needed to know, everyone saw him: He came rushing down from the hilltop as if he'd been stung by a wasp, running like a lunatic, like a madman. Sonia felt her heart stop. Maria smiled: This is better than a movie. . . .

Mattia, left behind and all alone, kicked a stone and decided that everybody could go fuck themselves.

Alessio was shoving and elbowing recklessly, without so much as an *excuse me* to anyone. His one terror was that he might lose sight of her. He was laboriously forcing his way through the crowd; he didn't have any choice but to shoulder people aside.

He wanted to shout her name. But he couldn't do it. He wanted to picture her in his mind. He couldn't bring himself to do that either. He was charging ahead like a wild beast rushing through a forest. He wanted to see her, now. See her face, alive, intact, in front of him for the first time in three years.

He felt such a thrashing turmoil in his chest that somewhere along the way he said aloud: "I must be having a heart attack." But he kept going, step by step, shouldering and elbowing his way, insult after insult. She was still there, at the gate. He hadn't lost her. He felt hot; in fact, he was dripping with sweat and he was incredibly thirsty. But he made it to the gate, and he made it to the parking lot, too.

It was cool here, the sounds of the party were muffled, and a vast nocturnal silence pressed down from the dense branches of the pine grove. He could hear crickets and pinecones falling. She was walking a few steps ahead of him, and it really was her.

That was the way she walked. Those were her calves. Her slender waist, her back, her shoulders. Her bottom: No, he couldn't bring himself to look.

A car with the engine running and headlights turned on was certainly waiting for her. Because she was walking in that direction, and once she was close enough, the right-hand car door swung open. She held out her arm to grab the door handle; she was about to get in.

"Elena!"

A roar: Her name exploded in the dark like an M-80. She stopped short. The final *a* in her name persisted, dissolving only slowly in the night air. She lowered her arm; she stood motionless.

"Elena . . . ," Alessio repeated in a faint voice.

As if someone were holding her by the shoulders, she slowly turned around.

She turned: Her familiar profile was untouched by the passage of time. A warm chestnut-brunette profile, long hair, longer than Alessio remembered. Slightly wavy, pulled back by a clasp. She seemed older, perhaps. She seemed like the highest creature in the kingdom of life.

All the strength had drained out of Alessio. He couldn't feel his body anymore, only the ferocious uproar of his organs. He just stood there like a fool, petrified, in the center of an empty parking lot, his knees trembling for the moment when they could give way. His words had all flown out of his head and evaporated into thin air. In his cranium he could feel his heart muscle pumping and booming; his throat was drier than a desert. What could he say? . . . He was nothing but a heart and a pair of lungs going to shit.

This moment was impossible to take, impossible to live.

It was the same for her. She didn't hear the voices calling from the car; she didn't take a step in one direction or the other. She stood there, motionless, just like him, and felt her knees crumbling to bits. She thought thirteen thousand things, all at the same time. That he was magnificent. That it had been three years. That she'd made her decision. That it was a fucked-up decision. That it was right. That it was wrong. And she couldn't bring herself to move even a fingertip.

They looked at one another for an absolutely insignificant split second of time, vanishingly close to zero.

Then Alessio smiled. And his smile was so beautiful, happy, incredulous, and childish that Elena smiled in turn. And she felt as if all those years hadn't meant a thing.

They heard a car horn, the proverbial goddamned blast of a car horn.

Elena came to her senses. Time existed again. She had a plane to catch tomorrow, and now she had to leave. She didn't want to go; it cost her an enormous effort to feign indifference. And yet she raised one hand in a miserable token of farewell. She got into the car and it departed immediately, as if it were a jet.

A fog of dust sprang up into the air, and a dense cluster of clouds tore and tattered across the moon. Then everything returned to the way it was before. The branches in the pine grove went on rustling and tossing. The wind cleaned the air and the branches. Alessio, after taking a few blind steps, let himself collapse onto an overturned log and held his head in both hands.

He wasn't alone.

Not far away, concealed among the trees, Cristiano was holding his head in the same way. He was thinking about his son, James, and staring obstinately at a rock.

Piombino was pouring feverishly out onto the roller rink.

The speakers were booming out "Rhythm Is a Dancer." Francesca and Anna had danced to that song a thousand times in the bathroom, behind a locked door, side by side in front of a mirror.

You can feel the, you can feel the . . .

Now there were bleachers packed with people instead of the window across the courtyard. The wheels of roller skates by the hundreds, by the thousands, were scratching the floor. And under the beam of the main spotlight every adolescent was highlighted, glowing magnificently, bathed in bright white light. Francesca was tossing back her mane of hair, and she couldn't know who she resembled as she twisted sinuously around the flagstaff of the faded Italian banner.

Lift your hands and voices, / free your minds and join us / You can feel it in the air . . .

They all shouted together: *Ooh, it's a passion.*

For an instant they fooled themselves into believing that their friendship was still intact.

CHAPTER 17

There was a guy at the bar; you couldn't tell if he was a priest or a parish volunteer. He was probably just a religion teacher at a local middle school. So he was sitting there, shaking his head, and saying: "What do we give these kids? What do we teach them?" While he was talking he was looking out onto the roller rink at all those bodies spinning here and there like on a tilt-a-whirl. "They have nothing! They don't think about anything!"

Mattia, left alone in the bar and feeling like a fool, had to sit and listen to him, adding insult to injury.

"They just do drugs and waste their lives. It was almost better when we still had to deal with the Communist Party."

"Like hell!" someone blurted out.

Mattia, in disgust, ordered another Sambuca. Alessio and Cristiano could both go fuck themselves, or each other, because he'd been waiting for them for the past fifteen minutes. Then he told himself that frankly he had no desire to go look for them, much less sit around listening to the rantings of old men. They could all do what they wanted: for tonight; he'd given as much as he felt like giving.

So, whistling as he went, he walked down from the man-made hillock. As he eyed the pretty girls he met along the way, he quickly regained his good humor.

He wasn't the kind of guy who bears a grudge or broods gloomily over some injustice. He was a guy who was equally indifferent to God and country. He hadn't stepped into a voting booth once in his life, and when he was eating dinner, if the news came on, with all those deaths and wars and massacres, he just changed the channel.

That's just the way Mattia was; he wasn't a bad guy at all. Of course, if the others found out the reason he'd left the country three years ago, right then and there they'd find it disturbing. But robbing a post office and shooting out a couple of automatic speeding cameras doesn't automatically make you a criminal.

Now he was strolling around the roller rink in search of inspiration. He had absolutely no interest in skating, much less in dancing. He just liked to watch things. The devil is in the details, he'd once heard someone say, and he truly appreciated that phrase.

He leaned on the railing, at the least crowded point, and stood there following the trajectories of the skaters with his eyes. He had just the time to light a cigarette and run his hand back and up through his hair when, bingo, in all that noise and confusion, he spotted her.

She went hurtling past him. Once, twice, three times. And each time she went by, wafting lightly but at high speed, that tiny pink miniskirt lofted and fluttered, uncovering a naked, velvety stretch of thigh; a bright, soft patch of crotch. And a pert, luscious, teenage ass darted left and right, back and forth, while the legs gave muscular thrusts forward.

Each time, in this sequence, she went by. The luminous parts of her went past. Right leg, left leg, arm, mass of rushing hair, a slice of nose. A smile.

By the time he counted to ten she had zoomed at scorching speed halfway around the rink.

Anna hadn't noticed that Mattia was there and that he was watching her. She'd practically forgotten about him; she was completely absorbed in skating faster than everyone else. If anyone dared to do a spin, she'd replicate the move instantly, only more gracefully. As soon as somebody performed a jump, she'd copy it, but higher. And in her competitive frenzy, so vastly out of place at that roller party, she showed no pity to the countless admirers who tried to take her hand or, somewhat less chivalrously, grab her ass.

Mattia made a mental comparison between this daunting Amazon and the embarrassed little girl that he'd surprised in her pajamas that morning. He was enchanted by the similarities, and he was glued to the rusty railing she sailed past every minute or so.

Every time that miniskirt fluttered up in the air, he suddenly felt, throughout his body, as if he were thirteen years old.

He was thunderstruck, hit by a bolt of lightning, and the girl had just finished junior high school. If someone had told him this story he never would have believed it, never in a thousand years. In Ossetia he'd even lived with an older woman. He really had slept in the depths of a cargo hold, he had dueled in the garden of a house that didn't belong to him with a Neapolitan mastiff, and he had skillfully eluded not one but four policemen in the middle of a roundup.

Those recollections flickered through his mind like quick cuts in a Tarantino movie, while the living image of her, her microskirt made of light fabric, triumphed unbeaten over everything. As if his life was now. Before this it was all a blank slate.

Mattia finished his cigarette in three quick drags. She'd been buzzing around his mind for twelve hours now. Now he couldn't control himself anymore. His eyes were practically aching from staring at her, studying her, waiting for her. . . . What was it that was so extraordinary about her? Who was it she reminded him of? Definitely not his mother; not his Slovenian ex-girlfriend either. And what did he care about who resembled whom? Forget about figuring it out. She just had an instantaneous physical effect on him, an effect that was visibly stretching his trousers.

What should he do? The million-dollar question. He didn't know whether he should call her name, catch up with her on the rink, or get the hell out of there and forget about this whole absurd situation. Should he invite her to have something to drink or ask her to go for a stroll in the pine grove? . . . Sure, in the pine grove! As if she'd just up and go for a stroll with him in the pine grove.

Then there was a problem. A major problem: Alessio.

He would club him to the brink of death. He'd destroy him. Worse: He'd drown him in a mill crucible full of molten steel. Okay, let's not exaggerate. Whatever: He'd be furious. He'd definitely punch him out. And he'd warn him to steer clear of his little sister in the future.

What a mess. No doubt, if he called her name right now, if he persuaded her to go hole up somewhere, alone, together, he would have a mess on his hands. But at the same time, who knew where Alessio was right now, and she was clearly getting tired of skating, she was gradually starting to slow down. . . . She was just too nice to look at. She had some fucking effect on him that he couldn't figure out. And he told himself that his intentions were honorable. He convinced himself that all he had in mind was to get to know her a little better, spend some time talking, find out what was inside that curly head of hers, and maybe, just maybe, hold her in his arms for a few minutes. He really didn't want anything more than that from this young, ridiculously hot, way too brazen . . .

"Curly!" he shouted.

Anna slowed down and turned in his direction, peering into the crowd. Jesus. She was spectacular.

That adorable face, curiously searching for whoever called her . . . was fantastic!

Sure, he'd take his beating, he'd explain what had happened, and then he'd take the rest of the beating. He'd start trying to explain a second time.

Anna saw him. She recognized him. And she suddenly skidded to a halt.

Mattia. Mat-ti-a. Leaning over the railing, as handsome as Brad Pitt in *Thelma & Louise*, as handsome as Riccardo Scamarcio on the cover of the latest issue of *Cioè*.

There were a couple of seconds of bewilderment, followed by raw, unrefined, ecstatic joy. Then Anna recovered. She tried to get over to where he was standing but that was easier said than done: Dozens and dozens of skaters were whipping around the curve like lightning bolts, and Anna had to be careful to avoid their trajectories unless she wanted to be knocked to the ground and skin her knee right in front of . . . Mattia!

For three or four minutes, they stood there: One over here, the other over there, making funny faces at each other, laughing in embarrassment, at the absurd situation, at the sheer itch they had to be next to each other. . . . But there wasn't anything they could do, with a steady stream of human rocket ships on the horizon.

Anna was so cute every time she tried to take a step and was then forced to jump back, puffing out her cheeks in annoyance, expelling a lungful of air. He stood there, cigarette stub smoldering between his lips, asking himself the reason for all this.

When she finally reached him, she leaned on the railing alongside him.

"We made it," she said, panting.

"Well, I have to say you're comfortable on skates!" he laughed.

Anna didn't know what to say in response. *Do you realize what's happening to you? There are people who have never had something like this happen in a lifetime.* Anna didn't know what to say, because she wanted nothing so much as to throw her arms around him and kiss him right then and there, but at the same time nothing terrorized her like the possibility of that kiss.

"I'm incredibly thirsty."

"You want me to take you over to the bar?"

He had that smirky little grin that made you want to hit him, like a criminal in a gangster movie. One of the good-hearted criminals, of course.

Anna climbed over the railing, as if it were the most normal thing in the world, and Mattia couldn't help but take a peek at her panties.

"No, I don't like the bar," she said, sitting down on a step, intent on taking the roller skates off her feet, "and I don't feel like staying here anymore."

"Well, where do you want to go?" he asked in surprise.

Anna was contorted on the floor, she couldn't seem to get the skates off her feet, and at the same time that diabolical miniskirt was hiking up yet again, for the umpteenth time, for the millionth time. Mattia was asking himself just what an Italian girl from a working-class neighborhood might have done, might know about life, at that age. Because Slovenian girls and Russian girls, of course, are precocious. . . .

"Well? So where do you want to go?"

"Out of here!" Anna exclaimed, getting to her feet.

Now barefoot, she hardly came up to his shoulder.

"And you just trust the first guy who happens to walk by?"

"But you're not the first guy who happened to walk by. . . ." Anna giggled, the way she did.

Mattia shook his head in amusement: He wasn't expecting her to be quite so enterprising. But he also knew that she wasn't genuinely enterprising; she wasn't much more than a little girl.

"Anyway, if you act like a jerk . . . I'll tell my brother!"

It was clear that she was just kidding, but when he smiled, it was still a tense, drawn smile.

"Come on. You think I'd say something to him?" Anna burst into laughter.

He felt a wave of relief. He also felt tricked, ensnared, and infected by that young girl's enthusiasm; young girl though she might be, she had a pair of tits on her. And so, discarding recklessly any scruples he might feel, tugged along by an unexpected and adolescent yearning for fun, he held out his arm jauntily and said: "Let's go, princess. . . . I'll take you wherever you command!"

Anna burst into laughter again and pushed him aside with both hands.

But he'd already taken her arm in his, and they were walking arm in arm now. Suddenly he felt ten years younger.

"Wait, I don't have my shoes!"

Mattia stopped, looked down, and realized that Anna's feet were bare on the ground; in an overexuberant outburst of energy and imagination, even before she could open her mouth, he took her in his arms and lifted her bodily, cradling her as he said: "I couldn't bear the thought of a pebble wounding your lovely, delicate little feet, ma'am. . . ."

So Anna suddenly found herself scooped up in Mattia's arms like a newlywed, gripping his shoulders and dazed, carried in triumph through the ecstatic crowd, all the way to the skate rental booth, to the locker where she'd left her sandals.

During that journey, Anna simply couldn't think. She let herself be rocked into a reverie by the movement of that body on the gravel, by the warmth that it emanated, by the dark brown smell of nicotine and alcohol and something else, could it be? . . . seaweed.

She perceived, with a blend of enchantment and fear the tension in his muscles, the blood surging through his arteries, the pulse of his circulatory system. She glimpsed with a mixture of astonishment and revulsion the tufts of dark hairs on his chest. And she plunged headlong into that physical contact.

Suddenly Mattia said: "What have you been up to?!" With astonishment in his voice: "Your hair is full of blades of grass!"

The devil's in the details.

Francesca had seen them.

She'd seen everything.

Anna slowing down on her skates, moving toward that guy, *the* guy. She'd skidded and spun to a halt immediately, and for a few minutes she'd had to hold tight to the railing in order to get her breathing under control.

She'd gradually moved closer, without attracting attention; she'd mingled in the crowd. She got to within a few feet of them. And she'd seen: Anna climb over the railing, unlace her skates and take them off, climb up into the arms of that man.

Suddenly she couldn't feel her arms, her legs, her heart. Only her stomach made itself felt, as it contracted and twisted, as if it had been sucked up and then pumped out and then once again lurched to a halt in a dizzying whirl.

She'd followed them. She'd spied on them from concealment until they reached the rental booth, tiptoeing miraculously on her skate wheels, slipping and slaloming through the gravel, barely staying alive under the furious sledgehammering of her heart as it pounded at a rate that couldn't last.

In fact, she couldn't take it: the sight of those two, laughing together in the rental booth, his helping her on with her sandals, or *pretending* to help her put on her sandals but tickling her as he did, and Anna laughed in a way . . . in a way that disgusted her.

They went outside. She'd followed them, to the bitter end.

Until they vanished completely into the darkness of the pine grove. And that was when she felt sick.

Leaning against the iron palings of the fence, a first wave of retching had swept through her. Then another, and another. She'd covered her mouth with one hand and, gathering all her strength, went running toward the bathrooms.

There was a long line outside. She'd been forced to butt ahead of six or seven people and hear some pretty foul abuse directed at her. She'd stood outside a locked door, desperately waiting. And when the door finally swung open, Francesca had thrust her head down into the urinal.

She'd thrown up.

Snorted noisily as she inhaled through snot-clogged nostrils.

Sobbed uncontrollably, locked into the square yard of urinal redolent of piss.

Someone was outside, knocking on the door, urging her to hurry up. Some lunatic started kicking the door, shouting: "You slut, get out of there!" For ten full minutes she sat in that squalid cubicle, in a daze. Only once she'd finally emptied her stomach and her eyes, when she felt that there was nothing left of her emotions, did she emerge.

She went and took a seat on the bleachers, curled up in the corner that seemed darkest and most isolated. She wrapped her arms around her knees and plunged her head between them, decided that from that exact moment forward Anna was dead.

Alessio was veering, now to the left and then off to the right.

He was trudging along, dragging his hump, at random, arms dangling at his sides, chin pointing at the ground. He was walking like a refugee escaping from a war zone. He went on, pushing his body through the pine forest, for half an hour, an hour, who could say. Until he finally tripped over a branch and fell face first. When he looked up, he recognized Cristiano.

He was huddled, hunched up on a rock. His eyes were dilated and grim.

They exchanged a glance: hard to say which of the two looked worse.

A tense minute passed, because they were both surprised and pleased to run into each other in the same pathetic state, but neither of them wanted to admit it.

Alessio straightened up, started brushing off his jeans.

"You were right; she's a whore," he said, looking off into the distance.

So now he'd made the first move.

Cristiano, as if he'd been holding his breath, quickly made the second move.

He walked over to Alessio, laid a hand on his shoulder: "Don't say that, not even as a joke. Elena is a girl . . . the best girl you could hope for."

"The best I could be dumped by, you mean?"

"She'll come back, I swear to you." He put a hand on his heart. "And if I said those things . . ."

"Forget about it."

Friends again. Total time elapsed: three minutes.

"I'm a shitty father." Cristiano kicked a pinecone furiously.

"You'd have to try being one first; it's too soon to tell."

They embraced vigorously; they crushed each other in a bear hug. They were alone in that pine forest; they were a pair of miserable outcasts. Alone, forgotten, but together. Just like always.

Cristiano used his ATM card to straighten out on an otherwise unmarked surface a conciliatory line of coke, the fatted calf of narcotics.

"I swear this is the last line. I swear for the rest of my life. From tomorrow, I'm going to be a father!"

"Me too, I swear. From tomorrow . . ." Alessio thought for a second. "I'll go back to the crane and fuck 'em all."

They hunched over the lines of coke, snorted with the usual ten-thousand-lire note rolled up into their nostrils.

"I have to say, though, James is a fucked-up name," said Cristiano as he raised his head.

There was a smile full of tenderness on his face now. He snorted massively and reflected on the thought that down there, in that blinking constellation of streetlamps, there was a tiny creature depending on him. A tiny, whiny little creature who he could teach how to stand up, how to walk, how to lay rubber and peel out on a motor scooter.

Actually, though, they weren't alone at all in that pine grove.

If Alessio had imagined what was happening just one hundred feet or so away, he wouldn't have sat there laughing like an imbecile. Not at all. If

he'd had even the remotest suspicion of who was hiding among the trees—
with pine needles in his hair, with his sister.

It was less than half an hour until the fireworks went off.

Francesca had been curled up on a tier of the bleachers the whole time.
She'd fallen asleep.

A harsh sleep mixed with waking moments in which real sounds mingled with imaginary sounds; every so often she was forced to start and open
her eyes, only to drop off again. They were confused, monotonous night-
mares. There was her father, silent, sitting in his easy chair, suddenly rising
to his feet and rummaging through a drawer in the kitchen. It was at this
point, zooming in on the blade of the kitchen knife, that her eyelids suddenly snapped wide open.

She lay there half conscious, in a fetal position on the reinforced concrete
of the bleachers, until she heard someone nearby speaking to her and shaking her. Her head was exploding.

She opened her eyes. Reddened, sleep-crusted eyes. Little by little her
pupils began focusing on the silhouette of a person, a female, outlines that
were familiar yet unknown.

She blinked her eyelashes repeatedly. Lisa was running her hand over her
forehead to see if she had a fever. Lisa was holding her wrist to check her pulse.

Lisa?

When Lisa had come back up to take her seat on the bleachers, she'd
immediately noticed something blond huddled on the uppermost tier, so
abandoned and ignored that she'd assumed someone had fainted or was
having a seizure. She moved a little closer and was absolutely flabbergasted
when she saw that the unconscious, filthy person was none other than Francesca.

Francesca, unrecognizable, sitting up now and weakly rubbing her eyelids. She was weak, like someone who had just had a traumatic encounter
or was emerging from the blurry effect of some kind of narcotic.

"Hey . . . you all right?"

She didn't answer. She went on rubbing her eyes and straightening her
hair and her clothing. She repeated the same gestures over and over again,
mechanically. A slight pool of saliva frothed at the corner of her mouth.

"Do you want me to call you a doctor? I saw an ambulance out in the
parking lot. . . ."

Francesca seemed to surface.

"No," she said.

Lisa began to consider her: She was looking at her with large, blank, expressionless eyes.

It was hard for Lisa to imagine that such a pretty girl—and she was pretty even now, with her hair a mess, her face a wreck, the mascara smeared around her eyes—might be unhappy, might suffer.

She looked like one of those children who've just escaped with their lives after a flash flood, who blink their eyes in astonishment against a background of mud and rubble while the television cameras zoom in on them for a close-up.

Lisa almost felt like wrapping her arms around her.

"I can go get you something. . . . A glass of water?"

But she was embarrassed.

"No, I'm fine now," said Francesca.

There was a hint of embarrassment in her voice as well: She was returning to the real world, her cheeks were regaining color, and she realized that she'd been caught unawares in a state of utter misery.

"Should I go get Anna for you?"

To Lisa it was the most logical question imaginable. She'd already gotten to her feet, she'd turned to look, peering through the surging crowd of skaters in search of the curly-haired figure in a short pink skirt. But she heard Francesca say, in a tone that smacked of pure ice, of total indifference, and therefore of the most earthshakingly unexpected:

"No," sharply.

Lisa turned in astonishment and looked at her. Francesca was calm and motionless.

"Did something happen with Anna?" she asked, in spite of herself.

But it was beyond Lisa's conception of the world to link that state of misery with a quarrel between friends.

"If you see her, tell me." Francesca said it flatly, without any apparent emotion. "I don't want to talk to her."

"No, I don't see her. . . ." Lisa sat down again.

They were sitting side by side, with no real idea of what to do or say.

"What time is it?" asked Francesca.

"It's almost midnight. Do you need to get home?"

"No, my father's at work."

It was nothing more than a scrap of information. But she had confided in Lisa; Francesca had given her a tiny detail of her personal life. And Lisa felt something close to a physical wave of emotion.

The two of them were together, alone together on the highest and most deserted tier of the bleachers. The people down there were dancing and leaping and pirouetting, distracted, unaware of what was going on around them. None of them knew that Lisa was sitting next to Francesca, her knee grazing Francesca's knee. That proximity gave her a sense of vertigo. She was ardently hoping that Francesca wouldn't decide to stand up and walk away.

But Francesca, too, once again aware of her surroundings, was not entirely indifferent to the situation. From time to time she glanced sidelong at the strange companion sitting by her side, and she was surprised to discover that she didn't find Lisa distasteful. As if she had reemerged but into a completely new life, and Lisa was the first new thing.

"I know we've never really been friends," Lisa said, out of the blue, "but anyway, if you want to talk about it, I'm right here."

She gulped: It was the bravest thing she'd ever done in her life.

"After all, we've known each other since nursery school, . . ." she ventured.

Francesca wasn't expecting a statement of that kind. She turned sharply and stared at her, blinking in astonishment, practically with a smidgen of joy. A tiny fragment of joy, followed by a shy smile.

Lisa was forced to think that perhaps a moment like this was something that she'd long dreamed of, in her wildest and most unconfessable dreams, if now, at the sight of that smile, she felt herself quiver with happiness.

"Francesca, are you sure you don't want to talk about it? Did you have a fight with Anna?"

"We're not friends anymore," she said, simply, "but I don't want to talk about it."

Lisa nodded. There must be a serious reason if that girl, who was so tough, and, frankly, such a bitch, that girl who had never bothered to glance at her, was now sitting with her on the bleachers, up here, apart from the crowd. They sat in silence for a short while. Lisa seemed to be swimming through a blossoming love, a torrid crush.

Francesca measured every corner of her face, from head to foot, that strange surrogate for Anna, that funny living creature who had never meant a thing to her, while Anna had signified everything. She looked at her for a full minute.

Lisa: No one cares about her; her sister is in a wheelchair.

Lisa: big nose, thick thighs, zits.

There she was, barely able to keep her excitement bottled in.

A nerd who'd be going to the *liceo classico*, who was going to spend the rest of her life in the gray silence of a library, at a desk, behind a lectern. In September Lisa was going to be in the same classroom as Anna.

That was the decisive factor.

"We're friends," Francesca suddenly decided, aloud.

Anna had replaced her with a big handsome boy.

Now she'd replace Anna with this homely dog. It was all perversely appropriate.

In the meantime, Lisa was openmouthed in disbelief: Me? I'm her friend?

They stayed there, seated, almost until it was time for the fireworks show.

They exchanged a few timid observations about the party. Lisa said that she'd never seen so many people in one place, and Francesca answered that she'd liked the songs. Lisa explained that she'd never heard those songs before; she didn't say that actually she knew them very well because she'd spied on Francesca and Anna from the window across the courtyard.

They talked about school, again shyly. Lisa said that she couldn't wait to start back to school again, and asked Francesca where she'd be going. Francesca answered that she'd enrolled at the IPS, that she didn't even know what she'd be studying there, and she didn't give a crap. So Lisa changed the subject. But there weren't that many subjects.

They'd been classmates for eight years, and they didn't know each other at all.

Every time silence fell, Lisa racked her brains to find the next thing to say. Excessive excitement, in the end, ensured that each time she'd choose the wrong thing to talk about. But Francesca was barely even listening to her.

At five minutes past midnight, a little late, a pyrotechnician ignited six or seven fireworks that went off as soon as they were fully aloft, and then vanished, dying away in the darkness. That's when Nino and Massimo appeared.

Lisa blushed immediately. They were astonished to find her there, with Francesca. As usual, they didn't even pretend to say hello to her.

They asked what had happened, where Anna had vanished to. Francesca answered with the utmost tranquillity that Anna was with "other people," and that now that it was past midnight, they could all go dancing.

Massimo and Nino both looked astonished, exchanged a glance as if to say: Is this for real? Then they wisely decided not to investigate further.

They rushed down the tiers of the bleachers. Francesca leaped to her feet, grabbed Lisa by the arm, and dragged her onto the dance floor. She seemed to be reborn; she seemed to mean what she said.

At a quarter past midnight on August 16, 2001, Lisa Cavini, the loser, was dancing in a discotheque in the middle of the floor with Francesca Morganti, Massimo Righi, and Nino Greco.

At a quarter past midnight on August 16, 2001, Lisa, to all empirical evidence, had taken Anna's place.

They looked everywhere for them.

Alessio was out of his mind, furious, shouting: "Where the fuck is she?"

He was especially pissed off at Sonia, who was supposed to have been keeping an eye on her. Meanwhile, Cristiano dialed and redialed Mattia's cell phone number, and the phone kept repeating: "The number you have dialed is not in service."

Alessio was acting like a lunatic. And he still hadn't put two and two together.

It was one in the morning. The roller rink was emptying out.

Sonia kept telling Alessio to calm down, not to worry, that Anna was certainly somewhere nearby, that she'd show up any minute. But Alessio wasn't calming down, he was shouting louder and louder.

"Francesca! Do you seriously mean to tell me that you didn't see anything? For Chrissake, you guys were together!"

Francesca, sitting on the bench next to Lisa, barely deigned to shake her head no.

"I'll go," Massi said, as he got to his feet. "I'll go take a look around in the pine grove."

Aside from the fact that he couldn't take Anna's absence any longer, he was eager to make a good impression on Alessio, who, whatever else happened, even though he might be freaking out right now, was still the most highly respected young man in the quarter of Via Stalingrado.

"In the pine grove? What the fuck would she be doing in the pine grove? If something happened to her . . . If somebody touched a hair on her head, I swear . . ."

He never finished the sentence. Anna emerged from the trees, her hair all mussed, a big smile on her face. As if nothing at all had happened, as if her clothes weren't all rumpled and askew.

She said: "Don't swear, I'm alive."

Right behind her was . . .

Everyone fell silent.

Anna was smiling.

Alessio wasn't smiling.

Mattia, who had been smiling, wasn't smiling anymore.

From the bench, Lisa was starting to understand a few things. Nino decided that now a brawl might be about to break out, and he was on Alessio's side, without a doubt. Massimo finally had the confirmation that Anna was never going to be his girlfriend. Sonia, Maria, and Jessica decided that Anna had really put her foot in it this time, and that at the same time, she had gotten away with something big. Cristiano, aghast, said only: "Shit."

"Is there something you want to tell me, Mattia?"

Alessio's tone of voice was unmistakable. As was his face, actually.

Mattia, with great dignity, replied: "Not here. Let's get in the car."

And he walked on ahead toward the Peugeot.

No one breathed. There were even a few people who pretended to look away.

As Mattia walked off, Alessio made a gesture to Cristiano as if to stay: You stay here. He'd be walking home again. But he lacked the courage to object.

Alessio started walking toward the car, then he suddenly turned and looked back at Anna.

"You," he decreed, "go home now, and wait up for me until I get back. Understood?"

Anna didn't blink an eye.

"UNDERSTOOD" he roared.

Anna nodded yes.

Sonia and the other girls walked over to her, to take her home. Alessio shot them an evil glare. Then he went over to the car. Both guys got in. The headlights switched on, the engine turned over. And everyone watched as the Peugeot with the three spoilers peeled out in reverse as if it were a jet taking off, and then vanished into a giant billowing cloud of dirt.

Francesca hadn't drawn closer; she hadn't moved.

Anna turned to look at her: She was sitting next to Lisa, holding hands with Lisa, and she was staring at her with an unsavory smile.

Anna barely had time to open her mouth, turn pale, look back at her with an incredulous, helpless glance. Then Sonia dragged her away.

CHAPTER 18

One week later, at 3:00 in the afternoon, Rosa rang the Sorrentino family's doorbell. And Sandra came to the door.

One week later was August 22, Anna's birthday.

But Anna wasn't home, and Sandra, as she was pulling her rubber gloves off her hands and walking toward the door, expected anything but that visit. In all those years Rosa had never once come by to see her, in spite of all the invitations and encouragement.

But there she stood, on the landing, on the doormat with WELCOME written on it. She seemed hesitant to step through the door. She hadn't even called ahead to announce her visit, and that was completely out of character for her.

Sandra greeted her with a smile and said: "Come in, come on in, sorry about the mess." It didn't take her long to understand from Rosa's demeanor that this was not just a friendly drop-by.

"Have a seat." She pointed to a chair as she walked into the kitchen. "Shall I make some coffee?"

Rosa nodded, and then, shyly and a little awkwardly, she sat down at the kitchen table. In effect, the place was a mess.

"Sorry about all this. I got back from work at two o'clock, and what with one thing and another, I haven't even had time to wash the dishes. . . . Hope you don't mind."

Rosa gestured with one hand as if to say: Please, it's not important.

She didn't have a job and never had, and her house was always neat as a pin. No sooner had Enrico broken something than she was sweeping up the pieces and tossing them into the trash can.

Sandra put the espresso pot on the stove top. She hurried to wash a couple of cups she'd pulled from the dirty dishes piled in the sink. Even though her back was turned, she had no difficulty imagining the expression on Rosa's face and guessing the reason she'd come by.

After all, everyone knew. Everyone in the apartment building talked about it, cautiously, in hushed voices.

Sandra didn't ask any questions. She did no more than flash her a reassuring smile when she turned around and met her gaze. She set out the bare minimum for company: a couple of paper napkins, two small espresso spoons. She set the sugar jar in the middle of the table and, considering the tension, lit a cigarette while she was pouring the hot espresso into the demitasse cups.

"Thanks," Rosa whispered, as she set down her cup. It was the first word she'd spoken.

Sandra sipped her coffee and took a drag on her cigarette. She wondered whether she ought to break the ice, ask her a question. But there was no need.

Rosa turned her eyes toward the open window: The sun was bright and hot, and you could hear the shouting of the kids all the way from the beach. Then she started talking. She spoke calmly, without sidestepping, without hemming and hawing, practically without interruption. She spoke without stopping for ten solid minutes. Probably, in her whole life, she'd never had so much to say.

"Sandra," she began, "you know why I'm here, you can imagine for yourself. . . . The truth is, I can't take it anymore. Today I decided that I had to talk to someone. . . . I have to deal with this situation, I can't avoid it anymore. And not just for myself. Believe me, I'm thirty-three years old; in the village where I grew up, I'm considered an old woman. It doesn't matter about me. I'm doing this for my daughter."

She gave Sandra a long, pleading look, a look of mute despair. Sandra felt an overwhelming sensation of understanding and respect for that woman who, with an enormous effort, was doing her best to express her pain, her sorrow, her grief.

"They went to the party, as you know. . . ." Rosa sat rigidly as she spoke, without moving her hands or any other part of her body. "I gave Francesca permission to go, without saying anything to her father. Because Enrico would never have let her go. He was working the night shift on Ferragosto. He was working a double shift for the overtime, and he wasn't supposed to come home, even for dinner. I told Francesca to go ahead, not to worry, that I'd cover for her, that her father would never find out about it. . . ."

She turned once again to the window, half closing her eyes for a moment of distraction in the heat of the summer sunshine, the lively, undamaged sound of children jumping into the waves.

"I don't want Francesca to wind up like me. . . . I don't want the same thing that happened to me to happen to her. I want her to be able to go out, to have fun like a normal girl. . . . I want her to continue her studies so that one day she can leave, get as far as possible from here. I want her to find a respectable job, a man who really loves her. I've never been to a party in my life, did you know that?"

Sandra nodded. Her blood was running cold as she listened to that woman's cool calmness, the underground strength of that woman who now—enunciating each word clearly—was rebelling.

"So this morning he found out. I don't even know how. Someone must have told him. Because he came in at six this morning and woke us both up. He refused to even speak to me. He just locked me in the bedroom. Then I heard him going into Francesca's bedroom. . . ." She clenched her fists in her lap. "And I couldn't do anything to stop him."

Sandra reached out for her, but Rosa recoiled.

"I could hear the thudding of things. I could hear the thumping of his hands. Francesca doesn't cry, did you know that? She won't cry anymore; she won't say a word. . . . She's become just like me. I could hear the thudding of things, Sandra, I heard them until seven o'clock this morning. And I never heard Francesca's voice. . . . Then he unlocked my door, put on his jacket, and left."

The shouts of children down in the street floated up to the window, and intermittent gusts of wind tossed and straightened the white curtain.

"When I went into her room I saw my daughter lying on the floor. Her face was all bloody; he'd broken her nose. I helped her up from the floor. She wouldn't even look at me. Sandra," she stopped, "you can't imagine what it felt like to pick my daughter up off the floor for the hundredth time."

Sandra took her hand, and this time Rosa didn't flinch away.

"At eight o'clock we took the bus. In the emergency room they asked us lots of questions. I said to her: "This time, we're reporting him to the police, this time we're reporting him to the police." But she kept saying: "No, no, he'll kill us." She was scared out of her mind. But I don't think they believed us in the emergency room. They're going to send social workers to our house. . . . They're going to send social workers to our house, and I have to tell you . . ." She looked up at Sandra—now her eyes were bright—"let them, I'm happy to have them come."

"You have to report him, Rosa. I'll go with you if it would help. We could go now, or tomorrow, whenever you like. . . ."

"Francesca was too frightened, I couldn't bring myself to go to the police. But I want to do it, Sandra. And if he's going to kill me . . ."

"Don't even joke about that. They'll protect you!"

"Where I come from," she smiled, "they don't protect women like me."

Sandra felt a surge of fury. She knew perfectly well that's how it was, that women let their husbands beat them to death and no one says a word. Because it's true that we're in Italy, but Italy is a piece-of-shit country.

"I don't care what happens to me, I only want to make sure that Francesca is safe. That's why I came to ask you . . . When I go to file the complaint—because I'm going to go, this time I swear that I'm going to do it—so when I go, can Francesca come and stay here with you? Can she stay here if there are problems?"

"You shouldn't even have to ask me that, Rosa."

"Thank you, Sandra." Her eyes were veiled with a slight quaver.

"You don't have to thank me."

Rosa stood up.

She was still pretty. At her age many women were still unmarried: they had jobs, traveled, went to the movies, ate out, went dancing.

Sandra stepped over to hug her, and Rosa let her.

"You're a brave woman," Sandra said. "I'll go with you to the police station; you'll see, things will change. . . ." She stroked her hair.

Rosa looked her in the eye. There was something approaching joy on her face now.

"You know," she admitted, "it's strange to say it, at this age, but you're the first real friend I've ever had. . . ."

Even though Sandra was a woman with a strong back, she had a hard time stifling a sob.

"Call me, come see me at any hour of the day or night. Seriously. Whenever you want, I'll go in with you," she said again, at the door.

Rosa nodded. Then she vanished.

Sandra wondered if Rosa would really do it. Go in front of a policeman, sit down, swear out a criminal complaint against the most important person in her life after her own father. Tell things to a stranger that for years she hadn't told anyone, perhaps not even herself. Leave her apartment, find a job, bring up Francesca alone. And maybe, someday, find another man, find something like love.

It was necessary, Sandra thought. At Rosa's age, it was truly necessary. But what about Sandra: Where did she get off giving advice? In all these years . . . what had she ever done?

She let herself drop into her armchair.

It's too late for me, at this point.

She wasn't going to construct a new life for herself. She knew that. She was going to grow old alone.

She didn't feel like washing dishes. She went to look out the window, full of light, where the comforting chirruping of children came in with the sunlight, just like sunlight.

For today, the place could just stay a mess.

She picked up the receiver, dialed her lawyer's number as fast as she could. That was the right thing to do, the only decent thing to do. If not for herself, for her children. For the future, for the children playing on the beach who haven't the slightest idea of how hard it is to do the right things.

CHAPTER 19

On August 22, Anna turned fourteen.
Mattia looked at her ass, the way it switched from side to side under her white sarong. He pushed his way through the leaves of the canebrake and wondered where she was taking him.

The light was brutal, overwhelming.

They'd agreed to meet in the basement stairwell at two o'clock in the afternoon, when everyone was napping. Anna waited for him in hiding, her feet bare on the dirty floor. She smelled of dust and pollen. She'd whispered in his ear: "I know a place."

Now it was a constant, rhythmic repetition. The whining of insects, mosquitoes behind the ear. Mattia was walking along, bare chested, jeans rolled up to his knees. He was obsessed by the hot, curving silhouette of her hips. Her bottom in motion sledgehammered away at his loins.

He was sweating, his calves plunged deep into the muck. The sun was slow-cooking the piles of seaweed. Where the hell is she taking me? He was expecting the dark, close interior of a cabana, or a cellar, with the key turned twice to double lock.

The sun was pouring straight down like a cascade of molten metal onto the sand.

He followed her through that barren wasteland he'd never seen before. A veritable cemetery of boats and empty diesel tanks. A deafening silence, and cats curled up, concealed in the shadows. Mattia was anticipating a secluded, dark spot. He assumed that young girls, for their first time, were afraid to see and to allow themselves to be seen in their details.

That was the hottest day, according to the television weather report.

Relative humidity was 95 percent; the sky was heavy and swollen. Anna slipped off her white pareo, let it slip down onto the sand.

"There's a membrane right at the beginning," she'd said. "A translucent membrane that can look different in different people. I've tried looking at mine, but I couldn't see it."

She smeared her legs with muck where the waves were lapping. She carved holes into the wet sand with the tip of her toe; the water quickly filled them. She was waiting for him.

"I looked up the verb in the dictionary," she'd said, "you say to *deflower*. Remove the flower." As if he didn't know all these things. "It's a funny verb, isn't it?" She'd smiled, childish, mischievous, naughty.

Anna walked into the sea up to her knees. Her swimsuit bottom was riding up in the crack between her ass cheeks; her hair was wet and spattered with sand. She stood still, backlit, rapt as she stared at Elba with one hand in front of her eyes.

Mattia took off his jeans, tossed them onto a rock. The scent of rust, the sun in his face. At 2:00 in the afternoon people hole up in their houses, nodding off on the sofa, their sweat-drenched heads lurching gently.

He caught up with her. He let himself fall into the dark, earthy water of that unfamiliar section of coastline.

"Let's swim out to the buoy," Anna suggested.

Mattia watched her dive in and then bob to the surface, her body spread wide.

He felt uneasy. Like the young boy he'd been when he'd slipped between a woman's legs for the first time, in a sleeping bag. It had been nighttime then; he hadn't seen a thing. There was a little cluster of his friends not far away, smoking marijuana and waiting for him to finish.

Now he and Anna were swimming side by side. They reached deeper water. The sea was warm and still, like the back of a sleeping animal.

It had been eight or nine years since his first time. Years of legs spread-eagled against tiled bathroom walls, in restaurants; against locker doors in gymnasiums, dressing rooms, in other people's king-sized beds, on piles of scattered clothing. So many things Anna had yet to learn about, things that she might do one day, maybe with him. Female students in roadside diners on school field trips. Older women against the dashboard of his car. The nauseating red glow of the private rooms at the Gilda. Possibilities that Anna didn't even suspect.

They swam together, arms reaching in parallel strokes. They bobbed and glided inside the white foam, the currents alternating cold and warm. Mattia spied on her from underwater, the way she unfurled legs, arms, and pelvis in the bare naked seawater. He was good at it, knew how to surge straight down to the sea bottom until he could touch with his fingertips the bed of kelp that was so like a beard.

They reached the buoy; they held on tight to it.

She had told him, as if it were an earthshaking piece of news, that before going to sleep she'd slip her fingers into her panties. Every night she brought herself to a tiny, mute orgasm.

They looked one another in their salt-reddened eyes, their eyelashes dense with water. They braided their legs together under the yellow buoy.

"Tell me something: Who did you used to come here with?"

Anna shot a glance at the beach, at the rubble of a cement floor. Where the cats would congregate, but not now, later . . .

Who was bringing them scraps now? Who knows if the cats still waited for the girls after dinner. The packages of pasta rolled up in a pocket.

"With no one," she answered.

"I don't believe you."

That wasn't the kind of place people go to play hide-and-seek.

The light was blinding. He peered underwater in search of her tiny feet. He ravished her with his eyes. He knew how to flush octopuses from under the rocks; he even knew how to kill them from a considerable distance with a harpoon. He knew how to creep up, move cautiously when necessary.

"Do you like to fish?"

Anna said: "Yes."

"And what else do you like?"

She was blooming. She had something indecipherable in her eyes. Quite simply, she was neither one thing nor another.

He swam over to her, grabbed her hair. Now that he was holding her still, she let him caress her close to her crotch. She was smiling, her lips parted slightly. Mattia nudged aside the hem of her swimsuit bottom underwater, and she squeezed shut her eyes.

"Wait," she said, pulling away from him, "I have to pee."

Mattia watched her, stunned, as she moved away from him.

"You can't come near me," she laughed, "or else I can't pee. . . ."

When they got out of the water Mattia went over to lie down on the overturned hull of a boat.

His body was dark, poised, impatient. He let himself drip in the sunlight, expecting at any moment that Anna would come over. This had been her idea; she had brought him to this place, this redolent broth.

But Anna stayed where she was. Instead of coming to his side she started trying to flush lizards out from under the rocks. She roamed around among the rubble of a pavement, crouching down to pick something up. She was doing it on purpose.

Mattia's nostrils were full of rusty iron and rotten seaweed. He rolled over onto his side to watch her.

Now she was picking up a branch. She had that damned swimsuit knotted on her hips, climbing up her crack, leaving both ass cheeks entirely uncovered. The humidity was unbearable; the light was massive and unchanging. It was like a jackhammer crushing his temples. It was intolerable to watch her padding around barefoot, roving to and fro like a half-pint predator. She was doing it intentionally.

"Come here," he said. Alessio was working this shift, 2:00 to 10:00. Cristiano was on the far side of Piombino, at Torre del Sale. And that little brat was catching a jellyfish, pulling it out of the seawater with the branch, carrying it to a pile of rocks, where she watched it dissolve. Pretending she hadn't heard him.

She wanted to be looked at; there was no other explanation: She liked being looked at. Anna was tormenting the liquefied body of the jellyfish, and as she did she was keeping track of Mattia out of the corner of her eye. She was barely suppressing that lethal smile of hers.

He'd jacked off endlessly to that smile. He had brutalized, in an absolutely violent and sadistic way—in the morning the minute he woke up—that mocking smile of hers. To her it was a game, like learning to ride a motor scooter, like trying to be the fastest on roller skates, at reckless speeds. She wanted to be the first of all her girlfriends. Mattia was no fool; he'd figured it out.

He was ten years older than she; he had fewer romantic illusions about life. He know how to handle weapons, manipulate tension, let himself be led literally by the nose by a half-undone swimsuit clinging to the incandescent body of a playful young girl.

"Leave it alone; it's dissolved."

She didn't have even the slightest suspicion that he might just be able to hurt her. She clearly gave the impression of someone familiar only with the nicer side of the world. The air of having been pampered so far in life. But enough is enough. "Come here," he said, with a tone of voice that clearly conveyed that he had no intention of saying it again.

Anna took a few steps toward him; she pointed out the protuberance that had appeared in his bathing suit. She burst into laughter.

The air was stifling; tomorrow it was going to rain. The sunlight was battering straight down from overhead at 2:30 in the afternoon; tomorrow he'd have to work in that fucked-up factory. Loading and unloading rebar, metric tons of steel fresh from the furnace, still enflamed, red-hot, incandescent.

"Come on," he said. "Forget about the cats, come over here."

This time Anna obeyed. She went over to lie down next to him.

She looked at him with her big eyes, flecked with yellow.

She was done with games. She stood still and wordless at the edge of the boat. Mattia was untying the top of her two-piece; he was undoing the knots of her swimsuit bottom. He slipped it off her legs. Now he could clearly sense all her alarm.

She wasn't ready. He had to hold her steady as he mounted her, his body dark brown and heavy. The sunlight was flowing down onto his back. He held her steady and slowly, gently moistened her. Now you could see the details. Her chestnut hair, her inner pink. The dark, swollen veins of him. You could smell the odor of the details—sharper, more acrid than the smell of seaweed.

He spread her legs, felt with his hand on her belly all her fear. He had to hold her still and caress her. He was sweating, sweating onto her. The sun in her face, the empty sky, the cats lurking in the shadows.

She was old enough; she had the body to do this. But she wasn't ready. Like at the doctor's office, on the examination table. She let herself be touched and waited for something unknown. He was forcing gently, moving gently. It was her birthday. This was her moment.

There was no point in looking up words in the dictionary. *Remove the flower.* This was real; this was much simpler. It hurt like a splinter, like a blunt object that doesn't cut, just thrusts. And the membrane split down the middle, like a fruit.

Anna had her eyes open; she was looking at him like a child seeking reassurance from the wrong person. She'd never been so *together.* She was tumbling softly, smiling quietly, yielding to that full yet indistinct thing. A rocking cradle. A motion like a thousand other things on earth. Warm and constant.

Mattia had sworn, one hand on his heart, a split lip, crumpled on the hood of the Peugeot the night of Ferragosto. He'd sworn an oath.

But Alessio couldn't know, would never understand, how his sister's body writhed, how she moved her pelvis in the hot sunlight. Her soft spots.

He'd never experience that briny acrid scent of hers. The way she knew how to move and give in and come with a childish smile.

She no longer belonged to her brother; she no longer belonged to anyone else.

He'd watched her grow up in the courtyard on the Via Stalingrado, seen her play with Barbie dolls with her little blond friend. He remembered her with her backpack and her little pink checkered school smock. He'd watched her splash in the plastic baby pool on the roof of the apartment building, with a thousand other little kids.

And now he was watching her come.

Watching her lift her head, bring it close to his. Her eyes rumpled, sweat on her face, the incandescent sunlight on her damp face, and that lethal, wonderful smile. Come inside her, unflower her. Anna felt something like a sudden explosion of ants from underground. And she sank back, her head dropped.

Mattia pulled out at the last instant—he ejaculated onto her tummy. He collapsed, his heart blown to bits, on Anna's white breast. An element returning to its place. Alessio was on the crane right now, hoisting mill crucibles brimming with molten steel, his back bent, his forehead pearled with sweat.

While Mattia and Anna were getting to their feet, brushing the sand and the seaweed off themselves, Rosa was ringing Sandra's doorbell and adjusting her hair to bolster her courage.

While Anna was looking around in bewilderment and going into the water to wash the white fluid off her belly, Alessio was snorting another line of coke in the control cab with a coworker, a new hire.

Anna was huddling, her whole body wrapped in Mattia's arms. They'd hidden beneath a boat, like cats. The sun was scorching; a breeze had sprung up. And part of Elba was burning, as always in the summer, in a black spot on Monte Capanne. Anna was peppering Mattia with questions, and Mattia was laughing instead of answering.

Cristiano was watching the forest fire and the black smoke rising from a not otherwise identified point on the island. He didn't know the names of mountains and he detested the Elbans: Let them all be burned alive.

He was sitting in a plastic chair, in the shade of a beach umbrella. They'd gone to Torre del Sale, the beach between the ENEL power plant and the Dalmine-Tenaris steelworks. His first family outing.

They were surrounded by other families. The men were talking about the fires in tones of concern, gesticulating animatedly. Cristiano looked away from the island and turned up the volume on his radio to hear the latest news about the major league soccer drafts.

Jennifer was stretched out on her back in the sun; her hips and ass were now slightly shapeless. She'd definitely lost her body; she no longer resembled the reed-thin, fifteen-year-old girl who had let him make love to her standing up in the basement stairwell or in her parents' darkened changing cabana.

Cristiano held the whining baby in his arms. He'd bought the baby a pair of tiny golden Nike running shoes, a model that was very fashionable right then. He'd spent a huge sum of money on those baby shoes for his tiny man, and yet they were still too big for him: What did he know about baby shoe sizes? He'd told the cashier: "You decide."

Cristiano shifted his gaze back and forth from Jennifer stretched out, with the earphones of her Walkman in her ears, to the snot running down his son's face. He didn't really know what to say or think. He pulled a cloth wipe out of the diaper bag and he cleaned off tiny James's nose. The baby seemed to want to tell him something, but of course he didn't know how to talk yet.

Cristiano couldn't understand a damn thing the kid was grunting. The tiny little eyes made him feel uncomfortable. It was tough; it was heavy. He didn't want to wind up like those forty-year-olds with massive guts, cooler bag always within reach, who waste an hour talking about how Elba catches fire in the summer.

But what could he really become? How the hell would he wind up there, in Piombino, breathing in filthy shit, sitting on top of the excavator at the Lucchini plant, going to the beach on Sundays with his little family . . .

Armed robbery. He could talk to Mattia about it. A post office, the local branch office of a bank. Weapons leveled. Surging adrenaline. And then disappear; go spend your days doing nothing in some bitching faraway place. He smiled. He caressed James's little hairless head.

"Papa's going to take you to Brazil," he whispered in his ear, "to see the carnival!"

But James was born only six months ago; he didn't understand words. And without warning James started wailing like a psychotic, obliging Cristiano to call Jennifer, to shout to make himself heard through the earphones of her Walkman.

CHAPTER 20

As soon as she got home, Anna slipped into the bathroom without even saying hello to her mama. She went straight to the toilet and sat down, lowered the bottom of her swimsuit and began scrutinizing it carefully. In fact, there was a stain.

She took the bar of soap and scrubbed furiously in the bathroom sink, eliminating the stain that no one could see. A little, she was sorry to see it fade. But then she realized: It was only fading; she couldn't get it out entirely. She had no desire to stand there scrubbing for half an hour. She balled up the swimsuit bottom and went and hid it under her bed.

When she emerged and walked into the kitchen, it was unmistakable that there was something new about her. On any other day Sandra probably would have noticed immediately. She would have put two and two together, drawing a line between the mess in the bathroom, the missing swimsuit bottom, the rumors about that young man who'd come back from Russia, and the aggressive smile on her daughter's face. She would have figured it out, at any other time.

Right now she was sitting in the armchair, her head plunged between the pages of *Liberazione*. But she wasn't reading. When she heard Anna's bare feet padding closer to her, she raised her head and folded up her newspaper. She saw a yard-long trail of sand mixed with other trash on the floor she'd just swept.

"How many times have I told you to rinse off your feet?"

Anna grabbed a peach from the basket of fruit and sank her teeth into it.

"My God, you're a mess," said Sandra, shaking her head. "You don't even bother to peel it?"

"I like the peel," Anna said, with her mouth full. "It's fuzzy!"

She spit the peach pit directly into the sink. Sandra stood up from her easy chair, visibly angered. What kind of manners are these—is this how I taught you to behave? But before she could say anything, Anna focused her gaze straight at her: "When is *your husband* coming home?"

She'd caught her off guard, the sly little devil. The classic, arrogant little face that drove Sandra crazy with irritation.

"I don't know when *your father* is coming home." She slapped the newspaper onto the ground. "He called yesterday, muttered something. . . . He said to say hi to you and to keep an eye on you."

She forced herself to laugh. "Oh, you're doing a great job of keeping an eye on me. . . ."

Sandra picked up the broom and started sweeping up the sand on the floor. Anna watched her pensively.

"Is he okay?"

Her mother was sweeping furiously, in the corners and under the furniture.

"Oh, he's fine. . . . How would I know?! He's alive," she hissed, "he's got his business deals, he has his artworks. . . . And why not? He's a busy man now, right? But I don't even want to know what he's doing. I'd rather not know! Anyway, he says he'll be back tomorrow."

Anna, when she heard the word *tomorrow*, felt a sort of sudden joy that she did her best to conceal.

Sandra put down the broom, rummaged through a side table and a kitchen drawer in search of a pack of cigarettes.

"I don't believe for a second that he's coming. . . . He's living the good life now, what do you think? Somebody saw him in San Vincenzo, they told me about . . ." She stopped brusquely: It wasn't right to say those things to her daughter. "I hope he comes back," she tried to adjust her approach. "I hope he comes back soon, because otherwise, . . ." but she couldn't correct course. "Your brother's an idiot, that's what! He went in and put a down payment on the VW Golf—he's taking out a loan to buy a car! So why do I always have to work my fingers to the bone? Just a tiny bit of brains, that's what I say, just a little intelligent thought, Jesus Christ!"

Whenever Anna heard her mother talking about money problems, she felt a sense of annoyance, practically of mortification. She had no desire to be depressed, today of all days, but she felt a wave of gloom sweep over her all the same. Let's hope he really does come to lunch tomorrow. . . .

She turned to go back to her bedroom. She needed to think it over, to reason it out, and she wasn't sure exactly what: whether it was Mattia, her crumpled swimsuit bottom, or her father whose only presence at home for the past month had been phone calls. She was about to turn and leave and pull the door shut behind her when Sandra said: "Wait, I need to talk to you."

Anna turned in alarm and looked directly into her mother's eyes. She'd been seized with a sudden, entirely irrational fear that she'd been discovered: the swimsuit bottom and everything else.

"Francesca's mother came by today. . . ."

Anna froze to the spot.

"There are some things I need to tell you. Sit down."

She sat down mechanically, her heart racing.

"I don't know what Francesca has told you about . . ." she exhaled hard, "her father."

Anna made a blank face, as if to say: Yes, but go on.

"Anyway, Enrico found out that you went to the party, and he beat Francesca. He broke her nose. Apparently, this is hardly the first time. It's become a habit for that pig. . . ."

Anna's hands began tormenting the edge of the table.

"Rosa wants to report him to the police, file a criminal complaint. I completely agree. I'm willing to go with her, to testify, whatever she needs." Sandra raised her voice, in the face of injustice. She would have to take up the issue at party headquarters, start a discussion about violence against women. Not the violence of Romanian thugs in the street, but this nightmare, in the apartment downstairs.

She calmed down. "Rosa wants Francesca to come stay with us for a while. . . . She's afraid, which makes perfect sense. She thinks that once she reports him to the police, Enrico might do something crazy. I can understand." She finally lit the cigarette and took a deep drag of nicotine.

"This morning, she had to take Francesca to the emergency room. . . ."

There was no need to say more.

Anna leaped to her feet. Her hands, her eyes, and her lips were all quivering with rage. An overwhelming sense of guilt. Her face was incredulous, incredibly pale, a chasm opened in the center of her chest. She looked at her mother for a few seconds. She was disgusted with herself. She made a dash for the front door, threw it open, and ran out without even closing it behind her. She went scrambling down the steps as fast as her legs would carry her.

Asshole! She kept shouting it at herself as she went. She was taking the steps two at a time. She felt like slapping herself in the face, plunging down the steps, and cracking open her head. How the fuck could she have ever left her alone? Pretending to ignore her for an entire week. . . . Just because Francesca had put on a sullen face, just because she'd made friends with Lisa.

And now she'd done what she'd done with Mattia, she'd taken him to that place. . . . She'd betrayed her friend, betrayed her world! Now Francesca was a mass of bruises. He'd beaten her up, that monster. Anna believed that she alone could rescue Francesca. The only one who knew, the only one with the power . . . What power? She wished she could shatter her body by slamming into the cement, feel an immense physical pain that would drown out whatever it was that was gnawing at her lungs, her stomach, and her heart.

She went galloping down the stairs barefoot, covered with sand, her eyes glaring with rage, filled with desperation, swearing over and over, a thousand times: *To hell with Mattia, I'll give him up, I'll give up anything. . . . Right now I have to hug Francesca, now I have to make sure nobody can hurt her again.*

She came to a stop in front of the door. The door that was always dark, always closed, the threshold she was never allowed to cross. *I don't give a damn, I'm going in there now.* She pressed down on the doorbell with her index finger for a good long time. *You're not tricking me again; this time you have to let me in.* But no one came to the door. *God damn it to hell.* She redoubled the ringing. Once, twice, ten times she leaned on that fucking doorbell, hammering away at the inferno where her Francesca was confined, an inferno that had to end once and for all.

Enough is enough. Now Francesca was coming to live at her house. Like a real sister, the way things ought to be. They'd sleep in the same bed together. Arms wrapped around one another. They'd eat breakfast together every morning, they'd go to school by motor scooter. And she'd wait for Francesca after school, outside the front gate of the IPS.

I don't give a damn, she was shouting in her mind, with her finger glued to the doorbell. *I'm not budging from here, I'm not leaving until I see her. And when I leave, she's coming with me. That monster is never going to see her again. He's going to jail, and he's going to rot there. They're going to toss him in prison, and he'll be covered with mold in his cell, like the black mold that he is. I'll kill him if someone doesn't come open this door.*

She heard steps. She heard the lock turn. The door swung open, no more than was necessary to glimpse a face.

Two eyes gleamed in the half light, with a dark and chilly glitter. Those weren't Francesca's eyes; they weren't Rosa's eyes either.

Enrico was staring at her without a word.

He was a giant. A mottled face of red flesh, mute and enormous.

Anna staggered slightly as she stepped back. It was only with enormous effort that she managed to say, stammering softly: "I was looking for Francesca. . . ."

The man didn't blink an eye. Maybe he sensed the terror of the little girl standing before him. Maybe he didn't. He seemed like a giant empty shell, a massive body, a human firearm. He didn't seem to feel any emotion, any thought. He seemed incapable of speech.

"Francesca's not here," he said. "Francesca doesn't keep bad company."

He shut the door.

Anna covered her mouth with one hand. To keep from screaming, to keep from sobbing, to restrain the fury and the fear that she was experiencing. She turned and ran away, as fast as she could go, down the remaining three flights of stairs.

When she came out into the courtyard it was 6:00 in the evening. It was still light out. She burst into tears of despair. The girls clustered around her, asking her what was wrong. Anna was sobbing as if someone had just died; she weakly punched Sonia and Maria as they tried to calm her down.

But Anna refused to calm down. She went on struggling and sobbing loudly. She went on for a good long ten minutes at least. Then she shoved the other girls away, went over to the bench and collapsed on it, on the bench where they had written their names in pink uni-POSCA. She was weeping softly now. She was weeping silently. Her hair was full of sand, there was seaweed stuck to her calves, her sarong was dirty and damp. She looked like the barefoot little match girl in the fairy tale by Andersen.

From her window, behind the curtain, Francesca watched her cry and wept along with her.

She'd heard when Anna rang the doorbell. She'd heard her father answer the door.

Her mother was knitting in the living room. She was locked up in her bedroom. Francesca's body was covered with bruises. Her nose still hurt. She'd felt a tremendous twinge when she'd recognized Anna's voice.

But now, as she peered out from behind the curtains, she wasn't crying about her father anymore, she wasn't crying about the bruises and the beatings. She was crying because it was all Anna's fault.

CHAPTER 21

The summer was ending; the light of each day was growing shorter. September was beginning. Anna went to Mattia's house to make love—a small, dark apartment at the far end of the Via Stalingrado that was always a mess.

In the end, Alessio had given in. He'd sat each of them down, his friend and his sister, and he had delivered a little lecture. "Kids, you have my blessing. But no fucking around as long as she's a minor," he had warned them in a paternal tone of voice. And Mattia had hastened to agree: "Of course, you kidding?"

Now Anna would go and wait for her boyfriend to get off work outside the main gate of the Lucchini steelworks or else tell him to come by and pick her up downstairs from her apartment. Alessio was no idiot, but he preferred to think that all they did was sit holding hands and gazing into each other's eyes. The truth was, though, that every chance they got they made love: on the big unmade double bed, with the shutters pulled down; in the bathroom, on the toilet or in the shower, and even in the hallway, against the door.

Alessio watched Anna get into his friend's car, all made-up and giddy: She planted a kiss on Mattia's lips, fooled around a bit with the car radio, turned the volume all the way up, and then they'd race away, tires screeching. Alessio would softly begin cursing and roll a joint.

One day Mattia told Anna that his mother was dead; it had been a brain tumor. That his father was somewhere in the world, but not here. Confiding these things had brought them much closer together.

Mattia would smoke a cigarette after they made love, he'd tell her pieces of his life. He even told her that he'd done bad things, made mistakes, committed crimes, but now he had no intention of falling back into that trap. Anna was filled with admiration as she listened to him. She'd also secretly started smoking.

Every time Francesca saw Anna she'd walk straight ahead, her eyes lowered and a little fake smile on her lips. In fact, for ten days or so, Anna had obstinately waited for her in the courtyard, on their bench, and had tried to talk to her; more than once she'd actually seized her by the arm and dragged her aside. But Francesca never stopped, never wanted to hear a word. She kept on walking, entered the ground-floor door of building number 8, and rang Lisa's doorbell. Until one day, after lunch, Anna wasn't there in the usual place. And then, even if she'd never admit it to herself, she felt a pang in her stomach.

Francesca spent every afternoon at Lisa's, just like Anna spent every afternoon at Mattia's. Only Francesca wasn't making love, had no interest in doing so, and had broken things off with Nino, too. She hung out in Lisa's bedroom, letting Lisa admire her, and playing *scala quaranta* and *ramino*—variations on gin rummy. Francesca had taught Lisa how to put on makeup, and she'd taken her to the open-air market to buy some decent clothes. Lisa had talked and talked to her about Donata, who was in the room next door with the sheet pulled up, her pills on the bedside table, and the shutters permanently pulled down.

Lisa's sister was doing worse. She couldn't even move her arms or mouth anymore. She could no longer smile that strange smile of hers. She no longer smiled; she only drooled out a few incomprehensible words. No one in that house mentioned Anna's name. No one in that house wanted to admit that Donata was dying.

One day in September, the second or the third, she'd gone with her mother to the Coop to buy a desk diary, a pen and pencil case, and notebooks for the new school year. Mattia was sitting at a table outside, at Aldo's, the bar at the marina of Salivoli.

He was smoking a cigarette and looking at the clear early autumn sky, sipping his Negroni without haste. At that time of the morning there was practically no one around. The foosball table was silent. An old man was reading *Il Tirreno,* his eyeglasses perched at the tip of his nose, half a cigar dangling from his mouth. A Maghrebi immigrant was hitting the levers of the video poker slot machine, but he wasn't winning. Even the radio was turned off.

Then Mattia saw Cristiano coming toward him. *Oh, what a tremendous pain in the ass*, he thought. Cristiano was walking the way he usually did, lanky in his baggy thug jeans. His hair was spiky and tufted with gel, and there was a new piercing beneath his lower lip. He looked like he was heading straight for him: that was the last thing he needed.

Cristiano sat right down at his table and ordered a glass of whiskey. Mattia had no desire to talk with him. If nothing else, he just wanted to be left alone, to think for himself about his own concerns.

Instead Cristiano wanted to talk; it was clear that he'd swallowed a tab of amphetamine.

"I'm working the night shift today," Mattia replied. "They've got me working rebar, but they might be moving me over to the converters. . . ."

"The converters are so much better!" Cristiano said, emphatically. "You don't have to lift a fucking finger!"

Mattia didn't feel like talking at all, least of all about the Lucchini plant.

"How's your kid?" he asked distractedly, just to change the topic.

Cristiano covered his face with both hands: "It's out of control, Mattia. That kid cries every blessed night. He starts crying while I'm fucking, you understand? Every single time, god damn it. And she always gets up. Just let him cry for a while, right?"

Mattia wasn't listening to him; he was just looking at him blankly.

"But in the end, it's not the kid who's getting on my nerves. He'll grow up, he'll mind his own fucking business eventually. . . . He can even be fun, sometimes. No, it's Jennifer that's been busting my balls. I made a mistake when I moved in with her, and she lives with her parents, just to make things worse! You can't imagine what a pain in the ass her parents can be. . . ."

He talked without stopping for fifteen minutes.

Mattia drank off the last of his Negroni, looked at the faces of the customers entering the bar. Little kids wearing flip-flops who wanted tokens to play foosball. Millworkers in overalls, old men who claimed they had no need of Viagra. Mattia put down his glass, looked over to see how the Maghrebi was doing on the video poker machine. Cristiano just went on talking frenetically. He wasn't a bad guy, he was just tiresome. And Mattia had practically made up his mind to pay for his drink and leave.

"Listen," Cristiano said, lowering his voice and his chin toward the table. "I came here because there's something I need to talk to you about. . . ."

Cristiano had an almost serious expression on his face now.

Oh great, thought Mattia. Then he decided that he could make this extra effort, and he sat back. He started toying with a plastic straw.

"You know you can trust me, right? I don't run my mouth, and after all, I'm not exactly . . ." he smiled, "a saint. You know, the coke dealing, various things . . ."

"Get to the point." Mattia was already growing impatient.

"No, that is . . . I know that you're in contact with certain guys from Follonica. . . ."

Mattia's expression changed.

"I know that those guys are professionals, and I've heard that you know what you're doing, too. . . . I heard all about it, the robbery in 1998, a nice little job done right. . . . I'm sick of this life, Mattia, I am sick to death of the Lucchini plant and Gianfranco, who busts my balls if I'm a minute late to work but has stopped even paying me overtime; in other words . . . So what I'm saying is I'd be interested, that is, in giving it a try. And I know you can give me a hand."

"No way."

"Come on, Mattia. . . . Everyone knows that. . . . Don't be a jerk. All I'm asking is to let me pull a job with you, something small. . . . I'm no beginner; I know what I'm doing."

"I don't do that kind of job; you must have been misinformed."

"Shit, I told you, you can trust me!"

"I don't know anyone from Follonica." Mattia was speaking in a tough, calm voice, but he was clearly uneasy.

"All I need is a handgun and a phone number. . . ."

A handgun? He's lost his mind, thought Mattia. He's completely fried his brain. This guy is the last idiot on earth who could pull off a decent armed robbery.

"Forget about it," he said, in a tone of voice that meant the discussion was over. "You don't know what you're talking about."

"Oh, I don't? Yes I do." He seemed a little frenzied and wrecked. "I'm very well informed, my friend. You may not like it, but I'm in, Mattia, and I know a lot of things. For instance, I know that your little sweetheart's dad? He's their hookup here in Piombino."

Mattia sat there, openmouthed, the straw forgotten in his hand.

"Just don't say anything to Alessio, though, do me that favor. He'll go ballistic if he hears about it."

He'd turned pale as a rag, and now he was ripping the straw into small pieces.

"I thought you knew that. I was sure of it. . . ."

Mattia stood up from the table and went to settle his bill.

"Let me tell you as a friend," he said, walking past him as he left. "Forget about it."

Cristiano sat there, like a small child who's put his foot on it and realizes it only later, and is starting to feel a little ashamed of himself.

Mattia got in his car and slammed the door hard. He wanted to go straight home and wait for Anna. He'd never have imagined. He sincerely hoped that this latest information about her father was just one more case of Cristiano spouting bullshit.

Anna was moving busily among the shelves in the store, filling the shopping cart with things that Sandra systematically evaluated in terms of cost and utility, after which she returned many of them to their shelves. Anna rummaged frantically through the bins of pen cases, in the throes of some kind of enthusiasm. She was convinced she could sort out everything at any time.

The new school year was starting. She only expected the best things from this year. She'd learned to drive her brother's Aprilia SR. Mattia had given her lessons in an empty parking lot, and she'd become an expert driver. She'd been to the health clinic, and now she had a prescription for birth control pills. She was convinced that any minute things would return to normal, the way they had been. That it was just a passing thing. That Francesca would ring her doorbell, any day now, and they'd throw their arms around one another.

Anna stood in line at the cash register, convinced that she was the same as she'd always been.

CHAPTER 22

The weatherman was announcing temperatures eight to ten degrees higher than average when the doorbell rang.

It was Sunday morning, the last Sunday of summer.

They stopped, in the middle of breakfast, cookies poised over their bowls of *caffellatte*, and exchanged quizzical glances. The voice of the weatherman, a colonel in the Italian air force, announced sunshine over the length of the Italian peninsula. A presentiment shared by many. Sandra got up and went to the door.

The sound of rubber soles on the floor. Brisk, syncopated steps.

Arturo came in, sheathed in a memorable pinstripe that wafted a scent of dry cleaning. A tray of pastries, nicely wrapped, in one hand, a pearl gray jacket draped over the other.

"*Buon giorno*," he said.

His children sat, frozen in surprise, in their chairs. His wife appeared in her dressing gown behind him and went over to lean against the doorjamb.

"It's nice to see you all looking well!" As if he hadn't abandoned them, alone and dealing with an array of problems, for almost the entire summer. He was glad to see them looking well: They glared silently.

Arturo dropped his overcoat on the sofa and then sat down, crossing his legs. The theater had lost a natural talent. Not even a threadbare excuse, not even the shadow of a modicum of shame.

"Go on, open the pastries . . ."

He was as excited as a punk kid who'd just stolen his first motor scooter, who can hardly believe that he's gotten away with it, overjoyed even though he knows he's done wrong.

Where had he slept? Did he have a lover now?

Arturo smiled a rogue's smile.

Sandra had to make a tremendous effort to control herself, to conceal her embarrassment, the discomfort that she felt in the presence of his new clothing, the impeccable pleat of his trousers (who had ironed them for him?), this new husband who, no matter what, even polished to a dazzling gleam, remained a miserable scoundrel, a half criminal.

Anna timidly nibbled her cookie.

There wasn't the slightest, even the most distant family resemblance between the tailored fabric of his suit and the upholstery of the sofa, the tablecloth, his wife's rumpled dressing gown. The sunlight poured in, high and bright in the sky, through the white curtain, and Sandra straightened her hair and did her futile best to neaten her disheveled blouse and get a grip on her nerves.

The clarion theme music of the morning news program rang out.

"I'm back," he said with a gulp, "for good."

Alessio had lost his appetite.

"Look, isn't this still my house?"

Silence of the grave.

Then Arturo slipped his hand into the inside breast pocket of his jacket. This time he'd really show them something that would amaze them. It was the grand gesture he'd been waiting all his life to make, the culminating scene in the movie he had in his mind. He pulled out of his pocket a little red-velvet ring box. He had that gleaming smile stamped on his face and a healthy glow on his cheeks, and it clashed colossally with his wife's compressed lips, his son's icy surprise. Anna held her breath in anticipation at the sight of the red snap box.

He opened it. He pulled out what was in it. He showed it to Sandra.

The ring that Arturo held in one hand was the most precious thing she'd ever seen.

"I'm back for good," he said again, "to give you the lives you deserve."

Sandra was dazzled, in spite of herself. She didn't want to be swept away, but she could feel herself giving in. In violation of all the beliefs she'd endorsed in a lifetime of party activism, union meetings, and rallying cries, she slipped the diamond ring onto her finger. Her husband was smooth shaven, the foulard neatly wrapped around his neck was scented with cologne.

Alessio stood up from the kitchen table, shoving his chair noisily across the floor. The playacting was more than he could stomach.

"Where are you going?" his father cried in alarm.

"To the bathroom," his son replied, in disgust.

He'd always been like that, troublesome and argumentative. Arturo had never understood him. His son had always tacitly blamed him for something. But for what? He didn't have a crystal ball, how could he say?

"Listen. Your car is parked downstairs," he hastened to say, with the confidence of someone who knows he has an ace up his sleeve and is about to play it. "Here are the keys."

He vigorously slammed down a key ring with an enormous Volkswagen logo on it.

"It's been paid for," he smiled triumphantly. "It's all yours."

Alessio turned to look at him. Incredulous, this time.

The incredible power of money.

"I parked it downstairs, right outside, by the dumpster."

Alessio's expression had changed. He hated his father, but his expression had changed all the same. His father smiled enthusiastically at him.

Alessio stood there without moving for a few seconds, torn in a way that he had rarely experienced. He didn't want to give his father the satisfaction; he didn't trust him. Arturo was looking at him, a mixture of arrogance and tenderness; suddenly he had become the generous father that he'd always imagined himself to be.

"Come on, at least go take a look . . ."

He looked at him beseechingly.

His son couldn't refuse to go take a look. He grabbed the car keys, walked right out of the apartment in his pajamas.

Sandra was doing some reckoning in her head. He unwrapped the pastries nonchalantly, walked around the room offering. And as he moved she was doing some rough accounting. She added up hypothetical sums with multiple zeros; her head was roaring like an oven, rounding off, upward or downward, depending. She hadn't the faintest idea what a diamond might cost. That is, if he'd paid for it. . . .

She didn't want to know. She wasn't interested. In the days that followed Arturo continued to pull gifts out of his jacket pocket, as if performing a recurring sleight of hand: money for the rent, including the back rent; money to pay off the dishwasher and the car radio. Each time, she'd see wads of cash appear, and she would avoid asking questions. She—his wife—would pocket the money, which kept popping out like rabbits from a magician's hat, without ever asking (even to herself, even in her mind) the simplest and most obvious question.

"Are you happy?" he asked her, gesturing for her to stand up and reaching an arm around her waist.

She was going to call her lawyer, tell him to drop the divorce proceedings, and as she did so, she'd feel a faint sense of shame. She was doing it for the money. And not only. The yearning to believe in something she couldn't really believe in. Sandra dove into her husband's arms. It was a Valium effect, the automatic church bells that rang the hour. The Mass was over, the Mass that no one had attended.

Anna had said nothing the whole time.

"What about me?" she finally demanded. "Didn't you bring me anything?"

After lunch Alessio took his father for a drive in the new VW Golf GT.

There was a pine-shaped car freshener dangling from the rearview mirror emanating the scent of the eighties. Alessio was maintaining a steady thirty miles per hour. His father was leaning back comfortably into the anatomically configured passenger seat, his necktie loosened, a pair of sunglasses. They talked about women and cars, with a hint of awkwardness in their voices.

Alessio was driving, caressing the steering wheel, caressing the engine with a sharp and attentive ear. He drove raptly, the sun off to one side, tinted glass in the rear windshield, which only the coolest guys have. The tires glided over the asphalt imperceptibly, gracefully, and the upholstery absorbed all noise. The interior was muffled and climate controlled.

Arturo was looking out at the spreading landscape, the way the colors of September glittered in the sun. This is what he wanted. The cheerful gardens where small children played unfurled alongside him, the couples sitting on benches or out walking their dogs. He too was on the right side of everything now. The clean, slightly blurred landscape of families on a Sunday afternoon.

This is what counts. A new car, polished and gleaming, with the clouds, the trees, and the houses all reflected on the hood. That's the sign of achievement. Air-conditioning. Waving to pedestrians through the glass of the passenger window as they slow down in Viale Marconi. Drive along next to the sidewalk: we're people with nothing to fear.

Alessio was driving, gauging the performance of his dream in silence. He turned onto the state highway that skirted the perimeter of the steel mill for about six miles or so. They were father and son now; it was sort of an embarrassing thing. He switched on the Clarion car radio and kept the music low, in the background. It was nondescript music, a radio station he'd tuned in at random. Blurring past on the right were the red-striped smokestacks, the translucent flames of the converters. Looming over all, grim and rusted, stood the tower of A-Fo 4, the one thing that never stops.

"Why do you keep on working in this shitty place?"

"Because there aren't any alternatives."

His father turned to look at him through the dark lenses of his Ray-Bans.

"I don't understand you. . . . You could do anything else you set your mind to!"

He let the bigger cars pass him. There were big SUVs with Milan and Florence license plates that flew past with a distinctly violent manner.

"I get unemployment insurance."

There were the last tourists of the day: They'd just left the ferryboat from Elba and were in a hurry to get back home.

"I get a monthly salary," said Alessio, shifting gears and accelerating.

He suddenly felt like annoying the driver of a BMW X5 who was tailgating and flashing his brights at him.

Arturo lit a cigarette, rolled down his window, and the screeching noise of the factory invaded his small and obtuse kingdom.

"Anything," he said, looking scornfully out the window, "is better than being a factory worker."

"I don't know what else I could do."

"You lack initiative, you lack a willingness to accept risk. . . ."

The radio was playing "Fotoromanza" by Gianna Nannini. What he lacked, what he really missed, was Elena, and it was like a hole in his heart. He avoided telling his father that the hardest work was to find it in his heart to forgive him.

"When I was your age, I had ideas, I had dreams. I was hungry for success. . . ." He smiled. "And as far as that goes, I still am! Anyway, anything is better than working at the Lucchini plant."

Alessio turned toward San Vincenzo, the factory shrank in the rearview mirror. The exact translation of his father's dreams had been this: an 850-square-foot apartment on the fourth floor of a giant public housing project, and two foreclosures. They were in the hills now. The signs by the side of the road: CANTALOUPES AND WATERMELONS: 1 EURO/2,000 LIRE.

Arturo tossed his cigarette butt out the window, lowered the sun visor, and took a look at himself in the makeup mirror. His son had become a factory worker; he'd acquired the mind-set of the loser who pays his taxes and takes it up the ass.

Alessio let slip a bitter little smile.

"Let's go to Baratti," he said, just to change the subject.

"If I were in your position, I'd give it a try."

"You'd give what a try?"

"Getting a different job!" his father raised his voice. "Get into business, try taking a little fucking initiative! Or else keep taking it up the ass the way you're doing; you'll get cancer, you'll be old by the time you're forty, if you even get to forty. . . ."

Arturo had punched the dashboard with his fist. Alessio had a bitter taste in his mouth.

He turned left, heading for Populonia. The Etruscan tombs were rocks surrounded by crowds of tourists. It was September, and there were still long lines of people waiting to visit a necropolis of assholes who'd lived three thousand years ago.

"You and me are not the same," said Alessio, pronouncing each word clearly. "Accept it. I like taking it up the ass all right, I like pouring molten steel into the mill crucibles, I like being seen as a loser in life. What I don't like is ass-fucking my fellow man."

The indicator on the speedometer shot forward from forty to fifty-five miles per hour.

His father sat without speaking now, barricaded behind dark lenses. But his hands had begun to torment the seat stitching.

"And what have you ever done, eh? You bought me a car?" Alessio spat out. "I guess that makes you pretty smart."

Arturo said nothing. The surging tide of things unspoken churned inside him.

That evening he'd listen carefully to the late-night edition of the local news report. He'd wait to hear a specific news item, and in fact he heard it. He'd make a phone call in the middle of the night. He'd make another phone call, his heart rate soaring out of control. And then he'd lie awake, unable to sleep.

CHAPTER 23

Francesca was crumbling a slice of bread; she had no intention of eating it. She balled up the white crumb with minute attention until she had reduced it to so many tiny spheres of something resembling Silly Putty. As she did she watched her father's hands, noticing how delicate they could be with gears and cogs, how they could almost caress them. Careful, precise movements, entirely unconnected to his brain, which was incapable, no matter how hard he tried, of understanding what was broken and how to fix it.

Enrico was focused on one thing: fixing the juicer. Next to him was his toolbox, with every tool neatly stored in its proper compartment. He pulled out a screwdriver, a wrench. He immediately put them away.

Francesca kept an eye on him, under her lashes. With his eyeglasses on, he looked older. She was sitting next to him in the chilly kitchen. The sun never shone into that room, no matter what the time of day. That morning at least she was hoping for a word from her parents, anything, such as: "Have a good first day at school." But it never came. All she received were the usual silent nods of the head.

Her father stood up and walked over to plug in the juicer. It didn't work. He sat down and began disassembling the juicer again. He was endlessly patient when it came to this kind of job.

"Don't worry about it; we'll buy a new one. . . ."

Rosa's voice was a feeble mewing drowned out by the clinking of wrenches.

He said nothing in reply; he just started over.

Francesca despised breakfast: the way her meal was set out impeccably on the floral tablecloth. Her hatred was calm and orderly: the napkin neatly rolled in the napkin ring, the coffee cup in the matching saucer, the juice glass on the coaster. Francesca wasn't old enough to smile at certain things. She lost her appetite when school started and her father wasn't working the 6:00 A.M. to 2:00 P.M. shift.

The television was broadcasting the morning talk show, *Uno Mattina*: Luca Giurato was showing how to bone a chicken. His was the one human voice that could be heard. Francesca kept her eyes on the table while she ate her helping of marmalade and spied on her father and mother.

Nothing was happening.

Rosa was sitting in her armchair, as usual. But she'd demanded a kitten. That's right: a kitten. She woke up one morning with this idea in her head, and for the first time in her life she'd insisted on having her way. She'd kept on throwing little tantrums every day, all day long. This was such an unprecedented thing that in the end Enrico brought her a kitten: a black-and-white kitten that he'd found deep in the basement of an industrial shed at the Lucchini steel plant. He'd come home with that little feral beast wrapped in a towel. The ogre, suddenly catapulted into a Barilla commercial.

Rosa was knitting a scarf. The animal was perched in her lap. The cat was always with her now. This was the main new development. Maybe, if she'd gone to the police two weeks ago instead of going to the doctor, she wouldn't have insisted on a cat—a cat that covers everything with fur and rips up the upholstery of the sofa.

Enrico reassembled the juicer for the fourth or fifth time. He hadn't shaved in days. Francesca didn't let down her guard; she nibbled off tiny flakes of cookie and chewed them as slowly as possible. There was a minimum time necessary, which she had learned to calculate and observe, in which to eat breakfast without offending anyone. She had to eat everything, or slip it into her pockets, ward off nausea and keep her eyes down; she had to pretend to listen to the television, wait at least a quarter of an hour, and then get up, taking special care not to scrape the chair legs on the floor.

Her family had never gotten around to buying those little pads that you can attach to the bottom of the legs of furniture. But that was no reason for Francesca to take a slap to the head.

If her mother had only had the sense to go to police headquarters, instead of to her public health physician . . .

Francesca looked at the clock and wiped the orange juice away from the corners of her mouth with her napkin.

The doctor was the same bastard who'd stitched up her wrist. But in Rosa's mind—what Rosa had learned in the godforsaken village in the Aspromonte where she was born—is that a doctor is the one who really knows. What do policemen know? Doctors have graduate degrees and make lots of money.

One Monday morning Rosa had gathered her courage, put on her only decent outfit, and gone to wait in the crowded medical clinic. She'd waited hours for her name to be called; she'd rehearsed in her mind what she needed to say. She'd said it over and over a dozen times, nodding her head, the way you practice an oral report for school. When the time came to say the words out loud, though, in front of the doctor's desk, she got flustered, then burst into tears, and then actually started laughing.

A depressive crisis, the doctor had concluded. He'd prescribed Prozac and sleeping pills.

Francesca walked over to the sink and set down her cup; she swept the crumbs off the tablecloth. Enrico had finally managed to get the juicer working, with a timid half smile, like an insecure child who has worked out a multiplication problem.

She could have contacted the city social workers; she could have gone to get advice from a lawyer. But Satta, the doctor, wasn't there to solve family problems, *unsolvable* family problems.

Rosa always smiled the same way these days, vague and remote. She made no distinction, smiling equally at her daughter, at the cat, at anything. And Francesca had started to hate her. Francesca had started doing the housework because her mother was always tired now.

But she could hear them, at night. The dull, recurrent thuds through the door, coming down the dark, stuffy hallway. The blows coming faster. The raucous grunts. Those walls were too thin; they were hollow. Francesca lay motionless, head hidden, sheet pulled taut, motionless like a hunted animal. To keep from hearing the noises, the acceleration, the horrible gasps that came from her parents. The effect of Prozac.

Francesca put on her jacket, picked up her schoolbag, and waved goodbye from the threshold of the door. A bottomless sense of disgust for those two sorry beasts. She closed the door quietly, carefully behind her. At eight o'clock she was supposed to meet Lisa in the courtyard. They'd pedal their bikes together all the way to Montemezzano, uphill all the way, to the complex of high schools. On last year's schoolbag Anna's uni-POSCA scribblings could still be seen.

. . .

The bell rang at 8:15 A.M.

Ten years ago the high schools were all downtown, old three-story buildings with windows overlooking the sea, and at recess everyone went down to the port to make out or smoke a cigarette. Now they'd moved the high schools out onto the state highway, between a balding soccer field and a gas station. Four cube-shaped cement blocks.

Across the street loomed the Lucchini steelworks, with its blast furnaces.

Francesca said good-bye to Lisa at the entrance to building number 1, the *liceo classico*. She'd glimpsed Anna's Aprilia SR parked by the front door. She said good-bye, taking care to barely graze her cheek, without kissing her. Then she ran to the front door of building number 4, the IPS.

The school bells all rang at the same time.

No sooner had she entered the new classroom than she heard howls and wolf whistles from all sides.

"Damn, what a piece!" was the chorus as she edged past the desks. A herd of morons.

She went and sat down in the back, near the window.

Familiar, interchangeable faces, bodies sprawled out on the teacher's desk. They were nearly all male, many of them had been held back from last year, many were from Via Stalingrado. They were kids who went to school to cause trouble, warming a chair because the law required them to warm that chair.

Two years, maximum, and they'd all be working in the steel mill. Hoisting mill crucibles, losing arms, making steel.

Francesca opened her backpack and arranged a notebook and a pen neatly on her desk. She ignored the comments of the boys, the obscene words that the boys with porn mags in their pockets were calling out. She couldn't say what she was doing there. The law wasn't a good enough reason; a government decree makes little sense if reality is completely at variance with it.

She didn't bother to turn to look at the face of the person sitting next to her. She didn't care: Whoever it was, it wasn't Anna.

She made a point of looking out the window, with big dark eyes. She didn't respond to questions: "What's your name? Hey, I'm talking to you. I said, What's your name?" She wasn't interested in the world maps hanging on the walls, or the periodic table. She wasn't interested in learning the name of the girl sitting next to her.

She was interested in the building next door.

They were identical: the cement cube where she was and the cement cube where Anna was. Separating them was a chain-link fence, a ramshackle fence that had been repaired here and there. Evidently somebody had tried to get over to the other side.

That's not possible. The two worlds aren't interconnected. You can't just cut a hole in a chain-link fence and stick your head through it to have a different life.

Anna was on the other side. Anna was hidden behind one of those windows.

She didn't know which window, but later Lisa would reveal floor and location to her. Once she knew she'd gaze in that direction every morning in hopes of seeing Anna: a bit of head, a shoulder, a flurry of curls in the glint of the glass. She'd never speak to her again, that much was certain. In fact, she'd hate her, unrelenting and forever. Every so often she amused herself by trying to imagine how Anna would react if she died; she'd fantasize about hanging herself just for the pleasure of guessing the look on Anna's face when she found her, dangling from a pillar in the courtyard— her crushing sense of guilt.

She'd stare at her window every day for the entire duration of class, without ever looking away, deciphering all the shadows, and sooner or later she'd see her. The silhouette of a dead person. On the other side. For five solid hours, Francesca would remain glued to the window glass, waiting for Anna.

That same day Elena woke up in her family's home in Campiglia Marittima. She looked out the big picture window in the living room at the panorama of fields, olive groves, and vineyards stretching all the way down to the sea in the distance, to the colossal industrial plants.

From up there, from that privileged vantage point, the Val di Cornia was a peaceful, well-ordered place: farmers over here; steelworkers over there; fishermen down in the distance, at the harbor. From her family villa you could even see the silhouette of Elba, a mist-shrouded rock in the sea.

Elena evaluated the options open to her for what seemed like the thousandth time as she sipped her coffee. There was no reason to move away to

Pisa or Florence—those fields, that sea, the sweet line of the hills all the way down to the tower of Populonia were her home. So she got dressed and brushed her hair, inserted the key decisively into the dashboard of the car, and drove toward Piombino, ready for her job interview. Rooms lined with gleaming wood and brass. The largest company in the region: Lucchini.

She had an MBA, had graduated with distinction. She was perfectly aware of the opportunities that degree offered her. She was the young, hardworking, beautiful daughter of the city hospital's chief physician.

Elena was driving calmly toward the huge steel mill. She still had no idea, though deep down she had a presentiment, that before long she'd be doing the hiring for a steel mill that makes railroad track for all of Europe, and even for the United States.

Alessio was sleeping comfortably, worn ragged by an eight-hour night shift with A-Fo 4 the rebellious, A-Fo 4 the mythical, funereal furnace. Molten steel flowing into the mill crucibles, incandescent steel becoming a marketable product, profit, salary, links between cities, places, time. Spontaneous generation and regeneration of the ends. What is the end, actually?

He couldn't imagine that in just a few weeks the great love of his life would be occupying an office in the executive office tower. And that she would hire and fire, reckon and calculate the lives, hours, and days of men like him.

He really couldn't imagine that in just a few months yet another of his coworkers would die, and that he'd be waving a FIOM union banner against her, who would be—for all intents and purposes—on the other side.

Elena was driving in utter tranquillity, and parked at the main entrance to the vast factory. She was confident that she'd be hired, confident that Alessio would be happy about it; because she'd never seen a mill crucible she had no idea what one looked like, and in her mind Via Stalingrado was something out of a comic book.

The sun shone its rays down on the hardworking city, on the glass of thousands of windows concealing people bent over tables, bent over desks covered with sheets of paper adding numbers, doodling with a pen, on the two thousand people who make the blooms, slabs, and billets—the steelworkers who have to take care not to slip and fall, not to lose their focus, not to be immolated under the continuous flow of molten metals, glass, iron, and cement.

2001. That day was the tenth of September.

CHAPTER 24

The next day seemed like summer.

Mattia had gone to pick her up outside the school. He was leaning on the door of his Fiat Panda, double-parked, waiting like any
of the dozens of parents. He had the day off and wanted to take her to the
beach for the last swim of the season. He saw her emerge from a multicol-
ored crowd of runts with oversized backpacks, rulers protruding.

Anna jumped into the car, hurling her backpack into the backseat. She
rolled the window all the way down and stretched her legs out on the dashboard. She felt good. She was reviewing the Greek alphabet in her mind
while Mattia drove with one hand and stroked her knee with the other. The
countryside flowed past outside the window: a land of hills and factories
glittering under the still-warm rays of the sun.

They went to Torre del Sale, the white sand beach between the ENEL
plant and the Dalmine-Tenaris steelworks. It was practically empty when
they got there. There was clay on the sea bottom. There were two or three
office girls stretched out catching some sun, their work clothes piled up
beside them. Lunch break: last chance to get a tan. The sun was intense
and brassy. It was shining as if this were the beginning, as if everything
were about to recommence: the summer, the games, Francesca stretched
out on the wet sand, in the waves. . . . Deceptive sunlight.

The water had turned a few degrees colder. Anna dipped the tip of her
toe into the waves, then pulled it out with a series of wracking shivers. But
Mattia came running and tossed her into the water. Mattia was eager to
take a swim and make love in the saltwater. They kissed for a long time,
the way lovers do, in the muck, in the slow and regular pulse of the waves.
They ate a sandwich and a piece of fruit. Then they went back to kissing,

the fragrant sand sticking to their skin. It was 2:49 in the afternoon. The office girls were putting their clothes on to go back to work. The two young people were pressing their bodies together in the hot sun, in the smell of diesel fuel from the exhaust fans of the nearby factory.

"When are you going to take me to Elba?" she asked him.

"Soon," he answered.

Now, after a swim and an orgasm, life had returned to normal. September. All the people were holed up again in their offices. The week was punctuated by the names of the days, the constant rhythm of a world duty-bound to produce. There was an emptiness now. Anna and Mattia noticed it, but barely. Something had happened inside the routine, inside everyday life. On the empty beach you could sense the absence of little kids playing ball, the ball that rolled all the way to your towel. The children had all gone back to preschool. And the sea slithered back and forth sleepily, entering into hibernation.

Something extraordinary had happened in the silence. A freighter moved slowly across the horizon toward Sardinia, slowly blurring into the sky-blue distance.

On the way back Mattia drove along the dirt road by the quail field. Anna looked out the window at the perimeter of the Dalmine-Tenaris property. The straw bales, the high-tension lines.

"What happened to the wires?" Anna pointed to the high-tension towers.

Mattia was putting the suspension of his beat-up Fiat Panda to the test, jouncing over potholes and rocks, kicking up a tremendous cloud of dust. He smiled.

"How come those electric lines don't work anymore?" Anna insisted.

"Let's just say that your brother took care of that. . . ." It was 3:30. Mattia drove calmly along the state highway, on the peaceful promontory after lunch on a Tuesday. Industrial sheds, with trucks entering and leaving. Shops with the shutters rolled up for cleaning before reopening for business in the afternoon.

"You want to drop by Aldo's?"

Anna nodded unenthusiastically: The place was dirty and depressing, and there were too many grown men. But that was the time of day when retirees and young guys with nothing better to do congregated in the bar. It's normal on the outskirts of town; it's normal to sit around shooting the shit in a neighborhood where everyone knows everyone else.

Mattia parked sideways on the sidewalk. They got out of the car with wet hair, flip-flops, feet covered with sand.

"Life is good, ain't it, you lucky dogs," called out an old man as they walked into the bar.

Mattia leaned an elbow on the counter and ordered a Sambuca and a fruit juice.

"Hey asshole," Alessio shouted, laughing. He was sitting at a table with Cristiano and a few others, playing cards.

There was a father with a couple of kids buying a handful of lollipops for them and ordering a Fernet Branca for himself. As usual there was a Moroccan immigrant furiously feeding coins into the video poker machine, never winning so much as a cent. The foosball table was the center of a mob scene; the ball crashing into the goals was making a tremendous racket. A plainclothes policeman was smoking a cigarette. There were steelworkers still dressed in their mill overalls, and others about to start their shift. It was a little before 4:00 in the afternoon. At the far end of the room the television was tuned to Rai 1.

Anna was sitting on Mattia's lap and happily drinking her fruit juice. People were talking and talking—they never seemed to stop. Anna watched her brother, talking cheerfully about things that meant nothing to her. Words like *bamba*—cocaine—flew across the room, projects that they called *storie*, and that they planned to carry to completion in the coming weeks in order to obtain the *grana*—cash—that they needed. An unspeakable stench of tobacco smoke. She was proud of her brother; she was proud of her boyfriend. She was at peace. The guys who knew her greeted her by pinching her cheek.

She was proud of her world, even if it was filthy and smelled bad. A few minutes later, Maria and Jessica showed up, too. Yes: Her solid, elementary world; she was proud of it.

"I had a customer today that I was ready to murder," Jessica said.

The two young women hunted around for a couple of chairs so that they could sit with them.

"She wanted to buy a thong, and I said to her: 'Signora, we don't have anything in your size.'" People came in and out. "And she gets all offended, and she acts like it's my fault! 'I'm so sorry,' I told her. 'Why don't you try the store across the street?' What can I do if you're fat? is what I wanted to tell her. What an asshole!" The old men were talking about Ukrainian women. No one was listening to Jessica and her story about the fat woman who wanted a thong. No one was listening to anything anyone said, unless it involved sex and money.

The theme song of the evening news broke in.

At this time of day? Aldo pointed to the television screen and waved for everyone to quiet down.

Special report. Decks of cards rattled on the stained tabletops. Huge piles of dead cigarette butts filled ashtrays. No one paid any attention.

"God damn it! Shut up so I can hear!" shouted the owner of the café: He'd rolled up a rag to clean off some tables, and now he stepped over by the television. He turned up the sound with the remote control.

The news anchor was a seldom seen face, one of the reporters that substitutes for better known colleagues at Easter and Christmas.

Special report. One by one voices fell silent and heads swiveled toward the television set.

The news anchor muttered something incomprehensible for a few seconds. Then the screen filled with a picture of two skyscrapers and a dense column of smoke. At the top of the screen was written: LIVE. WORLD TRADE CENTER, NEW YORK.

"What is it?"

The video poker kept churning away.

"I don't know; it's in America. . . ."

Someone put down their glass.

Someone else held their glass in one hand, forgetting to drink. And the children kept shouting, "Del Piero!" and "Pippo Inzaghi!"

"Sssh!" said Aldo. "Let me listen to this."

Now everyone was still.

Anna was tired of chewing her strawberry and cream–flavored bubblegum, so she stuck the wad, unseen, under the café table.

"What is it? Did someone shoot the president?"

The half-finished card games were arrayed in scattered decks of cards; some of the cards had fallen to the ground, along with the ashes and the receipts. Children kept playing foosball until they sensed that it was too quiet, that something must have happened. Then they let their arms fall to their sides, and the ball rolled on for a few seconds until it came to a stop.

The voice of the news anchor stuttered and fell silent. The image blacked out and then reappeared, same as before. Two skyscrapers and a billowing column of smoke. Zoom in on the skyscrapers: There were two columns of smoke issuing from two holes. At first no one could grasp that the eviscerated surface was actually a wall of office windows. No one could imagine that the black dots falling through empty air were human beings.

Cristiano turned toward the front door. A couple of Carabinieri in uniform were entering the bar.

"What's going on?"

"No idea. It's a special report from the United States."

The two Carabinieri leaned against the bar and started watching, but only after ordering a couple of espressos with a shot of Sambuca.

"The two planes crashed into the buildings this morning," the voice was saying. "A Boeing 767 that had just been hijacked and was obviously . . ." There was nothing obvious about it. "Eighteen minutes later, another airplane hit the building." No one could understand a thing.

Nothing was happening in the picture. The only thing moving was the smoke.

"Is this live?" someone asked.

"Any updates, Borrelli?" asked the news anchor. The face of Giulio Borrelli, his colleague on the ground, appeared live from New York, a familiar face attempting to provide an explanation to Italy from that distant corner of the world. "Well," he said hesitantly, "this is the biggest disaster, the worst terror attack ever unleashed on the heart of America."

There was a general silence, an uncomfortable silence and the thrills you get from an action film. Cristiano said: "If you ask me, it's just *Real TV.*" He started shuffling the deck. "You know, those bullshit American shows. . . ."

But it was a news report.

Conversations resumed, slightly subdued. A few people gave up trying to figure out what was happening and went back to their poker games, went back to stacking up thousand-lire coins. There was sand in Anna's swimsuit and it was irritating her. Alessio was watching the television screen intently, but by now he was one of the very few doing so. People were going about their business, and a few were heading home.

Forty-two minutes went by like that, with live feeds, monotonous scenes, journalists talking about the Islamic courts, a third airplane that had hit the Pentagon.

Aldo had stopped serving customers; he was doing his best to connect this piece of news with the fabric of the world, his world. People didn't give a damn, they could care less what happened in America. Boeing 767s crash into the buildings of world finance, 110 stories of people at work in their offices: a Hollywood fantasy that no one could believe.

Mattia was tickling Anna behind the ears. And Anna was saying that she needed to learn the Greek alphabet and study her Latin nouns for the next day at school.

"Will you take me home?"

The two Carabinieri phoned in to find out something from the main barracks. But over at the Piombino barracks, an old building with a flaking plaster front and two palm trees outside, they knew less about it than in the café.

After forty-two minutes the picture on the screen suddenly sprang into action.

They saw the skyscraper come tumbling down. It came down like the column of sand inside an hourglass. And then the other skyscraper came down, too. Everything collapsed to the level of the soil. And then inside the bar in Salivoli someone started shouting, shouting in astonishment and disbelief, while the screams of the Americans crying out for help reached all the way to their ears, live.

"Christ!"

It was something absurd, something happening on the far side of the ocean, on the far side of the world. Maybe it was happening *outside* of the real world. Alessio and Cristiano looked each other in the eyes. Everyone in the bar was incredulously staring someone else in the face, now that the Americans were screaming like wild animals, now that the skyscrapers had vanished from view.

"Is this live, for real?"

"Is this really happening or are they all high?"

Dozens of people in Piombino, from Aldo's bar, suddenly began sending text messages and making hurried phone calls.

"Oh! Turn on the television!" they said to their wives, their children. "Hurry, the world is falling down!"

Francesca, at Lisa's house, was sitting staring at the television screen, too. She was watching the Twin Towers come down, the collapse replaying over and over, dozens of times. The repetition of something out of the ordinary is somehow incomprehensible, and it took Francesca a moment to understand that this was history.

Aldo set a glass down on the bar. "People," he shouted, "the Americans just got a royal ass fucking!"

A few people applauded.

Mattia smiled at Anna as if to say: You see? Here we are, together, while something important is happening.

"They tore them a new one this time, boys!"

Alessio shook his head, stunned: "I mean, do you get it? They just slammed into the buildings, as if an airplane flew down low and crashed into the blast furnace. . . . It would be a disaster, the whole Lucchini works would blow sky-high. . . ."

There was a sense of exaltation, like during a FIOM-CGIL general labor strike. It was impossible to believe that there were real people dying in that absurd image.

"Will they make us work a regular shift today?"

"Yeah, right," one of them laughed. "Something happens in the U.S. and the Lucchini mill shuts down!"

Lots of people were laughing by this point.

"Damned capitalists!"

It was a fact that wasn't a fact, an event that hadn't really happened: It was a movie.

Anna, watching for what seemed like the hundredth time as the cement giants came tumbling down in the heart of Manhattan, felt that this was history—that vast and incomprehensible thing that is history—and yet she was now part of it.

Anna found herself in the midst of history and was astonished, but most of all, she realized that she missed Francesca. And she realized that she wished Francesca were here right now, with her, as if what was coming endlessly over the airwaves were a wedding or a funeral, one of those events where people have no choice but to grow close, and quarrels are forgotten.

Francesca at Lisa's house was experiencing the same thing: She was missing Anna, Anna's small hand, while the Twin Towers were collapsing for the tenth time. Staying apart made no sense.

The banner headline on the front page of *il manifesto* read: APOCALYPSE.

That night in Piombino the streets were empty. Everyone was at home staring at the television set, sitting close together on the sofa or around the kitchen table, with the adrenaline that comes with witnessing something that will go down in the history books. Sandra was on edge; she kept phoning party headquarters. Elena was in a state of turmoil; she felt like sending a text message to Alessio. But what would she write him?

And Anna and Francesca, each in her bed, couldn't help but think about the other and yearn to see the other, and couldn't help but hate each other a little.

So Anna got out of bed, turned on the overhead light, and started leafing through last year's diary. She reread all the phrases that Francesca had written, with spelling mistakes and little hearts dotting the *i*'s. Those scribblings, and the letters filled with curlicues, were every bit as significant as the fact that now there was a hole in the ground in Manhattan and the world was about to change direction.

Alessio was listening to the radio from the crane. Hundreds of radios and television sets were turned on in the sheds and buildings of the Lucchini plant, all tuned to the same frequency: the attack on the Twin Towers. Terrorism had defeated the West in just a few hours, and amid the fires, the mill trains, the giant incandescent ladles and crucibles, thousands of tiny men in overalls were melting iron and carbon, steel and pig iron to make the rails, the ships, the weapons of Europe and the United States.

Only Enrico, inert in his easy chair, kept changing channels. He stumbled upon a strange cartoon, and then a western with Clint Eastwood in it. He was thinking about other things. He was thinking about his daughter's body caught in his fishing binoculars. Cut off clean inside the lens: her back, the tip of her breast, backlit, in the water. The summer was over, and he had put the optical instrument away in a secure place in the apartment. The United States, a world away, the fall. His daughter cradled in the palm of his hand. He had held her, whole, odorous, in the palm of his hand when she emerged from the incubator.

And he fell asleep, alone.

PART THREE

CHAPTER 25

It's pouring down rain. That's a fact.

Arturo stares at the motion of the windshield wipers; fragments and stubs of thoughts float through his brain. He's in a state of extraordinary tension; he's inside his car. He turns to the left, turns onto the state highway. He may be safe.

They were plainclothes officers; they pulled handguns. Arturo is driving slowly to escape notice; he can feel surges of adrenaline in his arms and legs. They ruined a deal worth a hundred thousand dollars, maybe more, but they didn't catch him.

Something's happening now. The car in front of him brakes sharply and turns on its emergency blinkers. Another event has intervened, forcing him to slow down and stop. Arturo's not moving. What is it, an accident? That's the last thing he needs.

It's been pouring since last night.

It was raining earlier, on the wharf in the harbor at dawn when the raid exploded on them. And it's raining now. Traffic is stopped. Water's pounding down on the hoods of the line of cars. People are going to work; people honk their horns because they have to punch in on time. It's 8:30 in the morning. Water is flooding the sewer mains. It's running down the stems of the leaves, the few leaves still on the trees. It's shaking the bare branches of the trees along the side of the road.

Arturo can't seem to think. He has to decide where he should go, find a place to stay, pull something out of his hat—then, maybe, he can phone Sandra. Arturo stares at the windshield wipers and thinks about how many millions of facts, events, there are in the world, linked one to the other, unconnected and yet connected. He is one of them, one of so many. A living, thinking fact in the limitless, indifferent chain of events.

Water runs down the stems of the leaves, down the gutters of the industrial sheds along the state highway at the Piombino exit. It only takes an instant to lose control. Water backs up, overflowing the sewers and manholes, forming puddles on the cracked asphalt. It only takes an instant to slide down the back of that chain, to wind up in an unknown constellation of events. There's no time.

It's raining on the overturned motor scooter, and on the body of a man flat on the pavement.

Arturo stares at the windshield wipers, then he takes a quick glance at the rearview mirror and turns pale: There's a police car right behind him.

He turns on the heater. The windows are fogging up.

Pasquale . . . poor devil. They're definitely taking him to Livorno right now, sirens wailing, inside a police car just like that one, handcuffed . . . and he missed being right next to Pasquale by a hairsbreadth.

He stares at the motion of the windshield wipers, from left to right, from right to left. No one knows if the body stretched out on the asphalt just a few hundred yards away is alive or dead. People don't know how to drive in the rain, Arturo thinks. People get caught off guard.

Hydroplaning is the term. When you lose control and slam into the guardrail, you get injured. There are thousands of ways to get injured, though. It's called an accident. We call the facts that we slam into, crash into, land on top of—*accidents.*

You can't tell if the man stretched out amid the crumpled metal is a corpse or if he's still breathing.

It's raining down on the industrial sheds of the Lucchini S.p.A., on the smokestacks ringed in red and on the conveyor belts loaded with pig iron. Arturo stares at the automatic motion of the windshield wipers, and he knows that off to his right the spectacle of industry is spread out over four square miles. But he doesn't want to look at it.

Only a few minutes have gone by. The proper phone calls still have to be made. They haven't realized yet that someone is lying on his back in a heap of twisted metal, and that someone should call for help. Arturo tries to use the heater to defog the windows; he thinks that the man stretched out on the road is dead, while he's alive. Or maybe it's exactly the reverse.

On his right the Lucchini steelworks is drenched and dripping and burning fuel. He knows that, but he doesn't want to look. It's been raining on the blast furnace since last night. The thing that never stops. The water hammers down on the metal without stopping: the billets and slabs laid out in the yards waiting; the trucks lined up; and the steelworkers sheltering under improvised canvas shelters. All the Caterpillar bulldozers and power shovels are parked now, motionless like the cars on the state highway and the body of the man stretched out on the ground.

"Cristiano, go on home," his boss tells him. "We're not doing anything useful today."

The rain isn't stopping. The bulldozer is just piling up mud; it can't separate recyclable material from the slag. In a few minutes the ambulance will be there. Alessio and Mattia are taking turns driving the locomotive of the mill train. They're drenched to the skin, they're swearing uninterruptedly. They can't see on the state highway, but there's some poor devil who crashed on his motor scooter; it isn't clear if he's dead or alive.

That could have been my son, thinks Arturo. But he doesn't want to think, he wants to stare at the windshield wipers—the simplest piece of evidence in the fabric of the world. It's raining down on the hood of his car. The car behind him is a police Alfa 147 with its emergency lights flashing. The blue of flashing police emergency lights under a sky so dark it looks like nighttime. But it's morning.

Arturo looks at them and starts to panic. *Those policemen are certainly discussing the raid down at the port; for sure they're saying: There was a fifth man, but the bastard got away.*

Alessio is unloading mill crucibles from the mill train, and he doesn't know that the fifth man is his father.

His father is thinking: *If Pasquale tells them about me, it's over.*

They caught the others at dawn, red-handed, while they were unloading the freighter. And he's safe, maybe. It's raining on the body of a dead cat that nobody's bothered to pick up. The ambulance is slow getting there. Cristiano gets on his motor scooter and looks with annoyance at the traffic jam that's formed on the state highway. Alessio and Mattia stop to chat under a canvas cover, their overalls filthy, with lighted cigarettes.

"What shitty weather." They laugh.

The regular motion of the windshield wipers, a reassuring rhythm. The car is stuck in a traffic jam but the windshield wipers keep going.

That could be me, that dead man on the asphalt. Instead I'm inside a car that luckily doesn't belong to me, and I can breathe. Stop to focus on the bare essentials, on the minimum chain of existence. Did I turn my cell phones off? Yes. I threw away the SIM cards. And the guy on his back on the pavement, the guy who might *be alive or might be dead, is too big to be my son.*

Arturo glances at his rearview mirror again. *There are two men in front* *and one in the backseat. In the police car caught in traffic the man at the wheel is* *talking, while the one in the passenger seat is trying to light a cigarette. The third* *man is talking on his cell phone: He looks young and slightly overexcited. Maybe he* *was there this morning at dawn, maybe he was one of the policemen aiming his* *revolver . . . and maybe this successful raid will win him a promotion!*

The traffic jam isn't getting any better. A welter of car horns and sheet metal. A clogged traffic jam of water backing up. And so the policeman at the wheel loses his patience, turns on the siren, and forces his way through the cars ahead of him, which part to allow him through.

Arturo pulls over; his hand is trembling on the gearshift. *As long as* *Pasquale keeps his mouth shut . . .*

The ambulance arrives. Arturo pulls into the emergency lane.

They're loading the body onto a stretcher. Two more minutes and he can hit 100 miles per hour, even 120 miles per hour if necessary. He'll take the superhighway to Florence, no, better, the one to Genoa. He can meet with Sandrini, his lawyer, in Viareggio, and then there's that friend of his who owes him a favor. . . . Sandra will never understand all this.

At last the traffic jam breaks up; he can finally get moving again. There's a question that he really ought to be asking himself: "What the fuck am I doing?" But he doesn't have the nerve.

Piombino vanishes rapidly in the rearview mirror: the smokestacks, the industrial sheds, the roofs of the public housing projects, all gone, the familiar domestic settings. Maybe they'll go search his house, but he's clean. Maybe they'll want him for questioning, but what evidence do they have?

Pasquale, I beg you, don't mention my name!

The Lucchini steelworks goes racing past him, with its steelworkers drenched with rain. Maybe—the thought flashes through his mind—my son was right.

Anna looks up at the sky from the window of her classroom. There's a swollen, heavy layer of condensation. It's raining indifferently on the roof of the school and on the heaps of rotten seaweed pounded by the winter waves.

Piombino turns into a city of the dead in November. It gets dark early, and only the usual suspects go out in the cold. Cristiano and Alessio collapse onto the little sofas at Aldo's, waiting for their shift to start at the Lucchini steel plant. Life is punctuated only by hot meals at home and the mimimum essential functions. But Mattia makes love with her under the prickly wool blanket; they make love for the entire duration of the afternoon. When night falls she goes home, her hair disheveled and an odor and a sheen of sweat under her heavy jacket.

The Latin teacher is explaining the third declension.

The teacher is making chalk marks on the blackboard, drawing vowels in perspective. One color for the root, another for the verb ending. Anna is paying no attention. She's staring out the window; she's watching the regular drops of water. *She didn't come to school again today*, she's thinking.

And so she turns to stare at Lisa taking notes on the far side of the classroom. She's seeking in her concentrated face the signs of some explanation—any explanation. Why Francesca's bicycle isn't with the others, parked at the front gate. Why Francesca hasn't come to school for more than a week, and who knows what the fuck she's doing, maybe she's sick. She's counted the days. She's marked them down in her diary. Lisa knows, Lisa definitely must know. And Anna stares at her insistently, the Latin teacher runs through the cases of substantives by declension, until Lisa finally senses she's being watched and looks up.

They've always scrupulously avoided looking at one another or speaking to each other. They've always avoided running into one another when school lets out.

But Anna knows that Lisa is spying on her every bit as much as she is spying on Lisa. She knows that every tiny detail will be recorded and reported back to Francesca. Her daily average grade, what she wears, how she does her hair, when she's moody and glum, when you can tell she's had a fight with her boyfriend, even the snack that she buys at the vending machine: Everything will be faithfully reported.

The teacher explains, uselessly, the third declension, and Anna decides that she really no longer has any desire to go on pretending.

She leans over her notebook and writes in the top left corner: "Imparisyllabic nouns with a double consonant prior to the genitive suffix in -*is*. Example: *mens mentis, pons pontis*." The genitive is the case of ownership and belonging, the teacher repeats; it's the case of generation, as the name itself suggests. Anna decides that maybe it would be best to go ahead and talk to Lisa during the break, to ask what happened to Francesca. The genitive indicates the substance. What happened to Francesca? What are things made of, where do things come from? An indication can be found in the way that the words end—in the endings of the words.

Then the bell rings and the Latin teacher gathers her books and closes her class register. Anna decides that for purely strategic reasons she ought to make friends with Lisa, even if Lisa disgusts her. Then the young history teacher comes in, and the usual idiot girls pretend to fall off their chairs.

There's something that Anna just remembered, something that might help. Something that might be better than turning to Lisa. She could give Francesca a present, write her a note, ring her doorbell, and be brave, stand her ground, even if Enrico comes to the door.

"It's November twenty-second, kids," says the cute history teacher.

"What does that date mean to you? Anyone?"

The class is silent and drowsy, except the usual idiot girls who wear jeans and tight-fitting sweaters whenever they have history class.

"Nearly forty years ago in Texas, kids, John Fitzgerald Kennedy was assassinated. Does that mean anything to you?"

Blank faces, basically: No, it doesn't mean a damned thing to us.

"Texas, kids. The land of oil wells, enormous business interests behind petroleum. It all comes around again. History repeats itself. He was the president of the United States, it was 1963, kids. Cold war. And now, as you may have deduced from the attack on the Twin Towers, we're at war again."

The handsome history teacher is just getting warmed up.

"This is important. The United States has always killed its presidents. . . ."

Predictable witticism from the back of the class: "So why don't we do that in Italy?"

Anna learns the story of the president assassinated by the factory worker Oswald and calculates that twenty-four years later, at the hospital of Piombino, in the province of Livorno, Francesca Morganti was born, underweight and with sparse hair if any.

Twenty-two: That's Anna's number.

Half of that is eleven, the mice. Twice that is forty-four, prison. And twenty-two is the madman, of course. Her father had taught her the Neapolitan *smorfia*, the game of betting and numerology.

"Kids, it's important," says the young history teacher. "Be aware of dates and events. Exercise suspicion. There's always a conspiracy behind a simple date and a simple event. Isolate the right way from the wrong way. But know that both of them make history to the same extent."

Anna thinks that the ten minutes of discussion of current events, the ten minutes to talk about the world today, is a ridiculous waste of time. Pure bullshit. All she wants is to open her book to page thirty, "the Battle of Salamis," and be left to doodle on the page in peace.

"Bin Laden and Lee Harvey Oswald," says the twenty-six-year-old high school history teacher. "Who can say who they really are? Are they behind what happened? Or was there a larger plot involving the government, big capital, and the whole system?"

"Anything else?" someone snickers.

But there's no holding the teacher back now: "The system, kids . . . What do you think about September eleventh, what conclusions have you come to?"

Eleven: the mice.

Dozens of wads of bubble gum stuck to the undersides of the desks and the chairs.

"I brought in a copy of *La Repubblica*; you need to read newspapers, kids."

The kids grimace. Anna detests the ten minutes of discussion in class on current events that are *relevant to us*.

And while he reads yet another article about the world going to hell, Anna is musing over the fact that November twenty-second is the day that Francesca was born, and September eleventh is the day that in Aldo's bar she first yearned for Francesca. And she's wondering why Francesca hasn't been at school for more than a week. And she says to herself that there's a right way and a wrong way. And that continuing to act as if nothing has happened is the wrong way. And that ringing the doorbell of her best friend is the right way. And that she doesn't give a damn about bin Laden and conspiracy theories.

All things considered, something good might actually happen today.

CHAPTER 26

For two solid hours Anna rode around town on her motor scooter in the rain, looking for the right store. A store that matched not so much an idea as a feeling.

She couldn't find it. She needed for it to be something extraordinary, something that said: We're friends. We're friends forever, no matter what. Even if we stop talking to each other, even if it's winter and it gets dark early, today it's your birthday and I'm coming over to give you something. Please accept it, because I can't find the words.

Anna was getting her jacket and her pants sopping wet as she drove. It just wouldn't stop raining today. She kept turning down the same streets in the center of Piombino for the umpteenth time; she kept pulling up outside the same stores, caught in traffic, unwilling to park and go on. Driving helped her to think, to focus down on Francesca and the one extraordinary present she was going to find for her. It was getting dark, and the streetlights all flicked on suddenly at 5:30 in the afternoon.

People were clustering, hurrying along past the brightly lit shopwindows, umbrellas dripping, striding briskly, splashing through puddles. It was just a month until Christmas; the city had already put up Christmas lights. Anna couldn't bring herself to park. She wanted something symbolic, if possible, something eternal. If possible, for ten thousand lire.

At seven o'clock she stopped at the flower store. That wasn't what she wanted. She was definitely getting this all wrong. But she hadn't found anything better, and she was expected home soon. She walked in and looked around at the flowers: They all looked the same, pretty unimpressive. But at least they were alive. A flower. Even if it dies, it's alive. She saw one that looked different from all the others. She pointed it out to the florist and the florist told her that it was a calla lily.

Anna would give it to her in person, this evening, after writing her a love-filled gift card.

She had the florist tie an outsized red bow around the jar, thus burning through her entire weekly allowance.

She drove home on her motor scooter with the calla lily perched on her knees, hammered by rain. She did her best to protect it with her jacket, but the rain was pouring down and there was a strong wind along the waterfront. When she got home, the stem was visibly bent and two of the leaves were broken. The first thing her mother said, in the midst of making dinner, was: "Have you heard from your father?"

"No," she replied, and headed straight for her bedroom.

She had other things on her mind. She tossed her water-soaked jacket onto her bed and barely grunted hello to her brother. Alessio was combing his hair in front of the mirror while his cell phone vibrated with text messages.

"What's this? Your anniversary?" Alessio pointed at the plant with a laugh.

Anna sat down at her desk. She started rummaging through her drawers in search of a decent sheet of paper.

"It looks like a dick!"

"Could you just mind your own business, you idiot?" She was irritable and eager for her brother to get out of her face.

Dear Francesca, as you can see, I haven't forgotten that today is your birthday. Even if we've had a fight, I want to wish you a happy birthday all the same.

Her brother was answering calls on his cell phone, shouting and laughing loudly in the small bedroom. Anna didn't know what to write next.

Why did we fight in the first place? I know this is only a flower, but it actually has a deep meaning. It means that in life, when two girls are best friends, fights don't really matter.

Her brother was shouting into the phone, and Anna was chewing on the end of the blue ink pen, drumming the tip of the pen on the top of her desk. She was struggling to come up with a fucking phrase that refused to surface in her thoughts.

Because I've never really stopped loving you.

"*Ale*, will you get the fuck out of here?"

"Oh, I'm sorry," Alessio spoke into his phone, "but my sister just brought home a dick-shaped flower. . . ."

Dear France, this flower is to remind you that you're still my best friend.

She didn't know what to write.

Dear France

How could she find the right words? To say what, exactly? She slammed down the pen, crumpled up the sheet of paper, and went in to dinner with a lump in her throat.

"Anna," Sandra said to her, "your father has had his phone turned off since this morning. . . ."

Anna bit off a piece of bread stick and replied, through her mouthful: "I don't know; he probably lost the phone."

"I'm worried," her mother told her.

It was eight o'clock; the pasta was almost ready. And Arturo wasn't home. *It's strange*, thought Sandra, *it's very strange*, and she picked up a pair of pot holders.

"I'm going to Francesca's for a minute," Anna said, turning on her heel.

She went into her bedroom and picked up the calla lily. She left the aborted personal note crumpled up on the desk and took a deep breath as she steeled herself.

"Where are you going? I'm draining the pasta!"

She closed the door and walked down the two flights of stairs that separated her from her best friend, her former best friend, her undying best friend 4ever.

She was holding the plant in her hands, but she couldn't bring herself to ring the doorbell. What if the ogre answered the door? She had no way of knowing that no one was home. She had no idea what had happened that morning. Not the slightest idea.

She did the most idiotic thing imaginable: She set the plant down on the doormat, rang the doorbell, and ran straight back upstairs.

The spaghetti sat in the colander for twenty minutes. It turned into a clumpy mass of cold strands, like matted hair. Still, Sandra couldn't make up her mind to throw it away.

"Your father's phone is turned off."

It was well past 8:30; the evening news was over. Anna stared at the television screen and realized what an idiot she'd been, not even to sign her name, not even a piece of paper stuck to the plant with "Happy Birthday" written on it.

Sandra was starting to get seriously worried: Since Arturo had returned home he'd never missed dinner once. Something had happened; she felt it.

At nine o'clock, Anna finished the bread sticks and was starting to complain that she was hungry. Alessio was done with his phone calls, finished spiking his hair with gel. He appeared in the kitchen, beaming and dressed to the nines.

"Have you talked to your father?" Sandra asked him. "He's had his phone turned off all day. . . ."

"And why the fuck would I care?" He stormed out of the apartment, slamming the door.

Outside it was still pouring rain, the kind of weather that puts a sense of foreboding in your heart.

Sandra dialed and redialed her husband's phone number, and systematically she heard three short beeps, followed by the silence of the tomb. Not even the voice of the Omnitel woman. Absolutely nothing. Rain brings forebodings.

"Not only is it turned off, but there's no recording telling me he can't be reached. . . . It's as if they'd pulled the SIM card out of the phone."

It was 9:30.

"Give me the phone; let me try."

Anna tried calling her father, but it was true: She didn't hear the usual message from Omnitel. Three quick beeps, then nothing. She looked at her mother, bewildered. They were alone in the kitchen. They'd turned the sound down on the television. Outside, the rain kept pouring down, and the wind was picking up. Sandra rummaged through the kitchen drawer for her cigarettes, and when she found the lighter, it slipped through her fingers and fell to the floor.

"Something happened. He was in an accident, I know it!"

Anna remained calm; she didn't feel like getting worked up. She didn't want accidents. She absolutely didn't want bad things.

"I'm going to call the hospital."

"What are you talking about?" her daughter shouted in annoyance. "Would you cut it out? You'll see, he'll be here any minute!"

Sandra was standing, white as a sheet, with the receiver in hand.

There was an ominous sense in the house, a sense of foreboding. The table was set, the spaghetti was cold, a gruel of yellow worms in the center of the colander. In the meantime, the wind was making the shutters clatter, shaking the masts of the boats, making them utter hostile sounds.

It was after ten o'clock when the doorbell rang.

"Oh! At last!" Sandra heaved a sigh and smiled. "He forgot his keys again. . . ."

Anna smiled, too. "You see? What did I tell you? You're always so melodramatic!"

"*Artù*, you really scared me this time!" she shouted as she went to open the door. "You no-good scoundrel!"—happy and relieved, as she took the chain off the hook and turned the handle.

There were three police officers. Two men and a woman.

"Signora Sorrentino?"

The smile continued to hover on her lips, but now it was a senseless presence.

She didn't answer. She was failing to distinguish any of the lines and colors in that vision.

"Is your husband home? We have a search warrant."

The woman showed Sandra a sheet of paper with some scrawls on it.

"Mama?" her daughter called from inside the apartment.

Sandra wasn't speaking, she wasn't moving, she wasn't breathing. The smile gradually dropped off her face, but she still couldn't grasp what was happening.

"Signora, I asked you if your husband's home."

"He's not here . . . ," she managed to stammer.

Sandra stood there, frozen in place, and the three police officers were starting to get annoyed.

"We don't have a lot of time; could you let us in?"

It was like being picked up bodily and without warning and hurled from your normal life into the midst of a police television procedural on Rai 1. It wasn't that Sandra didn't want to step aside; it's that she was physically incapable.

She looked first at one, then at the next, and finally at the third of the three police officers. She raised a hand to her mouth. She leaned against the doorjamb and emitted a gooey suffocated sound, a sound that had nothing human about it, while the police officers brusquely pushed past her.

Anna saw them troop into the kitchen, in uniform and everything. Everything included a toolbox of some kind, with flashlights, instruments to measure and detect. The handguns in holsters, seen up close, made a tremendous impression on her.

She stood there silent, aghast.

"Signorina," said one of the policemen, "let's try to make this quick. Are you the daughter?"

She nodded.

We aren't social workers, thought the policeman. Then he said, in a brusque tone: "We need to search the apartment. Where is your parents' bedroom?"

Anna could hear her mother sobbing softly in the hallway.

"This way," she said, leading the way. Not that it was necessary: The apartment was a total of nine hundred square feet.

Like when someone dies. At first, what do you do? You separate yourself from life and you do what needs to be done. You think only about the things that have become necessary and indispensable. Like when someone tells you that the police are there to search your home and that your father's really put his foot in it this time. You show the policeman where the bedroom and the bathroom are. You respond mechanically to the policeman's words; you don't even try to decipher them. You are absolutely incapable of deciphering the phrase: "We need to search the apartment."

She heard her mother shuffling into the kitchen. She'd stopped sobbing, and now she was talking to herself. A policeman was turning the drawers upside down, emptying them, and rummaging through the packages of cereals and cookies.

"Is there a safe or anything of the sort?"

"No," Anna replied.

"He didn't come home tonight, eh?"

"No."

The policeman smiled absently, then snapped to: "Have you ever seen him leave the house with a handgun, or hide a pistol anywhere in this apartment?"

Anna shook her head in bewilderment.

"What time does he usually leave the house?"

"Nine in the morning."

"And does he always come home at night?"

Anna had no way of knowing that the police had been keeping an eye on him for months. She couldn't imagine that they knew a hundred, a thousand times more about it all than she did. She did her best to answer their questions truthfully. She had to suppose that her father and the father that the policeman was talking about were two different people.

"Yes," she answered.

"He's never stayed away? For a week, for a month?"

Anna was confused, with the policemen turning the apartment upside down and inside out. If the two fathers were the same person, maybe she needed to protect that person . . .

"He's always come home at night," she said, after some time went by.

"Your father—did you ever notice anything odd? Strange phone calls? Strange comings and goings?"

The policeman was turning her mattress over, and he smiled at her winningly. As if he and Anna were in cahoots.

"No," in a flat voice.

The policewoman muttered something that Anna understood: "With a father like that . . ." But Anna didn't know if the policewoman'd actually said it or if it was just an auditory hallucination. She looked at her parents' bedroom, ripped apart, torn open. She saw her mother's panties fly through the air, her father's socks, and it hurt her to see those personal items uncovered.

"There's nothing here." The policewoman closed the doors of the armoire.

"Check for false bottoms," the policeman told her.

The policeman who had been in the kitchen went into the bathroom. Anna heard him and thought that she might have left a used sanitary pad on the washing machine. She ran to check in some alarm. There was no sanitary pad on the washing machine. Just the bathroom sink, slightly smeared with toothpaste. A normal state of affairs, but Anna was still deeply ashamed, while the man in uniform emptied the bottles and jars in the medicine cabinet.

She heard her mother curse.

Anna stood motionless in the middle of the hallway like a wary animal; she'd suddenly developed the sense of hearing of a mouse, and she could perceive even the tiniest of sounds, the rustling of clothing in the dirty clothes hamper.

Sandra stuck her head into her bedroom and saw the way they were turning the place upside down. There were drawers ripped out of the dresser, clothing scattered on the floor, and a policeman standing on a stepladder who appeared to be examining the top of the armoire.

"He has nothing to do with any of this!" she shouted.

She had made up her mind, now, to stand up to them.

"Signora," said the policewoman, "we're very sorry, but we have to do our job. . . ."

"He hasn't done anything wrong!" she screamed, as if she were being butchered.

"No doubt . . . ," laughed the policeman at the top of the stairs. "But a little birdie told us that your husband has been dealing in stolen paintings and passing counterfeit bills."

Sandra took in that information the way you take in the content of an advertisement.

Then she shouted: "It's not true!" with all the strength in her body.

"You don't know anything about your husband's illegal activities, ma'am? Are you sure?" They took her for a fool. "Sorrentino is an old acquaintance of ours. We know all there is to know about his exploits. . . . Would you happen to know when he'll be home?"

Sandra blinked her eyes in disbelief. She still couldn't bring herself to accept that there were three policemen in her home.

"Are you tapping our phone?" she demanded indignantly.

One of them smiled as if to say: Signora, that's an incredibly stupid question.

Then he added: "If you happen to talk to him . . . could you ask him to drop by police headquarters? Let him know it's in his own interest to come in of his own volition."

"You wouldn't happen to know his friends, would you?" the other cop broke in. "Maybe they're the ones who got him involved in this. . . . What can you tell us about them?"

Sandra sat silently in the corner. This wasn't a nightmare. This was really happening. Her husband hadn't come home and three policemen were wrecking her home.

"There's not a fucking thing here, god damn it!" shouted one of the police officers, after he was done dismantling the master bedroom.

"He's smart, the son of a bitch. . . . He's going to get away with it again, you want to bet?"

Sandra thought back to the stolen paintings, the counterfeit money. . . . All charges that fit perfectly with what she knew about her husband. That's where the diamond and the VW Golf GT came from . . . "The bastard!" Sandra let it slip, through clenched teeth. Now she really wanted to break something.

They left well after midnight, empty-handed.

After locking the door behind them, Sandra hurried to check the green watermark on the hundred-thousand-lire bills that she had in her wallet. They seemed real; that was a relief. . . . Then she went into the kitchen, where her daughter was standing, frozen, in a state of shock, and sat down.

A few minutes went by in silence. They looked one another in the eyes.

Anna was about to say something, but her mother shushed her immediately: "Don't say a thing, please, don't say a single word!"

She stood up, in a cold fury.

"Go to bed, you have school tomorrow."

Anna didn't budge.

"I told you to go to bed! Beat it. I've got to get this place cleaned up, can't you see that?" And she swept her arm to indicate the typhoon that had just roared through the rooms of their apartment.

Anna looked at her as if to say: You're crazy; the whole bunch of you are crazy.

Then she thought: *But how is any of it my fault?* She couldn't take it anymore: She burst into tears.

"Are they going to arrest him?" she mumbled between sobs.

Sandra regained her senses and embraced her daughter. "No, they're not going to arrest him, don't worry. . . ." she started saying, tenderly, to reassure her. But then the thought of the counterfeit money, and the diamond purchased with the counterfeit money, and the stolen paintings—and they'd even come to search her house—made her eyes bloodshot with rage. She lost her temper once again.

"That piece of shit! That bastard! Enough is enough. Go to bed. . . ." She looked around—the drawers, the pots and pans and forks and knives, the linen tossed everywhere on the floor. "He should rot in jail! If they don't send him to jail, I'll send him there myself! He'd better not show his face around here again, if he knows what's good for him!"

She was screaming, and they heard her upstairs and downstairs. Everybody would know about it, and tomorrow nobody in the whole building would talk about anything else.

Anna watched, big tears welling up in her eyes, as her mother cursed and swore, picking up the mop and then laying it aside, then grabbing the broom and putting it down: Sandra didn't know where to begin.

She watched her mother wrap her fist around the spray cleaner as if it were a pistol and spray it everywhere, on the table, on the cabinet doors, inside the cabinets, on the countertops. At this point Anna decided it was time to go to bed. The spaghetti was ice cold, still sitting there in the colander. When her brother came home from a night of clubbing, tomorrow morning . . . She could just imagine what Alessio would say. Things would start flying again.

Meanwhile, on the A12 superhighway, Arturo was slowing down, turning on his right-hand blinker, pulling into the Autogrill.

He had an appointment here with his lawyer from Viareggio. He got out of the car, looked around at the dark parking lot. He was shitting in fear. He was waiting impatiently for Sandrini, as if Sandrini were some sort of wizard. If nothing else, with all the money he'd given him, he'd straighten things out.

But it was unnerving to wait.

He walked into the Autogrill and ordered an espresso with a shot of Sambuca. There were two truck drivers chowing down on a pair of enormous breaded-cutlet panini. There was a scantily dressed young woman who was unquestionably a prostitute. And then there was a phone booth.

It just takes an instant to slip from the right road onto a completely crooked road. *But*, thought Arturo, *it was a priceless feeling to have made the police look like fools, gotten away scot-free, sipping an espresso in an Autogrill late at night. . . . If only Pasquale keeps his mouth shut, I'm safe.*

The crooked road: It takes a special vocation to follow it. And his friend who owed him a favor was involved in business on an international scale. . . . A couple of months and I'll come home in style! Not one, but *two* diamonds is what I'll be bringing Sandra!

Arturo reached the phone booth, lifted the receiver, and dialed his home phone number. Then, on the first ring, he saw his lawyer walk in, and he hastily hung up.

CHAPTER 27

He was undergoing emergency surgery. Factured ribs and verte-
brae. One hand crushed. A hematoma to the brain, swelling that
they were doing everything possible to reduce.

The man had lain unattended for too long on the asphalt, stretched out
in the rain, losing blood. Blood and senses flowing away into the sewers, in
a chorus of car horns.

The ambulance had taken forever, and the emergency room at the Piombino hospital is no better than it should be.

Operating room number 3, fourth floor. Enrico'd been wheeled in the
door like a bag of meat.

"My love," said the woman sitting in the hospital ward. The woman was
puffy-faced from sleep and Valium, the suffocated lament of someone little
prepared to react. A woman from southern Italy, dressed head to foot in
black. Calf-length skirt, strict and sober, sweaty feet in a pair of moccasins.

My love.

Rosa looked older and fatter in the fluorescent light, while they were
operating on her husband. Rosa stirred a wave of revulsion in her daughter,
sitting poised beside her. The mother short and dark; the daughter dizzyingly tall and blond.

"Doctor," the mother moaned.

She'd brought a rosary of some kind and was holding it in her fingers.

The doctor said that he had no real news.

The odor of bleach and disinfectant. The drab color of the tiles. The
windowless wall of the hospital ward. The high-pitched squeaking of the
gurneys. Francesca liked the smell of disinfectant, because beneath something that kills there's something else that's alarmingly alive.

Francesca was still and silent. She felt like ripping the rosary out of her mother's hands and forcing her to swallow it along with fifteen or twenty bottles of Valium. Down her throat. All of them, one by one. Rosary, Valium, Prozac. *You're fat*, she was thinking. *You're disgusting.* The ward was half empty and the hours went by excruciatingly slowly.

The sounds of gurneys, with bodies on them that were incapable of keeping in fluids.

Francesca was shining in the midst of all this. If possible, she was prettier than usual, because there was a light in her face, a milky glow in the darkness of her eyes. Her pupils, tense and serenely still. The living, trusting pupil. The implacable joy of those who are strong, healthy, and marvelous.

A millisecond in which the light came to the surface. The intermittent beep of the word circulating through her neurons.

Die die die die die die die.

She went into the bathroom. She leaned against the tile wall. She got a thrill out of being there. In the heart of her birthday that no one had remembered. *That's what I want, that's the gift you can give me: Die.*

She went back to the ward. Rosa ran her fingers over the rosary and chanted in a low singsong voice. Her Calabrian upbringing always came out on this kind of situation. *Life is made up of two feelings,* thought Francesca. *Slavery and liberty.* She remembered her grandmother, who couldn't speak Italian, only dialect; her grandmother who would slap her mother openly even after she was married. She remembered the hut in Calabria where they'd grown up, while the doctors cast a pitying glance at Rosa.

She was a woman who chanted in a low singsong but stumbled repeatedly because she couldn't remember the Ave Maria. But what does "ave" even mean? A word that makes no sense, a ritual word. She'd had Francesca when she was nineteen. She'd practically ruined her life to give birth to her. She'd only married him because that pig had knocked her up. *And now look what's become of you.*

Francesca brought her a cup of water, and a cup of coffee from the vending machine.

Rosa was saying: "If I'd had a job, too, we'd have fixed the car, and he wouldn't have had to take the motor scooter. If I'd had a job, too. I said that to him, before he went out. 'Don't take the motor scooter; it's raining.' If I'd had a job, too, we'd have had the money. The money. Ave Maria."

Francesca was spying from under her eyelashes the mobile gazes of the two male nurses. She could feel her legs from ankles to calves tingling with pins and needles, from their eyes. She couldn't sit still.

He'd said to her: "You're not going back to school again!" He'd said to her: "Stay at home and help your mother with the housework." He was convinced that there was no legal requirement for her to attend school. He was convinced that there was no law but his law. It was true; there was no other law. And she hadn't gone back to school.

But if he were to die now . . . The world suddenly flung itself open in an infinite array of possibilities.

They're jamming pieces of metal into his skin. Scalpels, shears. They're stitching him and boning him. They're pumping oxygen and injecting substances into him. The difference between slavery and liberty is a magnificent difference.

Francesca pictured it in her mind the way it looks in certain made-for-television movies she'd seen on Italia 1. Flat on his back on a gurney in an operating room with lots of spotlights focused down on him. She got drawn in. The hours went by, and she imagined in detail everything that she could do if her father were only dead. Modeling competitions. Rome, Cinecittà, Canale 5. Anna would see it all on her television set. Francesca couldn't manage to sit still. Francesca couldn't manage to remain seated. Until, finally, Anna would understand that they couldn't live separate lives, and she'd dump her boyfriend. Just you and me, Anna would tell her.

Boom: He's gone; he no longer exists. Nowhere on earth, no place in time. You wake up one morning and you know that he no longer exists. Francesca was walking up and down the ward, doing her best to suppress the light, the feverish excitement, the desire. Until the doctor finally came out and said: "We've had to amputate one of his fingers."

They spent the night in the hospital. The calla lily sat there on the landing. The stalk, already damaged by the ordeal of the wind and the rain, finally bent over entirely. They spent another night in the hospital, without even coming home to pick up a few bare necessities. The calla lily withered rapidly, resting its concave petal on the edge of the jar, the oblong cone of pollen turned dark. They spent a third night in the hospital, without brushing their teeth or bathing their armpits. The calla lily couldn't withstand the weight of the dust and the hours. The following morning the cleaning crew picked up the vase and tossed it into the black plastic trash bag.

CHAPTER 28

Neither the Sorrentinos nor the Morgantis celebrated Christmas that year.

When 2001 turned into 2002, there were no corks popping out of bottles of *spumante,* no fireworks rocketing into the night sky. The shutters on the fourth and fifth floors of Via Stalingrado, building number 7, on New Year's Eve remained shut while all around them the neighborhood was rejoicing. A washing machine was thrown off a balcony into the courtyard; ten or so injured partiers had to go to the emergency room, and one kid lost his hand.

At Anna's house there was an empty place at the dinner table. Alessio went out dancing and didn't even bother to call at midnight to wish them a happy new year. Arturo took the risk of calling, but his wife just shouted something indecipherable into the receiver and then hung up without another word.

Sandra and Anna, alone, dropped off in front of the television while Fabrizio Frizzi led the countdown.

At Francesca's house they all went to bed well before midnight. Enrico was in bed by seven, after slurping a spoonful of broth. Now he had to be hand-fed and cleaned. He wanted to be waited on, but only by his daughter.

Francesca went into her bedroom and shut the door, and then doodled in her diary for a long time. She was sketching the outfits that she'd wear one day, in prime time. She was listening with one ear to Rosa coddling and babying her cat in the living room, the children setting off firecrackers in the courtyard. "I'm bin Laden!" one of the kids shouted. "I'll kick your asses!"

Both Anna and Francesca fantasized about slipping out, reaching the landing, and meeting in the darkness glittering with fireworks. Watch them together, leaning close against the glass. Neither of them did it. They both just imagined it, under the covers, and they jammed their heads into their pillows to crush down that thought.

There was a father on the run from the law now. The other father was rotting in his easy chair. And anyway, it had been months. Their friendship had turned into something that had failed to launch, like the dud firecrackers found on the sidewalk the next day. You can lose an eye if you try to pick one up.

Anna was sitting at the kitchen table; it was an ordinary February day. Her notebook was spread open, the Latin dictionary in front of her. Something was gnawing at her. She was looking up words without looking for them. Time was standing still.

Words don't love each other; words don't change you. Words don't fix things.

Anna was bored. It was the first time. The fact is that she had never been alone for so long, staring at the inert things that surrounded her, the way that things are dead in the present, a present that really couldn't care less about you and your misfortunes. The fact is that in the winter in Piombino there is shit to do. No one goes out, the streets are empty, the people are holed up inside, dressed in tracksuits in front of their PlayStations.

It seemed to her that the summer afternoons on the roof, surrounded by sheets drying on the lines, showing off their tits to the neighbors, were extinct, gone for good. Francesca's naked breasts, blooming at the window. Extinct.

She got up suddenly from her chair.

When does something become irreversible? She went over to the refrigerator and opened it; she peeked inside. She grabbed a package of ground beef; she wet a piece of bread and crumbled it up; then she mixed it all together.

She found herself detesting time itself, and this was what she could do to fight against it. She wrapped up the meat mix in a triangle-shaped package of aluminum foil. She slipped it into her jacket pocket. Go see what's still out there, what's survived . . .

She left her house. The fact is, you alone aren't enough for you.

Outside. There's a well-known poem that goes: *February is a rascal. / None of the slumber of great winter, / it pinches, it plays the pranks / of burgeoning spring.* Outside there wasn't a damn thing burgeoning. The teacher used to ask her and Francesca to recite that poem by heart, in front of the class, in third or fourth grade.

She missed her, there were no two ways about it. She went galloping down the stairs, narrowly avoiding a little girl squatting down and peeing while boys made fun of her from the floor below. She missed Francesca, she missed something like being two people instead of just one. So she glided along over the empty sidewalk. Not even a souped-up motor scooter parked across it. She crossed the street at a dead run.

The sea had washed up every sort of garbage imaginable on to the shore. Empty gas canisters, used sanitary napkins, glass and plastic bottles. Anna walked over it, the soles of her shoes crunching on the sand, buttoning her jacket because the wind was picking up and it was cold out.

All that was left of her beach.

The metal shutters of the café were rolled down, the tables and umbrellas chained together off to one side, drenched with rain. Anna's face emerged slightly from the hood of her windbreaker, trimmed with artificial fur.

She walked by the cadavers of things. There were broken dishes and fruit juice cartons. There were plastic spoons and forks and shredded plastic plates. The rusty showers up there, and here a broken toy pail. She wanted to believe that in just a few months everything would go back to the way it had been. Barefoot little boys with towels rolled up on their shoulders. Lisa and the other girls playing cards. Nino and Massi playing beach soccer. Why shouldn't it work again?

It always worked before. The season begins again. The bar opens its shutters; everyone crowds around calling for popsicles. At the beginning of June you go to the market to buy a new swimsuit, the skimpiest, lowest-cut swimsuit, one that you can see through when it's wet.

It wouldn't work. Anna took off her shoes and socks and rolled her jeans up to her knees. The swamp water was icy cold, but she splashed in, plunging her feet into it.

She pushed her way through the reeds. Desuetude, piles of rust. This is the red boat where I made love for the first time. That's the sky-blue boat I used to sit on with Francesca. They were there, but they were carcasses. Anna ran her hands over all this.

Places cling to you. Places become extraneous to you.

She placed two fingers in her mouth and whistled. A long, cadenced whistle. Even she didn't believe in it; she didn't really have the slightest hope they'd come. When something's broken, it's broken for good. Her father hadn't come home since November; every so often he'd check in by phone, and her mother wouldn't even let her talk to him; she'd just slam down the receiver in his face. A bastard, a reckless good-for-nothing . . . Not her, your, their father.

My father.

To her surprise, they emerged. One by one, and in packs. From under the boats, from behind the bushes, from inside empty oil drums. Lots of them. There were exactly twenty-one cats.

Anna bent down and unwrapped her packet of scraps at the center of a ring of meowing and erect tails. The things that come back, the things that can never come back. She couldn't bring herself to smile, she just couldn't do it. You're convinced that you have to have more, more, and more, with every passing day. That that's the way things work. Instead what happens is that you have less and less, with every passing day.

The cats were alive and lame. Anna worked out how many months it had been since she and Francesca had last gone out to bring them food. Five months. But those wild creatures could survive anything. They wriggled into pipes, under the rubble, extended their claws and showed their fangs.

Why isn't Francesca here with me? Why am I all alone watching these stinky cats hiss at one another over a piece of meat? Today Elba was covered with clouds. There was so much humidity in the air that you couldn't see a thing from here to there. Not even the silhouette of Monte Capanne, the broken outline of the iron quarries.

Anna turned and looked behind her; she sensed a presence but couldn't see who was back there sitting on a rock over the reef. Someone was down there, just a few dozen yards away. But the sun was going down, mist was rising from the sea; there was no point in trying to make out who it was.

She wanted to imagine that it was Francesca. A pale specter, a phantom Francesca, perched on the rocks where the waves crashed. Like in the legends.

Francesca was a whore. Anna had called her the minute she'd heard about Enrico, but that bitch didn't answer the phone. So Anna had gone downstairs and rung her doorbell, but she hadn't come to the door.

Why was she so stubborn?

She was jealous and morbid, god damn it. *Lesbian!*

The idea that that might be her, the silhouette sitting on the farthest cluster of rocks, melted Anna's chest into a rivulet of heat.

Even if it was her, what could she possibly say? Words never fix a thing.

CHAPTER 29

They ran into one another one Saturday morning in the little grocery store at the far end of the Via Stalingrado.

It was a tiny shop, one of those shops that was doomed to vanish over the next few years: a single room with vegetable crates scattered on the floor and packages of snacks and cookies jammed on the shelves, packed so tightly that at any minute it might all come tumbling down.

Sandra was ordering a pair of rolls and a baguette when she heard the chime ring at the front door, and she turned out of curiosity to see who had entered the shop.

She saw Rosa emerge through the draping curtain of beads.

At first she was flabbergasted. Rosa had become an old woman in the few months since she'd last seen her. She'd always dressed badly, that Sandra remembered, but her face had still been fresh, her black hair had still been neatly combed. . . . Now frizzled gray wires had sprung out on her temples and crow's-feet framed her eyes. Her cheeks were swollen, sagging around her neck; her complexion was an off-yellow that didn't bode well at all. She was dragging a floral-patterned shopping cart behind her, the kind with a rubber handle and rubber wheels, the kind that not even her aunt used anymore to do her grocery shopping.

Rosa lowered her eyes as soon as she recognized Sandra.

"Ciao," Sandra said to her, with a note of embarrassment in her voice.

Rosa responded by ducking her head, and she turned quickly to examine the leaves of the celery bunches.

She clearly was trying to avoid her. Sandra grasped the concept, asked for two more rolls, said, "That's all, thank you," put everything into her shopping bag, and hastily paid the shopkeeper.

Once she was out in the street, though, she decided that she'd behaved like a coward, and stopped. She sat on a low wall and waited for Rosa to come outside.

She remembered that day so clearly, when Rosa had barged into her house and told her all about Francesca. Sandra hated injustice, couldn't tolerate it. That's why she was a militant member of Rifondazione Comunista, that's why she handed out flyers and pamphlets, put up posters, and grilled sausages at the Festa dell'Unità and the Festa della Liberazione. To tell the truth, once her comrades had heard about her husband, they started to give her funny looks and launch barbed comments.

Even if there had been no indictment, no arrest warrant sworn out against him, even a child could see that Arturo was a good-for-nothing. And she'd married him.

Rosa came out of the shop a few minutes later and saw her sitting on the low wall, waiting for her. At first she got a scared look on her face. She didn't want to talk, to Sandra or anybody else. Rosa was a woman who had nothing left to say, or at least that's what she thought.

Still, after hesitating for a few moments, Rosa went over and sat down next to her. After just a few steps, her knees were already hurting.

"How are you doing, Rosa?" Sandra had decided not to beat around the bush.

"I don't know how I'm doing," Rosa replied. "I take a bunch of garbage, these days, medicines . . . that in theory are supposed to make me feel better."

"You shouldn't take them; they can be addictive."

"I know."

Both women stared straight ahead into the middle distance.

"I heard about your husband, heard about his accident. . . . I wanted to come by to say hello, but I didn't really know . . . How is he now? Is he better?"

"He's like a dead man, is how he is," Rosa replied, without a note of emotion in her voice. "Always on the couch, never lifts a finger. My daughter has to serve him and revere him; he calls her every five minutes; she's like his wet nurse, taking care of him like he was a baby. . . ."

Silence.

"At least he doesn't beat us anymore," she added.

"You could still leave him, you know." Sandra suddenly felt a burst of energy. She turned to look at Rosa, grabbed her by the arm, gave her a shake. "You could still kick him out and demand a divorce. The city would give you the apartment. . . ."

Rosa smiled. "Well, I've thought about it. I say to myself: Pick up the phone, call Sandra, ask her if she wants to take a walk. I say to myself: Why not go take a walk in the center of town? But then I don't bother, and the phone never rings. . . ."

Sandra broke in: "Believe me, trust me on this. Go to city hall and submit a request, I'm sure they'd assign the apartment to you, and kick him out, out into the street!" She was getting worked up: "You understand? The apartment and alimony . . . You just have to find the courage!"

Rosa turned and looked hard at her. "I really would have liked to go shopping downtown with you, you know." Now, there was an accusatory note in her eyes. "I wanted a friend, Sandra, someone you can talk to for a while and afterward you feel better. I know, it's my fault, too; I'm ignorant. I don't know all the things that you know. . . ."

Sandra said nothing for the moment, nonplussed. She couldn't see what Rosa was driving at.

"But I know one thing," Rosa started to get to her feet. "You talk and you talk, but in the meanwhile, you haven't filed for divorce. Your husband's out living the good life in Massa, in Viareggio. You think he's cheating on you? And you're still here dealing with your problems. . . . You're all alone now."

She hadn't expected that. Sandra listened in dismay.

"You talk, but actually doing things is a different matter. And I don't want to wind up all alone like you. I'd rather hold on to the dead man in my living room and take my medicines. Where I come from, Sandra, a woman all alone ends badly."

She walked away, dragging her shopping trolley behind her. Swollen legs at only thirty-four. And now Sandra felt like hitting her, but she stayed where she was, seated on the low wall by the food shop.

CHAPTER 30

N ino and Massi listened to him, rapt, staring into his eyes.
"Sending her flowers is a terrible idea! What you need to do
is grab her, spin her around, and stretch her out on the hood of
your car!" Cristiano was telling Nino.

He was shouting so loud that people at neighboring tables turned their
heads in amusement. Alessio was smoking and looking in the opposite direction, at the Corso Italia that was beginning to populate with adolescents.

"No, see, women want it rough! In the backseat, doggy style . . ."

"Okay, but I don't have a car!" Nino pointed out with a note of despair
in his voice.

"All right, what do you have? An Aprilia SR, right?" snorted Cristiano.
He knew all about things; he was a man who had lived life to the fullest,
and now he was wasting his time on this punk with a crush on the girl next
door—or across the courtyard. It annoyed him to a certain extent, but it
also thrilled him to explain to these two kids the way the world works.

Someday he'd explain it to James, and the thought filled him with exu-
berant pride.

"Then don't worry! Just bend her over the seat of your scooter, take her
out, and screw her in a field, in a parking lot, take your pick. But don't send
her flowers, for Christ's sake!"

Nino grew thoughtful.

Massi's head was starting to spin from the Jack Daniels at four in the
afternoon.

"But *France* . . . you don't know her." Nino shook his head. "She's never
done it, she's not easy. . . . She doesn't even think about me. She's not that
available, you know? It's a mess. . . ."

Cristiano lost his patience, slammed his glass down on the table with a theatrical thud. He'd been trying to explain to these two how you go about getting laid for an hour now. He lowered the sunglasses he'd bought from the Moroccan street vendor and said: "Sweetheart! Look at me, you know how old I am? With me"—he pounded his fist on his chest—"women last about as long as cats on the Via Aurelia!"

Alessio stood up to order another drink. He'd heard enough.

Nino and Massi sat there, silently reflecting. In their brains were images of cats hesitating as they looked out from under the guardrail, then at a certain point they gather their courage, they run as fast as they can across the lanes of State Highway 1, and at the last second: Wham! Crushed flat by a fast-moving car.

Try as he might, Nino couldn't seem to link that image with the idea of someday having sex with Francesca.

All four of them were waiting for something—for Saturday afternoon to fill the streets with mopeds and pretty girls; for a fight to break out; for Francesca to show up, dressed up in a way that was to die for; for Sonia, Jessica, maybe even Elena, to appear; for Mattia and Anna to come around after a week of being shut up in the house. In other words, for something to happen in this springtime that had just begun to unfold and bloom in that damned corner of the world.

They were sprawled out at a table outside the Caffè Nazionale in Corso Italia, their backs slouched down in their chairs, their legs stretched out under the table. Every so often they shot fierce and gratuitous glares at the passing pedestrians, as if to say: You don't realize who I am, who you're looking at.

All around them, at the other tables outside the bar, little knots of retirees were drinking too many grappas and smoking too many unfiltered MS cigarettes. Young girls in tight low-rider jeans that revealed their belly buttons were strolling by, wiggling their asses, arm in arm with other young girls, laughing too hard. They were walking briskly in their gold lamé ballet flats on a manhunt for the handsomest boy in their class. And the old guys, turning in their chairs to watch the girls go by, lived in the illusion that they were still on the dance floor, still in the game.

The four young men sat for a good half hour on the patio of the Caffè Nazionale—if you can use the term patio to describe a sort of shabby gazebo, set up slightly askew, between the street and the sidewalk. Across from them, in the Piazza Gramsci, a knot of kids were playing soccer, unfailingly kicking the ball against car hoods, while other kids hurled rocks at the monument erected in commemoration of none other than Antonio Gramsci.

Alessio watched all this while Cristiano unfurled a stream of advice about how to position a woman inside a car or over a parked motor scooter.

Three old women sat motionless on the bench next to the branch office of the UniCredit Bank, like three parked cars, their hair tinted, their faces smeared with makeup. Three widows, or three old maids, who sat there every afternoon, waiting for no one really knew what.

"There she is, there she is!"

Nino practically leaped out of his chair when he spotted her.

"Why are you shouting? Stop shouting!" Cristiano hissed. "Now when she goes by act like she doesn't even exist."

Doesn't even exist . . . Easy to say.

Francesca came floating along like a Greek goddess from the far end of the Via Pisacane, crossing the street in a miniskirt and stiletto heels, the sleeves of her denim jacket knotted at her waist, and Nino could feel his heart pounding from his heels to his temples. Francesca stood out, blond and distinct, from the crowd of people flowing along the corso, and not even that squat little toad, Lisa, who was walking arm in arm with her, could do a thing to dent her beauty.

Nino, Massi, Cristiano, Alessio, and all the drooling retirees who camp out at the Caffè Nazionale had turned to look at her—no, better: to claw at her with staring, inflamed eyes.

She ignored them. She was floating past, light as a feather, suspended in an aura all her own. Only Lisa furrowed her brow, gauging in astonishment the outsized effect her friend had on all and any males.

"Ciao!" shouted Nino from the bar tables, waving hesitantly with one hand.

Francesca barely glanced in his direction.

"Ciao," she replied in a faint voice, dripping boredom.

A "ciao" that was only comprehensible through an act of lipreading: She'd tossed it in his direction as an act of distasteful charity. He was thrilled all the same, and he bounced excitedly on his chair.

"You could wait ten years, I swear, you could wait twenty, and you'd still never make it with that one," Cristiano commented with a laugh.

But Nino wasn't listening now; he was gazing in a hypnotic trance down the sidewalk, where the crowd parted for Francesca.

Now she was standing in front of the plate-glass window of Intimissimi. She was pointing out bras and thongs to Lisa. That shopwindow must have been especially interesting to her, because she stood in front of it for a solid five minutes. And Nino thought of every possibility during that five minutes. Catch up to her, grab her, and kiss her then and there without asking. Even better: Slip into the store and come out with ten pairs of panties, beautifully wrapped, two fat shopping bags that would have made her faint in surprise. Nino pondered these possibilities intensely, but it didn't matter: he didn't have a penny to his name.

When he saw her step away from the shopwindow and vanish into the crowd, he stood up decisively from his chair.

"Let's go," he said to Massi.

They left without saying good-bye and, more important, without paying. Cristiano and Alessio watched them hurry off after Francesca down the corso and shook their heads.

"He's too stupid to ever make it with her," Cristiano snickered. "And Francesca is too hot to let him."

"Yeah . . ." Alessio had turned pensive. "You know, ever since my sister hooked up with that idiot, those two have stopped talking to each other?"

"I know. But your sister and Mattia . . . eh? What are those two up to?"

"Hell if I know!" Alessio snapped. "Don't make me think about it. . . ."

Cristiano broke out laughing: "Eh, your little sister . . ."

"Francesca is a little odd . . . ," Alessio resumed thoughtfully. "I've always seen her at my house, you know? They've been friends since they were two years old. I'm sorry about it. And it just doesn't make sense. . . ."

"She must be jealous of Mattia. She'll get over it."

"She'll get over it." Alessio finished his drink and turned his unblinking gaze on Cristiano. "But now, with that whole deal with her father . . ."

Enrico was one of those husbands, fathers, and heads of household who, even before the accident, never went to the bar. When Enrico wasn't at work he stayed home and watched television, or else he'd wash the car, or else dismantle and reassemble electric appliances.

"He's a pig," said Cristiano, suddenly serious. "*Ale*, remember this. That man is a complete pig, and I'd bet you anything that he pretends to be a retard just to put it to the Lucchini steelworks."

At four-thirty in the afternoon the middle and high schools of Piombino had already emptied their student populations into the center of town, where they strolled from one end to the other of the corso—doing laps.

Platoons of kids, wearing silver Nikes and jeans with rips at the ass, strode briskly and decisively toward Piazza Bovio, as if they were in a hurry. But then, once they reached Piazza Bovio, they'd perform an about-face and head back toward Piazza Gramsci. A tireless back and forth, up and down, from Gramsci to Bovio and from Bovio to Gramsci. Until they got hungry, and then they'd jam shouting into the already overcrowded and cramped fry shop.

They would try to pick up their female classmates en masse in front of the Cinema Rivellino or the Excelsior video arcade. Teenage girls dressed like Britney Spears, eye shadow and lipstick smeared on when their parents couldn't see, peering into the rearview mirrors of their motor scooters.

Some of them, made up like that, were even cute. The little punks clustered around, firing off the most shocking curse words they knew in an effort to pick them up. A pointless expenditure of energy, because these girls ruled them out from the get-go: They were interested in their older schoolmates.

In contrast, the boys reserved a different treatment for the girls who were approachable, and who were usually overweight and acne-pocked—they'd pull gobs of chewing gum out of their mouths and stick them in their hair.

Lisa looked at them, and she felt compassion for them and for herself, as she walked along, useless and invisible, beside Francesca. An unlovely accessory, a shopping bag: That's what she felt like. And she couldn't figure out why she should subject herself to this particular form of torture every Saturday: out for a stroll with the prettiest girl of the Via Stalingrado.

Why on earth did she do it?

Francesca didn't miss a single display window: Replay, and La Rinascente, and Benetton, and even Semaforo Rosso, which sells clothes for old ladies. Lisa was feeling guilty because, as usual, she'd left Donata at home.

"Could you get your ass in gear?" he shouted in annoyance.

"Just a second . . ."

Anna was perched on the saddle of Mattia's metallic 125cc in the middle of an exponential line of Phantoms, Typhoons, and Ciaos parked crosswise along the sidewalk. She was bent over the round rearview mirror, intently applying eyeliner.

Mattia was glaring at her impatiently.

"You look like you're ready for the circus," he said when she lifted her head.

"Go fuck yourself."

Anna was rummaging through her purse for her mascara, and before she could find it she'd extracted an industrial quantity of items.

"Who exactly are you getting made up for? I'm your boyfriend!"

Anna snorted scornfully and ignored him, focused as she was on finding the tube of mascara in the chaos of her purse.

"You even brought soap!" cried Mattia in exasperation.

"Sure. How else am I going to take off my makeup, huh? Let's just say that my father shows up for dinner. . . . He'll take one look at me and then you know what'll happen?"

"He ought to beat you silly!" laughed Mattia. Then he added, in a serious tone of voice: "Wait, is there news about him?"

"Who? The baboon? Even better!" Anna found her mascara and blackened her eyelashes heavily. "He called last week: He's always promising he's going to come home. But mama says that he's run away to Santo Domingo, and while we're stuck here, he's out there sunning himself under the palm trees. . . ."

Mattia listened in silence.

"Still, I know him, I know the way he operates," Anna continued. "That asshole might just show up without warning, any minute, poof! He walks in, he reels off his bullshit, he brings us a tray of pastries . . . and then he hits me over the head with a chair because there's makeup on my face!"

"Come on, your brother's waiting for us."

"Just a second!"

Anna snapped her purse shut, fluffed up her curls, twisted the handlebars to the locked position, and hopped off the motor scooter.

"Let's take a walk, though; let's not spend too much time with Alessio. I don't feel like it. . . ."

Mattia strode off briskly with some annoyance. Anna had other plans than to spend the afternoon at the Caffè Nazionale, breathing secondhand smoke, twisting plastic straws. Even if Anna wouldn't admit it to herself, she hoped to see her.

When they strolled past Calzedonia, Francesca insisted on stopping again. Lisa had no alternative, so she complied. At that exact moment, Mattia and Anna crossed the street. Lisa alone noticed, but she said nothing to Francesca.

"*Madonna*, what a fox!"

An old hick sprawled out in front of the Ice Palace (another Piombino bar equipped with a gazebo and a fauna all its own) glommed enthusiastically onto the sight of the blonde window-shopping for stockings.

"Hey, you know you're a little fox?"

Francesca didn't have any money to buy stockings, so she turned away from the shopwindow and resumed her stroll without bothering to dignify her spectators with so much as a glance, the jagoffs at the bar, reeking of Martini vermouth—you could smell it all the way over here.

"You don't have the only one in town, you know! . . ."

Francesca walked on, silent, dragging Lisa along behind her. She was willing to stop to talk only with older, well-dressed boys, and even then only to kill time. Even compliments bored and irritated her.

Last winter, on Saturday afternoons, she'd go to Corso Italia with Anna, and they strolled down the street, arms around each other's waist, hugging each other close, slipping hands into each other's jeans pockets as if they were girlfriends, but first they'd stop at the tobacconist to buy Big Babol bubble gum and cans of Estathé iced tea, then they'd stop by the *zonzellaio* to buy and gobble a thousand lire worth of *zonzelle*—deep-fried bread dough. And after all that they'd go over to the Gardenia store to shoplift lipsticks.

Francesca was the happiest girl in the world when she and Anna sucked Estathé through straws together, smiling at one another and whispering together, while all the boys walked by staring at them, shouting: "You guys are really good at sucking on those straws!"

Now she felt a sharp stab of rage. That bitch didn't even remember it was her birthday, she hadn't wished her a Merry Christmas, she hadn't even slipped a note under her door in all this time. And now she had to tie a bib around her father's neck and spoon-feed him. She hated everything and everyone.

Anna, too, who at that very moment was sitting at the Caffè Nazionale, forced to put up with her brother and his idiot friend, Cristiano—they were belching, rolling joints under the table, and talking about copper, cocaine, always the same things—wished she could rewind the tape of time and stop it on the snapshot of her and Francesca in front of the L'Oréal stand at the Gardenia department store, and then rewind it endlessly.

They had so much fun stealing lipsticks and eyeliners. They would put on an elaborate show before shoplifting. . . . Anna still remembered it. They'd play at being upper-class ladies: "Oh, try this one, Francesca, isn't it magnificent? Oh! I think that's just your shade! But no, Anna, can't you see how it clashes with my natural coloring? No, I have to say, it's not quite the thing!" And as they carried on with this pantomime, rather than putting the lipstick back onto the rack, they'd pocket it.

Anna remembered and smiled.

If she happened to run into her today, maybe she'd suggest they go shoplift something first thing. And maybe Francesca would say yes, and they would scamper off together to a perfume shop, the shelves of the Coop. . . . Together, like always, as if nothing had ever happened. Impossible. You can't reel time back. But really, when you get right down to it, what fault was it of hers?

Anna watched thirteen-year-old girls go sailing by down the corso, decked with ornaments like so many Christmas trees. She watched her own Mattia taking a couple of tokes on his joint before passing it to Cristiano, and Cristiano laughing like an idiot. God, what a pain.

She didn't want to admit that everything was better before, when they were still friends.

The stereo speakers, inexpertly secured with wire at the corners of the gazebo, were playing Renato Zero. *It must be that the two of us are from some distant planet.* And Anna was listening. *But the world from here just looks like a secret trapdoor. Everyone wants everything.* That's true, thought Anna. *We won't be like other people . . .*

"You guys, I could eat a horse!"

Cristiano was suddenly swept with a wave of the chemical munchies.

"Yeah, me too . . . ," said Mattia. "What should we do? Want to go to Pizza Più?"

"Nooo, I want a gelato. . . ."

"Then let's go to Topone," said Alessio, getting to his feet.

For the record, the *topone*, Italian for "fat rat," is the top one gelato shop.

"What are you doing, Anna, thinking it over?" Mattia shoved her roughly. "Get up, move your ass!"

Anna stood up, angry, as Renato Zero was singing *I migliori anni della nostra vita.* "The best years of our lives."

After more than an hour a retiree sitting at the Caffè Nazionale had given in and made up his mind: He went over to offer a cough drop to one of the three old women, the old maids perched on a bench in front of the

UniCredit Bank. The chosen one suddenly livened up and, concealing her cane behind her back, burst into an open, fantastic laugh.

"*France* . . . you know what I was thinking?" ventured Lisa in front of the plate-glass window of the Semaforo Rosso clothing shop.

A normal person would have said, at the very least: "No, what?" But Francesca didn't open her mouth.

"I was thinking," and she gulped uneasily, "that next Saturday Donata could come with us, too."

Francesca went on comparing prices, mute and indifferent.

"I don't want to keep leaving her at home."

Silence. Francesca disengaged and started walking away.

"She's my sister," Lisa protested feebly.

Francesca stopped abruptly.

She turned on Lisa and leveled a pair of burning pupils straight into her eyes.

"Listen to me, and listen good," she said. "I don't want that living abortion around me. There is no way."

She walked on, brisk and straight as an arrow.

Lisa hung back for a moment. She'd felt something crumple and then snap in her chest. Something that was pain, yes, in its rawest most natural state, but also fury. This time, no, this time she couldn't forgive her.

"I want some ice cream," said Francesca, as if nothing had happened.

Lisa walked after her, but this time she'd taken offense, and deeply so. For that matter, she couldn't imagine what was lurking behind that nonchalant mocking gait, behind that movie star face.

She'd never been to Francesca's house.

When they walked into the Topone they had to push their way through the crowded *gelateria* to the ice cream counter. Pistachio, chocolate hazelnut, Smurf, black cherry . . . Francesca carefully studied all the flavors before making her choice. Then she went to stand in line at the cash register, where she ran into Jessica and Sonia.

"Hey, *France*! What's up?" Sonia asked her.

"Nothing," Francesca replied. She didn't want to talk to them.

If she'd looked to her left she'd have seen Mattia and Alessio pretending to butt heads.

"How's school?"

"I quit school."

"Ah!" said Jessica. "You working?"

She'd dumped Lisa somewhere in the crowded ice cream shop, she couldn't remember where.

"Looking for work," Francesca replied curtly. She definitely wasn't telling those two about her own fucking private business. She turned to go.

Suddenly, when Francesca least expected it, there she was, right in front of her.

She felt her heart leap in her chest and suddenly turned completely pale.

Anna, who was struggling to keep her footing in the crowd, nearly jumped in the air. She, too, had turned around and discovered her—her lifelong best friend—standing right in front of her nose.

It was objectively so unsurprising to run into one another on Corso Italia on a Saturday. To tell the truth: Each of them had been hoping for nothing better. But now that it had really happened, they both had the same absurd expression on their faces. There they stood, inches apart in the crush. Now what the fuck should I do?

A second or two went by, no more, when they were pressed together, elbows touching elbows, knees touching knees, and it tickled like crazy. A second or two went by: They stared at each other, incredulous. In their heads were so many things to do and say that, in the end, there was nothing.

Anna felt like shouting out, in a rush and without a single interval between words: "*France*, I'm sorry come live at my house enough is enough let's run away together Mattia is an asshole your father is a monster I can help you tie him up and gag him let's go shoplift lipsticks together what flavor ice cream do you want?" Instead she said nothing, and her throat was dry and scratchy.

Francesca, meanwhile, thought how much she wanted to hug her and hit her and kiss her and rip all those curls off her head. Because when they were friends—no wait, make that sisters, not friends—everything was good and clear, and now everything is a river of shit, and her father was a monster, but she still had to spoon-feed him, and it was all Anna's fault.

Anna didn't even notice that a smile the size of a house had spread across her face. Francesca was about to give in and return the smile when Mattia appeared and her face darkened instantly.

"Whoa! Look who's here!" Mattia exclaimed.

Anna turned pale. She looked daggers and rifle bullets at him.

Cristiano and Alessio suddenly emerged from the crowd, along with Sonia and Jessica, the whole merry crew, with their eyelids at half-mast and the off-kilter grins of the simpletons that they were.

"*France*, it's been forever!" shouted Cristiano. "Jesus, she's turned into a babe, whoa!" And he elbowed Alessio.

Francesca started turning frantically in all directions.

Anna, instinctively, reached out to grasp her hand, but at that very instant Lisa showed up and Francesca practically leaped on her.

There, in front of the gelato freezer counter, amid all the people raising their hands, she cried: "A cone! A cup! Two flavors, no make that three . . . Excuse me! I want milk chocolate, not Swiss chocolate. . . ." In the midst of all this flurry of activity Anna had reached out to touch Francesca's hand, but Francesca hadn't noticed.

Now she clung tight to Lisa, clung to her for dear life. Lisa, on the other hand, was absolutely furious, glaring at Anna with eyes aflame. "You really should have kept her for yourself, this bitch," she wanted to tell her.

Francesca took to her heels without saying good-bye to anyone. She ordered her gelato, dragged Lisa out by one arm, and was gone.

She wanted to go home immediately. She walked toward the bus station in Piazza Verdi. She was deeply moved. They'd brushed against each other! Francesca was in turmoil, and was practically running. No, she'd never forgive her. When she got to the bus shelter she tripped and fell on the sidewalk.

"You are such an idiot!" Anna shouted venomously at Mattia.

He just snickered and barely noticed.

"Jesus! You could see we were alone. . . . What the fuck did you come over for?" She was furious.

Everyone was giggling.

"You're just a bunch of drugged-out jerks. . . ." Her voice started to break.

Sonia handed her a cone with pistachio and vanilla gelato.

"I don't want ice cream anymore!" Anna took the cone and hurled it to the floor in the middle of the mob scene in the overcrowded *gelateria*.

"And you . . ." Anna turned to Mattia, "you . . ."—her eyes were brimming over with tears—"you've ruined everything!"

CHAPTER 31

L isa caught up with Francesca at the bus shelter.
  She was walking deliberately, fists clenched. She was no fool; she saw how things were now. She'd certainly made a huge mistake: She should have chosen Anna for a friend, not Francesca.

Francesca was getting up from the sidewalk where she'd tripped and fallen.

"Damn it, I got a run in my stocking. . . ."

"That's your fucking problem!" Lisa snapped.

Francesca looked at her in surprise, but an instant later her face darkened: "Look out, little girl, don't mess with me. . . ."

As if to say: I'm in charge here, and don't you forget it.

Lisa wasn't having it this time: "I'm sick and tired of you, *France*. What do you think? That I'm completely unaware that you're using me to make Anna jealous?"

Francesca stood openmouthed.

"I've had it with you, okay? You can take the bus by yourself! I'm walking back . . . ," she blurted. "In fact, you know what? From now on, we're not friends."

She turned to stalk off.

Francesca turned a series of colors: No one, much less a pimply loser, had ever dared to talk to her that way.

"Well, who needs you? Go screw yourself!" she shouted after her. "Have you looked in the mirror? You big fucking whale! Go on, walk home. . . . It'll do you good: You might lose some weight!"

Lisa stopped short in the middle of the bus station. She headed straight for Francesca, walking fast and angry.

Not even she knew where this sudden wave of courage came from.

She stopped in front of her and spat in her face: "You're not worth Donata's pinkie finger."

This time she turned and walked away for good, leaving Francesca standing alone under the bus shelter.

When she turned into the Via Petrarca and found herself walking under the porticos, her tension suddenly dropped. Nice work, Lisa, she said to herself with a broad smile: one to nothing.

Francesca stood frozen to the spot.

For a few seconds she couldn't move a muscle. Go fuck yourself, Lisa. You can all go fuck yourselves.

Yes, she really was alone now, totally alone in the world. The bus wasn't coming, and she had a run in her stocking. Anyway, where did she want to go: home?

Maybe it'd be better if the bus just never came.

She sat down on a bench and rested her head in her hands.

All this pain. . . . No matter how beautiful she was, it didn't help her in the slightest. She hated the world. There wasn't a single asshole, on the whole fucking planet, who loved her even a little. That's what she was thinking, and even though she didn't want to, she burst into tears.

Actually, there *was* someone who loved her. In fact, there was a poor miserable fool who was so head over heels in love with her that he'd been looking for her all afternoon, and now, the minute he saw her—alone and in tears on the bus shelter bench—he practically couldn't believe his eyes.

He ran straight toward her at breakneck speed and came to a halt, panting and exhilarated.

"Go away!" shouted Francesca when she saw him.

Nino took a step back. *Why did she always have to be so difficult?*

"What's wrong?" he ventured to ask.

"Nothing," she mumbled, resting her face in her hands.

"As long as I've known you, all you do is cry and say 'nothing.' . . ."

"Then go away and leave me alone!"

"But I can't stand seeing you like this. . . ."

Nino was crushed; he didn't know what to do next. He gathered his courage and sat down on the bench by her side.

"I told you, you just need to leave me alone," Francesca said, her mouth gummy from weeping.

But Nino wouldn't let her finish, he implusively wrapped his arms around her and hugged her tight.

Francesca stayed there for a while, resting in his arms, because it's nice to have someone close to you, holding you tight and keeping you warm. She didn't want to go home, she'd had her fill of Via Stalingrado, of Piombino, of cleaning the corners of her father's mouth.

She came to her senses. "Nino, really . . ." and tried to shove him away from her.

"But *France* . . . Why don't you want to be with me? Why do you take it out on yourself like this?" He couldn't hold that question in any longer. "I've told you every way I can think, but you just don't want to understand me. . . ." The time had come: "Can't we be together, you and me?"

At that moment the bus arrived.

Francesca leaped to her feet.

"You can't always treat me like this!" Nino said, reaching out for her arm. "Don't go. . . ."

"Nino," she said, shaking off his hand. "Nino . . . ," she repeated calmly, "I don't like men."

She got on the bus and the bus pulled away.

If she'd hit him in the head with a sledgehammer, it wouldn't have stunned him so completely.

While all this was going on, Anna was crossing Piazza Verdi without noticing a thing. She turned into the Via Petrarca and went striding briskly down the street. Enough is enough! she kept saying to herself, I'm done with Mattia. This time I'm dumping him. He's too much of a jerk. He's ruined everything for me!

She was furious and desperate. She wanted Francesca back. No more pretending. She was going home now, and she'd wait for her in the courtyard, sitting on the bench with all the graffiti, where you could still read, in block print "Anna & France together forever." She'd confront her, once and for all.

"So? What is it?" she'd say to her. "Is the problem Mattia? You don't like him? No problem. I just broke up with him."

But when she got to Piazza Costituzione, outside Bar Pinguino, she noticed a black car double-parked with the emergency lights blinking. It was a big Mercedes, polished to a gleaming luster, an E-Class with Livorno license plates. She drew a little closer, read the numbers carefully.

Shit. That was her father's car.

Anna froze to the spot. She peeked in through the tinted windows: There was no one inside.

Still, he had to be around there, somewhere, the baboon. He must be in the immediate vicinity: The emergency blinkers were on. . . .

Anna hid behind one of the pillars in the portico and waited. It was completely absurd, no question. But for sure that damned baboon wasn't in Brazil or Santo Domingo.

She waited, with her heart in her mouth, spying from behind the pillar, with a clear line of sight on the car.

Five minutes later she saw him. It was him!

Arturo emerged cheerfully from the bar, with his unmistakable loose-limbed gait. He carried something, an indecipherable package of some kind, in one hand, and he was laughing loudly as he walked. That bastard was laughing. He hadn't come home in four months, and here he was, walking nonchalantly through the streets of Piombino. . . . That wasn't a package that he held in his hand: It was a bottle of *spumante*!

What an idiot, thought Anna. *What a complete bastard.*

At that moment she felt like stepping out into the open, grabbing him by the lapels, and shouting: "You shit! Why don't you come home? Because you're a complete asshole!"

But he wasn't alone. There was another man with him.

They were both well dressed: black trousers and jackets, white shirts with the collar unbuttoned. Both of them swaggering and laughing, both wearing sunglasses.

Anna watched her father get into the car with that other man, steer out of the parking place, and take off.

Suddenly she felt a knot in her throat; tears started welling up in her eyes. She couldn't take it anymore.

At the first phone booth she found she inserted her phone card and dialed Mattia's number. "My father's an asshole!" she shouted into the receiver, sobbing.

But Mattia, who was stoned out of his gourd, couldn't understand a thing she was saying.

"Mattia! I saw him! Don't you get it? He's in Piombino! And he can't be bothered to come see us. . . . Mama's going to hit the roof if I tell her. . . . Mattia, what should I do?" And she started weeping and sobbing and pounding her fist on the glass walls of the phone booth.

CHAPTER 32

You remember it, *Cri*? That time it snowed. What year? Uh, '94, or was it '95? It came down heavy, you said. It was a massive snowfall. How fucking old were we, anyway? Fifteen, sixteen tops. And you were an asshole, such an asshole. There was all that fluffy fucking snow. Snow, it's snow, you kept shouting, it's *bamba*—cocaine! We slipped and fell on the sidewalks because nobody had the right shoes.

Snow. Who'd ever seen snow? We'd seen plenty of cocaine; it was snow we'd never seen before. And at a certain point you grabbed a handful, you held it almost all the way up to your nose, and you said: *Ale*, fuck! *Ale*, get a handful of snow and look at it! What do you see? No, not like that, look inside the flake. And I even listened to you. I can't see a thing, *Cri*. No, look closer, look at the symbol, the hieroglyphic that's inside it. I don't see. . . . What do you mean? Don't you see the logo of the Ilva company?!

You turned to look at me under the white sky with a magical smile. And all around us—the street, the courtyard, the concrete pillars— everything was breathing quietly. What was it, *Cri*? A joke, something to make me laugh? Or something else. The beaches were all white, we had snowflakes in our hair and eyelashes. We weren't cold. It was all flour and milk, all silent, suffocating gently. Another world.

Now Alessio was standing, in the middle of the vast deserted space that was the steel billet yard, holding the latest generation of cell phone in one hand. As he thought back to all this.

It was called Ilva, back in '94 or '95. His grandmother was named Ilva, and so was Cristiano's grandmother. The grandmothers of lots of people, if they were named after 1918: They were all named Ilva. It was the steel mill that changed its name. The steel mill could afford to change its name. Slip between and around words as if it were the most natural thing on earth, avoid any definitive baptism.

You know what it means? Elena had asked him one day, after making love. They were stretched out on the bed, tangled in sheets and teddy bears in her little bedroom. Why, does it mean something? Elena had laughed, the way she did, partly mocking, partly because she was in love with him. The way she knew how to laugh, the way she knew how to say: Everything means something

Ilva, she had said, laughing, half naked. It's the ancient name, the Etruscan name, for the Isle of Elba.

Christ! It's like saying that paradise and shit are just the same word, he'd blurted out in astonishment. He was holding her slender body against his rough and harsh one.

And you know what it was called, at the very very beginning? Come on, take a guess. In 1865, when it was founded, it was called *Officine Perseveranza*.

My ass! *Perseveranza . . . perseverance . . .* It sounds like something out of a poem by Carducci.

By the time he was hired, in 1998, it had become the Lucchini steel mill. Nobody seems to know if the name is feminine or masculine. But at least paradise and shit no longer have the same name.

I assure you, I looked up "steel," and it doesn't mean shit. It's an alloy, she'd said, a light frown furrowing her brow. Yeah, but I looked it up in the dictionary, and it doesn't mean a thing. I mean, it's not a word with another word hidden inside it. It means that thing. And nothing else.

It's history, *Ale*. It's the fact that there were iron quarries on Elba, and it all started there.

Now Alessio was standing in the middle of the yard, with the sun in his eyes and his cell phone in his hand, and even he couldn't say why all that had surfaced in his memory.

Cristiano was shouting as he explained to him what he had to do to record video.

"Press that!" he shouted. "Not now, afterward! But press that button, on top!"

Cell phones that take pictures and movies were a new thing, and Alessio didn't understand how it worked. Cristiano was taking off all his clothes and acting like a fool. He climbed up, buck naked, onto an enormous Caterpillar and started waving his arms.

"Now, *Ale*! Now!"

Alessio pushed the button and the image appeared on the screen of the cell phone.

The moving image of a pink body, dick flying in the air, inside a black-and-yellow cage, like some science fiction animal.

"Come on, we'll post it on YouTube!"

Two or three millworkers had stopped and gathered to watch at a distance: the demented show of one asshole filming and the other asshole zooming back and forth with a power shovel with the bucket elevated high in the air.

He put it in reverse, as if getting a running start with that who-knows-how-many-ton monster. He made it rear up on the two back wheels.

"Look! He's doing wheelies with the Caterpillar!"

While Alessio was filming, he was shaking his head in amusement.

Cristiano was shouting like a demented lunatic. It exalted him to risk his life on a power shovel, and he extended the bucket arm as far as it would go, like the antenna of a giant grasshopper.

All around, everyone was astonished. The steelworkers left their posts, abandoning machinery and cranes unguarded and idling. They looked up to enjoy the scene, and called to one another to run, come see.

"What an idiot you are," one of them shouted. "Look at what a fucking asshole he is!"

Mattia came running. "Come on, flip it over!"

Cristiano kept popping wheelies, rearing the excavator up on its two rear wheels, but he didn't turn the machine over, he wasn't crushed to death under the massive weight of the power shovel. He controlled it like a bucking bull, and people started clapping.

"If he flips it over, I'll just laugh," said Mattia, as he caught up with Alessio.

"He's doing it for his son," Alessio replied.

"He's doing it to put it on a porn Web site."

But at a certain point Cristiano did much more than merely pop a wheelie on his Cat.

He spun the massive thing around: once, twice, three times. Spinning doughnuts, fast as a spinning top, the dust rising in a cloud, heaps of iron filings floating up into the blue sky. He spun around, on the enormous wheels of the yellow steel beast, and then jammed on the hand brake for a fourth time. Everyone went wild. That's when the floor boss showed up, ready to break Cristiano's nose.

Ilva is the secret name of Elba. The secret that holds the steel mill in its fist.

Alessio saw the floor boss grabbing Cristiano by the nape of his neck, as if he were a cat. He saw the vast expanse of industrial sheds and smokestacks, with the slag crusher in the middle. A sort of robotic scorpion fish that chewed away, crushing slag, the rubble of smokestacks, and rejected partially finished steel products through a massive saw-toothed proboscis.

But he really couldn't manage to link all this in his mind with a dozen or so Etruscan rafts transporting iron, diminutive men casting war axes. Something like a millennium. And Cristiano, naked as a worm, trading punches with the floor boss, a well-placed punch right in the middle of his eye.

"I swear, I'll get you fired, you dickhead!"

CHAPTER 33

A t nine o'clock she got him out of bed. "Careful," she told him.
He had creaky bones and skin hanging flaccid from his arms. The sheets, the ones from the wedding dowry, with the initials embroidered on the hem, emitted bad smells. She had no intention of washing them.

She helped him walk into the kitchen. She helped him get seated; she tucked the napkin in over his pajamas. He'd eaten nothing but broth, for lunch and dinner, for months now. His muscle mass had imploded.

"Should I help you?" she asked him, seeing how he held the spoon.

He wasn't yet used to handling objects with four fingers instead of five. He shook his head no. He looked up at his daughter and then lowered his gaze to the bowl. He checked the level of milk in the container. With the tip of his tongue, he tasted to see that it wasn't sour.

He wanted to move it, slip it into the handle of the cup. It's a simple enough movement, the difference between a prehensile hand and a paw. But there was no middle finger. There was just a hole, with the wrinkled skin inside it.

In March, they'd sent a team of psychologists to see him. He'd answered their questions with silence and a pale, sunken face. The fact is, he didn't understand what they wanted. The steel mill came to see him, the steel mill sent public health physicians to examine him. Lucchini S.p.A. was losing its patience and wanted to understand this case clearly. Wanted to see clearly inside a clump of hieroglyphics: He was incapable of deciphering the questionnaire that they had given him to fill out.

His daughter was standing next to the table, keeping an eye on every move he made. It was pathetic, and comforting, for her to see that he was unable to put sugar into his milk.

The loss of a finger is a symbolic loss for the patient. Depression, but that's only a hypothesis. The giant had shrunk in size, lost weight, buried himself alive inside his flaking apartment, which didn't even belong to him but to the city. The others, the people who lived on either side of him, had mocked him at first. Then he wasn't even a first and last name anymore.

Whatsisname, he'd become.

She took the teaspoon out of her father's maimed hand and sugared the milk for him.

The subject rejects the therapies. The subject is suffering from a trauma-induced illiteracy.

A-Fo 4. Why 4? Enrico was linking together fragile threads between one segment of his memory and another. Because it was the fourth blast furnace, but it was the only one left. Enrico had become a case to resolve and a clinic file. The decline in the price of steel on the world market over the past two decades had forced the steelworks to dismantle A-Fo 1, A-Fo 2, and A-Fo 3.

They were gone now. Like his finger. An enormous hole in the toxin-saturated earth.

Enrico was slurping milk from the cup.

"All of it, drink it all."

He was losing hair in the middle of his head.

Francesca wiped the corners of his mouth with a napkin. She walked him to the bathroom and helped him to lower himself to the toilet. She tore a length of toilet paper for him from the roll. And when he was done, she led him to the living room. She positioned him on the sofa, where her mother was finishing a doily, the cat curled up on her knees. Seated in front of the television set, Enrico sank his cranium back into the headrest and lowered his brow.

It was early April before it dawned on them that he wasn't faking it. Enrico really had regressed to that pathetic state of helplessness; his daughter really did need to feed and clean him. A state of biological rot. Perhaps there's a treacherous gene somewhere on which it's written that you're rotten.

It was Elena's job to take care of it. She had moved Enrico Morganti's file from one desk drawer to another during those months. What mattered to the company was to establish once and for all that they had no legal liability in his case. What exactly is a zero when it sinks into depression? A man who can be replaced by any of twenty thousand Moroccans, Romanians, or Italians waiting in line outside the steelworks. One day an executive walked into Elena's office and told her to fill in the form for early retirement.

A zero in the depressed system.

That morning Francesca polished off her chores in the kitchen even more hastily than usual. She did a sloppy job of washing the cups and saucers, didn't bother to dry them, and jammed even the stained cloth napkins into the kitchen drawer. She swept the crumbs up from the floor just to give an idea of cleanliness, even though she didn't care a bit if that disgusting hovel was clean or not. She hurried to make the beds.

Time, in that house, passed through the mysterious channels of the dust piling up underneath the furniture. *Cats*, we call them: gray wool where nests of parasites make their home. The passage of time encrusted the corners of the shower and the ceiling with lime scum and mold. Now Enrico smiled whenever the cat climbed into his arms and curled up, purring.

It wasn't hard to find an excuse. To say that she'd been out for half an hour when in fact she'd been gone for two hours. "We need milk" was all she needed to say, or else: "We're out of aspirin. I'm going to pay the registration, the insurance bill, the gas bill at the post office." It wasn't hard to get out of the house, especially at night, especially now that her father was taking sleeping pills, and was in bed fast asleep by seven.

Once she was done making the beds she went into the bathroom and locked the door behind her.

She squatted over the bidet and shaved off her pubic hair. This was the first time she'd ever done it. She thought, for no particular reason, that it was appropriate. She shaved her legs and armpits and waxed her arms. She smeared large quantities of lotion all over her white body. That morning she overdid it with eyeliner around her eyes, and red lipstick made her lips look huge.

These days she wore high heels everywhere she went. She stood nearly five feet eleven inches in heels. She walked like the skinny tall figures you see in roadside circuses. The stilts that people once used to gather cherries from the high branches. Every Wednesday morning, at the open-air market, she bought short skirts, close-fitting T-shirts, and elaborate lingerie from a vendor who also offered sex toys at his stand.

It was enough to bring him his morning coffee; it was enough to hold the cup up to his lips and pass her hand over the top of his head, and he subsided, as if he'd been masturbated, into a state of lassitude.

That morning Francesca left the house at 11:30. In a hurry, and with a knowing smile on her makeup-caked face. She liked to tell herself that she never thought about Anna, that she'd become like a package of cookies that had been left open for too many nights. A stale pastry that draws flies.

She walked out, into the sunlit world, and turned down Via Marconi. On her left, the surface of the sea was full of movement and life. The light cascaded down onto it, creating silver, movement, a nascent state. She bought miniskirts with the money budgeted for medicines. She skimped on food to buy corsets and bustiers and G-strings studded with rhinestones; then she modeled them for herself, all alone, in front of the mirror.

Now she was walking briskly toward Aldo's bar on the stiletto heels that hurt her feet. It was one of those days when Elba stands out distinctly against the two light blues—sky and sea. You can make out the villages in the inlets, the cliffs rising sheer over the water, and the patches of dark green shady vegetation. The island, unsullied, in this season falls into the hands of the animals, the elderly, the roots, and the seeds. Francesca didn't look in that direction.

She was convincing herself; she wanted to convince herself. She turned when a van full of plumbers or electricians slowed down to honk at her, and she flashed a smile.

The summer heat was returning. On tiptoes, but it was coming back. She could even take off her jacket and walk bare shouldered. April truly is the cruelest month.

Before going in she stopped to fix her hair in the reflection on the plateglass window. A stray lock refused to stay put behind her ear. The wooden cabin, the dank scent of wet wood. She didn't want to think about it. Francesca stood there brushing her hair in front of the bar window, with the midday sun glaring down from straight overhead and phantoms and specters rising from their graves. This was going to be our home one day. . . . Behind her the street was swelling with exhaust fumes and horns honking. A memory is just a dead piece of shit. She wanted to go in, but she remained on the threshold. The warm earth against her back and the moisture of the grass—even though she didn't want to, she remembered them. *But it's not something that can be part of my life,* Anna had told her that day. *It's something that goes against my whole future.* . . . So fuck you.

She walked in and was given the once-over from head to toe by the half dozen or so slackers bivouacking in the lightless reek of cigarettes.

She looked eighteen. She looked well aware that you couldn't look at her the way you used to.

The future isn't a tense, it's a form of selfishness. I don't give a shit about Anna's future and Anna's selfishness.

Yesterday she'd made that phone call, with the calling card inserted in the slot in the phone booth. She'd punched in the number she'd found in the classified ad in the free weekly. She'd gulped hard when they'd answered the phone.

The voice lurking inside the receiver had been courteous. The person had listened patiently while she provided her information, her details, her exaggerated measurements—thirty-six, twenty-four, thirty-six. And then the voice had even agreed to come to see her where she said, because it was a problem for her to come to Follonica.

Francesca sat on a stool near the counter, tapping her high heels regularly on the floor. She was terrified that the man might not show up at all. She stared straight at the door, and every so often took a sidelong glance at Aldo from under her eyelashes. Aldo was a typical proprietor of a bar with a shady clientele—with a firm determination to ask no questions. There was an underage girl sitting at his bar, instead of being in school, and what's more, she hadn't ordered a thing.

This wasn't the first time it had happened. This girl had been showing up in his bar for some time now, at unpredictable hours of the day and night, striking up conversations with this customer or that. Once or twice Aldo had seen her walk into the bathroom with adult men.

Her father was no longer capable of beating her. He couldn't even go to the bathroom by himself anymore. And there was no physiological reason. No logical explanation. The little cabin, after the winter, must be submerged in nettles and mud. . . .

Now she was drumming her fingers on the marble countertop of the bar. She stubbornly stared at the front door, counting to ten. Then she started re-counting to ten.

The man came in.

Francesca shuddered and stood up, to make sure he could examine her from head to foot. He was a distinguished-looking gentleman, elegantly dressed, wearing a black suit jacket and trousers. A sunlamped face and a pair of flashy Ray-Bans.

He walked toward her, held out his hand in a way that was relaxed and professional at the same time.

"Roberta? No. Francesca . . . Francesca, right?" He flashed a generous smile.

The man took a look around at the seamy little bar and ordered a non-alcoholic strawberry cocktail.

"Two," he added a second later.

Francesca's face pinkened with a healthy blush. You could see her panties, but she didn't seem to notice. She was sitting with her legs akimbo, across from a grown man, and she'd never even made love.

"Well?" said the man as he sat down.

He wasn't interested in knowing—it wasn't part of his job—why such an attractive young woman had made an appointment with him in such a lurid bar.

"Forgive me, I don't have a lot of time. . . . Tell me exactly what you know how to do. Or maybe I should say," he smiled, "what you're willing to do. . . ."

Francesca was surprised to discover that she was awkward and embarrassed. She'd never been particularly glib, and now her tongue was stumbling across her palate; her hands were trembling on her glass. *That's not a good sign*, thought the man. Francesca corrected herself repeatedly, in a succession of "that is-es," "I means," and "basicallys" that lasted a solid ninety seconds, before getting to the point.

"I can only work nights," she finally managed to say.

The man sucked loudly on the straw jammed into the slush of strawberries and milk that Francesca couldn't bring herself to swallow.

"That's not a problem," he wiped his mouth. "Quite the contrary."

She wanted to say something—she was racking her brains—something to win him over, anything to keep him from offering her a position as a waitress or a scrubwoman. He was elegant, so poised. She wanted to be rescued, taken, and adored by that man, by a stranger, by anyone.

"The Tartana is my dream," she found herself saying.

The words fell flat. She bit her lip and immediately felt ashamed that she'd blurted out such a monumentally stupid phrase.

The man inspected her, investigating her from behind his dark lenses. She could always count on her body.

"I'd like to work as a club girl," she said, correcting her aim, "I'd like to dance onstage, in the private salons. Well, really, anywhere you like. But I want to dance."

That expression on her face—the look of a small hunted animal. He'd never encountered such a pathetic case. Still, she was damned pretty.

"You're not a minor, of course. . . ."

Francesca shook her head. Everything about her was yielding and slippery. *No defenses*, the man thought. *This one, you could just grab, turn her face to the wall, and she'd say thank you afterward.*

"You're pretty," he told her, without taking off his sunglasses, "very pretty," with a voice that managed to be velvety and sandpaper harsh at once.

"The Tartana, you said. It's a nice club. . . . We're well-known all over Italy, and even outside of Italy."

Francesca smiled in embarrassment. "Well, to tell the truth, I've never been there. But I've seen pictures. . . ."

A girl like this—she'd take it anywhere, and she'd thank you for the privilege, wagging her tail. The man laughed, showing white teeth, a light milk mustache over his lips.

"The only problem is that I don't have a car; I don't have a driver's license yet."

"That's not something you'd have to worry about. We'd take care of these things . . . of everything."

Remarkable. A much more spectacular piece of ass than he'd ever expected. Fine legs, nice butt. Tits, maybe a bit small. But that's not a deal breaker. An obviously underage Italian girl is something you can take to the yachts moored off glittering Punta Ala, something you can pass around for half a million lire a shot to the wealthy and the powerful for their orgies, on the luxury boats that matter.

The man set down his glass and took off his sunglasses to look her straight in the eye. He had swollen circles under his eyes, a couple of bulging bags.

"The thing is, I have lots of girls at the Tartana already, I can't hire another girl. I hope you don't mind too much," he flashed her a bastard grin.

Francesca swayed on the stool. She did her best to keep down the slushy coagulate that she could feel rising from the pit of her stomach.

"But I do have another club, also in Follonica. . . ."

She pinned all her hopes on that phrase. She couldn't say why she was so determined to get that job: She didn't even know what the job was. Even she was incapable of reading deep inside herself, the clump of indecipherable desires that anchored her there, clutching the counter. The man in the jacket and tie, for that matter, was thinking about something else. He was thinking that a girl like this might even want to kiss you while you were fucking her.

"It's a wonderful club, let me assure you, well-known. . . . Even better known than the Tartana." The girl was literally falling at his feet. "The people who come to this club are people who matter, people you see in the celebrity pages every week. *Novella* 2000, you know, serious stuff. . . ."

"I'd like that," Francesca smiled radiantly. "I'd like to be on television someday. . . ."

"Right!" said the man as he stood up. "The road is long, but you have to believe in yourself, and I assure you, I'll help you as much as I can. . . . You're lovely, what was your name? Francesca . . ." Clearly, the man was thinking about other things. "You're marvelous, Francesca. Remember, only the people that count come to my clubs. You need a jacket and tie to get in. People from Milan, from Rome, lots of agents in the television business . . . and I know them all personally."

He stood up from the stool and invited her with one hand to stand up as well.

He gave her one last once-over: "You might be noticed."

Francesca smiled in the fullness of her smile, a beautiful virgin smile.

"So it's a yes?"

The man pulled out a fat crocodile wallet and paid with a hundred-thousand-lire bill.

"I'll give you an audition." He put his sunglasses back on and went on grazing on her face through the dark lenses. "Next week. We'll give you a call, Francesca. Francesca what?"

"Morganti."

"Okay, Francesca Morganti. I like you. You've got talent. I've got instincts for this kind of thing. We'll do great things together, you and I. But first we're going to have to see you dance. See how you handle things in general terms. Would you give me your phone number?"

Francesca hesitated. Her home number. Worse than giving him a pair of dirty panties.

"Perfect, marvelous. You're marvelous. Remember, it's a long, tough apprenticeship, but in the end you'll make it, you'll see. . . . You'll be the blonde on *Striscia la Notizia!*"

Before he could vanish again behind his reflective lenses, Francesca called out to him, shyly.

"Sorry, but what did you say the name of the club was?"

He hadn't said.

The man turned one last time before vanishing into a jet-black Mercedes SLK.

"The Gilda. It's called the Gilda."

CHAPTER 34

The meadow in front of the *liceo classico* was spangled with daisies, the oleander bushes were blooming, and even the two crooked birch trees outside the window of the classroom were covered with leaves. It put her in a good mood to look at them. Lisa recognized that spring was blooming, and this fact infused her with courage.

That morning Anna hadn't come to school on her motor scooter. Maybe this was an opportunity. She'd noticed Anna, as she rode past on the bus, walking up the Montemezzano hill: her curly head of hair springy with sunshine; an enormous backpack on her shoulders.

While the Latin teacher was explaining the *consecutio temporum*—not that anyone was listening—Lisa made her decision. An irrevocable decision.

As soon as the bell rang for recess, she cleared her throat several times. Then she walked out into the courtyard. Anna was there, busy flirting with boys. Lisa waited for the right moment. She watched her coyly holding court in the middle of a little group of excitable guys, boxer shorts sticking out of their pants, and decided that Anna really was intolerable when she was playing the fool. Still, she waited for her opening. When Lisa saw Anna break away from the herd to light a cigarette, she said to herself: one, two, three. . . . And she walked over and stood right in front of her.

She'd prepared and rehearsed any number of topics in her head—she'd even written them down in her notebook during class—but when she found herself face-to-face with Anna, inches away, grim-faced and irritable, all her speeches flew out of her head. She just asked her point-blank: "You want to walk home together this afternoon?"

Anna, there and then, furrowed her freckled features into an expression of surprise. The last thing she'd expected was that kind of approach from Lisa the loser. Lisa the hunchback, the whale, the braces. Without thinking twice, she replied, "Okay." She said it as if she couldn't have been hoping for anything better.

As they went back into class they each eyed the other out of the corner of the eye with a certain subterranean excitement.

It was odd when they met at the front gate at one o'clock. They'd been in classes together their entire time in school; they'd always listened to each other's oral exams, hoping that the other girl would stumble or fail. It had taken nine years before they finally exchanged a shy smile outside the school building.

Lisa smiled from behind her braces, her fine wispy hair gathered in a skimpy ponytail at the nape of her neck. Anna, her hair wafting in the afternoon light, walked toward her: bewildered, but also a little curious, in the crowded confusion of motor scooters, boyfriends, and parents waiting for school to let out, intent on identifying in the crowd of students the one they love.

They walked side by side down the hill along the panoramic road of Montemezzano. The bright light swept clean the sea, the hills, even the factory, injecting a hint of the excitement of summer. They walked along briskly, one squat, the other slender. Elba, unattainable and radiant, hovered motionless on the horizon.

Anna walked in silence, waiting. Lisa was uncertain how best to begin.

Below them, square miles of reinforced concrete spread out in all directions, the workers' quarters of Salivoli and Diaccioni, Soviet in style, square hewn, teeming with people at every window and balcony, tiny dots that were women hanging out laundry on the roofs, and in the middle, the Coop shopping center.

Anna looked down on it all.

"How did you do on your exam?"

Lisa had thought it over thoroughly, then she'd decided to start with the exam on the history of the Punic Wars. An understated, neutral beginning.

"I think I did fine," Anna replied. "I even knew how many elephants Hannibal had with him when he left Spain. . . ." She laughed: "Thirty-seven!"

Not a hostile syllable in her voice. Lisa could go on.

"All the girls think Mazzanti is so cool. . . . I think he's a total asshole."

Anna turned and looked at her in amusement. "I think so, too! When he asks us to comment on articles about Berlusconi and says, 'Well then, kids, what do you think?' What the hell am I supposed to think, asshole! Why don't you teach us about Scipio Africanus, since that's something we're going to have to know on the final exam."

They were walking a little slower now. They exchanged a glance of amusement. Then they went back to looking at the silhouettes of the huge public housing projects, the ones on the Via Stalingrado taller than all the others.

"Do you want to go to the university, after *liceo*?"

Anna turned, her eyes lively and glittering. "I really think I do. And I want to go far. . . . To Turin, to Milan. I want to go a thousand miles away from here."

"Me too," said Lisa immediately, "I can't wait."

From time to time, as they were walking down the panoramic road, a car would honk and slow down, and only Anna would turn to look. Lisa eyed her sidelong, under her eyelashes. It was nice walking home with her.

"What do you want to do when you grow up?"

Lisa, shyly, embarrassed, gesticulating, made a series of funny grimaces. "I like poetry, novels. . . . When I grow up, I want to be a writer!"

Anna's eyes grew big and round. "But that's not a job! What would you write?"

Lisa's face lit up for an instant. In spite of her acne, her braces, her chapped lips, her thick, tangled unibrow, she almost looked pretty. "I already know the plot. I've even started writing it. . . . But it's a secret; I can't tell you."

When they reached the intersection with Villa Marina, they stopped at the traffic light sealed in a nest of crystalline silence. They waited for the red light to turn green.

Anna said: "Well, as for me . . . I'm not sure exactly what I want to do. I just know that I want to do something important. Maybe architecture, so I could design some beautiful apartment buildings, with rooftop gardens and balconies with verandas. . . . Maybe when they knock down the buildings we live in now, I could build their replacements. . . ."

"If only!" Lisa exclaimed.

They crossed the street.

"Or I could get a degree in business and economics, and then I could become the minister of labor." Anna was like a river in spate. "Mama says that they're taking away all the factories, moving them to Thailand and Poland. . . . And when they're gone, we'll be flat on our asses around here.

So, if I become the minister of labor, or of . . . what's that English word? Of welfare? Then I could stop all that from happening."

"I want to tell a story," Lisa said again.

It's a funny thing. Sometimes it takes an earthquake, a cataclysm. It's like during a solar eclipse, when everything turns upside down, all the animals flee, and nature goes wild. Opposing elements make friends.

When they came up to the Coop, teeming with people and shopping carts and bags of groceries, Anna gave in to a surprising impulse. She suddenly grabbed Lisa by the arm, turned down a side street instead of going straight, and said: "Come on, I want to show you something. . . ."

Lisa had no idea where Anna was taking her, but she followed along curiously, almost happily. Because the temperature had risen, they'd taken off their jackets, and all around them was a crowd of mothers holding toddlers by the hand, kids getting out from the preschool.

Anna stopped in front of a hedge, holding her breath.

"Through here," she said. And she slipped through a break in the greenery. The smooth aromatic leaves of the laurel bushes proliferated on the chaotic, tangled branches. Lisa followed her and emerged in astonishment in a tiny playground that had two trees in the middle, a slide, a merry-go-round, and two rusty swings.

Anna broke into happy laughter. "You see? Everything in the world can change, anything can happen, but nothing ever changes in here!" She dropped her backpack onto the grass. "This place will always be the same."

Lisa looked around her at the little rectangle of greenery hidden in the heart of the reinforced concrete. She couldn't understand, of course, she couldn't even imagine. A sweet little thing, a handful of yellow dots surrounded by knee-high grass.

They sat down together on a bench. Now Lisa expected Anna to reveal the mystery underlying that abandoned little park that had absolutely nothing special about it, but Anna lit a cigarette and sat, as if in a trance.

"It's exactly the way it was, I swear it," she said, over and over again, in a low voice.

It was as if Francesca were stretched out there on the unmown lawn with the tufts of wheatgrass. As if that park were Francesca incarnate, the sun pouring down in the middle, between the play equipment, creaking with every gust of wind. Francesca had felt safe and intact in this place that now made Anna laugh, and Lisa couldn't understand what was happening, because nothing was happening.

"That's the cabin!" Anna pointed at it, arm held out straight, index finger outstretched, and a sort of enthusiasm in her voice, as if she were cheering in a soccer stadium. "There's an anthill inside it! You have no idea how long I hid out in there. . . ."

Francesca emerged from the aromatic nest of damp wood.

"So you want to become a cabinet minister. . . ." Lisa returned to the earlier topic of conversation, because she was bewildered and didn't know how to act.

"Right," nodded Anna, with determination, "minister, member of parliament, legislator."

"And you want to save the Piombino steel mill, too?"

"Everything, I want to save everything! This little playground, too, and the Lucchini plant!"

Lisa had lots of things she wanted to tell her. That Donata was sick and getting worse; that she was no longer friends with Francesca. But right now, sitting with her on this bench, she felt happy.

There was no need to say her name. Anna recognized her, between the hedges, sitting on the merry-go-round. The blonde. The finest thing.

"What is your story about?" Anna gave Lisa a shove. "Now you have to tell me. If I brought you here, you absolutely have to tell me now!"

Lisa looked down.

They were horribly late, and at home there were two irate mamas who had drained the pasta a good long time ago.

"It's about a friendship," Lisa whispered. "A friendship between two girls, a blonde and a brunette, and at a certain point they quarrel."

The expression on Anna's face changed.

"But then they make up, they find each other again," Lisa hastened to add, "and then they discover . . ."

"Don't tell me," said Anna, standing up and grabbing her backpack. "I promise you that I'll read it, when you're done writing it."

"But who knows when I'll be done!" Lisa blushed. "I've only written the beginning of the story. . . . I'll finish it at the university . . ."

"Then we'll go to the university together," Anna smiled. "But now get your ass in gear, otherwise my mother will be furious."

In fact, when Anna got home, her mother was furious, and the pasta was overcooked.

Her brother was sprawled out, his feet on the chair across from him, channel surfing.

Sandra filled their plates and brought them to the table.

"*A*'," Alessio said, chewing a mouthful, "anyway, Francesca's in bad shape. . . ." He swallowed the mouthful of penne in a gulp and went on talking. "I heard some things about her. *Madonna*, if what they say is true. . . . I've heard some really nasty rumors. I don't know . . ."—he looked up from his plate—"but I really think you should go talk to her."

Anna sat there, her fork poised in midair. She hadn't taken a bite.

Sandra listened in silence, thinking back to Rosa, the way she'd acted all high and mighty the other day. Where did she get the nerve to preach to me?!

"*A*'," Alessio went on, "I saw her at Aldo's bar. . . . I didn't want to tell you about it, but, I swear, she was dressed like a hooker."

Her best friend. A hooker. Anna's stomach had shrunk and was continuing to shrink, into a tiny knot.

"Listen to me," said Alessio. "Go talk to her. . . ." Then he drained off a whole can of Coca-Cola and belched as if it were the most natural thing. "She's really turned into a whore."

Anna felt her face turn flame red. She would gladly have killed him right then and there.

"All right, fine," she shouted in fury. "Since you can never seem to mind your own business, now let me tell you something, and we'll see what you think! Two weeks ago, when was it? The Saturday before last . . . I saw our father in Piazza Costituzione!"

Sandra turned gray.

Alessio turned green.

"I saw Papa!" Anna stood up from the table in a frenzy of exasperation. "He had a bottle of *spumante* in his hand! So why don't you learn to mind your own fucking business, you idiot, and shut your mouth about Francesca. Just don't even mention her name."

Anna vanished into her bedroom, slamming her door behind her. She threw herself onto her bed in tears, while behind her in the kitchen pandemonium broke out. Her own Francesca, dressed like a hooker. . . . It isn't true! Enrico wasn't human.

Enrico was the only man in the world who lacked even a scrap of humanity inside him.

CHAPTER 35

fter his shift, he was filthy: the coal-black boogeyman they tell little kids about to scare them. He walked into group showers where old men and teenagers soaped up, naked, side by side. He had to scrape his skin with an exfoliating sponge, the kind women use, to get the coke and iron dust off his flesh. That shit gets everywhere, deep down: How could it make its way into his underpants?

He brushed his hair carefully before heading out. Kidded around with his fellow millworkers about the tidal wave of layoffs. Swore twice or three times when he was putting on his socks, but laughed as he swore, in the Lucchini locker room that hadn't changed since the seventies: The doors of the lockers were practically falling off their hinges, the faucets all leaked.

Outside it was a magnificent day in May.

At two in the afternoon the temperature was already in the nineties outside. The season had begun: The beaches were almost entirely free of seaweed; the beach clubs were open all up and down the coastline that tourists loved best. Beach umbrellas were springing up everywhere, canvas beach chairs and recliners, and guys in Bermuda shorts walked through the sand, yelling: "Coconut, nice cool coconut!"

Alessio punched out at the time clock and said a friendly good-bye to the old woman in the booth. He didn't notice that he was being followed. He climbed over the crossing barrier at the industrial vehicle entrance. He'd never liked tourists.

He walked past the blisteringly hot hoods of the cars in the half-deserted parking lot in the baking heat. The clattering din of the factory hovered over everything: He couldn't make out the footsteps of the person who was following him. The distinct clicking of high heels on the boiling hot asphalt.

He swung open the door of his VW Golf GT, polished to a dazzling gleam. He tossed his backpack with the bath soap and shampoo into the backseat, along with his greasy crumpled-up overalls. He heard the voices of various coworkers as they left: "Ciao, you piece of shit!" He'd dropped his keys under the seat; he had to crane his neck to find them. "What are you doing with your ass in the air? Oh! Little faggot!"

Then he heard a completely different *ciao*.

He looked up. He saw her through the windshield. She was smiling politely, in her close-fitting black business suit. Dressed that way, outside of the protective sphere of the air-conditioned office, Alessio could tell that she was dying from the heat.

He emerged from the interior of the car in slow motion (Don't make any sudden moves, Tom tells Jerry, turn around slowly and reach for the sky). He'd immediately felt a tingling sensation in both legs, a Pavlovian reaction. Take Alessio, put Elena in front of him, and you can be sure, whatever thoughts may be going through his head, he'll get pins and needles in his legs, an increase in salivation, an accelerated heartbeat, and, deep down, a string of oaths as he curses all this.

"Can I steal five minutes of your time?"

He looked at her with distrust. The formal tone she'd employed every time they met lately, those few times they ran into one another in the parking lot, always managed to put him in a bad mood. Tiny dots of perspiration pearled her forehead; the foundation was starting to run at the corners of her nose and mouth. She was still beautiful, no question. Executive manners aside.

"Were you heading home? Do you have a minute?" Elena didn't wait for an answer. "I have to talk to you, *Ale*. It's urgent."

Ale. What an effect it had on him to hear her use that nickname, that confidential name.

"I'm all ears."

"Well, maybe we can get out of the sun. . . ."

They took shelter in a scanty strip of shadow next to the wall by the entrance that read LUCCHINI S.P.A. PIOMBINO written in foot-high letters, black on white. Alessio left his car door open, with his wallet and cell phone in plain view. Elena unbuttoned her jacket and, with an unmistakable sense of relief, she was now dressed in a semitransparent, light blouse.

They stood facing one another. The lace on her brassiere was catching on the fabric of her blouse, making clearly visible the outlines of those familiar, remembered shapes, which were now reemerging, an unmistakable presence. Alessio tore his gaze away.

"It's about layoffs. The 350 positions we eliminated aren't going to be rehired. There's going to be another wave of firings. Our Russian partners are imposing some pretty harsh conditions. They want to diversify the company's product line, move part of our production chain to Eastern Europe, a pretty substantial part. . . . There's nothing we can do to stop them."

Talking with her about production levels and planned layoffs. Something new that irritated him beyond belief.

"Italy's expensive. You know all about it: labor costs, transportation, and materials are all expensive. . . ."

"Okay," Alessio started dangling and jouncing his key chain. "And this has what to do with me?"

Elena's face turned serious.

"It has a lot to do with you, Alessio." There she went, stabbing down on the main point like a fork pinning a piece of meat. "It involves you directly and personally," like a schoolteacher, like an executive schoolteacher, "because it's certainly not in my own personal interest; in fact, it goes against my professional responsibilities to inform you about the corporation's future plans."

"Well, let me be the first to thank you!" he exclaimed with that arrogant sarcastic face that he knew how to put on, and that he knew drove her crazy. "Long-term corporate planning, no fucking shit!"

Elena was certainly not laughing. She looked at him grimly, annoyed and impatient. But rigid as she was, in her blouse, sheathed in a knee-length skirt that wrapped tightly around her thighs and hips, and with all those things she held under her arm: the jacket, the file folders, the dossiers, her attaché case, all she could do was raise an eyebrow and snort in annoyance.

"*Ale*," forcing herself unsuccessfully to be understanding and patient, "what we're talking about here is your future, not mine. I want to be perfectly clear with you. I need to know what your real intentions are, whether you want to go on working for us, for our company. . . ." — for *their* company, no less—"in other words, clear and simple. . . . Do you want to stay with us until retirement or do you intend to look for some other position?"

"Why do you ask?"

"Because it matters. Because I'm in charge of hiring and firing, because I can decide what column to put your name into. Eliminate your name from one list, add it to another list." She leaned forward and said, in English: "*Do you understand?*"

The condemned and the saved. She was even trying to be funny. Jesus, what a powerful woman. . . . Hear ye, hear ye! What list to write my name in, or erase it, or rewrite it. She's the one who decides, get it? She really should have married that toad who had the job at the UniCredit Bank.

"This paradise? Who'd ever want to leave?" Alessio laughed bitterly. He was shimmering with pure hostility, pure anger. "I see that you've got yourself a nice little position here, in this paradise. . . ."

Elena ignored the jab, and went on: "Your name is on the list for the next wave of layoffs. I just want to help you."

Next wave of layoffs. Help you.

"Listen, Elena, let's talk straight. I don't want any favors from you. I don't need them."

She bit her lip: "Was I rude somehow? I apologize if I've offended you in any way. I certainly didn't mean to. . . ."

"So that's how it is? You can save my ass and stick some poor bastard on the list in my place, just because you've never met him, some poor bastard with a family, with kids?" He was starting to lose his temper. It was clear as daylight that he was losing his temper, and she should have counted to a hundred, not just to three, before opening her mouth.

"I heard about your father . . . ," she suddenly blurted out "I know that your salary is especially important now for your family, so I thought . . ."

"*You thought?* What the fuck did you think?" roared Alessio. "You'd better not fucking think about me, you understand? How dare you, you little bitch! My father?" Out of his mind now. "What does my father have to do with anything? Tell me what the fuck my father has to do with me?! Slut!"

Elena closed her eyes: Omigod, what have I done, omigod, what have I done?

"You misunderstood me, *Ale* . . . ," she tried to say. "I'm sorry."

But his face was bright red. He was now capable of hurling himself furiously against a street sign, against the mini-Dumpsters or a parked car, anything that came to hand, and simply destroying it: She knew Alessio well enough to know that. So she stepped closer to him to grasp his hands, she tried to calm him down the way she had millions of times before, until four years ago.

"Don't touch me," he snarled, wounded, shaking her hand off him.

"It just came out wrong, I swear to you." She put her hand over her mouth and then said, in a tiny voice: "I only wanted to help you. . . ."

"But I don't want to be helped. Fuck!" he shouted furiously into her face, distorted by the heat and fear. Then he fell silent.

He turned away. "See you." And started walking.

Elena tried to keep him from going. She grabbed his elbow with one hand and held tight. And he could feel the grip of her hand throughout his body. He didn't move.

"Your fancy job went to your head," he said.

Elena took a step forward, covering the four or five inches separating them, zeroing out the distance and pressing cheek, breast, and belly against his powerful back.

It was a spontaneous thing that left both of them rigid.

"Your fancy job doesn't authorize you to treat other people like beggars and bums. You don't know a fucking thing, just remember that."

A moment of incredulity at finding themselves, after all these years, in the middle of a full-blown fight, fully aware that they were now two impermeable strangers, inaccessible to each other, with a wall of bitterness between them.

The contact was warm, it felt good. He could feel her heart beating against his back. He could feel how upset she was, how terrified; he could feel her whole presence worming its way under his skin, roving freely through his circulatory system.

"Please," she said.

Without releasing her grip on him, she forced him to turn around and look at her.

"You really have changed, you've turned into a high-class call girl."

"Please." She held his hands and he let her hold them. "It's so hard to talk to you. . . . I didn't know how to approach you, so I made a mistake. When I saw your name on that list today, I was scared. Believe me, my heart was pounding in my chest. . . . And I promise you, the last thing on earth I was thinking about at that moment was my fancy job."

A second or so later Alessio broke out of that absurd embrace.

"Okay, Elena," he said, in the most neutral tone of voice he could muster. "You just do whatever you have to do, do whatever your conscience tells you to do. Now I've got to go." He turned toward his car. "So have a nice day," and he started walking.

"Wait!"

Alessio was walking briskly toward his Golf GT, and she was chasing after him in disbelief. She kept dropping papers from her files, they fluttered in all directions, and she was letting them fall and flutter. "I don't want this to be the way we say good-bye." She put a hand on the hood with determination. "Wait a minute. I don't want it to end like this, after all these years. . . ."

Alessio looked inside the car to see that his wallet and cell phone were where he'd left them.

"Can I ask you to lunch?" She was begging him. "Let's have lunch together, please, we can take some time to talk. . . ."

Take some time to talk? What is this, a public service announcement for fathers and sons, a line from a song by that pansy Michele Zarrillo? Elena was spewing one atrocious banality after another in a beseeching tone that was just ridiculous. She realized it clearly and was deeply mortified. But she wouldn't give up.

"Men ask women to lunch, where I come from," Alessio snarled.

The window was rolled down and he closed it. Put an end immediately to that pathetic scene, seal it hermetically out and away. He did his best not to look directly at her.

"Then why don't you ask me to lunch?"

Now she was leaning against the car, shouting against the window as it closed.

"This was a misunderstanding, *Ale*, please! You can't go. It can't end like this!"

He started the engine. Vroom: sharp and unequivocal. Key turned in the ignition, clutch, accelerator. He shifted into second, third, and fourth gear in rapid sequence, in fewer than 350 yards, emitting a tremendous roar that was still not enough to express his full fury.

This can't be how it ends, after all these years. That slut, that whore, she should have thought about that! Fucking bitch that you've become. With your fucking attaché case, your blouse, just fuck yourself! She wants to offer me charity. Goddamned pampered aristocrat. You can stick your fucking charity up your ass. "Stick it up your a-a-a-ass!" he shouted, alone, inside the speeding car.

Elena was standing frozen in the middle of the parking lot under the baking sun, on the boiling asphalt. She'd clapped a hand to her forehead; she'd managed not to shout. She stood there, motionless, her eyes fastened to the spot where Alessio's car had vanished in a cloud of dust. The steelworkers, variously ending and starting their shifts, stared at her curiously.

Slut slut slut slut slut! What the fuck did all that education, all that schooling, do for you, turn you into an arrogant slut? The power to change what category I put you under. She takes my name and she moves it, get it? The layoffs. Market pressures. "Our Russian partners are imposing some pretty harsh conditions," he aped her voice aloud in an angry falsetto. "Just go fuck yourselves, every last one of you!"

He stamped on the brakes at the intersection. The driver behind him was forced to swerve, and missed him by inches. Alessio stared at the yellow traffic light for a fraction of a second, just long enough for it to turn red. Then, once it was red, he accelerated again, and screeched around, making a reckless U-turn in the middle of traffic.

Alessio unleashed traffic hell outside the Bar Elba, triggering the deepest wrath of the motorists who were forced, variously, to jam on their brakes, run straight into a streetlight, a road sign. A furious chorus of horns, people staring out of the bar.

He went roaring back up the one-way street the wrong way, went rocketing into the parking lot where Elena was still standing, motionless in her Gucci suit, her attaché case dangling open, and her face that of a postmodern Madonna, like some sculpture by Cattelan.

"Go on, get in," he said, throwing open the door.

A Madonna, her face twisted, dressed as a top manager, like something out of the Venice Biennale.

"Get in, I'm hungry."

He was acting tough, playing the hard-ass, with one hand on the gearshift and the other on the wheel, not looking at her and jamming his foot on the accelerator so that she could hear the anger of the engine. Elena flopped down into the passenger seat, got a run in one of her stockings, and Alessio roared off even before she could close the door. A gust of wind scattered pink slips all over the parking lot.

Now they were sitting wordless in the car that smelled of Magic Tree car freshener.

At the exit from the parking lot Alessio yanked up the hand brake, like in the old days. The car whipped around in a 360 degree spin, and Elena couldn't help but smile—reckless, affirmative. Affirmative of what? That she couldn't say, that she didn't care to know, as she hastily fastened her seat belt because he was charging like a bull, hurtling cross-country through streets, on ramps, through intersections clogged with traffic.

They were risking a fender bender every twenty yards or so, they were risking far worse. Alessio was driving and not looking at her. She wasn't looking at him either, but she had a crazy urge to throw her arms around his neck. A semidemented desire to tell everyone to go fuck themselves. She had a run in her stocking, her makeup was smearing, her blouse was half unbuttoned. What do I care? She was next to him while he was driving; he could have gladly driven into a bridge abutment.

The city, the houses, the shops, the newsstands, the balconies, mothers with strollers, old men with dogs, toddlers, children letting out from school: the world was zigzagging against the car windows, leaping from one sheet of glass to another, from the windshield to the rearview mirror. A huge mess. Alessio made turns fishtailing, and Piombino became Guernica.

Elena was holding her breath, but only because she was having the time of her life. Alessio knew it, that she was smiling in the passenger seat. That she was the passenger.

Her heart was doing what it wanted, her lungs likewise, and her leg muscles were completely shot. How long would it last? Fifteen minutes, half an hour, a whole afternoon? It didn't matter. Time was outside the car door, along with profit, capitalism, the mill crucibles. The past, the future: *ciao*.

"What time do I have to get you back to your office?"

"I have the day off."

Alessio turned to look at her.

They looked at one another, in total complicity, while the sun shone gleaming into the interior of the car that was scented with Magic Tree.

"Let's go to the Vecchia Marina," she ventured.

She was overexcited; she was too alive to notice.

"Are you joking?" he asked her.

"No, not at all."

Alessio pushed the automatic doorlock, shot a quick and contemptuous glance at the red-and-white sign that stated, clear as day, LIMITED-ACCESS SECTOR, then turned to look at her . . .

There was silence in the old part of the city. The silence of fishnets abandoned on the piers, pocket fountains carved into the marble, and small wooden boats bobbing in the water. La Rocchetta was the ancient refuge of fishermen and adolescent couples going steady on Saturday afternoons.

In Piazza Padella, a piazza no bigger than a broom closet, Alessio and Elena had kissed for the first time.

As they walked into the restaurant, the kitchen was just closing.

"We'll make an exception for you," said the waiter. All around, on the empty tables, there were crusts of bread, rumpled napkins, and carafes with an inch or so of wine in the bottom. A man who looked to be in his sixties was finishing his meal alone, diligently cutting something with knife and fork.

They sat down. Not at the table where he'd asked her to marry him, another table . . . but still overlooking the island.

Elena's hair was a mess; she was tormenting a bread stick. Alessio grabbed the menu and started reading without understanding a thing. There wasn't a single subject, not a single one in that whole boundless region of subjects, that they could talk about.

They ordered two plates of spaghetti with clam sauce and a bottle of white wine—a Greco di Tufo.

For a while they looked at one another; for a while they looked at the silhouette of Elba and the way the sun coated it with silver at that time of day. The tension dissolved in the alcohol; the solitary gentleman set down his empty glass of *limoncello* and stood up, putting on his jacket.

It was peaceful now, in the empty restaurant. They felt the calm and the sense of surrender. The waiters loosened their uniforms, the cook took off her apron; the calm and surrender of the afternoon hours, in a place out of the past overlooking the sea.

Actually, there was one thing to talk about, one thing to say. But neither of them said it.

They got up at almost the same instant. Alessio went to pay the check, Elena remained by the table, afraid to stop him.

They left the restaurant and walked side by side toward the lighthouse, the point that was as close as Elba got to Piombino.

The VW Golf was still there; they hadn't towed it. But there was a ticket, clearly visible under the windshield wiper.

The woman walking next to him now, in her black designer suit and satin blouse, was the director of personnel for the Lucchini corporation. The man walking along next to her was a specialized steelworker, jeans loose, riding low on his ass. Still, somewhere on that bench, their names must still be there, carved into the wood.

They leaned over the granite balustrade. The piazza, dedicated to

Giovanni Bovio, distinguished devotee of the creation of an Italian republic, a man of the Risorgimento, a crusader for the idea of a just world, had over the course of time become a terrace for people in love.

The waves were breaking on three sides. It seemed as if they could touch it, as if they could reach out across the waves and seize it . . . Ilva.

The secret name, Alessio said to himself softly, the meaning.

CHAPTER 36

The lights snapped off.

"Tits! Tits! Tits! Tits!"

In response to the raucous stadium cheer, from the left side of the room, came another, from the right side: "Pussy! Pussy! Pussy! Pussy!"

She could hear them banging and shouting from behind her door. Livestock jostling against the fence of the corral. She could hear them pounding their fists on the table, rattling their money on the counter. One, two, three . . . she was counting.

She held her ear glued to the door. She heard a couple of glasses break, the onset of a brawl. Then the intervention of the big, bearded, Bud Spencer–looking bouncer.

When she reached ten she scampered out of the dressing room, ran on tiptoe through the tables. A light breeze, taking care not to trip.

She walked onto the runway. The clamoring audience could make out her silhouette moving though the dense, foul-smelling darkness. They started to quiet down. The soft flickering of her G-string in the light of the cell phone screens entranced them. The chants died out.

She took her place on the pedestal. She seized the metal pole with outstretched arms and slid into her starting pose.

Rhythm. She tilted her head back. *Rhythm.* She spread her legs.

The spotlight in the middle of the ceiling suddenly turned on, blazing her into existence.

You can feel the, you can feel the . . . Drenched in hot white light.

Massed, sweating. There were more than two hundred people.

They emitted a collective grunt of surprise. A second later, the music exploded. *Rhythm is a dancer.* Her song.

And she was nude, and all eyes were on her.

If it had been last year, if she had been looking out the window of the fifth-floor bathroom of building number 7, then Lisa would have been spying on her from behind the curtain with her heart racing furiously, and her uncle would have made a point of interrupting his breakfast.

But this is a completely different situation; this place is full of drunken steelworkers clapping and breaking glasses. It's in front of all these men, here and now, that she achieves fulfillment.

She orbits, unveiled, around the steel pole, in stiletto heels and a G-string. Nothing else.

She isn't like the other girls. She's alive. She's beating time to the music with her lithe pelvis. Nothing's holding her back. The candor of a little girl under her eyelashes. When she lifts her leg, higher and higher until she can touch her ankle to her temple, then she really is your limber daughter on the foam mat doing an artistic routine at gymnastics.

Moving aside the hem of the G-string with her index finger. You can see that she's afraid to do it. She smiles in embarrassment. It's her embarrassment that is frightening; it's her loveliness that unleashes the steelworkers from the Lucchini and Dalmine plants. It's deeply moving to see a grandfather, open-mouthed, hand losing its grip on his glass, because basically she doesn't know how to do her job. She fumbles the crucial point, the G-string.

She grabs on to the pole, lets herself swing around, her silky hair flying free. Cheers and applause. She's happy, she looks like a radiantly happy whore. She rubs her ass cheeks on the pole, getting down on her knees. Once, twice, three times. The steelworkers are going crazy; they get up and wave their money. This is their holiday.

There's a fury in her as she dances. There's the determination and the insecurity of her first dance audition. Sometimes she bursts out laughing, when she makes a misstep: That's something that nowhere in the world, during a strip show, you will ever see happen. You have to come here, to this fucking backyard of nowhere, to this moldy cellar auditorium, to see something like that, something that moves, a true thing that sometimes falls down, gets back up, shakes her ass like a wild animal.

She knows it perfectly well: The talent scouts from Canale 5 will never see her. They don't come here. This is a dive. The people who come here do hard labor for eight-hour shifts, don't wash often enough, have a family at home in a disgusting little hovel. The strategic vantage point from behind the curtain.

She likes to be seen, likes to be looked at. But not by just one man. She knows the sound of groaning from behind the door, the hand slipping into the trouser pocket, rubbing the genitalia. She knows that it's because of her. She knows it's her fault. But here, on the stage of the Gilda, she's having fun.

Lisa's uncle, multiplied by a hundred. The man hiding in the building across the way, behind the door . . . She's not like *that other one*. She's not playing around. She pulls in a crowd of two hundred men to this club every Friday night, and she manages to extract more money from their fat wallets than all the other girls put together.

A vulgar smirk on the clean face of a high school girl. That's not all. She's the pearl in the slimy, drooling texture of the mollusk.

You can feel it everywhere.

The hidden man. The unconfessable thing with a mottled red face, unzipping his fly. They were all tremendously proud, fiercely fatherly: the owner, the manager, the city councillor in charge of tourism, and the delirious crowd of tourists, the steelworkers, the retirees with one foot in the grave.

The first guy gets up on the stage, breaking the ice. She bends over and rubs her ass in his face. She wants a serious bill. He slips it in. She bends over again. She wants more money. The demented old idiot, maybe Gianfranco maybe someone else, is bewildered, confused. He slips banknote after banknote into her panties.

The cash register clinks. Applause bursts out. She's the unrivaled queen of the Gilda.

Long, dizzyingly long legs. A slender, angular torso. That face, the face of a movie star from the thirties, framed by a golden vaporous cascade. It doesn't take a graduate degree to figure out. The rivulet of her aroma, the adolescent motion of her body squirming against the pole. The embarrassment, the blush of the mischievous girl next door. She's universal.

They take her to parties, sometimes to yachts docked off Punta Ala. They buy her elegant clothing to show her off, so no one can tell where she comes from. Her employer deflowered her in a motel one afternoon in April, and she lay there underneath him, impassive, eyes wide open, staring at the ceiling.

But once she's on the stage, it's a completely different thing. The song fills her up. "Rhythm Is a Dancer" is her triumph. It tickles her, makes her arch, makes her arch her back, and she wags in joy. Look at her. She's laughing. She's riding and singing, full-voiced. *Ooh, it's a passion.*

Look how she plays . . . like any adolescent girl dancing in front of the mirror, and imitates Britney Spears, and undresses, locked in the bathroom.

Halfway through the show, Cristiano walked in.

He stumbled through the darkness and confusion, his eyes were stinging from the smoke. He couldn't see a damn thing.

He groped and shoved his way to the front row, where Gianfranco was sitting, after bumping into five or six tables. He'd spilled most of his Negroni by the time he got to the front.

"Hey, jerkoff," snickered his boss when he noticed him.

Cristiano was taking a seat. There were six or seven other workers from the same company, all of them drunk as kids, wasted as kids. But he was stone sober, fuck it all. He'd had to channel Houdini to get away from Jennifer's bed, make it out of the apartment without waking her up. It had been no laughing matter to ask Alessio to borrow the Golf.

"This one's unreal," his boss said, hooking his head in her direction.

Cristiano shot an absent glance in her direction; he was still trying to remember where he'd parked the car: Was it a legal parking spot? He couldn't afford to have them tow Alessio's Golf: That would be catastrophic.

"I'd fuck this one, Jesus Christ. I'd screw her standing up!" shouted Gianfranco in a frenzy, in a pink checkered shirt and the same enormous belly as last year.

"Because she really has that expression that says 'come fuck me,' right? She really has that kind of a face, like she wants it. . . ."

Everyone laughed.

Cristiano was thinking, trying to remember exactly whether or not the place where he'd stuck the car on the sidewalk was legal. Was there a no-parking sign or not? While he struggled to remember, he saw a pair of legs moving to an unusual rhythm.

"She has class," said someone. "I don't know where they found her, but she's better than any of the others."

"She's going straight to Canale 5!"

Cristiano looked up.

"Look at the way she moves. . . . Forget about Canale 5; I want her in the Italian parliament!"

He observed the ass moving right in front of him.

"Election! Election!"

A pair of round buttocks, firm and flying, a rare sight. And a wonderful back, smooth white skin, slightly undulating along the spinal cord. The tidal wave of hair, spilling over first one shoulder then the other.

Cristiano started smiling like an idiot. They were right. This one knew what she was doing; she moved her body to a spectacular rhythm, and it was obvious that she could ride you like a horse, hard and fast, for an hour at a time.

She turned around.

She gyrated, turning her slender torso, her narrow hips, her small muscular bust.

Her face.

Cristiano was paralyzed. A rivulet of gastric juices seeped up his esophagus. It can't be. . . . He sat there with a mouthful of Negroni, but without the courage to gulp it down. He was afraid to spit it out, spit out everything. A clear feeling of fear.

"Francesca," he stammered under his breath.

A feeble thread of a voice that no one could hear.

CHAPTER 37

"**W**e went to Milan last Thursday, on a maintenance run," Mattia was saying, just talking to hear the sound of his own voice. "The plant was smaller than ours, but in much better shape. After our shift, we went downtown to take a look around. It was insane. . . . You know what I saw?"

"What?" asked Anna, indifferently.

She was lying on one side, her back to him; she didn't even bother to turn her head.

"I'll tell you, there was everything you could think of, in the clubs up there. Amphetamines, ketamine, MDMA, a ton of shit at ridiculous prices! Huge crowds, even out in the street . . . It's not like here, where everyone is in bed by eleven-thirty." Anna was listening and ignoring him at the same time, slightly stunned by the hot sunshine. "So we finally wind up in this big piazza, with a church, a campanile, and everything. There were kids stretched out on the ground, people with guitars and bongo drums at one in the morning. . . . So you know what I saw? You won't believe it!"

"What?" she yawned.

Mattia exploded: "Two girls kissing each other!"

June 2, Italy's Republic Day. The beach was infested with children and fat families sprawled under beach umbrellas. There was leftover lasagne in aluminum pans, and other garbage, like apple cores, tossed onto the sand. Everyone was there, everyone from Via Stalingrado.

Everyone except for *one person*.

Anna raised her eyebrows behind her sunglasses, behind the new screen that gave her a different air, the look of a young lady, a signorina. She rotated onto one hip, looked at him without commenting.

"Two girls, two females!" He was working himself up. "You should have seen them, A', sitting under a fountain, hugging in the moonlight, . . . sticking their tongues in each other's mouth!"

She remained motionless in that position, riveted to the spot. Her heart started racing in an absurd, unjustifiable manner.

"That kind of thing can only happen up there. They're crazy, I'm telling you; it reminded me of Amsterdam. But two girls kissing in front of everyone. . . . That's just going too far."

She had immediately started scanning the beach for her: as she was walking down the steps; as she strolled along the walkway between the cabanas; and then again as she was laying out her beach towel and slipping out of her sarong.

To find her there, at the water's edge, in the place she'd always chosen for herself.

Mattia was telling her how absurd Milan was, with all that money, all those transsexuals lining the sidewalks, how the people all seemed to hate the Romanian immigrants at the bus stops, how some young guy had died in a discotheque—over just one tablet, from just one knife wound—the crime reports, and the only thing that seemed absurd to her was the fact that Francesca wasn't there.

But maybe she hadn't looked carefully enough. Maybe in the past ten minutes, while Anna had been stretched out basking in the sun, *she* had arrived.

Anna sat up again. She started searching under every umbrella again, on every beach chair, in every corner of the bar where she might possibly be hiding. As if the two girls from Milan might have something to do with it. As if the animal had suddenly reawakened inside her.

Mattia is just some guy, an ordinary guy.

Yeah, a guy who doesn't wonder about things.

Have the basic courage to look at what's right in front of you. Not on the beach towels, not where the old people, the losers, the young couples are rotting away—and where you are now numbered among them. Look straight ahead of you, at the sea. At the rings of adolescents playing ball. Recognize.

The island went on sleeping, inviolate, on the blurred line of the horizon.

She could pick out Nino and Massi. They were playing in the water, just like last year. Their heads drenched, hair tousled, muscles tensed. She saw Nino kick the ball skyward, and then watched it describe a perfect parabola that came to an end when it met Massi's heel.

She could hear them yelling "To me! To me!" even if the voices only came to her faintly from down there.

The sun straight overhead, beating down on their shoulders. Their eyes were reddened from the saltwater, their pupils were narrowed fissures. It was perfect. The crystalline movement of developing bodies; young girls running in a nascent state. Anna saw one young girl shouting because she had sand in her swimsuit bottom, and then duck into the water to slip it off.

Broad circles of kids, assembling and reassembling. A ball, skipping along fingertips, outstretched arms that were victorious as they drove home a point over the volleyball net. And the chaotic din, so typical of little girls, still half children, taking running starts to fling themselves into the waves. They dive in, they resurface.

Nino and Massi had girlfriends now, but nothing serious. They'd picked up a couple of little girls from upper middle school, girls who were pointing at them from the water's edge, who clapped if they kicked in a goal.

Anna saw one of them whispering in the other's ear. They were slender, shapely. Their long hair dripping, hanging down to their butts. Breasts still small, hips nonexistent. Anna noticed that one had her triangle top in disarray, her round derriere almost entirely revealed. She saw them leap and lunge without warning. Rush into the scrimmage and latch on to the backs and shoulders of the boys.

Mattia had stopped talking; he was leafing through the pages of *La Gazzetta dello Sport* now. Maybe he'd asked her something. But she had no intention of replying. No intention of interrupting that form of torture: sitting there watching the realm to which Francesca no longer belonged. To which neither she nor Francesca belonged now.

And no one had even noticed they were gone.

Anna stared out at the skyline of the horizon, that damned island that she'd never reached. She felt a powerful wave of anger swelling up from inside. She felt herself glaring resentfully at those two younger girls, standing on their hands underwater, their legs breaking the surface and pointing straight up at the sky.

Bounced out of the game. Ejected. Like in nursery school, when they point a finger straight at you and say, grimly: "You can't play." An experience with which Anna was completely unfamiliar. An experience that was incomprehensible to her. Because she wasn't one person, she was two people. She wasn't "you," she was "both of you." Neither of you can play. *Annafrancesca* can't play. And you can just imagine how little they cared: They had secret beaches all their own, wooden cabins, basements, benches, the entire coastline of Salivoli to monopolize.

They're cruel, thought Anna. The adolescent girls walking toward her now, hand in hand, focused only on taking their idiotic stroll on the beach, their marvelous walkabout to show off their ass, their tits, everything they possess that can unleash envy and hormones.

Let's turn cartwheels, let's see who can stay underwater longest! Time is a horrible thing. Francesca was right. Now, where is she? What could she be doing now?

Mattia pulled out a deck of cards. "Want to play a game or two?" he asked with his dopey smile.

To be at the center of life and not know it.

Anna picked up the hand of thirteen cards, sorted them rapidly, deftly, between her fingers. She started playing *scala quaranta* with her boyfriend.

It's not something you waste. It's something that wastes you.

Mattia kept playing new hands on the beach towel: three jacks, sequence of spades, three queens. And she sat there, passive, watching the grains of sand scatter between the cards, her focus broken by the shouts of the new little sluts on the beach, and she couldn't make up her mind to discard.

Maybe if the two of them had been born in Milan. . . If they'd moved to Milan, maybe they would have kissed in front of everyone, in the middle of a vast piazza, with the moon peeking out from behind the bell tower of the church.

"Three to nothing," Mattia exulted.

In the distance you could hear a shout: "Goal!"

"I don't feel like playing anymore."

Anna tossed her cards onto the towel and lay back down.

"Oh come on, what's with you?"

He climbed on top of her, started massaging her back: just a pretext to slip his fingers under the material of her swimsuit.

"Cut it out," hissed Anna.

"You're turning into a prude. . . ."

He got up, went back to where he was sitting, but for another five minutes kept groping her, whistling happily all the while. He was contented, no question about it. He was at peace with the world.

"Let's go for a swim!"

A year ago those were words that nobody even needed to say.

Mattia leaped to his feet, started running across the scorching hot sand, then turned and called her again.

Anna didn't feel like getting up. She didn't feel like doing anything. It would be better to stay at home with the shutters pulled down: Then maybe she wouldn't hate him.

She started walking listlessly toward the water's edge. He was swimming blissfully, as if nothing were wrong. Anna stepped into the water. First she wet her belly, then her shoulders, and she shivered with the cold. She took a couple of strokes to get warmed up. She caught up with Mattia: the average guy, the man who was at peace with the world who was now ready to fuck underwater. She waved her finger no at him.

She let herself float on the surface. The dead man's float. She let legs and arms spread out in the water like a weightless corpse.

Where was she now? Where do things go when you lose them?

Her running shoes under the hull of the boat, on the seaweed-covered beach . . .

Anna closed her eyes. If she concentrated, she could make out Francesca's voice pointing out the buoy down there, a tiny bobbing yellow dot, a microscopic destination, but for them, in 2001, immense. . . . Francesca flying in a flat trajectory straight into the water, headfirst, and then surfacing to shout: "Come on, let's go to Elba!"

CHAPTER 38

A lessio was walking briskly, backlit, at six in the morning.
This is the feral time, the hour of the tapered snouts. They
creep out of the sewers, climb up the pipelines—the secret creatures of the Lucchini steelworks that teem under the industrial sheds.

Alessio saw one of them, a survivor, emerge from behind a withered
hedge, and he stopped short. He had nothing to offer it. He bent his knees,
dropped into a squat. He liked the noses those animals had, the damp pink
triangle. The tabby cat froze, gazing at him with its large yellow eyes. Its
tail was a severed stump. Alessio extended his hand until he was almost
touching it, but the cat arched its back and vanished.

The sun was rising, casting four square miles of steel mill shadows.

Alessio reached the crane, his own personal beast, and thought that
maybe today his father would come home.

He greeted the coworker whose shift was ending as he headed off to
bed. He wrapped his hands around the control panel, checked to see that
all the crane's gearing was turning properly. Okay, Private Ryan, get to
work: Hoist mill crucibles, move them, mentally send them to hell.

Alessio jammed the earbuds of his MP3 player into his ears. The hard-
core music he listened to basically fucked up his eardrums. It's no simple
matter to synchronize the timing of your life with the time frame that steel
requires to become molten, solidify, and take a shape.

No question: It takes a line of coke.

He leaned into a corner, brandished his tactical hand mirror, rolled up a
five note, and ingested through his respiratory tract his daily dose and his
salary. He took up his position in the ongoing daily warfare, and in fact he
took pride in it. And in fact he even managed to enjoy himself, with the

hard-core punk pumping out to the rhythm of the mill crucibles. He'd have been able to do it again today if Elena hadn't started tormenting his brain.

A mile away Mattia was hurrying up, out of breath, to the rod mill, the rolling mill that turns a billet of steel into a bundle of steel wires and rods with an exponential specific weight. It was his job to load them, fresh out of the blast furnace, onto the fork, and to transport them to the industrial shed where surface quality checks were performed.

He waved hello to Eva Henger, Miss June. He climbed onto the forklift, parked there especially for his convenience, so that he could climb aboard and spend the next eight hours comfortably earning a living.

The light shot down hot and fecund between the smokestacks and the gantries. Mattia was thinking about Anna, his little girl, sleeping peacefully, pressing her freckles and her curls into her pillow. Her summer pajamas, the ones she'd been wearing the first time. Her bright groin. Mattia was thinking about Anna, warm and wafting under the sheets. And his body reacted.

It happens, it always happens when you're loading tons of steel at a time, that your body rises up inside your overalls. You can feel your vital sap rising all clumpy from the depths, your arteries dilating and pumping away. The hidden muscle, the least civilized muscle of them all. You have to go find a bathroom; you have to seek out a corner behind a hedge. You have to unzip and rebel.

In a completely different quadrant, over on the western perimeter of the factory grounds, Gianfranco was dressing down Cristiano for showing up late this morning—for the thousandth time.

"You've got to stop going to the Gilda!" he was shouting. "Just take a look at yourself. . . . Look at this mess!" He waved a hand at a mountain of scrap and rubble. "Why don't you go wash your face, god damn it to hell!?"

Cristiano was yawning, stroking his spiky eyebrows.

"Calm down, boss . . . ," he managed to mumble. "I was there a couple of nights ago, not last night."

"Then you're a complete jerkoff, is what you are!"

The thought of Francesca had kept him from getting any sleep for two nights in a row. He saw her nude in his mind's eye again, fluorescent under the spotlight, and he couldn't reconcile himself. Because he knew that she was fourteen, not eighteen. She was his neighbor, goddamn it. He'd seen her going off to school in a checked smock, hand in hand with Anna. Tiny toddler girls, with brightly colored backpacks on their shoulders.

But right now there was a magnificent Caterpillar power shovel waiting for him. A heap of scrap and rubble fifteen or twenty feet tall, straight out of the crusher. These were the problems he needed to think about: rubble and slag.

He poised the bucket of his power shovel, then plunged it in, raking up a load overbrimming with all sorts of material. Rubble from demolished smokestacks, iron rebar, worn-out refractory brick, dead rats, and even a few chunks of copper.

Copper: In situations like this the categorical imperative demands that a millworker turn off the engine, carefully dismount, extract the three thousand lire per kilo from the bucket, and hide it somewhere safe until it can be smuggled out through the main factory exit.

Cristiano implemented that imperative, with Kantian zeal.

This morning, as usual, after barely fifteen minutes at work, he discovered an upwelling of sentimentality. Sweat dotting his temples, dirt filtering into his mouth, and the distinctive taste of iron shavings on his tongue, had that effect on him.

He called Jennifer, made her get out of bed, and told her to bring the kid to him. At mile marker 3, near the gas station.

Alessio was on edge. Mattia was sleepy. Cristiano couldn't wait to spin doughnuts with his Caterpillar in front of his son. Seven A.M. June 3, 2002.

It was a great piece of luck that they were all working the same shift that morning. They had planned to meet at two in the afternoon in the vintage locker room, under the hiccupping showerheads. They'd all three head out for the beach at Via Stalingrado; they'd make their powerful entrance through the beach cabanas: Look out, people, here we come!

A nice mill crucible: 19.6 metric tons. Alessio hooked it on, hoisted it, transported it, and so on until noon, then it was time to eat lunch, and then another hour of ball-crushing boredom and irritation. June: the curvy brunette from *Striscia la Notizia* arching over backward on the rocks by the water.

The sun was rising rapidly over the promontory. From here you can't see Elba. You can see the gulf that stretches out from the mill toward Follonica, the silhouettes of the Dalmine plant and the ENEL power station in the middle. The procession of naked high-tension towers. The way that Cristiano and Alessio, alone, are able to modify a landscape.

"Okay, tomorrow I'll call you and let you know." That's what Elena said in her message yesterday.

Why don't you call me? Because you haven't gotten out of bed and eaten break-fast yet. . . . But he couldn't wait. The night before he'd worked up the nerve, he'd asked her if they could have lunch together today, and it had taken him an hour to enter that fucking text message on the keypad.

Alessio lifted his eyes and gazed vaguely among the diesel fuel tanks, the red and purple vapors that superheat the atmosphere. Then he went back to his lever, the elementary movement. Something that exerts pressure on something. Something that serves as a pivot.

He was sweating, breathing lead, cursing the 2,800 degree Fahrenheit temperature required to melt the metal. Incandescent mill crucibles went past him. Get too close to one and your overalls can catch on fire.

The only time you can really enjoy it is when you go to the train station. You board an Intercity, look out the window, and hear the screeching of the steel, the friction, the crackling spark of your journey. In your mind you review all the phases of production: from the coke furnace to the blast furnace, from the blast furnace to the steelworks, and from there to the converters, to the crucible ovens, and to the rolling mills . . .

The track your train is running on: You made it yourself.

Alessio was waiting anxiously for her call. The sun was hammering down on his head. The cell phone wasn't buzzing. The muggy heat condensed into a rust-covered swamp between the structures. Where could his father be right now? *I wonder if that good-for-nothing really is coming home. How dare he show his face? It takes some nerve.* No, he definitely couldn't forgive him.

It's eight in the morning. The mill crucibles keep up the pressure. The shadows shorten by an inch, an inch and a half at a time. And you've got your own shitty problems in your head. Your hand grips the control panel nervously, with irritation; you have this frenzied need to know if that asshole of a father of yours is coming home today, if Elena is going to eat lunch with you in the company cafeteria at noon. You can count the passing minutes by the arrival of one mill crucible after another. You hate them, the passing minutes. Your hand jerks forward, angrily. And now you're jerking the goddamned mill crucible on its cables. Now the steel cables are tangled, you can see them snagging. . . .

You catch yourself swearing like a deranged sailor. "Fuck fuck fuck fuck fuck fuck!"

Alessio shouted and hurled the control panel to the floor.

Keep calm. It can happen. It happens that a mill crucible bounces at the end of the cables, that the cables ride over one another and get tangled, that you're forced to shut it all down to keep from making things worse. It can happen at any time. But just not today.

He was swearing.

The cocaine circulating in your blood vessels, your father called yesterday and he might show up today, and you have this overwhelming need to forgive him. He ripped the earpods angrily off his head. This was the last thing he needed: an extra hour or two of work. This is the kind of crap that just makes you furious. Because you want to see Elena at lunch, you need to see her, and you don't want to miss that opportunity because of a fucking mill crucible.

Now he had to lower the hanging load, unhook it from the winch, and then walk around swearing furiously, in search of the section foreman. Whatever the situation, even if you're about to lose control, you have to remember to follow safety protocols. Alessio was following safety protocols. Head down, snorting, he was looking for the section foreman.

He found him twenty minutes later, a huge hairy beast of a man, a guy who spent a lot of time in Aldo's bar, sitting in a patch of shadow on a folding chair.

"The cables got tangled on me," he said.

"What a pain in the ass," the guy complained.

His belly comfortably resting on his open legs. He was dripping with sweat, just sitting there.

"Let's try to get this fixed quickly." Alessio coked to the gills.

"Sweetheart," the huge animal belched, "just keep calm, and I'll get maintenance over to you fast enough."

It took him at least three minutes just to get to his feet. All of that fat, melting in the intense heat, must be difficult to move around. The man pointed to the Maxim calendar hanging on the door of the industrial shed. An ass and a cascade of red hair.

"Cute, eh?" with a toothless leer.

Alessio wanted to push him against the wall and shoot him.

Jennifer appeared, sleepyheaded, with the baby in her arms at 8:30 in the morning. The minute Cristiano saw them he jumped down from the bulldozer and ran straight toward them, pogoing with joy on the way. James regurgitated a tiny mouthful of milk onto his mother's blouse. They talked through the iron grates of the fencing.

"He's been vomiting all morning," she hissed.

"Little man! Little brute!" Cristiano was saying to him. "Look at this, watch me . . ."

The baby was green in the face. Whatever he might be thinking, his eyes were only asking for mercy, for a chance to fall back to sleep. By the tenth funny face his father made, he was on the verge of tears.

Cristiano, all enthusiastic: "You want to see Papa's big, bad mastiff?" In a fluting voice: "You want to see Papa's snorting bull?"

Neither Jennifer nor James had any wish to see Papa's bull.

But Cristiano, as we all know, ran to the bulldozer, turned on a portable radio full blast, and started running through the circus routines that by this point everyone knew by heart.

"Let's have a race, let's have a race!" he shouted at his coworker. "Let's have a race, so my son can see us!"

"You're sick in the head," his coworker replied.

James was puking on Jennifer's blouse. And Jennifer was simultaneously partly annoyed, partly disgusted at the vomiting, and a little sick to her stomach herself.

Five minutes later mother and son both headed home. Cristiano watched them leave and turned off the engine. They hadn't even said good-bye.

Two old guys, two decrepit repair guys. That's what they were sending over, after he'd waited for half an hour, after he chewed off every skin tag on his callused hands.

"Let's get this done in a hurry," Alessio immediately demanded.

"Hey," said one of them, as he climbed up onto the gantry, "I'm not the one who broke the thing!"

He watched the two old men from maintenance climb up onto the crane, wide-eyed and furious with impatience. By the time these guys unwind the cables, straighten them out, and roll them back onto the winch drum, I'll be ready to shoot myself.

He was watching his lunch break drift out of reach, his one chance to sit at a table in the cafeteria with Elena and hear people whispering behind his back: "You're sleeping with the boss, you filthy bastard."

"Well?"

The maintenance guys had just squatted down over a drum to unbolt it. "Stay calm, son. . . ."

Stay calm my ass. He had no intention of gulping down a sandwich on the crane to get back up to speed. No intention of missing out on the spectacle of Elena in her designer suit in a cafeteria filled with pathetic losers. He watched them work, whipping them in his mind.

A leak in the system, just one tiny leak. And then everything gets shot to hell.

Why don't you call me, bitch? It's almost 9:30.

"How much longer?"

They stood up, their knees creaking: "Ehhh. . . . An hour, at least." "Maybe two . . ."

"Two hours?" Alessio ran his hand through his hair.

Anna was calling him. Mattia answered, clamping the cell phone between shoulder and jaw. He was driving the forklift on a zigzag route between the industrial sheds. Steel rebar piled up to and over the windshield. He couldn't see shit.

"Mattia, I'm going out of my mind with fear. About what? About if I don't get at least an eighty on this test, I'm in trouble. What are you saying? You know that subject inside out. . . . No I don't! Look, we haven't been able to fuck for the past week because you had to learn every one of those damned verbs. What are you saying? I'm just saying. You can't understand. . . . What's not to understand? The third conjugation . . . Would you rather be driving a forklift through this hellhole? Baby, I can hardly hear you. I'm over near the converters. . . . I'd better get back to class, the witch is sitting down at her desk."

Good luck. Yeah, right.

He was blazing with rage. He was blazing with impatience. And he couldn't stand still.

"I'm going to go take a walk. . . ." Alessio shouted through cupped hands.

"Good idea," the two guys replied, "and cut back on the drugs."

The sun had become a disk of reinforced concrete over his head. The helmet is just an optional. It's like a motorcycle helmet: If you wear it, you're a pathetic loser. That is, if they give you a helmet, of course. That is, if they're willing to detract three or four thousand lire from their fantastic mountain of profits.

Two thousand bodies pulsating to the rhythm of the mill. Alessio was walking through the middle of it, in torment, cell phone within easy reach. Elena wasn't calling him. Brutally thirsty.

He headed for the rod mill. He needed to blow off steam. *That guy's an asshole, his whole life has been one failure after another . . . Still, he bought me the VW Golf—don't you see? He committed grand larceny to get me that Golf GT.*

Mattia would definitely understand.

No doubt, he'd be scratching his ass. He'd be smoking a cigarette, sprawled out in the cool of the shade. No doubt, he'd be leafing through one of those miserable magazines: how to give a woman pleasure, how to find her G-spot with confidence and give her multiple orgasms. No doubt, he was doing anything you could think of but working.

Alessio stepped over the rails of the mill train, walked under the all-powerful cranes and the conveyor belts loaded with coke. Mattia was only a mile away. His sweat-drenched overalls, the sun that melts you and crushes you underfoot. But Alessio felt such a fury in his chest that walking, running, sweating . . .

Listen, Mattia, I have something I want to tell you. You remember Elena, the bitch, the one who can save us or fire us? Right. You know her? I hate her. I detest her, but I'm head over heels in love with her, god damn it, I feel like I was thirteen again! Let's go get a beer, he'd say. There's a gas station right over there that sells beer.

Why don't we pull off a robbery? If the cables get tangled, and the Russians dismantle your job and the place you work, you can't move to Poland to work there!

He was giving it some serious thought, or maybe he should say, some semiserious thought. He was thinking about the gantry crane undergoing maintenance, about his miserable father, and about his ex-girlfriend who, right now, he would have liked to back into a corner, against an incandescent mill crucible, and tear away her nice clean blouse, her nice shiny briefcase, and strip her bare, entirely in his possession.

He got to the quality control shed. There was a pile of rebar as tall as the apartment building he lived in. There was a guy smoking a cigarette. A guy that maybe he knew.

"Is Mattia around?"

"He's on the forklift," the guy answered, taking a look at his watch. "He went over to the rod mill to load up, half an hour ago. . . . He should be back here any minute."

"Don't tell me he's actually working!"

The other guy laughed. Then he looked a little closer: "Wait a minute, I think I know you. . . ."

"Oh, yeah?" said Alessio, looking up for a second from the cell phone that he was holding in front of his face like an idiot, waiting for it to vibrate.

"Didn't you go to the Body Gym last year?"

"Yeah." He didn't give a damn about the Body Gym.

"I used to go to that gym; we fought in a kickboxing match together!" He smiled. "Sure, you're Mattia's friend, of course. We ran into each other at the Gilda, I think. . . . Alessandro?"

"No, Alessio." He couldn't stay put, he couldn't take part in that bullshit conversation.

"Okay, I've got a phone call to make." He waved. "Later."

He started walking around in circles like a lunatic, up and down outside the quality-control shed, obsessively staring at the screen of his cell phone. Why don't you call? Come on! What would it cost you? You're killing me here, god damn it. Call! Okay, I'll call her.

Alessio dialed Elena's number, the office number, so that he could be sure that she'd answer. The June sun in the middle of the blast furnaces, even at 10:00 in the morning, drills through the top of your skull. It's like being inside the furnace, exactly the same thing. Only now Elena's voice was blossoming from the earpiece of the cell phone.

"Hello? Elena, this is Alessio." *"Ale* . . . I was going to call you later. I'm up to my neck in things right now. . . . But I don't have any time! What? I can't hear you . . . Wait a second, let me move. . . . Where are you?" "I'm at the rod mill; there's a huge amount of noise here."

Alessio was shouting, he was squatting down, crouching close to the ground to avoid the apocalyptic noise that kept surging up toward the smoke-masked sky.

"Are you there?" "Yeah, I'm here." "Look, I can't spend much time on the phone; if they catch me, they'll kill me. . . . Are you there?" "Of course, I'm here."

Mattia was thinking that tomorrow, his day off, he might surprise Anna and take her to Elba.

They'd been talking about going for a year. He'd buy two tickets at the Toremar office later today. He lit a cigarette. To tell the truth, he couldn't see a fucking thing. He'd loaded fourteen metric tons of wire rod instead of twelve so that he could be done sooner and relax in the cool of the shade. Anna's soft summer pajamas . . .

Mattia was driving and thinking, and as he drove, emptying a water bottle over his head. The sun shreds you to pieces, molten steel, incandescent steel under the sun directly overhead. It chews you up.

"So are you going to be there today?" "*Ale*, I wanted to ask you to forgive me. . . ." "Forgive you for what?" "For the other day, when I told you about the layoffs. . . ." "Wait, I can't hear you . . . Layoffs?" "What the fuck are you talking about?" "No, not you! That is, I meant to say. . . . We're not going to fire you!" "Ah! Okay, that's good . . . But then are you going to be there today?" "To tell the truth . . . I can't do it." "What do you mean you can't?!" "*Ale*, I can hardly hear you . . ." "Wait a minute, let me move . . ."

Mattia was driving toward the quality control shed, driving with the instinct of memory, and meanwhile he's taking deep drags, filling his lungs with the smoke of his Pall Mall Blue cigarette. He couldn't see a fucking thing, but he knew the route by heart. The steel jungle, the incessant screeching, roaring, the ejaculations of the mill.

Alessio was moving around; he went somewhere else and crouched down there.

"What were you saying?" "I was saying that it's a problem today, I have too many forms to fill out and I absolutely have to finish by this evening . . ."

Alessio squatted down on his knees and put his hand over the other ear to be able to hear Elena's voice in the midst of the maelstrom, in the patch of baked earth in the midst of the titans.

"You've turned into such a bureaucrat, why don't you tell them to fuck themselves for once? Just this one time, your damned bosses . . . Come on, I really want to see you. Just half an hour, just five minutes . . ."

Elena was stalling, hiding behind the receiver.

"Elena, god damn it, will you answer me?" "Okay, let me see what I can do. . . ." "Come on, what would it cost you? I have something important I want to tell you. . . ."

Mattia was accelerating because he wanted to relax in the shade, gulp down a liter of cool water.

"Say you'll have lunch with me. . . ."

Alessio was tormenting a mangy tuft of grass with an impatient hand, a hand that wanted to touch something other than threadbare grass.

"*Ale*, listen . . ." Elena's heart was racing.

"No, wait . . . how about this! Instead of going to lunch in that fucked-up cafeteria, let's take the ferry and go to Elba!" "To Elba? *Ale*, what are you saying?" "I don't know what I'm saying." He laughed.

Mattia was jamming down the accelerator with his foot and thinking how much fun Anna would have on Elba. . . .

"We could go to Elba, just for the day . . ." "Why?" "I don't know." "All right, we'll see, maybe the day after tomorrow." "Then are you going to have lunch with me?" "I don't know." "Why don't you kno . . ."

Something like a noise. But not an identifiable noise. A thump. A malfunction. Right. Some sort of interference . . . "*Ale*, hello? . . . Alessio? Alessio? Hello? Hello! Hello hello hello hello hello . . ."

How many times can you say it, how long can you go on repeating this senseless word, knowing that on the other end no one's listening to you? You can do it for an entire minute before slamming down the receiver and turning pale.

A whole minute: Alessio's cell phone transmitted Elena's voice for another minute that morning, between 10:06 and 10:07.

Anna overjoyed on the ferry to Elba . . .

Mattia felt something hard and bulky under the treads that forced him to stop short. At first he didn't understand. It took him a few seconds before he turned off the engine. He got down from the forklift, stunned by the heat. He was about to lose his temper when he noticed a rivulet of red seeping out from under the treads.

The sun was beating down exasperatingly. Mattia stood there, his arms hanging limp at his sides, watching. A blind fury mixed with astonishment, because he expected a rock, a beam, some bastard thing or other that he hadn't seen with all that rebar covering his windshield. He stood there like that for a couple of minutes, drying the sweat off his brow with his forearm.

Then he heard someone call him from behind.

"Mattia!"

Someone had stepped out of the industrial shed to yell at him: "That friend of yours was here, looking for you . . ."

Someone came walking over at a fast clip, and then the footsteps slowed. He was saying: "Alessio was around here somewhere . . ."

Silence.

"What happened . . . ?"

A gust of breeze. It was snowing down iron filings along with tree pollen.

"I think I ran over a cat."

A cat. One of those hairy, tailless, earless gadgets. One of those fucked-up little animals, eyes covered with cataracts who live in the pipes, under the industrial sheds, and who sometimes, from living in this toxic environment, are born without a paw. A cat. It was just that the rivulet of red kept spreading, forming a deepening puddle under the scorching sun.

"Move the forklift, please," the throttled voice of his coworker.

Mattia, without a word, climbed up onto the forklift, started the engine, put it in reverse.

He got down again. When you crush a cat it doesn't put out that much blood. A sole. Something like: a human shoe. And the scorched filigree of hair.

He saw that shapeless heap. He really couldn't understand. He saw his coworker blanch, start looking around, start shouting: "Alessio! Alessiooo!" Behind, in front of the industrial shed. "*Ale*, Alessiooo!"

Call the floor boss. Come back, come back to his side where he was standing, anchored, next to the forklift. Say: "My God."

Say: "What have you done? My God."

Not a thought. The shell of a thought fluttering through the brain, like in a shower drain. *This, this puddle of oatmeal here, that's a cat.*

What have you done? Someone was muttering something, in a steadily fading voice. Eyes wide open, staring at the puddle of blood glimmering in the incandescent sunlight. Clumps, shavings of bone scattered along with the steel rebar, the gleaming, silvery tons of metal. *That couldn't be a man.*

Elena had been left sitting at her desk, holding the phone receiver in one hand and a blank gaze focused on the office wall in the cool of the air conditioner. Then, in slow motion, she got to her feet. She shot down the stairs. She was running, faster and faster, stumbling on her high heels. She'd started to shout to her coworkers, to anyone. She was shouting, on the verge of falling: Please, get me a car. Shouting, stumbling down the stairs. Immediately, please. She got back to her feet, she was shouting. To the rod mill, please.

Petrified, Mattia stared at the glimmering red void. The puddle, the detritus, the remains that surely belonged to a cat. *One of those small calico beasts covered with scabies, all of them identical from years of inbreeding, mangy, AIDS-ridden, rabid. Or the fox, the one that only comes out at six in the morning, the fox from the pit that Alessio always talked about. Alessio, who everyone was looking for.*

Not him, everyone else.

Mattia didn't need to look for him; he knew where he was; he was at the crane. They were supposed to meet at two o'clock in the locker room, so that they could catch a smoke together after lunch outside the cafeteria, and he knew that the shoe, the puddle of blood . . . His brain kept saying *cat.* His brain kept repeating just one word: *cat.* Nothing more.

His coworker went to call over to the crane. At the crane, Alessio wasn't there; the maintenance guys answered the phone. They'd seen him leave half an hour ago. The coworker had seen him three, four minutes earlier.

He was here, damn it! God, he was talking on the phone! He was shouting convulsively to the floor boss.

God, don't say his name. *Don't forgive us*—they wrote on the fifth page of *Il Tirreno*, tomorrow, his coworkers from the rod mill. *Ciao Alessio, and don't forgive us.*

Someone put a hand on his shoulder. But Mattia was standing there sweating like a dissolving apple core. Mattia was fixated on the word *cat.* And the coworker went running to call for help. People were running around now, ten, then twenty people, calling Alessio's name, taking roll call the way people do on a class field trip when someone gets lost.

Gradually, every steelworker in the mill looked up. They turned off their machinery, left their workplace, gathered in the area between the rod mill and the quality control shed where someone had been phoning but now there was no one.

"What the fuck are you saying?" Cristiano snarled at Gianfranco.

He turned off the engine of the Caterpillar.

Gradually, the entire rod mill sector ceased functioning. The rumor spread; word filtered out to the other departments. All the steelworkers hurried over to the place where Alessio had stopped living, had stopped being a human body, where Alessio had become a puddle of blood, spreading between the scattered steel rod, a blinding pool.

Not Alessio. A cat.

Who is it? Along the entire production process, the manufacturing cycle, the mammoth collective effort. They showed up, panting, in overalls, from every corner of the Lucchini mill. They arrived in groups or one by one. On foot, on mill trains, in cars. The name. We need to know the name.

Elena got out of the car and pushed her way through the crowd, flinging her arms against the crowd. When she got there, she let out a single, inhuman scream. Time stood still. The steelworkers in a circle, faces cradled in their hands. Mattia the hub. Something exerting pressure on something else. All it takes is one thing, a single leak in the system is sufficient, a single moment of distraction. Call the morgue. The medical examiner's office. Alert the executive suites. The labor unions. The police. The mayor of Piombino.

"The name. We want the name."

And his name darted from mouth to mouth, bounced from wall to wall, flew up to touch the summits of the smokestacks and dropped back down to the pavement and dirt, scattered among the clumps, the unrecomposable, unreassemblable remains of a body that absolutely, absolutely had to be the body of a cat.

"What the fuck are you saying?" Cristiano stepped down from his bulldozer. "There's a thousand guys named Alessio. What's his last name? I want to know his last name!"

"I don't know that," Gianfranco stammered.

"Where'd it happen?"

"At the rod mill."

"Alessio doesn't work at the rod mill. Mattia works there." He put both hands up to his face. "Gianfranco, fuck it! What are you telling me? Alessio works at the crane!"

"Please, let's just go look for ourselves. The crane was undergoing maintenance. . . ."

You know it from the beginning. You've always known it, in your guts, in your blood. So you start running. So you don't get in the car with the others. You start running, at breakneck speed, and in your mind you repeat a single sound, a monosyllabic word, the last word that left your lips, the word that you really need to say, you don't even know who you're saying it to, you just know you need to say it.

No.

Cristiano was shouting and running down the endless boulevard dominated by the looming bulk of A-Fo 4.

The name hammering away. The name, hissing along the entire perimeter of the steelworks. They called the police. What's the condition of the corpse? Well, there really is no corpse.

He needed to wrap his arms around him, make sure he was okay. Those bastards scared me, my God, you have no idea. . . . A slap on the shoulder. That's all he needed.

Steelworkers, coming in waves. The section foreman, the crew captain, called an ambulance. They called the state commissioner for occupational safety, the representative from the FIOM metalworkers union. They called the CGIL, the CISL, and the UIL unions. What the fuck are you calling an ambulance for, idiot!?

Call the inspectors from the public health service. Don't touch, don't touch anything. The entire zone is off-limits, sequestered. The police, the Carabinieri arrive. The investigating magistrate will be down here from Livorno by this evening. Don't cluster, move back, let them through please, make way. . . . Someone should inform the family.

Mattia was standing there. He hadn't moved an inch.

Don't ask him questions, please, not now. He's the only eyewitness. Was he the one driving the forklift? Can't you see that he's in shock!

Cristiano arrived, out of breath. There were ten or so police officers and Carabinieri. The executive offices refused to allow the state commissioner for occupational safety to enter the factory grounds. Cristiano shoved his way through the crowd. Alessio. Where's Alessio? His head swiveled left and right. He was rapidly reviewing the faces of everyone he saw, eyes wild and rolling.

You remember it, *Cri*? That time it snowed. What year? Uh, '94, or was it '95? . . . It was snowing. You remember it? Snowflakes and inside, if you looked carefully, was the hieroglyphic for Ilva.

He saw him: Mattia standing there. He had to get to him. Cristiano hauled back and punched a Carabiniere who was trying to shove him away. He managed to make it to the forklift. He grabbed Mattia by the shoulders, shook him, stuck his own face close to Mattia's. "Mattia, where's Alessio? Listen, tell me where Alessio is, so we can all just go home."

Mattia swayed slightly. He was staring down at something that can't have a name.

"A cat," he said.

Cristiano felt a chasm split open in his chest.

Take him away. Give him a sedative. Take him away. Cristiano lowered his gaze to the ground now; he couldn't see anything but the puddle, the bloody oatmeal, the naked reality that was coagulating in the baking sunlight.

Then he let out a roar.

"That's not him!" pointing to the heap of ravaged flesh. Full-voiced: "That's not him!"

With all the strength that he had in his body and outside of himself, with all the strength that was in those shocked faces encrusted with pig iron and the Carabinieri in uniform who were clearing the area.

"That's not him. No way, that can't be. That's not him. You don't understand."

They were taking away Mattia. They were taking him away like a wooden log. Phone calls to city hall, the regional administration, the provincial government. Cristiano had his name in his throat. The Italian state, the district attorney, the investigating magistrates. It's not him. They had to move in, intervene. It took two, then three of them to restrain him. But Cristiano broke free.

He charged straight at the forklift, head down. He flung himself against the forklift, kicking it. He assailed it, kicking, punching, and head-butting it. Ten, twenty head butts, until he felt his forehead crack open and a gush of blood flow down over his eyes.

No one had mentioned his name, not even Pasquale. The lawyer had said to him: "Congratulations, once again you've gotten off scot-free!" Arturo was going home a free man, and a happy one. He ran up the stairs, taking the steps two at a time, he believed it: Starting tomorrow . . . He inserted the key in the lock, he turned it. Starting tomorrow, everything was going to be different. . . . His hand was trembling. He'd been waiting for this moment for months. From now on . . . he was convincing himself. Sandra, I swear it. . . . He was rehearsing his little speech in his head, he was working himself up, and he opened the door, and he was so happy to see his own floor, his hallway, his wife standing with the phone in one hand . . . Arturo stopped suddenly, the goofy smile faded from his face. Sandra dropped the receiver, she was telling him: "Alessio's dead."

The following day the mayor and the city council canceled the fireworks show planned for the celebration of the start of summer on June 21. The labor unions announced a strike at the steel mill from 4:00 P.M. to 10:00 P.M., with the participation of the subcontracting firms as well.

A six-hour general strike; only the blast furnace would be exempt.

PART FOUR

CHAPTER 39

The island bobbed in the middle of the water like a cookie. Anna leaned out from her balcony, elbows propped on the railing, and gazed at it.

Down in the street was a little knot of children, playing soccer with a brand new Super Santos soccer ball. The steel shutter of the grocery store a block or so down the street was screeching as it rolled up out of sight.

Anna watched, newly awake, in her pajamas. Her bare feet rested on the chilly tiles; she was rubbing her eyes. Elba was so close in that instant, in the clean air. The little villages clustered around the inlets, and the cliffs looming high over the sea, the boats scudding before the wind around the island.

Here, drenched in light, Stalingrado was beginning to stir and awaken. Coming out a window in building number 8, a television set blared at full volume about conflicts in Afghanistan and the Middle East. The clattering of coffee cups and utensils on the balcony next door. Anna followed with her gaze the arc of the soccer ball as it grazed a windowsill and then fell straight into an agave bush.

This, between Via Nenni and Via Togliatti, was her entire world. She saw the children suddenly rush, all together, to retrieve the soccer ball.

"No," she heard them cry a few seconds later, "it's going flat!"

Soon those streets and courtyards would be filled to the brim with adolescents, beach towels draped over their shoulders, and motor scooters carrying a rider and passenger but no helmets, women with tote bags filled with groceries, cars with the windows lowered. The notes of a song by Laura Pausini wafted up from somewhere, maybe from the fruit van that was driving down the street.

It was time to make peace. It was truly necessary; there was no other solution. Streets named after such stirring figures as Carlo Pisacane, the Roselli brothers, Karl Marx, had their shutters flung open or rolled up now, carpets were being hung out windows and beaten now, little boys were running roughshod through the quarter, busy playing pranks with apartment buzzers.

Anna watched as the garbage truck stopped to empty the little trash Dumpsters, a couple of Maghrebi immigrants jumped off the truck, dressed in safety-orange overalls. Reality demands it. Reality wins in every case, whatever you think or do. The kids went back to playing with the deflated soccer ball.

Now Jennifer was crossing the street with James in her arms. She sat down on the bench at the bus stop. Anna observed the scene, elbows on her balcony railing. And all things considered, she had no desire to leave this place. She could hear her mother bustling around in the kitchen, the tiny James clapping his hands and shouting as loud as he could the only word he was capable of uttering.

She imagined her. Somewhere, she didn't know where. Sitting at a café table having breakfast, or else under the blankets fast asleep. One floor down, with the fan blowing on her dresser, eyes shut tight. Or on some tree-lined boulevard in Follonica, teetering on stiletto heels. It didn't matter.

When they used to hunt crabs off the rocks, Francesca would catch them with a lightning lunge, and she was good at avoiding the snapping pincers. They'd shared a pail when they were little girls: First they'd fill it with sand and water, and after their hunting expeditions, they'd carry it home filled with barnacles and sunfish, determined to make a pasta sauce.

That's what mattered to her, right now.

That those kids were playing soccer in the middle of the street, in the middle of traffic, with their deflated soccer ball. What mattered was that Francesca was here, somewhere. Present, alive.

It was an ordinary morning. Sandra was mopping the floor. Rosa, one floor down, was watering the plants. And Anna stood there, looking out from the balcony in the barracks number 7.

Meanwhile, a bus was creaking along the Grosseto-Livorno provincial highway.

In the back of the bus, huddled in the last row of seats, the one passenger was staring out the window, her temple pressed against the glass.

There was a tractor on the side of the road, loaded with hay bales. In the fields, in the rows of watermelons and tomato plants, there were young men from Ghana.

The bus driver looked up at his rearview mirror: He was worried that his one passenger had fallen asleep. She was curled up on her seat, her knees pressed against her chest, rapt in a distinct silence all her own.

Motoring along from Follonica toward Piombino, the countryside became swamp and then scrubland. Low-lying, arid shrubbery. Hedgehog corpses lay here and there by the guardrail.

Francesca looked sleepily out the window. The ENEL and the Dalmine-Tenaris plants towered over the uninhabited stretch of coastline. Between one canebrake and the next, between one pine grove and another, in Torre Mozza, Riva Verde, and Pirelli, she caught glimpses of the sea; at this time of the morning fishing boats were navigating back to port. A cruise ship slid slowly past, heading for the middle of the Tyrrhenian Sea.

As the bus passed Gagno and they got closer to Cotone, Francesca could make out the cranes and the smokestacks. Huge steel arms and rusting blast furnaces, some active, some dormant. People were already starting to talk about reclamation, about dismantling the steel mills. Converting the local economy, focusing on tourism, the service industry. Francesca's eyes scanned the gap-toothed silhouette of the factory. Like the Colosseum, like the hulls of the fishing boats stranded on the sand, the blast furnace, too, in a decade or so, would become the property of the cats.

She was so tired. She rubbed her puffy eyes, her forehead pressed against the glass of the bus window, frosted with condensation. She was coming home.

At the exit for the ferry port, a line of cars inching forward. They were waiting to board the ferry. Bicycles strapped down on the roof racks, Jet Skis and windsurfing boards on trailers. Francesca looked away.

There were so many things, everywhere. Every corner was so jam-packed with industrial sheds, gas stations, and the little soccer fields where players were practicing, maybe even Nino and Massi.

She sat there, closed inside herself, between the empty seats, in her rumpled body. Her jeans, ripped at the knee, tennis shoes, and an oversized T-shirt. She bounced on rough patches, in the orange Menarini-built bus that had been operating since the eighties. She held her backpack next to her, with her things from the Gilda, her makeup case, her G-strings, her short dress studded with rhinestones and low-cut in the back.

Ordinary, indifferent things, balled up, things to stuff into the washer, to take home to the fourth-floor apartment where Mama and Papa spend their day on the couch, tablets dissolving in their drinking glasses.

The city emerged, with its dominion of chimneys and dish antennas.

If time could slip by unnoticed in the bedrooms, under the doors. If everything could culminate in that off-kilter angle of the head on the easy chair, hands folded in the lap, hands forgetful of all they had done, without a trace, as if they'd never laid brick or applied cement, shaped train track, pummeled and beaten bodies, carving deep into one's offspring, one's children.

Francesca yawned, wiping the condensation off the window with the sleeve of her sweater. Her long blond hair was gathered neatly in a bun at the nape of her neck, her nails covered with chipped red polish. She had no audience, right now. Except for the bus driver, who looked back at her in his mirror every so often, wondering what she was doing, that girl—half child, half young woman, forsaken in an empty intercity bus at that hour of the morning.

She had no one on earth but her. She could travel the world, from Milan to Palermo, she could shout and act out, misbehave and act as if nothing had happened. It hadn't been easy to spy on her from behind a cypress tree at the blue-collar cemetery, the one over by the slaughterhouse. It hadn't been easy to press up against the wall in the basement stairwell, once when she'd heard her go out. Even if she ran away, even if she never came back to Little Stalingrad: the place where they were both born. There was nowhere else. The bus braked at the stoplight, by the Piaggio motor scooter dealership. When the light turned green, the bus turned right, heading toward Salivoli.

Francesca stood up, pushed the button to request a stop. She looked out at the Lungomare Marconi streaming past in the bus window, the hedge of pink oleanders, the phone booths that had been smashed and beaten with bats. The sunlight poured in, pitiless and radiant, illuminating her creased, weary face. The road curved downhill in two switchbacks before reaching Via Stalingrado, at the boundary with the promontory.

She got out of the bus.

She stood there for a few seconds, under the bus shelter, dazed by the bright sunlight, the long bus ride. She saw a little knot of boys playing soccer in the middle of the street with a half-deflated ball. She saw Jennifer climbing up the steps of the bus, her baby in her arms, and James laughing, his only, tiny tooth. Clapping his hands he kept repeating in a strong voice the first word that all children learn to say. The trashmen were climbing back onto their truck and roaring off.

She looked up. Leaning against the railing on the fifth floor, she saw Anna.

Two cars sailed past her, followed by a bicycle, before she could cross the street. Before she could register.

Anna was leaning on the railing of her balcony, as clean as a sheet hanging out to dry. The only figure in the flaking gray wall. Small and curly-haired.

For a long instant they took each other in. In the early morning light, in the shouts of children kicking the soccer ball. And the ball bounced against the wall, landed on the bus stop bench, and one of the kids fell and skinned his knee, and another kid shoved a third, and it was all so real that Anna was looking out, like a girlfriend waiting for her, looking out for her as she returned home.

It was an instant. To Francesca it looked as if Anna, at a certain point, recognizing her, had smiled. So she waved her hand. Raised her arm, waved hello: It just came spontaneously. And it happened that Anna returned the wave. It happened at this time, just like that, without warning.

Francesca crossed the street and the courtyard. Without realizing it she was running. Now she was in a hurry. In a hurry to get to her room, to throw herself on the bed, to capture that moment and treasure it in her body. It was a day like any other. The date doesn't matter. Nothing had happened, in the ordinary way of things: She got off the bus, she saw Anna, she waved hello. . . .

And she was running. She was running to keep her turmoil under wraps. They'd only glanced at each other, waved at each other from opposite sides of the Via Stalingrado. There was a little crowd of snot-nosed kids being annoying: It was the normal thing for little boys to ring doorbells and run away.

Francesca climbed the stairs two steps at a time.

On the fourth-floor landing, once she'd located her house keys amid the dirty clothing, she suddenly froze. She had one hand on the door handle; she could hear the remote flickering of the television set behind the door.

It wouldn't take much. A flight of stairs consists of thirty-five steps. A year consists of 365 days. These aren't enormous numbers.

Francesca tiptoed to the railing and looked up the stairwell. Someone was shouting, "Slut!" at someone else. You could hear a sharp slap ring out, immediately afterward a little boy started crying. Francesca held her breath. A meow. The rustle of a broom across the floor.

The things that remain unchanged. The white foam of the sea, the foam in your arteries, and it was so clear and exact to think of it. It woudn't take much.

She climbed the stairs to the fifth floor. She came up to the door, saw the doorbell with a sticker, the name *Sorrentino* written in script on it. She rang the doorbell. It was real, that sound. The wicker doormat beneath her feet, with WELCOME written on it, was real.

Anna hovered motionless in the kitchen. It was just an instant of bewilderment, a moment filled with confusion and fear in which she and her mother looked each other in the eye. Sandra was setting the table for breakfast. She stood there, with a mug in one hand and the sugar bowl in the other.

The sun was filling the room with white light, and the room was fragrant with cookies and hot milk. In a shady corner of the living room, Arturo sat silent in his bathrobe. He was distractedly leafing through *La Repubblica*; he hadn't said a word in the past month.

The doorbell rang a second time.

"It's *France*," said Anna.

That word had been poised, frozen, for far too long in her throat, and now it left her lips with a sort of incredulous smile. Because it couldn't be anyone but her, and she wasn't waiting for anyone else.

Anna walked down the hall, barefoot, like any other day. She took the chain off the hook. She swung the door wide open.

It wasn't simple. Nothing, no feature of her face, was simple.

The asymmetrical freckles on her nose, her eyes flecked with yellow. To look at them, to see those eyes: chipped, yes, scarred, but present. And the dimples on her cheeks, her hair as soft and fluffy as meringue, and now a little disheveled. The face pale and splintered.

We're the same height. That was the first thing each of them thought. We're the same height and our hair is practically the same length.

While Francesca walked through the front door, wobbling slightly, they grazed one another—their arms and their clothing.

Anna closed the door behind her. She turned to look at her, as she walked down the hallway, shy and yet striding. The outline of her back, a hint of the contour of the spinal cord through the cotton of her T-shirt.

They emerged into the kitchen, with the apprehensive faces of truants caught red-handed by the schoolteacher. Sandra had set out the mug and the sugar bowl on the kitchen table. Her eyes widened as she looked at them.

Her hair was gray around the temples. Sandra had aged, her hands were shaky. But she could still smile.

"Ciao, Francesca," she said, "have you had breakfast?"

Francesca stood in silence next to Anna, looking at the pantry, the refrigerator with the magnets, the photographs hanging up next to the copper pots—Alessio with Cristiano on the bulldozer, Arturo holding a tiny Anna in his arms, and all of them, together, on the beach—she looked at the arrangement of the various objects on the mantelpiece, the hooks shaped like mushrooms, the pot holders hanging from them, the order of the ladles and wooden spoons over the sink: It was all exactly the way it was supposed to be.

She shook her head.

"Then sit down." Sandra pointed her to a chair. "You know what it's like at our house, we're kind of catch-as-catch-can. . . ."

She pulled open a drawer and took out another napkin. Her back was a little bowed now, that had changed. She'd put a photograph of Alessio from his first communion on the hood over the stove. Now she set another mug and a spoon on the tablecloth.

Francesca sat down next to Anna. She didn't want to look at her. She just wanted to feel her elbow against hers, feel her knee under the table. And her movements close beside her as they dipped their cookies into the milk.

Anna didn't turn to look at her either. But she pressed her calf against Francesca's calf, under the table. A flashing thrill that tickled. She gave her a little smack with her knee. And she knew that now Francesca felt, at least a little, like laughing.

"It's a pretty day," Sandra suddenly said, and looked her in the eyes. "Are you going to the beach?"

Both Anna and Francesca froze, motionless, cookies in hand. The expression of someone caught off guard.

"No, even better," said Sandra, as she was clearing the table, "why don't you go to Elba?"

Now they even stopped chewing. Each turned to look the other in the eye, at the exact same second. And then they both turned to stare at Sandra, silent, speechless, eyebrows arched.

Sandra laughed and pointed at the watch: "Look, you've got plenty of time. Just be home in time for dinner. It'll take an hour to cross over to Portoferraio. It's just a stone's throw from the port to the gravel beach, the Spiaggia delle Ghiaie, it's just a short walk. You take a swim, you catch some sun, then you come home. . . . It's nothing transcendental!"

They went on sitting there, wordless, looking at her, for another second or two. They were thinking. In fact, you just put on your bathing suit, your beachwear over it, you stuff a towel into your backpack, with a couple of bottles of fruit juice, some snacks, and you're ready to go. In fact, if they caught the bus, they could be down at the port in fifteen minutes. Then they'd buy tickets, then they'd board the ferry. And by 10:30 they'd be on Elba.

"I don't have a swimsuit," said Francesca.

"I'll lend you one," Anna hastened to say.

She leaped up from her chair and ran for the bathroom.

"Mama, get our backpack ready!" she shouted as she turned on the faucet, grabbing toothbrush and toothpaste tube. Meanwhile, Francesca drew closer, leaning against the jamb of the bathroom door.

Anna lifted her head from the sink, stopped scrubbing her teeth for a moment.

Francesca stood poised, balanced on the edge of the door, the most radiant of all the elements. They were leaving now. They were going to swim to Elba. Like the Germans, like the tourists from Milan and Florence. Surely there was a square with a church and a bell tower and everything, just like here.

They smiled; they didn't say a word. And one of them had a mouthful of toothpaste, the other had chapped lips, her mouth half open.

They fit together perfectly.